ANOTHER FIRST CHANCE

ALSO BY ROBBIE COUCH

If I See You Again Tomorrow

Blaine for the Win

The Sky Blues

ANOTHER FIRST CHANCE

ROBBIE COUCH

SIMON & SCHUSTER BFYR

New York London Toronto Sydney New Delhi

An imprint of Simon & Schuster Children's Publishing Division
1230 Avenue of the Americas, New York, New York 10020

Simon & Schuster: Celebrating 100 Years of Publishing in 2024
For information about special discounts for bulk purchases, please contact
Simon & Schuster Special Sales at 1-866-506-1949 or business@simonandschuster.com.
The Simon & Schuster Speakers Bureau can bring authors to your live event. For more
information or to book an event, contact the Simon & Schuster Speakers Bureau at
1-866-248-3049 or visit our website at www.simonspeakers.com.
Interior design by Krista Vossen
The text for this book was set in Minion Pro.
Manufactured in the United States of America
First Edition
2 4 6 8 10 9 7 5 3 1
Library of Congress Cataloging-in-Publication Data
Names: Couch, Robbie, author.
Title: Another First Chance / Robbie Couch.
Description: First edition. | New York : Simon & Schuster, 2024.
Identifiers: LCCN 2023051389 (print) | LCCN 2023051390 (ebook) |
ISBN 9781665935302 (hardcover) | ISBN 9781665935319 (paperback) |
ISBN 9781665935326 (ebook)
Subjects: CYAC: Secrets—Fiction. | Grief—Fiction. | Friendship—Fiction.
| LGBTQ+ people—Fiction. | LCGFT: Novels.
Classification: LCC PZ7.1.C6757 An 2024 (print) | LCC PZ7.1.C6757 (ebook)
| DDC [Fic]—dc23
LC record available at https://lccn.loc.gov/2023051389
LC ebook record available at https://lccn.loc.gov/2023051390

For the grieving ones

RIVER—MONDAY, JUNE 3, 2024

I drive by the billboard displaying my dead best friend's photo, just like I do every day. It looms above our town's pet groomer's on my route to school, the worst line in advertising history spanning its surface in bold, all-caps letters: DON'T DREXT LIKE DYLAN DID.

"Drext," if it isn't clear, is a combination of "drive" and "text." I'm not sure which Michigan Department of Transportation staff member invented that moronic marketing term believing that they're clever, but if our paths ever cross, I'll make sure to correct their thinking.

Dylan wore his favorite shirt that picture day. I bet even his parents don't know that, let alone the strangers who barely glance at the gigantic teenager staring down at them as they speed by with their drive-through coffees. But I do. They won't realize that the polo is bright red, not depressing gray, because the campaign decided to desaturate the photo.

I mean, I get it. A black-and-white photo is sadder and more ominous than one filled with color, and sad and ominous is exactly what these billboards are going for. Dylan Cooper was the exact opposite of sad and ominous, though. He was happy and magnetic, inspiring and optimistic. He was exactly what every kid should be striving to be more like—not the poster child of reckless teen driving.

My mom overheard me call the billboard "stupid as hell" to our neighbor the week it went up and lectured me on why I shouldn't say things like that out loud to people. They'd think I'm "strange," or "insensitive," or not dealing with Dylan's death in the "right way."

Joke's on her, though, because they'd be correct on all three counts.

Today I don't mind driving by it like I usually do, though, because Dylan's billboard got an upgrade overnight: a Mario mustache, freshly spray-painted right above his big, grinning lips. And while some people might call it vandalism, I'm certain Dylan would be dying of laughter if only he weren't already dead.

Plus, the mustache looks great on him, with his square jaw, dark eyes, and even darker hair thick enough that running a comb across his scalp could have been an Olympic sport (one he never came close to medaling in). He was the type of handsome that would steal your attention from across the room. Add a mustache, and you'd never get it back.

Still, I manage to tear my eyes away and spot that my gas gauge is almost on empty in time to pull into the one station between my house and school. I haven't even set down my can of vanilla-flavored coffee at the register when Roy asks, "Did you see it?"

Roy went to my high school a couple years ago. He used to be our school's mascot before he got busted for selling weed brownies to eighth graders under the bleachers in his Timber Wolf costume. He dropped out a week later and got a job at this gas station, where he still sells weed brownies illegally from behind the register, just not to middle schoolers or dressed as a wolf.

"Are you talking about the billboard?" I ask, as if I don't already know the answer.

Roy nods. "Who fucks up a dead kid's photo? And *today*?"

He has a point. Because everyone in town would've been upset by the mustache regardless of when it showed up, but the fact it appeared on Dylan's one-year deathiversary will incite enough rage to ensure it's the top-trending topic in Teawood.

Clearly, the vandal wants to send a message.

"I think the mustache is kind of funny," I say, responding to Roy with the exact kind of comment that my mom wishes I'd keep to myself.

Roy stares at me with his big, bloodshot eyes, surprised. "But weren't you two close?"

I nod. "I knew him better than anyone."

Roy scans the gas station to make sure we're alone and leans closer. "Did Dylan have any enemies working at Puparazzi-Ready?"

I open and close my mouth, confused. "Not that I know of. Why?"

Roy's eyes narrow on mine, suspicious that I know more than what I'm willing to share. "It's weird that the billboard just happens to be above the pet groomer's, don't you think?"

I stare back, unsure if Roy is attempting to make a joke or if he genuinely doesn't realize most roadside billboards have nothing to do with whatever business happens to be nearby. Is he suggesting Dylan was really mauled by a freshly shampooed Goldendoodle or something? If so, the staff at Puparazzi-Ready pulled off the cover-up of the century.

"I think Dylan's wrecked car confirms it was a tree on the side of the road that killed him," I sigh, "not a pampered puppy named Spot, if that's what you're implying."

I push cash across the counter and turn to leave.

"To be fair, a tree didn't kill him," Roy mutters with a soft snort. "*Drexting* did."

I freeze in place, drink in hand, as a bubble of anger rises in my chest.

See? One split-second mistake behind the wheel and a shaming billboard gets to define Dylan for the rest of eternity. A mistake that wasn't even entirely his fault, either.

My mind goes into overdrive concocting the perfect insult that somehow combines cannabis, middle schoolers, and mascots, but before I can get it out, Roy sees the look on my face and regrets going there.

"Bro, I'm sorry," he says sheepishly, "I'm just messing around—"

But I'm gone before he can finish his apology.

I blast off toward school, swallowing my frustrations with my first sip of overpriced canned caffeine. After parking in the student lot, I start walking toward the main entrance of Teawood High School for the fifth to last time, hopefully ever. It's a sprawling, brown brick building perched on a hill, covered in ivy, and filled with Dylan memories that still make every day I have to spend inside difficult.

I feel a pair of eyes glue onto me the second my shoes hit the pavement, and glance up to locate the source of the staring. Jacob Lewis, a quiet gamer who's leaning against the hood of his car, is inexplicably tracking my every move.

He loves comics, as evidenced by the Marvel-themed T-shirts he wears every day, but that's pretty much all I know about Jacob Lewis. His glaring would have weirded me out if it happened before last year, but I've gotten used to people reacting to me in strange ways since Dylan died. Especially after the billboard went up.

In theory, it was supposed to honor Dylan's legacy while encouraging Teawood teens to drive safely. But I think it mostly just keeps the tragic nature of his death fresh in our heads. Instead of remembering him for who he was, the billboard has turned my best friend into a statistic, prompting a wave of speculative questions about his death. Some of the curiosity has resulted in outlandish bullshit—like conspiracy theories involving villainous pet groomers—but even the more grounded questions have been unhelpful at best, slowly turning Dylan the Person into Dylan the Tragedy with each hallway whisper. And as the Best Friend of the Dead Kid at School, I've been roped into the spectacle through no choice of my own.

If the ambulance arrived sooner, would Dylan have survived?

It must have been bad if the Coopers chose to have a closed casket, right?

And the absolute worst one:

Who was he texting when it happened?

I push the questions and Jacob's weird stare aside and slither through hordes of students congregating on the school's sloped front lawn on my way to the steps that lead to the main entrance.

"River fucking Lang."

Now a sparkly jumpsuit slides into my line of vision. Unfortunately, the voice belongs to Goldie Candles.

"Who do you think did it?" she asks.

I take one of my earbuds out and pretend I didn't hear her question.

"I *said*," she begins again with added sass, eyes piercing me from two steps above, "who do you think did it? And don't even pretend not to know what *it* is."

I pretend not to know what *it* is. "I'm not a mind reader, Goldie."

She gives me a look confirming that *she* knows that *I* know exactly what *it* is, but she indulges me anyway. "Dylan's new facial hair."

"Oh." I shrug. "No clue."

She refuses to blink, observing me intently, like she's waiting for me to crack.

Goldie has curly, white-blond hair that reaches her chest, cobalt eyes the size of saucers, and a crackly voice that could carry across the Atlantic. Nepotism provided both her parents with cushy, grossly overpaid jobs with the University of Michigan football team, which explains just about everything you need to know about Goldie Candles—besides the fact that she hates my guts. So I'm not exactly shocked that she seems to suspect I had something to do with Dylan's mustache.

She continues to study my face suspiciously. "Interesting. You don't seem that upset about someone destroying our friend's billboard."

"Should I be?"

"*Shouldn't* you be?"

"On one hand," I say, "no one should spray-paint property that isn't theirs. On the other, you have to admit that Dylan looks . . . kind of great with a mustache?"

Her face twists with disgust. "You're a weird dude, River."

I consider the accusation. "I don't disagree."

"You actually *do* think the mustache is funny, don't you?"

I'm about to answer when Goldie's gaze drifts over my shoulder, begging me to follow it. I give her the win, glance backward, and see Dylan's girlfriend—*former* girlfriend—Mavis Meyers on the front lawn of the school.

Mavis is standing as still as a statue, her jet-black hair billowing in the breeze the only confirmation that she hasn't turned to stone. With a cluster of girls happily signing yearbooks on her right and wound-up jocks bent over in laughter on her left, Mavis's misery couldn't stick out like a sore thumb any more if she tried. Even from this far away, I can tell her hazel eyes are holding back tears. She's a shell of the girl that existed 366 days ago.

"See? Mavis is in hell today," Goldie says, "as any grieving girl-friend on the one-year anniversary of her boyfriend's death would be. Call me crazy, but . . . shouldn't people expect the same from his supposed best friend?"

I've been in hell *every* day since the accident thanks to the bill-board, the Roys and Goldies of Teawood, and the brutal injustice of the cosmos.

I turn back around and face Goldie. "What are you getting at?"

She licks her glossy lips. "You're smiling at the thought of Dylan's billboard getting destroyed, and the criminal hasn't come forward yet. What do you think I'm getting at?"

"I wouldn't say it was destroyed. I'd call it an upgrade. A little spray paint couldn't possibly worsen a billboard as terrible as Dylan's."

Her eyes squint into mine. "Well, then, who do you think did it?" She repeats the question, even softer and more menacing. "Because I have a guess."

"Well, I don't." I squint back innocently.

Goldie finally gives up, exasperated. "Just stay away from her. Okay?"

Although Mavis and I haven't spoken in a year, it still stings to hear Goldie request that I keep my distance from the girl whose friendship basically defined my childhood.

I can't let Goldie see me wounded, though, so I laugh. "As if we ever talk anyway."

"I mean, stay *especially* far away from her today." Goldie looks me up and down. "You already ruined her June third last year, you don't need to do it again."

She flashes a knowing look and barrels past me to Mavis. I take a deep breath and swallow hard, pretending her words don't feel like a punch to the gut. I'd be fine having to deal with Goldie's disdain from time to time, if only her hostility weren't really just channeling the passive rage Mavis has felt toward me since this day last year.

Because Mavis despises me even more than Goldie does, I'm sure of it. She just shows it by adhering to the strictest silent treatment I've ever experienced instead of berating me on the school's front steps.

But honestly? I can't say I blame either of them all that much.

Yeah, I'm the one who spray-painted the mustache on Dylan in the middle of the night, but infinitely more importantly, I'm the reason he's dead in the first place. And Mavis is the only one that I'm certain knows the truth.

2

DYLAN—SATURDAY, JUNE 3, 2023

I wore my favorite red polo for picture day. My grin went crooked as usual as the flash went off, which Mavis was quick to point out when we got the photos back. She teased me about it, but in a flirty way that I've learned meant she actually likes the way I look. It's been a while since I've seen that playful side of her and she'd probably say the same about me.

I'd like to think the photo, framed and shiny under the lights of the school's main hallway display case, feels like the real me. I guess to some extent it does. I am the driven, type-A student-athlete of the month for the junior class, which the label above my photo proclaims to all who walk by. But the guy in the photo isn't the whole me. Not even close.

I can't dwell on that right now, though, with so much to do. I turn around and face the silent main hallway, which is empty of people but full of the tables and chairs I've been setting out for Summer Sign-Ups. I sigh, realizing how much faster this would all get done if the other two Student Council members who volunteered to help hadn't bailed this morning. It has to all come together before Monday, when each table will be staffed by a different club recruiting students to join their activities for next year. Summer Sign-Ups was originally my idea, after all, and I plan on hyping it up in my college application essays, so it needs to be a continued success.

I blow up more silver and blue balloons and straighten out the

Quiz Bowl and Theater Club tables, but before I can move on to the streamers, I'm distracted again, this time by the new piano at the end of the hallway begging me to test it out.

It's still in transit to the band room, where it belongs, as evidenced by the moving blankets and packing tape covering most of its edges, but it's been at least an hour since I spotted the workers who initially brought it inside. My dad refuses to buy a piano for the house—he wants me laser focused on school and basketball—and the one I've been practicing on at Mavis's church has been broken for weeks. So the universe leaving the new one unsupervised at my fingertips means I'm practically obligated to play it, right?

I look to my right and left, ensuring no one's around to catch me, and then grab my sheet music from my bag. I crouch down in front of the piano, since the bench must be packed away somewhere else, and my fingers find the right keys. I begin to play the song that I've been trying and failing to learn for months, my hands struggling to keep pace with its quick tempo.

In the moments when I'm not butchering every other note, the music drifts throughout the surrounding hallways as if I'm playing in a cathedral somewhere far, far away from suburban Michigan. My anxious thoughts melt into the ceramic tiles beneath my shoes, which never happens when I'm dribbling down a basketball court or giving a class speech. It's like, I can feel the same parts of myself that are missing in my school photo vibrating through my chest to the music—which somehow makes both no sense and perfect sense to me.

I'm only able to get through the song once before a deep voice interrupts my playing.

"You're talented, Cooper."

I freeze and jump back from the piano, caught red-handed by Harry the custodian.

"Thanks," I say, trying not to look as startled as I feel.

"Not as good as your three-point percentage," he says matter-of-factly, "but still, impressive. That's a beautiful tune. Who sings it?"

My cheeks glow pink as I tell Harry more. I can hardly find time to practice the piano at all each week, let alone practice in front of other people, so it's rare that I hear compliments from a live audience in real time, even if it's just an audience of one.

"If it were up to me, I'd say keep the concert going," Harry continues, pushing a pile of dust bunnies past me with his broom, "but the movers asked me to make sure no one touches that piano while they're on break."

I step even farther away from the keys. Harry may be the beloved curmudgeon of Teawood High School, but he's not afraid to put both students and teachers in their place if he feels like it's called for.

Harry pauses next to the display case and leans on his broomstick. He examines my photo for a moment before pivoting his gaze my way. "Why are you here on a weekend anyway? Don't tell me the junior class student-athlete of the month landed himself in Saturday detention. . . ."

I gesture at the tables and chairs scattered down the hallway. "Setting up Summer Sign-Ups for next week."

Harry nods slowly, taking in the scene. "It looks bigger this year. I'm sure it'll be the best one yet, Cooper."

I feel a smile spread across my face almost involuntarily, even as my stomach twists with renewed dread. I've talked to the school counselor, Mr. Babcock, about this before—how my outward reactions to compliments often contradict my internal ones. I may smile to make sure Harry knows I appreciate his praise, but the praise mostly feels like the bar's being raised on me once again.

What if this Summer Sign-Ups *isn't* the best one yet, though? What if it's so disastrous, I can't even use it for my college application essays? Why do people keep moving the goalposts on me—and why do I keep letting them?

"You didn't ask for it, but here's a piece of advice." Harry leans toward me, calloused hands still clasped around the end of his broomstick.

I nod, sure it will either be something along the lines of *Don't rest on your laurels* or his two cents on what college I should commit to for basketball—an opinion seemingly every middle-aged man in Teawood feels obligated to share with me.

So I'm a little confused when he says, "Slow down."

I pause. "Slow down . . . doing what?"

"*Everything.*" Lines crinkle around his eyes. "If it's not basketball, it's giving speeches to the student body. And if it's not speeches, it's spending your last weekend before summer break alone at school, organizing an event without help from anyone else."

Is Harry . . . a mind reader?

I do the thing again and let out an awkward laugh to lighten the mood, even though his honesty has me on edge. "Sure, but I enjoy helping out, and I—"

"I'm telling you," he says, cutting me off, "your plate's too full for an eighteen-year-old."

"Seventeen."

He sighs. "Take it from me, Cooper, there's plenty of time to work. Stop and smell the roses while you still can."

Harry and the pile of dust bunnies at the end of his broom float farther down the hall as I stand there in silence, letting his words sink in.

River says I do too much all the time, but no adult at this school has given me that advice before. Mr. Babcock somehow convinced my dad that I should take one fewer AP class next year, so maybe that counts. But I guess advice from a candid custodian hits differently than class scheduling at the hands of a school counselor.

Even as Harry's words resonate, another voice speaks up in my head reminding me that he doesn't see the big picture. Of *course* it'd be nice to cut back on my extracurriculars and spend more time debating River on Pluto's declassification as a planet or learning more songs on the piano. But I won't get a basketball scholarship to Cascara if I don't play my senior year. Plus, like my dad always says, people count on me as a leader. What would happen if I quit?

If I can just get through this next year, then I can pump the brakes. River and I will be out west, starting a new chapter living in the same dorm together, and Mavis won't be that far away, either—assuming we make it past the bumpy road ahead. Maybe then, the whole me can shine.

The thought motivates me to pick up the pace and knock out the rest of the streamers so I can get to the most pressing, if not downright scary, priority on today's to-do list. Because even though I can't take Harry's advice and slow down this exact moment, I can do at least one thing to feel in control of my life again—even if it's a thing I've been dreading for days.

Once the hallway is in a good place for the sign-ups, I swing my bag over my shoulder and breeze through the school's main lobby toward the parking lot. I'm so caught up thinking about what I need to do now that I barely register the voice to my left saying, "Hey, Dylan."

I stop and look to where Brady Potts is tucked away next to the school's deteriorating Timber Wolf statue. He's wearing a purple tank top, glasses with green rims, and a dangling silver earring that nearly reaches his shoulder.

"Hi, Brady." I attempt to sound pleasantly surprised to see him, despite my mind being elsewhere.

"I love the new color," I say, eyeing his newly blue mullet, even though it pretty much makes him look like Sonic the Hedgehog.

"Same to you."

"Thanks?" I don't know what he's referring to, because my hair has never changed from its original dark brown. But after being in Spanish class with him, I've learned to roll with Brady's randomness.

"What are you doing here?" I ask, shifting gears.

"I left my Switch in Ms. Weiss's room yesterday," he says, "so I'm hanging around until she gets here for Driver's Ed so I can grab it."

I cringe, hating that I have to deliver the bad news. "Driver's Ed is every other weekend, and it's not today."

"Really?"

I nod and he hangs his head in defeat.

"Did you drive here?" I ask.

"I don't have a car. I walked."

"From where?"

"Boiling and Smith."

I mentally map out the intersection on the outskirts of Teawood. "Wow, that's . . . a *trek*, Brady."

He frowns. "Yeah."

I gesture for him to follow me out the door. "I'm giving you a ride."

"Are you sure?"

"Yes."

"But I think it's out of your way—"

"It's okay, Brady. There's no way you're walking home."

He grins and grabs his bag, turning a shade of red so dark it might be purple, and follows me outside. I'm so relieved when my phone starts buzzing on our walk to the parking lot, hopeful the call will eat into what's sure to be an awkward car ride, that I don't even check to see who's calling before answering. That relief fades quickly, though, when I'm greeted with, "What's this eighty-eight all about?"

It's my dad.

"Huh?" I reply.

"Your calc exam," he says. "You got an eighty-eight. Did you not know that?"

At the start of the year my dad demanded that he get weekly updates from Mr. Babcock, who rounds up reports from my teachers, as if I'm a failing freshman and not an upperclassman with straight As.

"What about your class rank?" my dad asks before I can get a word in. "Will Cascara notice if you drop out of the top ten?"

I reach my car with Brady in tow. "The eighty-eight won't affect my class rank, Dad. The exam is only ten percent of our final grade, so I'll still get an A in the class."

I tap my key fob, unlocking the doors, and gesture for Brady to get in, but I hang back for a moment in order to have some privacy.

"You're sure?" Dad presses. "Only ten percent?"

"You got the same syllabus I did at the beginning of the semester," I say. "You can check it yourself."

"Attitude, Dylan."

Anger rises in my chest, but I remind myself that I just need to put up with this for one more year and successfully bury it before it boils over. "Sorry."

But as he rants on, Harry's words come back to me. *Slow down. Slow down. Slow down.* With each repetition they become more tantalizing—yet with each word my dad says, more impossible. Thankfully, an incoming call beeps at me, interrupting the pressurized pulling and pushing in my head. I peek at the phone screen.

River.

I fall back against my driver's-side door, somehow instantly at ease. "Dad, I've got to go."

"Where are you?"

"Leaving school, about to go see Mavis."

He asks me to check in with him later, then we say our good-byes and hang up. I knew mentioning Mavis would get him off my back.

My dad needs to be constantly clued in on every detail of my life: my grades, basketball—even my friendship with River, although that has more to do with his homophobia than anything else. But the one area he doesn't micromanage is Mavis. He considers her an "acceptable" girlfriend, as he once put it. And to my dad, acceptable means someone who isn't going to be a distraction in the classroom or on the basketball court. If anything, Mavis's work ethic has kept me *more* focused on my own, which, aside from pleasing my dad, is one of the things that first drew me to her—and now, one of the things that are driving us apart.

I'm about to give up the one part of my life that's been free from my dad's prying, which only adds to the increasingly long list of reasons why breaking up with Mavis is the most difficult decision I've ever had to make.

3

RIVER

Between Roy's *drexting* remark and learning Goldie correctly believes that I painted Dylan's mustache, this may be one of the worst mornings of my senior year. And yet, when I walk into the school lobby and see rows of silver and blue balloons straight ahead, my heart sinks knowing that my not-great day is about to get even worse.

Because it's the start of Summer Sign-Ups.

Dylan may have won the league for our basketball team and single-handedly resuscitated the Astronomy Club, where we became friends. But having the idea for Summer Sign-Ups our freshman year, and then executing it flawlessly, might be his greatest claim to Teawood fame. It's become one of the most beloved annual traditions of manufactured school spirit in the four years since. Student groups claim it's a good way to get a jump on recruiting newbies for next year, but I think it's just as much about the unspoken, not-so-friendly competition between clubs over which one designs the most enticing recruitment table or recruits the most new members.

As much as I'd rather avoid the madness in front of me, Mr. Babcock might actually withhold my diploma if I'm tardy to first period again and trekking the longer route around the auditorium and pool will all but guarantee I'm late. So I put my head down and take a step forward into the chaos of silver and blue.

Almost immediately, I regret my decision.

From the looks of it, most tables seem to be trying to acknowledge Dylan in the same sad, sensationalized way the billboard does. Several are displaying his black-and-white yearbook photo with depressingly cheesy sayings printed over the image. The swimming team printed YOUR WINGS WERE READY BUT OUR HEARTS WERE NOT, typed in Comic Sans font, floating in the space above Dylan's head. Next to them, the bowling team decided to print a giant RIP over Dylan's eyes and nose next to a crying emoji that has bowling balls for eyes.

I try my best to swallow my frustrations as I beeline past clusters of students monologuing about why the tennis team or the Photography Club are "so much fun" or "look great on college apps." I'm careful to avoid accidental eye contact with the Astronomy Club members as I pass by, seeing as I didn't participate this year and still feel guilty about ditching their meetings. A quick glance shows me their table features a homemade solar system model with Dylan's black-and-white face taped over the sun. It's so absurd that I almost burst out laughing, then quickly look away and pick up the pace. They didn't intend for it to be funny, I'm sure, but Dylan would've thought it was even more brilliant than his new mustache.

I near the end of the sign-ups with even less school spirit and faith in our student body than I had walking into school a minute ago, but the last table on the right grabs my attention. There's a white posterboard taped to its front reading THE AFFINITY TRIALS, printed in jet-black ink. The only color on the board comes from four same-sized dots in green, blue, orange, and red, spaced out neatly beneath the text.

It's not only the lack of streamers or balloons that's strange, though; it's also the only one not being run by students. A guy old enough to be my grandpa is glancing around dreamily behind the table, a small smile planted on his face. He has a white, crinkly beard, gentle eyes, and glasses with smudges dotting the lenses. He reminds me of a more slender, professorial version of Santa Claus.

"Hello," he says, pleased to see that he's got someone's attention. "I'm Dr. Ridges."

Dr. Ridges, I learn as he rises to his feet wearing a tan tweed suit, is a giant.

I have to stare up at him as we shake hands. "Hi."

"And you are . . . ?"

"River."

"River." He nods knowingly, as if my name makes sense to him. "Your parents must appreciate the serenity of nature."

"Sure?"

"How are we doing this morning, River?"

"Fine. What are . . ." I glance down at the sign to make sure I read it correctly. ". . . the Affinity Trials?"

"I'm with Affinity Mind and Body," he says, slow and faint, as if he smoked a joint in the parking lot before coming inside—and who knows, maybe he did. "We're looking for twenty students to enter a weeklong study starting next Monday here, at the school. It's quite the opportunity for you to make history."

Make *history*? I snort—then realize he's being serious.

Dr. Ridges reaches into his pocket and hands me a business card. I expect to see his name and contact information, but it only reads *The Affinity Trials,* above the same four colored dots that are on the table sign. "Is Affinity Mind and Body the new yoga studio in town?" I ask, examining the card. "Are you guys sponsoring a club?"

This time he laughs, a soft chuckle that I can barely hear over the noisy hallway. "No, no, we're a research lab headquartered on the West Coast."

I glance around. "So then how are you allowed to be here?"

"Pardon?"

"Summer Sign-Ups is for student groups," I say.

He folds his hands together in front of him. "Superintendent James approved our table."

When Summer Sign-Ups first got requests from local businesses to sponsor tables and sell products freshman year, Dylan made a rousing speech that shut the idea down. It was important to him that the event be for student groups only—a stance the school supported. I guess it's just another thing that's changed without him here.

"Now, River," Dr. Ridges says, shifting gears, "may I ask you a question?"

"Sure."

"Do you have a friend?"

"Huh?"

"A friend." He stares at me. "Do you have one?"

My cheeks flush as I tense up.

It's kind of a dick move for anyone to ask that, let alone a bizarre old guy I met five seconds ago. It's even weirder realizing that I don't know what my honest answer is. *Do* I?

Growing up, I was always the type to have a few good friends rather than a hundred acquaintances, but that became even truer when me and Dylan got close freshman year. It's funny to think about it now, really, because at the time I knew him as Mavis's first and brand-new boyfriend, who I thought was stealing her away from me. Maybe that's why I was so quick to fight him over Pluto's erroneous declassification as a planet during the Astronomy Club meeting where we met—the first of countless debates over outer space we'd have.

It wasn't like we'd *only* hang out with each other and Mavis. A few guys on Dylan's basketball team were cool. Then there was Len, the former Astronomy Club president, and Dylan's neighbor, Matt.

But if I'm honest, all those guys were sort of more Dylan's people anyway. After he died, I felt each one of those connections slowly drift away like sailboats crossing the horizon—except for Mavis. Her cutting ties with me felt more like a speedboat beelining off the cliff of a waterfall. I'm not explaining any of that to this guy, though.

"I have friends," I answer, more forcefully than I'd hoped, "obviously."

"Terrific," Dr. Ridges says, sounding unconvinced. "Well, on the off chance someone you know is interested in learning more, we're encouraging any student between the ages of sixteen and eighteen who considers themselves to be struggling socially to apply. We think they'll benefit from the experience. On top of that, participants receive a two-thousand-dollar stipend after completing the trials." He nods at the business card in my hand. "The website goes into more detail."

Even if I'm struggling socially, I'm just a few days away from putting this place behind me for good. So I nod and smile as a way to say thanks, then turn to leave.

"Were you friends with Dylan Cooper, River?"

I freeze for a moment before turning back. "Why would you ask that?"

"I noticed his picture up and down the hallway," Dr. Ridges says, "so I asked a few students about Dylan's story. Some of them mentioned a River among the many loved ones Dylan left behind." He smiles sadly. "It's difficult to forget a great name like River."

My cheeks grow hotter. "He was my best friend."

Dr. Ridges shakes his head. "It seems like Dylan was a

spectacular young man with a bright future. Hard to replace. Anyone would struggle with that."

Out of nowhere, Dr. Ridges bends across the table and attempts to pull me in for a hug. His long, wiry arms start to wrap around my shoulders like the grim reaper, but I step out of reach.

"*Whoa*," I say, staring at him wide-eyed.

He seems confused by my reaction. "I thought you'd appreciate a hug—"

"You thought wrong."

It's awkward enough when one of my parents tries consoling me with hugs, let alone a slender, possibly-stoned Santa who I just met.

I back farther away from Dr. Ridges before swirling around and striding off.

"We're taking applicants through Friday!" he calls after me. "Visit our website and come see me tomorrow, River, I'll be right here!"

Once I escape, I start speed-walking to Mr. Babcock's office, making it just before the bell. As I wait for him to open his door, I flip Dr. Ridges's business card over in my hand and notice the other side has Affinity Mind & Body's apparent tagline, printed in small, curvy lettering:

creating the future of friendship

I scoff at its cheesiness, even as my stomach sinks in sadness. Because it's been difficult for me to imagine any future for myself without Dylan, let alone one filled with friendship.

4

RIVER

Instead of having a normal first period, my parents thought it'd be smart to "ease me into the day" (Dad's words, not mine) by spending time "getting a better grasp on my grief" (Mom's words, not mine) with the school counselor.

Technically, getting free therapy at school doesn't qualify as a credit, but Principal Fyres agreed to classify it as an elective course in the computer system to fulfill my academic requirements. "Guided Learning Hour" is a laughably inaccurate characterization of my first period with Mr. Babcock—he hasn't guided me toward anything, other than a stronger case of senioritis all year. But I guess "River Lane Is Still Not Over His Best Friend Dying and Needs Help" is too long to fit on an official transcript.

"So," Mr. Babcock exhales from behind his desk, the purply bags beneath his eyes looking extra purply today. "Today's the day."

I knew he'd want to discuss my feelings about today being the one-year deathiversary. But witnessing the planets rotating around Dylan's head at the Astronomy Club table and seeing a crying emoji with bowling balls for eyes hasn't exactly put me in the right headspace to confront my grief. So I try to lighten the mood with a little levity.

"Sorry, Mr. Babcock"—I tilt my head, pretending to be confused—"today's the day . . . for what? Oh, half-off subs at Big Bites!"

He hesitates, unsure if I'm being serious. "No. Dylan died a year ago today, River."

I sip my can of coffee with a grin. "Of course. I'm joking, Mr. Babcock."

His face drops in annoyance. "How are you feeling about it?"

"Dylan's deathiversary?"

He nods.

I puff out my cheeks and exhale slowly. "Basically the same way I've felt about it every other day you've asked me this year."

I haven't *hated* my sessions with Mr. Babcock, I guess—his lime-green loveseat is at least preferable to the plastic chairs in class, and his windowsill lined with fake plants isn't the worst view—but I *have* hated repeatedly answering the same set of questions the past two semesters. If I had a quarter for every time Mr. Babcock's asked me how I'm feeling about Dylan's deathiversary the past month, I'd have at least ten dollars by now.

Mr. Babcock scratches his chin, unsatisfied with my answer as usual. "Feelings can change day-to-day, though. How are you feeling about the significance of *today*, River?"

"Fine, I guess."

Mr. Babcock presses his fingers together and leans forward onto his desk. "You know . . ."

Please don't say it. For the love of God, *please don't say it.*

His eyes pierce mine. "It's okay not to be okay, River."

There it is.

I doubt Mr. Babcock realizes he's repeated that exact phrase to me at least twenty times throughout the past two semesters, each time delivered with the same intensity you'd expect from a corrupt televangelist asking for cash on Christian TV. Every time the words come rolling off his tongue, I imagine them on one of those quote cards that my aunt in New Mexico always shares to her Instagram Stories.

faith & family. they come first!

Live. Laugh. Love. AND DANCE.

It's okay *not* to be okay.

Mr. Babcock is nice enough, but whenever we talk about Dylan, his help comes off as vague and impersonal. It's as if he's reading directly from a grief guidebook, trying to help Student A mourn the death of Student B, when I wish he'd help *me* mourn the death of *Dylan*. I wish I could be more honest about the guilt I've felt since he died and why the billboard's made it so much worse, but after a year of first periods with Mr. Babcock, I'm no more confident in his ability to help than I would be in Goldie's effort to catch me during a trust fall.

"Well . . ." he says as he stands, a more serious tone in his voice. His round belly nudges the dusty diploma from Wayne State out of place on the wall as he circles his desk. "Do you want to talk about what happened?"

"Didn't we just do that?"

Mr. Babcock leans his butt back against the front edge of the desk, nearly toppling over a photo of his wife. "No, not the deathiver—" He catches himself. "See, now you've even got *me* calling it that. I'm talking about the billboard, River." He pauses, then adds seriously, "Dylan's new facial hair?"

I try not to, I swear, but I can't not grin listening to him mutter "new facial hair" as if spray-painting a Nintendo-inspired mustache is essentially a hate crime.

"You found it amusing?" he asks, seeing my reaction.

I pinch my lips to one side to help smother my smile, remembering my mom's warning about reacting strangely when Dylan gets brought up.

25

"I wouldn't say *amusing*," I lie, "no."

Normally, I don't adhere to my mom's warning, but maybe I should. Now that I know Goldie suspects I spray-painted the billboard, others could be out there, too. And if I'm caught as the culprit, could that jeopardize my scholarship to Cascara in the fall? The money is contingent on "good behavior," after all, and I'm pretty sure spray-painting a billboard would land me on the collegiate naughty list. I can't blow up my plans now that I'm so close to escaping Teawood, for me and Dylan both.

Mr. Babcock does the thing where he nods dramatically while searching for his notebook. "I think you should talk to someone else who loved Dylan about the billboard, River."

"Why?"

"Seeing his face vandalized like that, *today* of all days, is probably difficult for many of his loved ones," he says. "I think talking to someone else who knew him might give you a different perspective."

"Aren't I doing that right now, though?" I ask.

Does Mr. Babcock think I don't know Dylan spent a class period with him every day last year, too? To be fair, Dylan's elective was accurately classified as Advanced Career Development—an option for ambitious upperclassmen to get a head start on their post–high school plans—and not an hour of babysitting disguised as grief counseling. But still.

"I meant more of a personal friend of Dylan's, or someone in his family," he says, "not me. What about Mavis?"

My chest tightens. "Meyers?" I ask, as if he could mean anyone else.

He nods.

"Eh," I say, "I'd rather not."

"How come?"

Well, her friend just warned me to stay away from her specifically today, for one. But even if Goldie hadn't cornered me on the
front steps an hour ago, I wouldn't attempt to reach out to Mavis.
Not after what happened at Dylan's funeral.

Mavis didn't answer my texts or calls in the aftermath of the
crash, but I wasn't surprised. I couldn't fault her for not responding
to me with a left leg still wrapped in a cast and the trauma of witnessing her boyfriend die fresh in her memory. But when I tried
talking to her in the parking lot after the funeral service, she bee-
lined in the opposite direction. Message received, loud and clear.
That's when I knew *she* knew I was to blame, too. That Dylan was
replying to a message from me urging him to text back when his
car went off the road.

Sure, maybe I could argue that I wasn't the one behind the
wheel, so I shouldn't be blamed. But it's harder to argue that if I
hadn't sent that text, he'd still be alive today.

Mr. Babcock studies my face. I think he can tell how uncomfortable I am talking about Mavis and takes it as a sign to keep
pressing. "May I ask *why* you don't want to reach out to Mavis?"

"It's complicated."

"Try me."

"I'd rather not."

"Didn't you tell me she was the first person you came out to? At
lunch in eighth grade, if I'm not mistaken?"

I'm a bit surprised he remembers. "Yeah. I nervously spilled
soup everywhere."

He smiles. "So clearly she's a person you trusted—at least at one
point—right?"

Yes. But I can't admit that to him now without telling him why
that's not true anymore. "That soup spill was a long time ago. A lot
has changed."

I can tell he's contemplating digging in further, but after a glance at the time, he decides against it. "You don't need to talk to Mavis, but I'd like you to do something to acknowledge today's significance. It'll help. What about visiting his gravestone?"

"That's too cliché. Plus, cemeteries creep me out."

"Could you visit his family?"

"Dylan's dad is awful and his mom lives in Indiana."

"You could write Dylan a letter?"

"I know I haven't gone to medical school yet, but I'm pretty sure dead people can't read," I say, even as I shiver at the thought.

Mr. Babcock glares. "The purpose of writing it would be for you to process your feelings, funny guy."

"I'd rather be pen pals with the living."

"What about journaling about him?" he asks. "Sometimes, when your feelings feel too big, just getting them out of your head and onto paper can help. You don't even need to journal about Dylan for the practice to benefit you."

I stay silent, pretending to mull it over. Because the more time I waste, the faster I can escape this office.

"River," he breathes, "can I be candid with you?"

I nod.

"I'm happy you got the scholarship to Cascara. But with only a few days left of school, I worry going there in the fall may be tough."

I almost respond with a snort. Has he seen my GPA? "I know I can handle college."

"I know you can *academically*," he says, "but emotionally, I'm not as sure."

My cheeks redden as my eyes shift from Mr. Babcock to the window instead.

"You'll be on the West Coast," he continues. "Without Dylan as your roommate, you won't know anybody out there. I understand wanting to leave Teawood to start fresh, but I'm concerned you won't have the support you need in Oregon."

I stay silent, my eyes still glued to the distant clouds outside.

He's not wrong. But he doesn't get *why* I need to leave Teawood to start fresh. I'm not only going for myself; I'm going for Dylan, too. And I can't ditch our plan and stay trapped in Teawood forever.

"Have you heard about the Affinity Trials?" Mr. Babcock asks.

I perk up. "I met the guy with the beard at their sign-up table. Why?"

"Dr. Ridges came in here earlier to introduce himself," he says. "He told me a bit about the type of student they're looking for."

The type. Clearly, I fall into that category.

"Are you going to participate?" Mr. Babcock asks.

I sigh. "Probably not, no."

"How come?"

"Would *you* want to spend a week trapped in this school right after your final day as a student here?" I ask pointedly.

He shrugs. "If it came with a nice stipend, yes."

"How come businesses are allowed at Summer Sign-Ups now?" I ask. "That hadn't been the case before."

Mr. Babcock pauses, deciding how honest he wants to be, before lowering his voice. "When a business pays the school enough money to cover the rest of our gym's skylight renovations, rules become more . . . *flexible*, so to speak. But you didn't hear that from me."

One year later, and just hearing the word *gym* still plunges me into a pool of dread. It was my favorite place in this school before Dylan died, but I haven't stepped inside since. It reminds me of him too much.

"Hey," he says after I don't respond, "believe me, I'm not thrilled that Principal Fyres gave Dr. Ridges permission to use my office during the trials without running it by me first, but I'm focused on the greater good. And in this case, the greater good is students like *you* benefiting from a study like *this*."

Mr. Babcock lifts a small stack of business cards I hadn't noticed off his crowded desk and hands me one. I see the same *the Affinity Trials* text on its surface.

"I already got one from skinny Santa before first period," I say, "but thanks."

The bell rings, and not a moment too soon. I swing my bag over my shoulder and head to the door, grateful to have only four more first periods left with Mr. Babcock.

"River?" Mr. Babcock asks before I can escape. "Promise me you'll at least think about signing up for the study?"

I nod halfheartedly, unsure if it's a promise I want to keep. "Okay."

5

RIVER

I hear the door from the garage to the kitchen swing open and close, followed by the familiar sound of grocery bags landing on countertops, which means my mom's home and my after-school peace is about to be replaced with an onslaught of Dylan-themed questions.

"River?"

"In here," I answer her from the living room sofa, where I'm lying on my side and channel surfing.

I hear her bounce into the dining room behind me moments before feeling her presence hovering nearby.

"'We believe the trials will revolutionize the world's understanding of social connection among young people . . . '?" she reads off my phone. "What's that about?"

I grab it off the sofa cushion next to me. "It's just a thing from Summer Sign-Ups."

I got curious and looked up the website on Dr. Ridges's business card, but I'd rather not bring it up with my mom just so that another adult in my life can lecture me on why I should participate.

"I can't believe Summer Sign-Ups are happening again already." I can tell by the tone of her voice that what she's really saying is *I can't believe it's been a year since Dylan died.* "Tell me more about these so-called *revolutionary* trials you learned about today."

"They're looking for students for a study."

"A study on social connection?"

I nod.

My mom circles the sofa and gestures for me to scooch so she has room to sit, too. I move my legs and she falls into the space next to me, tossing her receptionist name tag onto the coffee table. Then she pulls out her hair tie with a sigh, as her graying blond hair falls to the side.

"Are you going to sign up?" she asks.

"No. The study website says I'd have to turn over my phone. Plus, I'd be on surveillance cameras there basically 24/7."

Being trapped at school for an entire week sounds awful enough without losing access to the outside world and being monitored nonstop.

My mom waits a beat before conceding. "Okay, that's a little creepy."

I really did try to be more open-minded about the study after Mr. Babcock encouraged me to consider participating, but five minutes on TheAffinityTrials.com made the idea even less enticing. The study sounds like a bizarre boot camp, with strict bedtimes, barely any info on what they're even studying, and vague descriptions about what I'd be doing in there for seven days. If I'm spending a week trapped inside the high school, I'd like to know a little more about how my time will be spent beyond just "games and group activities."

I go back to channel surfing and decide to rewatch the docuseries about the emerging science of black holes that Dylan was obsessed with. I've already seen it from start to finish four times, but it's loaded with so much info that I pick up on new factoids every rewatch. Besides, if Mr. Babcock wants me to find a way to remember Dylan today, learning more about the mysteries of dark matter feels way more in step with the Dylan I knew than visiting a grave site.

My mom hears the docuseries' dramatic theme music and sighs. Honestly, I can't blame her. As much as I love rewatching it, I'm sick of the intro, too.

"We didn't get a chance to talk about today before you left for school," she says.

Here we go.

While I've appreciated my mom's attempts to be there for me throughout the past year, I've gotten more anxious whenever I sense she wants to talk about Dylan. I haven't cried over him yet, which, coupled with my allegedly strange reactions to mentions of Dylan, basically guarantees the prodding will continue until I move out of the house.

But I get the sense she's increasingly determined to make one of these chats end with me floating in a puddle of my own tears, and I'd rather not force it. If I feel like crying over Dylan, I will. What's it to her, or *anyone*, if I haven't yet?

"Don't you want to talk about today?" she follows up. "I'm sure it was difficult."

I almost crack a joke about surviving Mr. Babcock's coffee breath being way harder than anything related to the deathiversary, but I stop myself. Sometimes I'm able to filter out my "inappropriate reactions" around my mom so she'll stop bugging me about them.

I seep deeper into the sofa.

"Hello?" she prods. "Earth to River?"

"I'm too far away for Earth to reach me right now," I say, watching a black hole eat a galaxy. "Try back next millennium."

My mom grins and pats my leg.

She still smells like the dentist's office where she works, an odd combination of disinfectant, toothpaste, and an overheating printer. She hates the smell even more than I do, and the fact she hasn't gone to change out of her work clothes the second after she walked in the door tells me she's been eager to have this conversation all day.

She nudges my side in another attempt to redirect my attention off the screen. "You don't have to guard your feelings so tightly, you know. Today must have felt *different*, at least."

"I'm not sure why everyone expects today to be so different for me than any other Monday. Dylan is on my mind *every* day, not just June third."

"I know, Riv," she says, "I know."

My mom slips her shoes off and gets more comfortable on the sofa as the series' narrator explains what the Big Bang was.

"I drove by Mount Marigold on my way home, you know," she says nonchalantly, trying to be clever.

Mount Marigold is the wooded area near the Meyerses' house where me and Mavis used to play our make-believe games growing up. My mom mentions it whenever she wants to bring up Mavis but needs a believable segue to do so. She drives past the hill on her way to work every day, though, so her strategy is much less subtle than she thinks it is.

"It reminded me of Mavis," she says, right on cue. "By the way, did you see her today?"

"Yeah."

"Did you two talk?"

I don't respond.

"Hey." My mom takes the clicker from my hand as a star collapses in on itself and turns off the TV. "I *asked*, did you talk to Mavis?"

"No."

"I think you should."

"Okay."

"Even if today felt like any other day to you, maybe it didn't for Mavis," she says. "I know you two aren't the best of friends anymore, which I still don't understand because you refuse to tell me why—"

"I *have*, Mom," I interject, feeling my heartbeat tick up, "because friends grow apart sometimes."

I can tell she doesn't believe my reasoning, yet again, and I honestly can't blame her. "All I'm saying is, you both meant the world to Dylan. She may appreciate a call—you know, just to check in."

Is my mom scheming with Mr. Babcock or something?

"Hey, guys," my dad says groggily as he emerges from his office at the end of the hallway. His brown hair is messier than usual, his under-eye circles are darker, and there are coffee stains on his checkered button-down—three signs that his Monday has also sucked. "Paige texted me about coming home in August for her birthday, but she wants to make sure we'll all be around."

My mom lights up, like she always does when we hear from my older sister. "Of course! We should plan a barbecue. Ask her if she'd like that."

"Will do." My dad grins and looks to me. "I wasn't sure about you, kid. Don't you leave on August twelfth?"

My stomach churns.

My flight to Oregon isn't until the twenty-fifth, but I know why the twelfth is probably stuck in my dad's head: it's the date me and Dylan had been planning to leave on our cross-country road trip to Cascara together.

"No, I'll be around," I reply.

"He leaves the last Sunday of August," my mom says, glancing at me. "I can't stomach thinking about you being three time zones away from us, you know."

My dad turns toward his home office again before remembering something. "Oh, did you guys"—he strikes a serious tone—"see it?"

It takes me a moment before I realize the "it" he's referring to is the same "it" Goldie brought up earlier. I swallow hard and try to look chill, knowing there's no world in which my parents would be on board with my decision to spray-paint the mustache, even if I explained my rationale for doing it. Thankfully, a knock on the door interrupts our conversation.

My mom and dad look at me, surprised.

"I'm not expecting anyone," I say.

My dad walks to the foyer and I hear the front door swing open, followed by his voice greeting someone, but I can't make out what's being said next. When he returns to the living room a few moments later, his eyebrows are crinkled. "Do you know a Jacob Lewis from school?" he asks me. "He wants to talk to you about something."

Jacob Lewis?

I sit up on the sofa, racking my brain for what this could possibly be about. I barely know Jacob, but his eyes felt like daggers this morning in the parking lot before school. Did I do something to piss him off without realizing it?

I walk to the open front door and see Jacob standing on the porch. Our eyes meet awkwardly.

"Hey," I say, stepping outside and closing the door behind me. "How's it going?"

"All right." Jacob is about my height and keeps his low fade impressively fresh. I can only hope the angry Hulk on his shirt doesn't match the energy he's bringing to the conversation he's about to have with me. "I'll get right to it." He glances around to make sure we're not being watched before reaching into his pocket and pulling out a business card. I recognize the four colored dots right away. "I saw you talking to Dr. Ridges this morning. I need you to sign up for the study."

"What?" I tilt my head with a grin, unsure if this is some weird joke. "Why?"

"Because I know you spray-painted Dylan's billboard," he says, eyes glued to mine, "and if you don't sign up for the trials, I'm telling everyone."

6

I say goodbye to my dad and answer River's incoming call.

"Jupiter's biggest moon," he says before I can even say hello, "quick."

I grin apologetically at Brady in the passenger seat as I drop behind the steering wheel with my phone wedged between my neck and ear. "That's easy. Ganymede. It's even bigger than Mercury."

"And Pluto."

"Which, as you know, is no longer classified as a planet—"

"But *should* be."

Every so often, River begins our phone calls with a planetary pop quiz. I once pointed out how needlessly competitive they've become, seeing as he'll be a neurologist someday and I'll be an engineer—two careers in which random space facts hardly come in handy. *But not everything needs to be about preparing for the future*, he argued back. Which is fair.

I start the car and drive toward the parking lot exit. "You watched Dr. Skelemont's episode on Pluto, right?" I ask River.

"Of course."

"Then you know it's not gravitationally dominant in its region. Which means, technically, it's not a plan—"

"We're *really* going to do this again?"

I laugh.

Brady points out the windshield and whispers, "That way, *that way*," as we exit the parking lot. I spin the steering wheel in the opposite direction and the wheels screech before I center the car in the correct lane. I mouth *sorry* at him.

"You good over there?" River asks.

"Yeah. I'm giving Brady a ride home."

"Brady?"

"Potts," I say, glancing to my right with a smile. But Brady seems unbothered by our phone call, practically entranced by the blur of trees and homes outside his window as if he doesn't see them every day.

"Personal chauffeur," River says. "Is that another responsibility for the juniors' student-athlete of the month that I didn't know about?"

"You know it."

"Want to come over after you drop him off?" River asks. "I'm finally going to watch that docuseries on black holes you won't stop raving about. Also, my mom is making chicken enchiladas."

"*Oof*, very tempting," I say, "but I can't."

"Why not?"

"I'm hanging out with Mavis."

"Tell her to come, too," River says. "I finished her copy of *Himawari House*, so she can get it back. She's been bugging me about it for months. Unless . . ." He pauses. ". . . you guys want some *alone* time?" He moans through the speaker.

I grin, glancing at Brady to make sure he didn't hear River's sultry performance. "No, I'm going to her house."

"On a Saturday?" He laughs. "Then I know alone time will not be happening."

I rarely spend Saturdays at Mavis's house. Mr. and Mrs. Meyers typically aren't home during the day, which you'd think would allow for more privacy, but the opposite ends up being true.

Mavis has three younger siblings, and without parental supervision, things tend to be even more chaotic around the house than they normally are during the week. So I get why River's surprised.

I don't have any better options to have the talk, though. Mavis is busy with church stuff all day tomorrow, and her teachers approved of her missing our final week of school to attend a summer camp for aspiring law students since finals already happened. Then when Mavis gets back on Friday, her family takes off for their camping trip up north—for the rest of June.

I can't put the breakup off for that long. It wouldn't be fair to Mavis. Plus, this way, she'll have time and space to process it, and maybe she'll be ready to talk to me once she's back in Teawood. We can spend the rest of the summer smoothing things over, adjusting to life as friends, and still have an incredible senior year. *All* of us can, together. Me, River, and Mavis—or, as Mrs. Lang once referred to us, "the three peas in a pod."

At least, I hope that's how this goes. I may not be *in* love with her anymore, but I still love Mavis, and I can't stomach the thought of losing her for good.

"This is the last day I'll be able to see her before she's gone the rest of the month," is all I say to River, though.

It's strange not telling him that I'm going to end it with Mavis, because of all the people in my life, I share the most with River. But I know it's the right thing to do.

Mavis and River have been friends much longer than I've been close to either of them, which I respect, and I'm not entirely sure how he'll take it. Plus, I have to consider what comes *after* I do it. I'm hopeful the breakup won't end disastrously, but in case it does, I haven't wanted to implicate River in my decision. I love both of them too much to pit my two best friends against each other. So for River, when it comes to this, I think ignorance really is bliss.

"I keep forgetting Mavis has that . . . what are we calling it again?" River asks. "Lawyer boot camp?"

"That might be what *you're* calling it," I say, "but no. It's a camp for aspiring law students."

"A camp for aspiring law students . . ." River repeats slowly and with a sigh. "I can't think of anything more boring or perfectly Mavis than that. Speaking of camping up north, though, I need to send you this link of the worst campgrounds in America."

"Why?"

"Because a bunch of the spots on the list contradict what we've been following in *Starlight Sleeps*."

"Yeah?" I perk up, shaking off the anxiety over what I'm about to do. "Do tell."

River starts firing off the names of overrated campgrounds to cross off our list for next summer's road trip before going on a tangent about which tourist traps we need to avoid and which might be worth it. Iowa's "largest bull in the world" statue is allegedly underwhelming, but a gourmet popcorn stand off the beaten path near Grand Junction is supposedly Colorado's best-kept secret.

Usually, I try to avoid thinking about next summer too much in an effort to stay focused on senior year. But between Harry's advice to slow down, my dad interrogating me about my calc exam, and the excitement bursting through my phone from River, I'd love to be able to hit fast-forward and take off on our road trip right now.

"Oh, side note, before I forget," he says, shifting gears, "I saw a whodunit graphic novel that takes place at a *law school*. Obviously it screamed Mavis and I almost bought it for her, but because I'm an amazing friend and want you to win some boyfriend points, I'll let you do the honors, if you want."

My gut churns again.

"Right here!" Brady pipes up, pointing to a red-and-white house on the left.

I jolt my attention back to the road and hit the brakes a little too hard. My wheels let out another screech as they turn into the Pottses' driveway and bring us to a stop.

River gasps. "What happened?"

"Nothing, just got to Brady's," I say, shifting the car into park. "Can I call you later?"

"Yeah."

I hang up and turn to the passenger seat. "Sorry for being on the phone the whole time . . . and also for almost taking out your mailbox."

Brady just smiles. "Thank you for the ride." He pulls the door handle but pauses before getting out. "Can I ask, what is *Starlight Sleeps*?"

The question catches me off guard because I doubted Brady could even hear what River was saying on the other end of the line, let alone care enough to listen in. I wonder what he thought about River's pretend moaning. "Have you heard of Dr. Skelemont?"

He thinks. "The space scientist?"

"Yeah. *Starlight Sleeps* is his book about the best campgrounds to stargaze. River and I are using it to plan our road trip to college next summer. We're going to be roommates at Cascara."

I brace for Brady to react.

It's not that I care all that much about what he thinks of me. It's just, this is the first time I'm telling another junior about me and River's objectively nerdy plans to spend our final days before college stargazing together instead of partying.

Brady stares at me in the same dreamy way he stares at *every-one*, all the time. But right now, it feels different. Like he's seeing a bit more of the whole me. "Wow," he finally says. "To be with your best friend under the stars? I can't think of cooler way to start a new adventure."

His words sink in like a warm hug.

I'm grateful Brady didn't do what my dad did when he first learned about our road trip idea and responded with a homophobic "joke" warning me not to share a tent with River or reenact a scene from *Brokeback Mountain*.

"Thanks," I say, "I needed to hear that."

The Pottses' screen door creaks open. Brady's frail grandma is leaning against the frame, an oxygen mask strapped around her freckled face. She still manages to wave and smile at us, though.

"How come you asked me to be your partner in class?" Brady asks out of nowhere.

I turn to him, yet again, surprised by his question. "Huh?"

"Fifth-period Spanish last year," he answers. "You asked to be my partner on our final project, even though I was barely passing the class. We both know partnering with me made your life harder." He laughs.

I forgot about that, honestly.

The truth is, Brady doesn't seem to have many friends at school, and he rarely said a word in that class—in English *or* Spanish. I felt bad, and I was trying to be nice.

"Well," he says after I struggle to answer, "it was a kind thing to do, just like driving me home today. And I like when people do kind things, especially when they're hard. Not enough people do."

Brady is already striding toward the front porch before I can respond. He hugs his grandma on the way inside, and the screen door closes with a creak and thud.

A twinge of guilt twists in my middle again, this time for having reduced Brady to being a loner with colorful hair when he'd probably understand me, the *whole* me, more than most. I'd probably understand him, too, if given the chance.

I back out of the driveway, extra careful to stay clear of the Pottses' mailbox, and head toward Mavis's house. I glance down at my phone, wondering if I should call River back right now and go ahead and tell him. But Brady's words stop me.

Mr. Babcock always spouts these cheesy sayings *live, laugh, love*–style, but one time he said that "a friend is someone who reminds you who you are when you've forgotten." It stuck. And a moment ago, despite us barely knowing each other, Brady gave me that reminder.

I love Mavis and River too much to drag River into my decision. The kindest thing to do is keep him in the dark.

7

RIVER

My blood runs cold as I struggle to keep my composure. "What are you talking about?"

Jacob is refusing to blink, his eyes piercing me on the front porch, reading me like a book. He doesn't seem angry, just stone-cold serious. "Don't bother pretending," he says casually, "I know you painted the mustache on Dylan."

"But—"

"So unless you want me to tell everyone, you need to sign up for the Affinity Trials, complete the weeklong study, and then give me half your stipend."

My jaw drops. A *thousand* dollars? "What for?"

"It doesn't concern you," he says, stepping backward off the porch.

"Wait, you're leaving?" I hiss, trying to keep my voice down. "Jacob, hold on—"

"We'll touch base once the trials are over so you can give me my half."

My brain is about to combust. Is Jacob Lewis actually black-mailing me right now? How does he even know I spray-painted the billboard? And how do I know he hasn't told anyone already? But also . . .

"Why do you think I care?" I challenge, all my frustrations from today bursting out of me at once. "Tell the whole fucking town. This is my last week of school anyway, why would I—"

I freeze, remembering my scholarship to Cascara.

The money would be revoked if word got back to the school about my vandalizing a billboard, I'm sure, and there's no way my parents can afford out-of-state tuition. I could apply for financial aid, but not in time for the fall semester.

I'm trapped.

Jacob waits another moment for me to finish my thought, then turns to leave.

"Wait," I call after him, hopping off the porch and crossing the front lawn. "What if I sign up for the study but don't get in? Skinny Santa was telling me that—"

"Who?"

"You know, Dr. Ridges? He said they're only accepting twenty kids." I think back to the requirements I read about on the Affinity website. "What if I fail the qualification survey thing we need to take—"

"You mean the A-Test?"

"Yes." We approach his car, parked on the street next to our mailbox. "It's out of my control if I don't qualify. You'd still tell everyone about the mustache if I'm not accepted? Which, for the record, I'm *not* admitting to spray-painting—"

"None of that is my problem," Jacob says, swinging his car door open. He hops inside and looks up at me through his open window. "So you better make sure you get in."

Without another word, his car roars to life and jets off down my street. And somehow, Dylan's already-terrible deathiversary just got significantly worse.

I try to play it cool walking back inside the house.

"That was fast," my dad says, his head shooting out from the office. He looks me up and down suspiciously. "Were you yelling at him about something?"

"It was just a bit." I round the corner and head for the stairs. "An inside joke."

"You have inside jokes with Jacob?" my mom calls after me from the kitchen. "Also, who's Jacob?"

I reach the top of the stairs and dash to my room, pretending as though I couldn't hear my mom's questions. I close the door, fall onto the mattress, and try to digest the disaster unraveling around me.

On one hand, I'm not ashamed of what I did. I'm proud to be the artist behind the mustache, because any driver-safety billboard with the tagline DON'T DREXT LIKE DYLAN DID deserves to be vandalized, for one, but more importantly, I know Dylan would've appreciated it, too. Screw everyone else in Teawood for feigning outrage as they text gossipy whodunit messages about possible suspects from behind the wheel themselves. But on the other hand, I desperately need to escape Teawood—for me and Dylan both—and getting caught as the culprit would tear up my ticket to Cascara, ending our dream of leaving.

I don't know what Jacob is up to or why he needs money badly enough to target me, but none of that matters right now. I don't have much of a choice.

I have to sign up for the Affinity Trials.

8

RIVER

Walking into school the next day pretty much confirms I need to do everything I can to keep Billboardgate an unsolved mystery, even if it means getting blackmailed. Because I've seriously underestimated this school's penchant for scandal.

Nearly every conversation I overhear is related to the mustache.

"I heard it was Seth Smith. He was always jealous of Dylan."

"Maybe the cops will find the person's fingerprints around the sign?"

"I bet Dylan died in a hit-and-run, and the spray painter is the guy who drove away."

Some of the conspiracy theories I'm hearing make Roy's suspicion of the pet groomers seem logical in comparison.

Entering the Affinity Trials is my only option to avoid the spotlight landing on me, given Teawood's growing hunger to find the vandal, but if Goldie is already suspicious of me and Jacob is somehow certain I did it, will it even matter?

If I was sloppy enough to be a suspect this quickly in the eyes of at least two people, who else might already know? Did Puparazzi-Ready have a surveillance camera in their parking lot I passed without having my hood up? Wait, *can* the cops search for my fingerprints near the sign?

I try to push past the anxious thoughts swirling in my head and walk down the main hallway to find a smiley Dr. Ridges dressed in another tweed suit (today's is maroon) standing behind the Affinity table. He's fielding what I can only imagine are bizarre questions from Brady Potts, whose spacey, awkward nature increases the chances he'll land one of the trial's twenty slots. I don't stop by, and I tell myself it's because I'll be late again to Mr. Babcock's if I wait around for them to finish talking. I can always come back before second period.

But Dr. Ridges calls after me before I can get away. "River, my friend."

Friend? I turn back.

"Did you want to talk?" he asks. "Because if you can wait just one more moment, I'm finishing up with Brady—"

"I'll be back before my next class," I assure him, pivoting away.

I don't know if it's nerves, procrastination, or dread, but I don't go back after first period. Or second . . . or third. It takes a full day of overhearing Billboardgate gossip and imagining a letter in the mail confirming my Cascara scholarship has been revoked over a dumb mustache to force me back down the main hallway again after last period.

Dr. Ridges stands to greet me. "I was hoping I'd see you again today."

I approach the table but stand at a safe distance, should there be another attempt at a hug. He seems to notice my caution.

"I apologize for trying to console you yesterday when you hadn't asked for it, River," he says. "I overstepped and I'm deeply sorry."

I . . . wasn't expecting that. I stand a bit taller. "Okay. Thank you." The genuine look of relief in his eyes surprises me.

"Did you get the chance to explore our website?" he asks.

I nod.

"Wonderful," he says, beaming. "What questions do you have for me?"

I think. "Everyone has to follow the no-devices rule, right? Including phones?"

He grins. "It's our most-asked question by far. Yes, everyone has to follow that rule."

"And cameras are recording us all the time? Everywhere?"

"Certainly not *everywhere*." His smile grows. "You'll have complete privacy in specific spots, such as the restroom. It sounds more unsettling than it will be in practice."

"What are you guys studying anyway?" I ask directly. "I know the site mentioned friendship and social dynamics, or whatever, but can you be more specific?"

"I can't divulge much more to potential participants," he notes. "As I'm sure you've learned in your science classes, that would bias the results. But should you qualify and decide to enter, you'd be placed into a group of your peers and given daily schedules that include activities, like art and fitness. All you need to do is enjoy the experience—and, critically, follow all the rules."

He tries to sound mischievous to sell me on it, as if the Affinity Trials are like the Hunger Games—not a study of social misfits stuck in a suburban high school for a week.

But I don't reciprocate his playfulness.

"That's really all you can say about what you're studying?" I ask, unimpressed.

I can't tell if Dr. Ridges is frustrated or amused by my stubbornness, but he holds my stare for an awkwardly long time before offering up a few more crumbs. "Our focus is social dynamics, as you noted, and we'll be analyzing many factors related to how participants who self-identify as struggling in this area behave, socialize, and change throughout the week of the study."

"Factors . . . like what?"

"All will be made clear, should you enter and complete the

trials." He slips off his glasses for a moment to remove a smudge. "May I ask how old you are, River?"

"Eighteen."

Dr. Ridges bends in half and reemerges with an overstuffed briefcase, which lands on the table with a thud. He reaches inside, pulls out a form crammed with tiny text on its front and back sides, and hands it to me. "Since you're eighteen, you don't need parental permission. But you do need to sign a consent form to enter the trials, and that needs to be done before you can begin your A-Test to qualify. I assume you also read about A-Tests on the website?"

I nod and glimpse at the first paragraph of the consent form, which is filled with so much legal jargon, I might as well be trying to read Mandarin.

Sensing my irritation, Dr. Ridges leans toward me. "You know, even some eighteen-year-olds have had their parents read through the consent form to ensure everyone is on the same page. Why don't you take it home tonight and run through it with them?"

Roping my parents into this any more than they need to be will only create more potential for them to discover why I'm really signing up. I haven't exactly been eager to find more friends this year, and my mom will already be questioning my change of heart after I panned the trials in front of her yesterday; I don't need to create more opportunities for the truth to surface.

"It's okay," I say, "I don't need to read it with them first."

"Are you sure?"

"Yes."

Dr. Ridges hands me a pen out of his briefcase. I skim through the rest of the consent form, deciding it looks somewhat standard, sign on the dotted line, and hand the form back.

"Excellent," he says, reaching behind the table again to grab a clipboard. "Would you mind printing your name here?"

I freeze, spotting two familiar names on the list.

11. *Mavis Meyers*
12. *Goldie Candles*

Goldie?

In what world would Goldie Candles ever be considered someone who's "struggling socially"? She has, like, a hundred awful friends at Teawood. And the cash stipend can't be all that attractive to her, either. From the number of new outfits Goldie debuts each week, I can't imagine her allowance isn't double whatever pennies she made at the ice cream parlor last summer before getting fired.

"Is there a problem?" Dr. Ridges asks, noticing my hesitation.

I gesture at the eighty-three other names listed on the clipboard. "About how many people will sign up, do you think?"

"For a school the size of Teawood, I wouldn't be surprised if by Friday we ended up having around . . ." Dr. Ridges pauses to think. "A hundred fifty, two hundred students, give or take."

"So if you're only taking twenty for the trials," I say slowly, trying to do the mental math, "the vast majority won't get accepted into the study, right? Maybe just ten to fifteen percent?"

"That's correct. As much as I'd like to accept everyone, we want to ensure every participant meets the criteria, so our results are useful and up to standards."

The study being incredibly selective means Goldie's chances of getting in are basically zero. But if they're searching for sad, disconnected teens, I can't think of a better candidate at this school than Mavis—other than possibly myself. We may not have spoken for a year, but that hasn't stopped my noticing her staring off into space in the hall between class, quitting the AAPI Student

Association, and leaving the bathroom dabbing at her eyes on more than one occasion.

I look back down at the sheet, weighing my options. Nothing about Jacob's demeanor yesterday implied he's bluffing about exposing me if I don't make the cut. But if I *do* get in, my guess is Mavis will, too, and that means a torturous week trapped inside the high school with a former best friend who now can't stand the sight of me. Still, I'd rather suffer through seven awkward days with Mavis than see my scholarship ripped away from me over some spray paint.

I scribble my name on the sheet.

"So," I ask Dr. Ridges, adjusting the straps of my backpack, "when is my A-Test?"

Dr. Ridges checks his phone again. "How about now?"

"Like . . . *now*, now?"

"Yes, River. Now, now."

I swallow. "I'm not prepared to take it, though."

"There's nothing to prepare for." He starts tapping away on his phone. "A student just canceled on us, so our research associate could see you in about five minutes. Classroom D12, Mr. Simpson's room, I'm told."

I look down the hallway, contemplating. I'm probably not going to get any more information out of Dr. Ridges to help my chances, so I might as well get it over with. "All right, let's do this."

"Magical," Dr. Ridges says. "Don't worry if the door is still closed and you need to wait a few minutes for the research associate to finish up. Just take a seat outside. I'll let them know you're on your way."

I halfheartedly thank Dr. Ridges and head off. When I enter Mr. Simpson's hallway, I see identical signs covering the windowpanes looking into a few classrooms, including D12.

RESERVED AFTER SCHOOL FOR AFFINITY MIND & BODY, JUNE 3–7. *I'm making the right decision,* I keep telling myself as I wait outside, although it's hardly quelling the sense of dread creeping through my insides. I'll survive the final days of school, get through this study, and then put Teawood and the worst year of my life behind me after I give half my stipend to—

"Jacob?" I blurt, seeing him appear in Mr. Simpson's doorway.

I startle him, but he regains his cool a split second later. "Hey."

Why would Jacob blackmail me for more stipend money if he plans on participating himself? And why would he only demand half? Is there some rare Captain America collector's item that's selling for three grand or something?

Before I can lob questions his way, Jacob disappears down the hallway, his bulging backpack bouncing against his spine. Being forced to spend a week with Mavis would be bad enough, but the potential combination of Mavis, Goldie, *and* Jacob? I might as well just go confess everything to Principal Fyres now.

"And you are . . ." A voice turns my attention back to Mr. Simpson's classroom, where a woman who looks just a few years older than me is standing in the doorway. She references the phone in her hand. ". . . River Lang?"

I nod, surprised a research associate could be as young as she is. I squint at her name tag, which reads MS. MEHTA.

"Ignore that," she says, noticing where my eyes are pointed, as she presents her hand to shake. "They want us to be *professional,* but Ms. Mehta is my mom. I'm Nora."

My expecting a female version of Dr. Ridges to run my A-Test was way off. Instead of a tweed suit, she has on a yellow hoodie that complements her deep brown eyes and skin. Her hair is spun into a messy bun that's unraveling strand by strand as we speak, and her faded blue jeans are holey at the kneecaps.

"All right, River," Nora says, gesturing for me to follow her. "Let's get started."

I walk into the classroom and close the door behind me. All the desks and chairs have been pushed against the walls except for a single set in the center of the room, placed next to Mr. Simpson's projector.

"That's all yours," Nora instructs, pointing at the seat.

I walk across the room and slide behind the desk. "How long will this take?"

"An hour-ish," Nora says, busying herself in the corner.

I let out an agitated sigh, which probably isn't a great look, considering Affinity likely wants students who actually want to be part of the study. So I try to think of a question I can ask to seem at least a little bit interested in the trials. "Why is it called an A-Test anyway?"

"Technically, it's the Affinity Assessment Test," Nora explains, "but we thought calling it 'AA' ran the risk of parents thinking their fifteen-year-old is going to an Alcoholics Anonymous meeting. One *A* works just fine."

Nora pushes a cart toward me in the center of the classroom. On its surface, I see a lopsided mountain of paperwork, colorful manila folders, and a large laptop with dozens of stickers littering the back of its screen. It seems as though Nora not only doesn't care about appearing professional but is actively fighting against it.

It takes me a moment to realize that a set of lime-green wires connected to Nora's computer is attached to an object that looks like a metallic black helmet sitting on the second level of the cart.

I stare at the apparent torture device. "What is *that*?"

"It's fucking bizarre, right?" Nora catches herself. "Shit, Dr. Ridges warned me about cursing in front of students—*damn it*."

I surprise myself with a laugh.

She pauses to collect herself as another loose strand of hair falls away from her bun. "Let me try that again." She clears her throat, pointing at the black helmet thing. "Their full name is Neurotracker-Yranigami Model 77490, but we call them the Neuro for short."

"The Neuro," I repeat, staring at it.

"Yes, sir. You'll wear the Neuro on your head during a portion of the A-Test so it can . . . well, tell me what's going on in your brain."

I perk up, intrigued but suspicious. Dr. Ridges didn't mention anything about the Neuro tracking my brain waves, and the Affinity Trials' scant website implied researchers are only studying participants' social behaviors.

"What sorts of things does the Neuro see?"

"Hoo-boy. Lots." Nora flips through some paperwork before looking up at me. "Didn't you read about it in your consent form?"

Oh.

I nod, as if just now remembering. "Right. Yes."

She reads her phone. "It says here that you submitted your consent form to Dr. Ridges, correct?"

"Yep."

"You're eighteen years old?"

"Yeah."

"How are you with needles?"

"Uh . . . why do you ask?"

She pauses. "For your sample."

"Sample of . . . ?"

Damn it, I scold myself, thinking the consent form probably answered that, too. Before Nora speaks up, I pretend to recall what she's referring to. I assume it's blood, because if not, I'm not sure I want to know what bodily fluid Affinity wants to collect from me using a needle.

She reaches into the lower half of the cart. In the blink of an eye, there are fresh latex gloves on Nora's hands and she's wiping my arm with a disinfectant pad. She pulls out a needle and focuses on where it should sink into my skin.

"Just a quick *poke*," she says, right as I feel it.

I watch dark red liquid slowly fill a small glass vial on the cart.

"Doing okay?" Nora asks, closely monitoring every drop.

"Yeah, but why do you need to do this?" I ask. "I thought this was like a social study—not a medical one."

Nora freezes, as if I've said something *very* wrong. So I attempt to clarify my question, knowing that I can't do anything to lessen the chances that I'll pass my A-Test. "I mean, it's totally fine that you need a blood sample," I say, grinning. "I'm just curious."

Nora slowly rests her pointer finger over her lips and whispers, "Let's pretend you didn't ask me that. After all, they could be listening. . . ."

What?

Just when I start to panic, Nora dissolves into laughter. "Just kidding, River."

I stare back in surprise.

She pulls the needle out and wraps a narrow bandage over the entry point, still tickled by her own joke. "To answer your question, we're taking samples so that we can look at a variety of metrics." Nora pulls off her gloves and tosses them into the trash.

"Metrics such as . . . ?" I follow up. When she takes too long to answer, I continue, "Because a blood sample can relay a lot of info, like diseases, glucose levels—" I shut up, realizing I'm mansplaining blood to someone with much more medical training than me. "Sorry."

She smiles, impressed. "Don't be."

I try to justify my nosiness. "I'll be premed in the fall."

That is, if Jacob keeps his end of the deal—hence the whole reason why I'm even here.

Nora's eyes fall back onto the cart. "Which part of your A-Test do you want to do first? The interesting part—which involves this scary-looking thing that's actually not so scary—or the boring part?"

"What's the boring part?"

"A long-ass survey—" She drops her head again. "A *long* survey, unrelated to butts."

I'm able to stop a laugh from escaping this time, but I do grin. Thus far, Nora is way more my speed than Dr. Ridges.

"Let's do the interesting part first," I say.

She lifts the Neuro high into the air, checking that each wire is plugged in properly. Hundreds, if not thousands, of minuscule holes dot the helmet's interior surface, barely visible.

"Is this thing like . . . a portable MRI machine?"

"Sort of? But not really," she says. "It's more advanced. It monitors detailed brain activity in real time. Are you ready?"

No, because my curiosity has now officially been piqued. "Can I ask more questions first?"

She laughs. "You seem very interested in this."

"I want to study neurology after high school."

"Aha," she says with a nod, "that makes sense. Let's hear 'em. But keep in mind the technology is proprietary, so I can't tell you much more than you already know."

I'd still like to shoot my shot. "What brain activity is it monitoring, exactly?"

"I can't answer that."

"Can it gauge electrical signals in real time? Or is it even looking at electrical signals?"

"I can't answer questions one or two."

I stare at the Neuro. "Is there any comparable technology already out there that I might know about so I can learn *something*?"

"You'll never guess my answer, River, but"—she shakes her head—"I can't answer that."

I concede to Nora's tight lips as she pats my shoulder and lifts the Neuro onto my head. I cringe, expecting it to drop onto my skull like a brick, but it's shockingly light, and its holey, soft interior feels strangely cozy against my scalp.

Nora grabs a red wire plugged into the laptop among the lime-green ones and inserts it into Mr. Simpson's projector. A large aerial photograph featuring a green park, a brownish-blue creek, and a strip of brick storefronts appears on the board in front of me.

"Is that downtown Teawood?" I ask, looking at the projector screen.

Nora glances up. "It sure is. Quite the charming suburb, I admit, even if one of your school's linebackers gave my brother a concussion last season."

Nora walks toward the wall of windows and pulls on a chain—the room gets considerably darker as blinds block out the sunshine—and then heads to the door and flips off the light switch.

"This photo of downtown Teawood establishes a baseline," Nora says, crossing the room as my eyes adjust to the projector's glow in the darkness. "Once I hit play, other images will start appearing and disappearing on the board in front of you, too, sort of like a slideshow. Some of them may stay for a few seconds, others might be gone in a flash."

Establishes a baseline. That probably means the Neuro will be documenting some aspect of my brain's responses to the various images. I consider confirming my theory with Nora but stop myself, as there's a 99 percent chance she can't tell me anyway and pestering her with more questions would only annoy her.

"The slideshow will last sixty seconds," she continues. "You don't need to be thinking about or concentrating on anything specific. Just focus on the images. Oh, and please avoid talking and don't close your eyes—aside from blinking, of course." She smiles. "Make sense?"

"Makes sense."

Nora tweaks the helmet's exact placement on my head and checks her laptop to make sure everything's in order. Once she concludes we're set to begin, she taps a key on her laptop. "Ready?"

"Yep."

"Three, two, one . . ."

Nothing happens for about ten seconds. I'm just about to ask Nora if there's a problem with the slideshow when an odd sensation starts trickling across my scalp. The Neuro is becoming warmer, I realize, and my whole head feels tingly. It sort of reminds me of the feeling I used to get when me and Dylan would put heating pads on our freezing feet after coming inside from ice-skating.

The aerial photo of downtown Teawood disappears, and a bright yellow sunflower standing tall against a cloudless sky takes its place. Then the sunflower vanishes, too, replaced by an old man sitting on a park bench. Then it's this year's Teawood basketball team photo. My instinct is to search for Dylan's face until I remember why he isn't in it. When it disappears, a gigantic, melty chocolate chip cookie being held by someone with orange fingernails fills the screen. Then there's the Golden Gate Bridge, half covered in fog.

The speed of the photo changes starts to increase.

The Timber Wolf mascot doing a backflip (there's no time to tell if it's Roy or not). A photo of my freshman year social studies teacher, Mrs. Steinberg, eating an apple. Raindrops falling on a window in a blurry big city. Japanese soccer fans cheering in a stadium. A crying toddler with mud on their face. I barely have time to register any of them, but a teal car, its entire front smashed in from an apparent accident, hits me like a punch to the gut. Even though the vehicle looks nothing like Dylan's, my chest tightens and I almost have to look away.

That's not Dylan's car, I tell myself, *that's not Dylan's car.*

The speed of the transitions continues to tick up. I wish I were doing a better job at computing what I'm seeing, but I'm still so flustered from the image of the car that I start to distrust my eyes.

A cruise ship on the open water, I think.

A steak knife, maybe? Or is it—

Whoa, smoke billowing across the New York skyline on 9/11.

A pan of mac and cheese—wait, no, a photo of a *puzzle* of mac and cheese?

Dylan's grayscale face on the billboard. *With the mustache.*

A painting of Michelle Obama, possibly.

Either a Chia Pet or someone wearing a green, bushy wig.

Was that really Dylan's billboard?

I start to feel nauseous—whether from seeing the billboard or the speed of the images changing, it's hard to say—just as the slideshow stops on the same shot of downtown Teawood.

A few seconds later, the screen goes black. Then the classroom lights are on and Nora is pulling the Neuro off my head. "You good?" she asks, setting it down on the cart. I nod, although I'm not so sure, as my eyelids blink rapidly to adjust to the sudden brightness of the room.

That couldn't have been Dylan's billboard. Right?

I guess it wouldn't be out of the question, given there were lots of pics in there taken around town or at the high school. But an image of the billboard *with* Dylan's mustache on it? That'd mean it was taken fewer than forty-eight hours ago. And if the Neuro is collecting information that determines our qualifications for the trials, I'd assume the photos in the slideshow were carefully chosen by Affinity over a matter of weeks or months, not thrown together overnight.

But honestly? I could have imagined it.

In the first few months after Dylan died, I kept seeing him appear and vanish before my eyes—rounding a corner at school or speeding through my subdivision on his bike. I was even convinced I saw him one morning sitting behind the piano in the band room while I ran to first period. I did a little research, legitimately scared that I was losing my grip on reality, and was relieved to learn that grief can play all kinds of tricks on our brains. Eventually, the Dylan sightings stopped. But could they be returning?

I know it's a shot in the dark, given Nora's tight lips regarding anything related to the A-Tests, but I decide to ask anyway. "Was that Dylan Cooper's billboard in one of the images?"

"You're not going to like my response," she says, adjusting the wires on the Neuro, "but I can't answer—hold up." She freezes, eyebrows furrowed in thought. "Dylan Cooper . . . why does that name sound familiar?"

I wait a few seconds for her to connect the dots on her own.

Her face lights up knowingly. "*Oh*, the 'Don't Drext Like Dylan Did' billboard? God, what a tragedy."

"Yeah," I say, my skin crawling from hearing the tagline aloud.

"What a terrible sign," Nora adds under her breath, returning her attention to the laptop. "Texting or not, shaming a kid for his own death feels gross." She glances up at me. "Don't cancel me for saying that, please."

Cancel her? I'd prefer to wrap her up in my arms as tightly as possible after hearing a comment like that. But having just been on the receiving end of a nonconsensual hug only yesterday, I decide against it.

"Now on to the boring part of your A-Test," Nora says, oblivious to how much her stock just rose in my book. "Can you confirm your first and last name?"

"River Lang."

"R-I-V-E-R, L-A-N-G?"

"Yes."

"And do you identify as male, River?"

"Yeah."

"Date of birth?"

"January 24th, 2006."

Nora asks me to stand so she can snap a photo of me, then takes my weight and height. After I sit back down again, she pushes a stack of paper and a pen onto the desk.

"This survey is a beast, fair warning," she says. "But it's critical you answer all the questions as accurately as possible. Okay?"

I nod and get to work, as Nora starts typing all my info in on her laptop.

At first, the questions are straightforward:

In what city and state were you born?
Ann Arbor, Michigan.

What high school do/did you attend?
Teawood.

What is your race?
White.

Then the questions gradually get more personal.

Do you consider yourself more introverted or extroverted?
Since last summer, more introverted. Prior to that, more extroverted.

Are you easily embarrassed?
Not really.

How do you label your sexual orientation (if you categorize it)?
Gay.

I'm ready to get out of here by the time I reach the midway point, my wrist throbbing from the amount of handwriting this survey demands. But the final few questions are annoyingly difficult to answer on the fly, especially when I have to be strategic in hopes of qualifying for the trials. I don't want to outright *lie*, because if I get in, that could come back to haunt me. But I need to be thoughtful about my answers.

I stare down at the next line:

Name your favorite spot to spend time with a friend and explain why.

I'm not even sure I *have* any friends now, let alone a favorite spot to share with them, as I realized yesterday during my talk with Dr. Ridges. I mean, it used to be the gym, but not since Dylan died . . . which is *exactly* the kind of answer I should include, I realize.

Affinity wants teens who are struggling socially? Because that, I can give them. I jot down why I've been avoiding the gym and my realization that I don't have friends, and move on to the next question.

Describe a place where an important childhood friendship truly blossomed.
Mount Marigold, a hill with trees and creeks where I used to play with a good friend, but we don't talk anymore.

Would you be more nervous or excited about going to a party where you don't know the majority of people in attendance?
Definitely more nervous. I probably wouldn't go.

Have you ever been in love? Regardless of your answer, how do you know?
No. Because I feel like when you're in love, you just know it. And I know I haven't been.

My eyes move down the page to the last question. I hope it's an easy one to answer, because I'm pretty sure my wrist will fall off if it's not.

Do you have a best friend?

My hand freezes in place, the pen held tightly in my grip.

Does Dylan still count?

The scientist in me says no, considering a living, breathing body is typically seen as a prerequisite to a best friend, but the idea of acknowledging that on my survey unsettles my gut more than the Neuro's quick slideshow transitions did. Having to write an *n* and an *o* makes Dylan's death feel more personal and permanent than his funeral or a stupid driving PSA or a sobbing emoji with bowling balls for eyes ever did.

"Don't stress it," I hear Nora whisper.

I look up. She's smiling down at me, and it feels like the warm hug that I wanted after hearing her thoughts on the billboard.

"The last question throws some students off, River," she adds gently. "It's okay if the answer is no."

I feel hot tears collecting in the corners of my eyes. And for the first time, I start crying over my dead best friend.

9

DYLAN

Mavis and I are lying opposite each other atop her fluffy white comforter. Her bedroom door is wide open due to the Meyerses' most important, and also most obnoxious, house rule. I'm not annoyed because me and Mavis can't hook up—I can't recall the last time we even kissed, let alone needed that amount of privacy—but the open-door policy means not having a sound barrier to insulate us from Mavis's younger siblings' laughter, tantrums, and video games set to full volume.

Mavis's eyes are on her sketchpad, but I know she can feel me watching her draw. "Can I help you with something?" she asks, looking up with an anxious grin.

"Nope," I say, smiling back and wondering if I'm hiding my nerves any better than she is. I take in her bedroom, wondering when—or even *if*—I'll be in here again. It's tidy, airy, and bright, with just one framed poster on the wall and a few healthy plants thriving by the window. It's exactly the kind of minimalist bedroom classmates at school would assume Mavis the perfectionist has at home.

She hops off the bed and opens the top drawer of her work desk, though, revealing a side of herself that Mavis shares with very few people: the secret comic book artist.

The drawer is an absolute disaster. I'm used to seeing it by now, but the first time I got a peek inside, I was shocked at how little

Mavis cared about keeping her assortment of knickknacks, art supplies, and how-to books on sketching organized in any functional way. She cleans the insides of her locker with disinfectant wipes every week and meticulously updates her Google calendar hourly; how could the same Mavis I know draw so diligently at a desk that messy?

It took me a while to realize that she wasn't drawing in *spite* of the mess but in part *because* of it—that creating comics was an area of her life that felt off-limits to the demands of the outside world. Just like I'm liberated by playing piano, even when I'm butchering note after note, Mavis is freed from the pressures of perfectionism when she's creating on a sketchpad at a desk in disarray.

She tosses her sketchpad next to the tablet she uses for Illustrator and shuts the drawer, then notices that I'm watching her. "What?"

"Nothing."

"You're being weird," she says, still grinning, but more suspicious of me this time.

I force a laugh. "Okay."

Mavis falls back onto the bed with a sigh. I try not to stare, knowing she can already tell something's up with me today, but I still try to steal glances, savoring the final moments before I start the big talk.

Just like she thinks my crooked grin is cute, the features Mavis considers flawed on herself are the same ones I tend to adore most: the ears that are a smidge too big for her face; the tiny birthmark on her neck that's shaped like an umbrella; the lone, deep dimple on her left cheek. *I should have one on each side or none at all*, she vented to me lightheartedly last year, standing in front of a mirror before the Homecoming dance. *I feel like a one-dimpled mutant.*

I hope I'll get to hear her laugh like that again after today.

Mavis is my first girlfriend, so I've never had to end a

relationship before, and I haven't been broken up with. I don't enjoy feeling like an amateur doing *anything*, let alone beginning one of the most consequential conversations I've ever had, so I take a deep breath and remember how I planned to start it off as Albert the cat comes rushing in—likely to escape Mavis's seven-year-old twin siblings, Ryan and Rachelle. He finds protection nestled against my side, and feeling his purrs on my hip helps put me at ease.

"So," I begin, my sweaty palms stroking Albert's belly, "I've been thinking about our senior year. Do you feel like you're under a lot of pressure?"

Mavis snorts, turning on her side to face me. "You're joking, right?"

I shake my head.

"Dylan," she says, like her answer should be obvious—and truthfully, it is. "Yes, I feel the pressure. I know you do, too. Have you met us?"

This is a big reason why losing her as a friend is such a scary thought. Mavis is the only one who understands how suffocating the pressure can be.

"Aren't you just . . . *exhausted* from it all?" I ask.

She waits a beat and glances my way before responding with a shrug. I can tell Mavis wasn't expecting to hear that from me, and I get why. Our shared hunger to go hard was what initially brought us together, the first and most important building block the rest of our relationship has rested upon since we got close in the library freshman year.

Almost every weeknight, me and Mavis would clock each other there between bookshelves and trips to the drinking fountain. I'd drop in after basketball to get my homework done without my dad hovering nearby; she'd drop in after AAPI Student Association meetings to do the same in the peace and quiet that Ryan and Rachelle would never afford her at home.

First, we made eye contact. Then we exchanged smiles. It wasn't long after that we were sharing a table and study note cards, venting about class to each other. I learned that she wanted to go to law school; she learned that my pet hamster Happy died on my eighth birthday. She bought me an expensive set of pens after noticing my old, crappy one had run dry; I got her an Andy Warhol bobblehead after I overheard her telling a friend that he was one of her favorite artists. I saw the same drive in her that I recognized in myself.

We became each other's biggest motivators. She pushed me to propose Summer Sign-Ups to the Student Council, even though I felt inadequate pitching such an ambitious event as a freshman. I encouraged her to try out for the debate team, knowing that she didn't believe she had the personality to do well. She grew into the best debater at THS. by the end of the year.

Albert abruptly abandons me, shaking me out of my memories, and runs to Mavis to rub his face against her chin.

"Where's this coming from?" Mavis asks, propping her head up using her palm. "I mean, I know the pressure can be a lot, but hasn't it always?"

I try to stay clearheaded, even as the dread of what I need to say rumbles in my stomach. "We're near the end of high school, though, and I don't want the pressure stopping us from doing what we want our last year. You know what I mean?"

"I don't know if I do." Mavis thinks, scratching Albert's ears. "Why, what do *you* want out of our last year?"

This is it: the opening I'd been hoping for to say what I need to say.

But there's a loud *bang* downstairs—it's anyone's guess which sibling caused it—followed by the scurrying of footsteps. A moment later, Ryan comes to a halt in the doorway. "Have you seen Albert?" he asks us breathlessly. "Rachelle dropped the air fryer. Loud noises scare him. I'm worried he'll run away."

Mavis slowly pulls a pillow across her bed to better hide Albert from Ryan's view. "I'm sure he's fine. That cat is even more scared of the outdoors than he is of you two maniacs."

"*You* dropped the air fryer!" Rachelle yells, bouncing up the staircase behind her twin brother. "He's lying, Mavis."

"I am not."

"Yes, you are!" Rachelle appears next to her brother. "He broke the air fryer and didn't want to get blamed."

I hear a door swing open and noise from a TV drifts down the hallway. "Please, for the hundredth time today, *shut up.*" It's Ari, Mavis's fourteen-year-old sister. "I'm watching the finale."

"Tell Ryan to stop lying about me, then."

"*No*, tell Rachelle to stop—"

But before Ryan can finish, Rachelle smacks him in the chest, starting the next World War. All four of the twins' arms are swinging at each other as the pair fall to the floor in a screaming match and roll out of view.

"Remember why Saturdays are awful here?" Mavis asks, sighing and hopping out of bed to break up the fight.

How could I forget?

The first few months we dated, I helped Mavis babysit on the weekends while Mr. Meyers worked security at the hospital and Mrs. Meyers knocked out shifts at the outlet mall. Mavis was appreciative but asked me to stop, claiming Ari was getting old enough to take on more responsibilities with Ryan and Rachelle. I think Mavis was more embarrassed by the chaos of her house, though.

Mavis stomps back into her room and slams the door.

"Won't the twins tell your parents that you're breaking their most important house rule?" I ask her.

"Let them. I've had it with those gremlins." She jumps back onto the bed and rubs her temples. "I love my family." She looks at me. "But I hate that they'd all fall apart without me."

My stomach sinks. I've known she feels that way, I just never heard her say it like that before.

"For the record, I think your parents would be okay with you spending more time doing what *you* want to do." I stare back, lowering my voice. "Your mom's always telling you to get out of the house on Saturdays because Ari can help out more with the twins. And during our drive back from Lansing, I heard your dad warning you about burnout again."

"It's not that simple."

"Maybe not. I'm just saying, it's not all on you."

"And *I'm* just saying, it's more on me than you think it is."

I hate this.

I've grown to resent the hustle mentality that first brought me and Mavis together, because I learned who I was working so hard for, and it wasn't me. I used to crave my dad's praises, but I'm sick of trying to be this unattainable caricature of his perfect son and denying my whole self in the process. And this is why I see me and Mavis's journeys eventually splitting apart.

Because if anything, she's grown more determined to hustle harder; to get straight As; to captain the debate team to states; to get into one of the best undergrad programs, then law schools, then law firms in the country. *Then*, she figures, her family will be in much more stable hands: her own. I'm not sure she's ever even questioned that that's the path her life needs to follow. Slowing down isn't an option.

To her, the messy art drawer needs to stay shut so it doesn't muddy her otherwise spotless room. Her parents aren't pressuring her to keep the drawer closed, either. She is.

"Well, don't you still want to take that graphic novel course this summer?" I ask.

She looks at me, confused as to why I'd be asking about it now. "Of course. At least in theory. Why?"

"Why do you say 'in theory'?"

She drops her chin. "You saw the price tag. I can't expect my parents to pay for that."

"Why not? They covered your prelaw camp next week after you asked for help."

"Yeah," she says, growing agitated with me, "and they both had to pick up extra shifts to do it. I'd never ask them to if the camp weren't an investment in my future."

"Would the graphic novel course *not* be an investment in your future?"

Mavis's phone starts buzzing atop her comforter. I expect her to answer it, but she keeps her eyes on me.

"I bet that's River," I say, trying to lighten the mood, as the phone continues to vibrate. "Speaking of graphic novels . . . he said he finished reading one of yours and wants to return it—"

"I want to go to law school, Dylan," Mavis cuts in.

The phone stops buzzing.

"Do you really, though?" I say.

She glares at me. "What are you getting at?"

Shit.

I've let the conversation get derailed, and now I'm coming across like a know-it-all dick. I take a moment to collect my thoughts. "I know you love to draw and you're incredible at it." I scooch closer toward her. "I just hate to see you deny that part of

ANOTHER FIRST CHANCE

yourself because of this bullshit pressure to be on the perfect path
to success—"

"So, let me get this straight," she interjects, eyebrows furrowed.
"Just because I'm not majoring in art as someone who likes to
draw, you think I'm *denying* myself?"

"No, I only mean to say—"

But Mavis's phone goes off again. We sit there for a moment,
allowing the temperature between us to cool, before she bends
over to see the screen.

Her face crinkles in confusion. "It's Goldie."

My eyes narrow on hers. "I thought you said she's working at I
Scream?"

"I thought she was." Mavis lifts her phone to her ear. "Hey,
Gold—"

But Goldie's voice immediately cuts Mavis off, exploding
through the speaker like a bomb detonated. A moment later, all I
can hear is sobbing.

10

RIVER

Now that they've started, hot tears won't stop streaming down my face. "Sorry, I didn't expect this," I say to Nora, which may be the understatement of the year. "I've never cried over him before."

"Are you kidding me?" Nora replies, handing me tissues from off her cart. "You have nothing to apologize for."

Out of all the moments that could've triggered my first Dylan tears to fall, I can't believe it was answering a stupid survey question that made the dam burst. After a full minute of choppy breaths and words of encouragement from Nora, I'm finally able to get the flow under control.

"Friendships are hard in high school," Nora says, shaking her head. "I mean, I *still* don't think I'm fully recovered from my friend Ruth moving to Cleveland when we were fifteen."

"Well, at least Ruth wasn't killed in a car crash—"

I freeze, very aware of how strange and insensitive my words sounded leaving my mouth, just as my mom had warned. I look at Nora, whose eyes are wide in surprise. "I'm sorry. That was an asshole thing to say."

"It's okay," she replies. "Dylan was your best friend, then, I take it? 'Don't Drext Like Dylan Did,' Dylan?"

I nod, then prepare myself for one of the countless unhelpful platitudes I've heard over and over since last June to come rolling off her tongue.

At least Dylan is in a better place now, River.

Time heals all wounds, River.

Or my personal unfavorite: *Everything happens for a reason, River.*

But instead she says, "Life is fucking dark sometimes, huh?"

She doesn't scold herself for cursing this time.

"Yes," I say, relieved, "it is."

"I'm sorry you lost your friend," she says. "It's shitty. It's unfair. And I wish I could say some magical words to make you feel better, but we both know those words don't exist." She reaches into her pocket, pulls out a watermelon-flavored lollipop, and offers it to me. "Sugar, however, usually can help."

I take it from her and smile.

Silence consumes the room. Whenever this happens with Mr. Babcock, he'll fill the void with repetitive discussions about Cascara or reminders that *it's okay not to be okay*. I like that Nora is comfortable just letting me be.

I use the sleeve of my shirt to dab at the remaining wetness around my eyes and then pick up my pen to finish the survey.

But Nora stops me. "You don't need to answer the last question." She takes the papers off my desk and turns back to her laptop.

I immediately think of Jacob standing on my front porch, though, reminding me what's at stake. "Won't leaving an answer blank hurt my chances of getting in?"

"Nah. I'll talk to Dr. Ridges about it."

"You're sure?"

Nora glances at me hesitantly. "Technically, I'm not allowed to confirm a student's acceptance into the trials. But after learning more about you and your story . . ." She leans closer. "I'd say you have a *very* good shot at getting in, River, if you catch my drift. You didn't hear that from me, though."

I smile and sigh as bittersweet relief swells in my chest, knowing that I'm one big step closer to getting Jacob his blackmail money. I just hope Nora didn't say the same thing to Mavis, too.

11

DYLAN

We both keep our eyes peeled for Goldie as Mavis's truck creeps through downtown Teawood, the line of aggravated drivers growing longer behind us.

"Do you see her?" Mavis asks, craning her neck to get a better view of the crowded sidewalk. "Damn, why is *everyone* and their mother out in downtown today?"

It is weirdly busy. Although, it's the first sunny Saturday at the start of the summer, which explains why seemingly every Michigander has been forced outside.

Cars start honking behind us.

"You've got to drive faster, Mavis." I peek out the back. "The speed limit is twenty-five."

"And?"

"And you're going . . ." I look at the dash. ". . . ten. Ten miles per hour. People are pissed."

"Good, let them be pissed," Mavis hits back, eyes never wavering from the sidewalk.

Mavis's loyalty to Goldie is as exhausting as it is admirable.

Their friendship stumped me when we first started dating. Mavis is ambitious, thoughtful, bookish; Goldie is bombastic, irrational, aimless. When I asked Mavis what they had in common, though, she told me about their middle school field trip to Detroit when Goldie threw her slushie at an old douchebag who'd gone on a racist rant attacking Mavis, and it all made sense. Loyalty means the world to Mavis, and she'll always have your back if you have hers.

It's one of the things that drew me to her, too. When it comes to her people, Mavis will show up when it matters most. Like when I got into a fight with my dad over taking piano lessons and within hours Mavis figured out a way for me to use the piano at her church to practice on. Or when she stayed up until 3 a.m. to help me study for a history exam I'd been completely unprepared for, even though she had an extra early morning with the debate team the next day. Maybe that's another reason why following through with this breakup has been so hard. It feels disloyal to end our relationship, but it also feels disloyal pretending it's the same as it used to be.

"Goldie could have gone home," I theorize as we continue failing to find her in the crowds. "Who'd want to wander around sobbing in front of strangers?"

"Goldie Candles," Mavis says at once.

The honking behind us is getting more aggressive.

"She told me she would be downtown, though," Mavis argues, her tone increasingly concerned as she glances at her phone to see if there are any missed texts. "But she probably wouldn't be up here near I Scream. Who would loiter outside the place that just fired them?"

Now it's my turn. "Goldie Candles."

No sooner have I said it than Mavis exhales with relief, pointing ahead. "*There.*"

Barely twenty feet from the ice cream parlor, Goldie is sitting on the curb dramatically with a wad of tissues in her hand. Mavis pulls into a parking spot on the side of the road and relieved cars zip by us as we hop out of the truck.

"Holy shit," I whisper.

When we approach Goldie, she looks and sounds like she needs to be sedated by a medical professional. Her sobs can be heard over both a roaring motorcycle at the stoplight and the hip-hop music blasting from a nearby storefront. Her wet cheeks are the same color as the pink tie-dyed apron around her waist and the matching baseball cap placed backward on her blond hair. People passing by do double takes, concerned for the crying I Scream worker who they must assume just received life-ruining news on her break, instead of getting fired from yet another job she doesn't need.

Mavis elbows my side, then takes the lead. "Hey, Goldie," she says sweetly, approaching her with the caution of an animal control officer helping a wounded rodent that could strike at any time.

Goldie opens her arms for a hug before she even looks up, and Mavis immediately bends in half to oblige.

"They *fired* me," she wails, chin tucked into the side of Mavis's neck.

Customers in line outside I Scream turn and look at us.

"I know, I know," Mavis says, rubbing Goldie's back.

"So what if I'm not the fastest person on the register?" Goldie argues. "I'm not the slowest, either."

Mavis lowers into a squat to better embrace her. "It's their loss, Gold—"

"They could have just had me refilling product or scooping flavors up front," Goldie says, eyes welled with tears again. "I'm good at those things! They didn't have to fucking *fire* me for being stupid."

Mavis and I exchange looks, confirming Goldie's emotional instability is worse than both of us anticipated. I still want to follow through with the breakup today, but my plan has clearly taken a backseat for now.

"You're not stupid, Goldie," I say, trying to be helpful.

"Yeah? Tell that to my now former manager, *Greg*." Goldie lifts a tissue to her nose and blows out what must be a pound of snot over Mavis's shoulder. I spot a little girl with an ice cream cone staring in disgust. "What kind of name is *Greg* anyway?"

As if on cue, a door on the side of I Scream's storefront blasts open, and a small, round man probably in his forties wearing the exact same tie-dyed hat and apron as Goldie comes storming toward us, red in the face.

"You need to leave," he hisses, shooing us away like we're vermin. "You're scaring off our guests."

"You're *literally* not the boss of me anymore, *Greg*, so screw you," Goldie fires back, still wrapped in a hug with Mavis. She looks up at me. "That's Greg."

I nod.

"How dare you speak to me like that," Greg roars, flabbergasted, as beads of sweat trickle down his forehead.

Goldie laughs, and I can practically see her tears turn to ice as she pulls away from Mavis to face her ex-employer head-on. "I lied last week when I complimented your haircut, just so you know. It makes you look like a tortoise."

Sensing that the tension is about to boil over, Mavis tugs on Goldie's shirt. "C'mon, let's go back to my house—"

"No," Goldie says. "It's a free country. If I want to sit on the curb outside the ice cream store"—she begins to shout so customers can hear her—"that just *fired me for no reason* and that *never cleans the disgusting cabinet in the back where we store the toppings*"—she lowers her volume—"then I can."

Wanting to help Mavis, I step closer. "It's really not worth it," I urge Goldie. "Let's go."

"I'll be here all night," Goldie says defiantly, wiping her nose on her apron.

My chest tightens, because if Goldie is here all night, Mavis will be, too.

Greg looks at me and Mavis. "She wasn't fired for *no reason*, by the way. She was fired because she got caught scrolling through her phone behind the register for the third time this shift while the line to pay was out the door." I'm pretty sure smoke is about to start billowing out of Greg's ears as he turns his attention to Goldie. "What will it take to get you the hell out of here?"

She opens her mouth confidently to answer—

"And there's *no way* I'm giving you your job back."

Goldie glares at him. "Fine. I don't want to work at this dump of an ice cream parlor anyway. Then I want—"

"You can't have your employee of the month headshot, either." Greg exhales, hands on his hips. "I've told you a hundred times that the photos are owned by corporate."

Goldie turns to Mavis, gutted, and whispers, "Sure, it gave mug shot vibes, but it was still the best photo I've ever taken."

Eager to flee the scene and get my plan back on track, I decide to step in.

"How about a free scoop of ice cream?" I suggest, my head shifting back and forth between Goldie and Greg. "Will that work?"

Goldie stares, disgusted with me. "Dylan, I'm not going to compromise my values as an abused wage worker in this late-stage capitalism economy just for—"

"I'll make it a pint," Greg interjects.

Five minutes later, we're driving in relieved silence as a subdued Goldie eats between me and Mavis from her pint of mint chocolate chip with a plastic spork.

But then we miss the turn to the Candles' house. I glance at Mavis, confused.

"I don't think Goldie should be alone," she says. "She's eating Saturday dinner with us."

I stop a groan from escaping, force a supportive smile instead, and look out the window.

Not only will Goldie be spending the rest of the afternoon with us, but I completely blanked on the Meyerses' Saturday dinner tradition: an hours-long feast with the whole family squeezed around the dining room table. My plan to end things with Mavis is melting away faster than the pint of mint chocolate chip in Goldie's hand.

12

RIVER

I look out the passenger-side window to avoid seeing the billboard as my dad speeds by Puparazzi-Ready. I haven't driven past the mustache with either of my parents since I painted it, and I'm not too keen on hearing my dad's two cents seeing it in real time.

Please don't say anything, please don't saying anything. . . .

"Principal Fyres has to be searching for the kid who did it," my dad says, "right?"

I swallow hard. "It's not really a school issue, so I'm not sure. Why do you assume it was a Teawood student, though?"

He scoffs at the idea of it being anyone else. "It appeared on June third, Riv. Either that's a big coincidence or it was a local kid who knew exactly what they were doing."

"News to me that adults don't know how to spray-paint."

He grins. "Fair point. But I can't imagine anyone over twenty-five has the flexibility to scale a brick wall and then take that rickety ladder up to the billboard," he mutters. "I hope they catch the kid."

My stomach shoots up into my throat. Would he feel the same way if he knew the kid was me? There's a small tree that's easy to climb, hidden on the other side of Puparazzi-Ready, and it makes getting on the pet groomer's roof surprisingly simple, but my dad definitely doesn't need to learn why I know that. I just have to get through this week, pay off Jacob, and put this nightmare behind me as quickly as possible.

My dad turns onto the street the school is on and pats my shoulder lovingly.

"I'm proud of you for doing this," he says. "I think it'll be good for you."

I force a smile in return as another spoonful of guilt drops onto the wave of feelings washing through me. If he only knew *why* I'm doing it.

When I got my official acceptance email into the trials on Friday, my parents were so pleasantly surprised that I'd taken the initiative to sign up for something, *anything*, after a year of rolling around on the sofa, that they hardly asked any questions about Affinity or why I wanted to go. Aside from my mom's concern that I can't communicate with the outside world throughout the week unless there's a medical emergency, they were all in.

When we reach the high school, I'm surprised to see a jam-packed parking lot. Hordes of jacked guys who I don't recognize are wandering around in shorts and tanks alongside rows of buses with the names of other schools that aren't Teawood. A couple of them are from nearby cities, like Saline and Ypsilanti, but I have no idea why kids from Muskegon or Petoskey would be here today.

"Oh, this was on the news this morning," my dad says excitedly, taking in the scene.

"What was?"

He points at the football stadium in the distance, where there are hundreds of tiny, flesh-colored dots throwing footballs back and forth. "The football camp."

"A high school football camp made morning news?"

"Apparently it's a big deal." We pull toward the front entrance of the school. "Lots of top players from across the state, college recruiters dropping in . . . even that quarterback from Ann Arbor Pioneer is supposed to be here." He says it as if it should mean something special to me.

"Why, is Pioneer's quarterback pretty good or something?"

My dad snorts. "If you watched ESPN with me every once in a while, instead of the same docuseries on black holes over and over again, you'd know that yes, he's *very* pretty good. Nash, something or other, one of the best in the country." He pauses, then glances at me with a grin. "I'm kidding, you know. I was grateful to be picking you up from Astronomy Club meetings with a head full of space facts, not football practices with a head full of concussions."

My dad puts the car in park near the front doors of the school. I try my best to push away my nerves, then grab my overnight bag and meet my dad on the sidewalk.

"Your mom is bummed she couldn't here," he says.

She may be bummed, but I'm relieved my mom couldn't get out of work. One fewer parent here means half the chances a question about the mustache or the trials will be raised and end up revealing the mess I've found myself in.

He starts to walk toward the entrance with me.

"It's okay," I tell him, wanting to make those chances even lower. "I can go alone."

"You sure?"

I nod.

He wraps me up in his arms and squeezes tight. "Mom wanted me to give you an extra big hug for her," he says, before getting back into the car and driving off.

I head to the doors. It's ironic, feeling like a naive freshman on their first day all over again after having just finished my senior year last week.

Inside, about a dozen students are in the lobby already, most of them accompanied by parents. Some of them look vaguely familiar; all of them look anxious. A few long tables act as barriers between the lobby and main hallway, each taped with the same THE AFFINITY TRIALS sign that was hung during Summer Sign-Ups, four colored dots beneath the text.

Behind the tables, I see a couple of well-dressed adults who I assume work for Affinity talking to parents, and a smiley Dr. Ridges is floating among them in a bright yellow tweed suit that must be visible from the moon.

Another set of doors from the parking lot swing open to my left, and my stomach drops. Because Goldie and her insufferable parents are marching through them.

How could *Goldie* have gotten into the trials? There's no way she's in the top twenty of socially struggling students. She wouldn't even be in the top thousand.

Thankfully, the Candles stride forward without noticing me. But the relief I feel from dodging that bullet is quickly dashed as I spot who they're walking toward.

Mavis.

I'm not at all surprised she qualified—I would have been shocked if she hadn't—but it still hits differently, confirming we're about to spend an entire week together, presumably in pretty close quarters.

We make eye contact for a split, incredibly uncomfortable second, and my stomach sinks even lower.

"Hey," a voice nearby calls.

I turn at once, seizing the moment to escape the awkward eye contact. It's one of the Affinity people calling at me, a stocky white guy who's probably in his thirties and has a butt chin and thick neck. I dash up to the table.

"You're here for the Affinity Trials, and not—I repeat, *not*—the football camp, correct?" he asks me. The look he gives me makes it's obvious he's had to suffer through multiple inconvenient mix-ups already.

"Definitely not the football camp," I answer.

"First and last name, please?"

"River Lang."

"Hi, River. I'm Rex, one of the Affinity Mentors."

"Mentors?"

"Don't worry, it'll make sense later." Rex begins scanning a clip-board lying on the desk. "River . . . Lang . . . *Aha*. And your parents are . . . ?" He looks up at me, then to my right and left, like my mom and dad are going to make a dramatic entrance any second.

"Do they need to be here?"

"Are you eighteen?"

"Yes."

He checks the clipboard again and nods. "Ah, I see you already signed your consent form. Can I see your ID?"

I dig through my wallet and show him my driver's license. Once Rex scans it and does some more scribbling, he gestures that I can put it away. "Do you have any questions for me before I take you back, River?"

If I weren't distracted, I'd likely have a million, but I want to escape the lobby without a run-in with Goldie or Mavis. So I decide against taking up any more time and shake my head.

Rex surveys the lobby, muttering, "I should take at least one more participant back with me. . . . Can you wait over there?"

I circle the table and shrink into the brick wall as he calls for another student to check in. While I try to be as close to invisible as I can, I spot Nora speaking with someone two tables down ful-filling the same role as Rex. I bet she's considered a Mentor, too, then.

Nora looks much different than she did during my A-Test, having swapped the broke college student look for professional attire. Her wavy hair is flowing down her chest against a dark gray dress, and the beige heels propping her up to nearly my height match the blazer hugging her torso.

She spots me as well, and I expect her manner to be more professional, too, now that I'm officially one of her lab rats. But she gives me a quick wink before redirecting her attention back to the parent in front of her. I'm relieved to see her, even if the relief couldn't be more fleeting.

Finally, an increasingly frazzled Rex reappears at my side along with Brady Potts.

"This football camp will be the death of me," the Mentor vents, wiping his forehead. He flips through his clipboard. "Do you two know each other?"

I nod and smile at Brady, who does the same to me.

"Yeah," he answers Rex. "We go way back."

I wouldn't necessarily put it that way, but we have always gone to the same schools, just like me and Mavis, so I guess he's not wrong.

Unlike with Goldie, I'm not at all surprised to discover Brady got into the trials. You only need to spend about a minute with him, let alone twelve years of school, to see that Brady's a bit of an oddball.

"You upgraded to pink," I say, eyeing Brady's hair.

The only reason I clock the change is because his bright blue mullet was impossible to miss in a sea of black at the funeral. I'd remembered Dylan saying Brady's hair reminded him of Sonic the Hedgehog, which made me snort out loud at the worst possible moment: *just* as Dylan's cousin began crying up front reading a Bible verse. Just like with the mustache, I know Dylan would've been laughing right there with me, but people at the funeral were far less amused—most notably, my mom. Come to think of it, Brady's Sonic the Hedgehog hair may have been the start of her worrying about my "inappropriate reactions."

My eyes wander from his pink mullet to the brown smudge on his chin. "I think you've got something . . ." I point at it.

Brady wipes the smudge away, embarrassed. "My grandpa just took me to I Scream. I probably shouldn't have gotten a triple scoop of Mackinac Island Fudge. Too messy."

"These are for you." Rex holds out two white duffel bags. "Everything you need for the next week is in there. Let's go, gentlemen."

Brady and I each take one and follow Rex down the main hall-way, practically jogging to keep pace. I'm not sure what all is being provided that I don't already have in my overnight bag, but Rex seems too hurried to be bothered by my questions.

He leads us around a corner and heads into a boys' bathroom?

Brady and I pause, wondering if we need to enter, too—maybe Rex just needs to pee?—but he holds the door open for us to follow suit.

Once we do, Rex walks toward the stalls and stops outside two with open doors. "May I?" he asks us, holding out his hands.

I'm unsure what he's asking before I realize he's looking at the bag I brought from home. "We have to hand these over to you?"

"Yes."

"But all my clothes and stuff are in there."

"Like I said," Rex sighs, "everything you'll need is in the bags I just gave you."

I reluctantly hand mine over and Brady does the same with his backpack.

"Now," Rex says, clearing his throat, "please step inside a stall, empty your pockets, undress completely, and change into what's been provided to you. No, Affinity's cameras are not filming you yet—and even once they are, restrooms are no-filming zones. Yes, you can request a different size if any items are ill-fitting to the point of discomfort. Your color, however, cannot be swapped. And no, I did not choose whatever color your uniforms happen to be; those are chosen at random."

"Our color?" Brady asks, glancing at his duffel bag.

But Rex ignores him. "You are not allowed to take anything—and I mean *anything*—you came here with into the trials, including any prescribed medications that haven't been preapproved by Dr. Ridges. As your consent forms noted, any attempt to do so will get you kicked out of the trials before they even begin, stipend not included. Okay?"

I feel my pulse pounding the insides of my throat, wishing I'd spent a bit more than five seconds skimming my consent form. What the hell did I get myself into?

13

DYLAN

As chaotic as Mavis's family can be, when we get back to the Meyerses' house after picking Goldie up from I Scream, I'm reminded that they do have one thing I wish I did when it comes to my dad: a general liking of one another.

Ryan and Rachelle are playing tag in the cramped kitchen as Mr. and Mrs. Meyers finish up dinner, toggling between being entertained and aggravated by their youngest kids. Ari is cutting up veggies while Facetiming her girlfriend, dropping spoiler after spoiler about whatever finale she was watching earlier. Every so often, she'll grab one of the twins so the other can catch them, prompting laughs from whichever sibling benefited and shouts of injustice from the other.

I'm seated at the dining room table by myself, watching all the action in silence, after being reminded yet again by Mrs. Meyers that I'm a guest who isn't allowed to help. I always feel guilty benefiting from dinner-guest privilege, but given that no one knows what I'm planning to do, that guilt feels extra gross today.

I may have avoided the Meyerses' full house lately, but knowing that this will be my last day over here for a while—maybe ever—makes me wish I'd taken part in more Saturday dinners. The closest thing to a loud, fun family meal at my house is me yelling answers to my dad's questions about basketball practice over the TV blasting NASCAR, lukewarm takeout sitting on our laps.

"Hey, no sneaking!" Mr. Meyers scolds, watching Ari steal a slice of pork belly. "Tell Jasmine goodbye and go sit down." He kisses her on the head as she floats into the dining room and falls into the seat next to me. "And stop assuming everyone else has seen the finale by now! I haven't."

"I haven't, either, though now I feel like I have," Mrs. Meyers calls from the sink. She turns her attention to the twins, who have abandoned tag and are now just running laps around the island together, giggling as they go. "Hold it right there!" She intercepts Ryan, who, to the horror of everyone who isn't Ryan, has been running with a knife in his hand.

"It'll be a miracle if those two make it to eighteen without losing an eye," Mr. Meyers mutters to me, setting a salad bowl down. "Where are Mavis and Goldie?"

"Upstairs."

He looks at Mrs. Meyers. "Why did she get out of dinner duty?"

Mavis's mom gives him a look like he should know. "Goldie's had another rough day. I think friend duty trumps dinner duty right now."

Mr. Meyers nods but wisely doesn't ask any further questions, and instead just calls out, "Hey girls, come eat!"

Mr. and Mrs. Meyers bring rice and pork to the table, followed by Ryan and Rachelle with bowls of kimchi and green beans cradled precariously in their hands.

Mr. Meyers is debating Ari about one of the spoilers he overheard when Mavis appears at the bottom of the stairs. She takes the seat next to me, followed shortly by Goldie, who drops into the chair across from us in a T-shirt and jeans she borrowed from Mavis.

"Everything good?" I ask Mavis quietly.

She nods with an exhausted sigh. Years of friendship has made

Mavis a pro at talking Goldie through her "rich white-girl problems," as River calls them. It's always annoyed me that Mavis tends to be the one Goldie goes to with said problems, not her dozen other *actual* rich white-girl friends. But I wasn't just asking about how Goldie's doing after her I Scream meltdown.

Mavis was clearly irked by my pressing her about art earlier and we haven't been alone since, so it's hard for me to tell if she's still peeved or not. I hate that I let the conversation go off course, although I think it would've been worse for all three of us had Goldie's tear-stricken call interrupted my explaining why I think we'd be better as friends.

From the looks of it, though, it seems Mavis has succeeded again in helping Goldie feel better about her first-world problems. Goldie's cheeks have returned to their typical shade from the stop-sign red they'd been outside I Scream, and she's noticeably more chipper than during the car ride home. If I hadn't witnessed it, I would never guess that barely an hour ago, Goldie had just been throwing the most public tantrum I've ever seen from anyone older than Ryan and Rachelle.

After Mr. Meyers says grace, everyone starts digging in.

"I heard your job called you stupid," Rachelle blurts with a giggle, wasting no time shining a spotlight on the elephant in the room.

"*Hey*," Mr. Meyers warns her.

"It's okay," Goldie says, struggling to smile at Rachelle instead of murdering her.

"You're the furthest thing from stupid, Goldie," Mavis's mom says. "Don't listen to that doofus. I can ask my manager if we're hiring part-time sales associates if you'd like. Have you worked retail?"

"Thanks, Mrs. Meyers," Goldie answers, "but I see myself more on the designer side of fashion, not so much in sales."

I catch Mavis's mom and dad exchanging quick, amused looks.

"I see," Mrs. Meyers says. "Let me know if you change your mind."

"The security team is hiring," Mr. Meyers chimes in with a grin, "although you'd be the only girl. And the only one under two hundred pounds—or younger than forty."

Goldie considers it seriously. "I don't know if that's a good fit for me."

"He's just messing with you," Mavis clarifies for her. "Please just tune him out."

"In all seriousness," Mr. Meyers says, "I think you need a job that brings out your strengths."

"Right? If Greg were a good boss, he would've let me run I Scream's social media," Goldie concludes, as if it should have been obvious. "I could have done a *lot* more for that business creating TikToks than scooping Moose Tracks."

"Do you still play basketball?" Ryan asks me, abruptly changing topics with a rudeness only a seven-year-old can get away with.

I nod, swallowing a mouthful of rice. "Sure do."

Mr. Meyers turns to me. "What's the plan for college? Still wanting to play for Cascara?"

I hate that *college* has come become synonymous with *basketball* for me. "Nothing's been confirmed in writing," I say, "but if they follow through on the full ride they said they'd offer, then yeah, Cascara it is."

"*Whoa*, won't you be under a ton of pressure?" Mavis ribs in a slightly mocking tone, pushing green beans around her plate. "I mean, a lot will be riding on your ability to throw a ball through a hoop."

She glances at me with a playful grin, but I can hear the passive aggression, if not downright hostility, in her tone. I guess I have my answer: Mavis is still irked about our back-and-forth.

I tense up. "I'll probably feel that pressure, yeah."

"Well, why don't you major in music instead?" she continues.

Ari laughs. "Wait, is that even a real major?"

"That's *right*," Mrs. Meyers says, as if remembering something, then sipping her water. "Mavis told me that you've been using our church piano to practice for a while. I had no idea you've been learning to play, Dylan. I love that."

"I do, too," Mr. Meyers adds, looking at me with a smirk, "but I don't think you should major in music."

I'm about to clarify that I'm not even entertaining that idea when Mavis cuts in. "Why not? He loves playing the piano."

We stare at each other tensely. I should've avoided the subject altogether this morning.

Mr. Meyers laughs. "Tuition is a lot of money to spend learning something that doesn't need a degree."

"So, what you're saying is . . ." Mavis trails off in fake deep thought, putting on a performance. "It's possible to enjoy doing a thing you're passionate about—like, playing the piano or drawing—without having to make a career out of it?"

The table lulls into silence as the rest of the family finally realizes they're being roped into a spat between me and Mavis. Even the twins can tell the conversation went awry, as they scoop food off their plates quietly.

"Anyway," Goldie laughs, attempting to break the tension, "these green beans are delicious, Mrs. Meyers."

I fidget in my seat, wishing I could snap my fingers and reset the day. Because as certain as I am that I need to end things with Mavis, it's crucial that I'm able to convey why I think doing so will bring us even closer as friends. And I'm not sure that understanding will be possible on a day like today.

14

RIVER

I step into the vacant bathroom stall, lock the door behind me, and open my new duffel bag as Brady presumably does the same on the other side of the divider.

Inside the bag are a small notebook and pen, an assortment of off-brand toiletries, flip-flops, and clothes. All the T-shirts, shorts, and pants are navy blue, and made from a similar material as the scrubs I see the dentist wearing at my mom's office.

I take a deep breath, take everything off, and pull on what's been provided to me. The shirt is a bit snug and the flip-flops are too long, but neither are uncomfortable enough for me to want to spend the extra time it'd require with Tyrannosaurus Rex to swap them out for different sizes.

Brady and I walk out of our stalls at the same time.

"Interesting," Rex says, as he looks us up and down. "Both Blue."

Brady and I look at each other and then down at our identical outfits.

"So, what does getting blue mean for us?" I ask.

"What other colors are there?" Brady adds.

But Rex stays mum as he unzips the bags we were asked to forfeit a minute ago. "Put the clothes you wore in here as well as anything that was in your pockets, all electronic devices, and yes, that includes your phone. It'll be stored in a secure spot and returned to you after the trials."

After we finish, Rex takes a step closer to me—*too* close, honestly. "Hands up," he says, just a few inches from my face.

"Why?" I say, raising my arms slowly and grimacing at Rex's bad breath.

Without answering me, Rex starts patting me down aggressively.

"*Oof*, okay, *damn*," I breathe as Rex's fingers dig into my chest and glide across my sternum. "I feel like you don't have to—*ouch*—press that hard in order to—is that *really* necessary?"

Rex gives me the stink eye and finishes up. Then he performs the same inspection on Brady, who doesn't seem to mind the intrusive pats, as he moves his head from side to side to see the profile of his mullet in the mirror above the nearby sinks.

"Does Affinity not believe in consent?" I fire at Rex, still flustered. "I must have missed the memo explaining that participants would be manhandled upon entering the trials."

"You should have read the consent form more carefully, then," Rex says, straightening back up, "because it underscored each step of our safety protocols, including this inspection."

Shit.

Rex watches me fumbling to think of a witty comeback. "You *did* read your consent form before signing it, didn't you?" he asks, eyeing me.

"Of course." I lie at once.

He stares at me a moment longer, then finally says, "Let's go."

Rex beelines out the door and takes off down the hallway. I hear Brady's stomach gurgling loudly and know that it can't just be from nerves.

"You okay?" I whisper at him.

Brady rubs his middle with a grimace. "Too much I Scream, I guess."

I smile supportively, but I'm cringing on the inside. There's no way I could've gorged myself on ice cream before coming here. I'm way too nervous.

I turn toward Rex. "Where are you taking us?"

"The E-Wing," Rex answers without looking back, "where the trials will take place."

"Do they *only* take place in the E-Wing?"

"Yes."

Damn it. I hate that section of the school.

The E-Wing is the biggest wing of the building, but it's also the oldest and most interior, too, with few windows, stale air, and dated classrooms. It is, however, the best area of the school to be in if your goal is to be cut off from the outside world.

"It's not so bad," Rex says, sensing my reaction. "You'll have access to the courtyard."

A spaced-out Brady perks up. "Nice," he says in pleasant surprise, as if after spending four years here he didn't know the courtyard is in the E-Wing.

"And the gym is there, too," Rex points out, "so we'll use that space for the trials as well."

My chest tightens and I take a deep breath.

I managed to successfully evade the gym throughout the past year because the number of Dylan memories in there is overwhelming. But now I'll be expected to face it anyway—*after* having graduated?

Yeah, it's the place where he sunk a buzzer-beater, upsetting Saline for the league championship, and where he gave a fiery speech that somehow made the dull topic of overpriced school supplies an issue that galvanized a mass protest on the front lawn. I couldn't care less about those kinds of moments, though. They may capture the Dylan this school remembers—or at least *remembered*, before Billboard Dylan distorted everyone's impression of my real-life friend. But the gym was to me and Dylan what Mount Marigold had been to me and Mavis.

It was the place where we truly became friends.

Freshman year, the Astronomy Club decided to move their meetings into the gym in anticipation of the new skylight that was supposed to be finished by Christmas. We were never *actually* going to get a good look at the night sky through it; school clubs aren't allowed to meet that late into the evening, and even if we were, the football stadium lights would have made seeing any constellation or planet impossible anyway. But the club decided that a skylight would make the gym a much cooler spot to nerd out on space topics than any classroom, nonetheless.

Principal Fyres's project estimations were about four years off, though, meaning the skylight remained unfinished until this past October, and neither I nor Dylan got to see it completed. But skylight or not, the gym became the place where I got to know Dylan each week.

Not the straight-A basketball star everyone in Teawood knew; the *other* Dylan few got to see, who geeked out on the mysteries of dark matter and mastering difficult songs on the piano. The Dylan who couldn't stand his overbearing dad but felt guilty letting it show, and who secretly dreamed of deserting Teawood and all the expectations with me someday, and seeing as many stars as we could during our drive west.

But despite all the good times, the gym is the last place I saw Dylan alive. And that memory, indelibly seared into my head, haunts me to this day. Because I can't remember our last moments together without remembering that he'd still be alive if it weren't for me—that he was texting me when the car slid off the road.

And if Dr. Ridges, Rex, or even Nora require me to step foot in there at some point during the next week, I don't care about forfeiting my stipend or Jacob telling the whole town that I was behind the mustache; I'm leaving the trials.

We approach the gray double doors to the E-Wing and the first thing I notice is that . . . they're closed. It's an odd sight, given they've always been propped open throughout the school day for seamless foot traffic between classes, just like the doors to every section of the building.

"Once participants step through, they can't leave prior to the end of the trials without losing their stipend." Rex pauses with his hand on one door, his eyes darting between me and Brady mischievously, as if he's the bouncer working the entrance of a haunted house. "Are you ready?"

I glance at Brady to gauge if that sounded as ominous to him as it did to me, but the same chill, spacey expression remains planted on his face.

I swallow hard, wipe off the sweat on my palms on my navy blue pants, and remind myself why I need to do this. Then I follow Rex into the E-Wing, Brady in tow.

Once we step through the doorway, two burly security guards dressed in all black appear out of nowhere on our left and right, startling me. They allow us to continue, though, after spotting Rex's Mentor badge.

"Will they always be there?" I ask, glancing backward at the two guards.

"Yes," Rex answers. "Affinity will have several guards on watch at all times throughout the E-Wing to keep non-participants from entering and participants from exiting—accidentally or otherwise." He glances at me. "Don't be alarmed. They're here to help keep you safe."

The four years I've gone to school here, we've never needed security guards outside individual wings, even when the semester was in session. Affinity wants to keep us safe from *what*?

The first sign of life we spot after the security guards is Harry the custodian, who I'm pretty sure has worked at this school longer than it's existed. He's always been ornery but nice enough, and seeing a THS. staple like him roaming the halls in an otherwise surreal situation gives me a surprising amount of comfort.

"Hello, Harry," Rex says as we pause by the collection of dust bunnies he's sweeping into a circle. Rex turns to us again. "Affinity requested an on-site custodian for the duration of the trials, so he'll also be staying in the E-Wing with us for the next week. But Harry isn't a participant or Mentor, so it's against the rules to engage him with anything more than a friendly hello."

Harry ignores Rex but acknowledges me and Brady. "You two are doing this thing?" he asks in a disapproving tone.

Rex is immediately on edge and wants to keep moving, I can tell.

When we nod, Harry shakes his head and sighs before returning to his work. I hear him grumble about the "weirdo scientist with a white beard" and have to stop a laugh from escaping my mouth as me and Brady follow Rex deeper into the E-Wing.

We come to a halt outside the band room. Rex motions for me and Brady to enter, and as we do, the lingering lightheartedness I felt from seeing Harry evaporates at once, replaced with a sweeping sadness.

I've only been in here a few times throughout the years, but seeing the piano immediately makes me think of "Dylan's Song," as Mavis and I had called it—the song he was hell-bent on mastering when he died.

Anytime we'd stumble upon a piano together, he'd make the

same mistakes in the same trickiest parts to play, over and over again. So now, whenever I hear it come on at random times in random places—like crackling over the radio in a convenience store or through the windows of the car next to mine at a red light—the correct version sounds weirdly incorrect. Like it's yet another way, along with the billboard, that the world is trying to erase the Dylan I knew. That isn't a rational way to think about it, I know, because when I once told Mr. Babcock that hearing the real version of the song got under my skin, he gave me one of those puzzled-meets-concerned looks my mom warned me about when I say something odd related to Dylan.

The pit in my stomach grows as I stand frozen at the band room entrance, realizing there's a chance I'll be having *many* emotional moments like this one throughout the next week. Affinity wanted kids who are struggling with friendships, after all. Will the next seven days be one giant therapy session? Because I'd rather be stuck in an elevator with Goldie than unpack my grief with Dr. Ridges, Rex, or some other stranger from Affinity who doesn't get me, never knew Dylan, and has no idea just how badly the billboard fucked up my senior year.

Unless that stranger from Affinity is Nora.

"River?" Brady says, pulling my thoughts back into the band room.

I smile at him, shake off my anxious thoughts, and step farther inside. Only then do I notice the band room looks completely different now that Affinity has had its way with it.

All the black music stands and instruments in their cases have vanished. The musically themed posters and marching band accolades on the walls are gone, too. The space feels big and sterile now that it's empty except for the piano and twenty chairs placed into four rows of five under the room's high ceilings.

I count five participants already seated with their backs to us, duffel bags identical to the ones given to me and Brady placed by their feet. Only one of them is wearing blue like us, a girl my age named Biggs. I don't know her that well, other than she's Teawood High's closest thing to an influencer. The other four are wearing either hunter green, burnt orange, or dark red.

The front whiteboard has been blocked by the room's projector screen, which reads *the Affinity Trials* above the now-familiar four dots, which are the exact same colors as the clothes we've been provided. That can't be a coincidence, but it still doesn't tell me anything about what the colors could signify.

I turn to ask Brady where he wants to sit, but he's already headed to the front row. I'm not a front-row type of person, so I search for another familiar face. That's when I realize one of the heads belongs to Jacob.

I tense up contemplating what to do. With just twenty of us in the trials, ignoring Jacob for the whole week is next to impossible. So should I treat him like a friend or foe?

On one hand, cozying up to the guy who's blackmailing me feels gross. I doubt Jacob would think I'm being sincere anyway. But on the other, staying on good terms with him could help me in the long run. If I can get Jacob to like me, it'd further dissuade him from letting my secret out. Plus, he may even tell me how he learned I'm behind the mustache, which could clue me in on how many others are capable of figuring it out, too—if they haven't already.

I'd be lying if I said I wasn't curious about what he needs my stipend money for, too.

I drop into the chair next to him in the farthest row from the screen. "Red, huh?" I whisper, eyeing his shirt.

He fidgets like I startled him. "Yep."

"What do you think the colors mean?"

He shrugs, keeping his attention on the front of the room. Clearly, getting to know me is not one of his priorities during the trials.

A handful of participants trickle in, accompanied by two other Mentors I saw in the lobby. As I watch them take their seats, I notice a small, blinking red dot on the wall: a camera that appears to be recording. I swirl my head around and see that there's one in each corner.

"Do you think they're listening to us, too?" I whisper to Jacob, nodding at the nearest camera.

He shrugs again.

We sit in silence as Dr. Ridges drifts into the room, followed closely by Nora and the final group of participants, including Mavis and Goldie. Goldie is wearing green, and Mavis, I notice as my heart plummets, is in blue.

Now I *really* need to know what these colors mean.

Goldie and I make accidental eye contact as she and Mavis take the only remaining seats in the room directly in front of me and Jacob. Her mouth opens to deliver some snide remark to me, I'm sure, but Dr. Ridges starts speaking before she can get it out.

"Lights, please, Jade?" Dr. Ridges requests, looking toward the door.

A middle-aged Mentor with short bangs and thick-rimmed glasses flips the switches off. The projector screen illuminates the darkened room.

"Welcome," Dr. Ridges says with open arms. "As all of you should know by now, I'm Dr. Ridges, and I'm so grateful that each and every one of you is here."

The greeting is met with lots of silent, anxious stares.

"I love playing pickleball, my granddaughters, and summers

in Nova Scotia," he continues, "but more pertinent to you, I'm the research manager at Affinity Mind and Body's Teawood trial. I'm elated to be here."

The Affinity Trials and the four dots disappear from the screen, replaced by a slide saying *Welcome to Headquarters.*

"Headquarters?" Goldie attempts to whisper to Mavis but fails to keep her voice down.

"Yes, Goldie, we are at Headquarters—formally known as the band room." Dr. Ridges smiles at her before his eyes bounce around the room. "You all have likely noticed that each of you were given a color to wear for the week. If you were to count, you'd find five of you are Reds, five of you are Oranges, five of you are Blues, and five of you are Greens."

A few participants peek around curiously, including Mavis. I notice her gaze lingers on the piano for a moment, though. Is she also thinking about Dylan?

"In case it wasn't made clear to you already," Dr. Ridges says, "the colors were dispersed at random in your bags, which were provided to you by four of Affinity's finest research associates—or, as we refer to them, your Mentors. They'll be helping me run these trials on top of being a vital resource to each of you. Nora, Rex, Jade, Dorian?"

Dr. Ridges signals for the Mentors to join him.

Rex bounces toward the front of the room the fastest, followed by Nora and Jade. The towering fourth Mentor bringing up the rear must be Dorian. He looks a few years older than Nora and has blinding white teeth and bulging biceps the size of car tires bursting through his white polo.

If I didn't know what a stereotypical research associate looks like before, I'm no closer to getting it now. Between Nora and Jade's big age gap and looks, and Nora and Rex's polar-opposite personalities, a blindfolded Dr. Ridges could have selected all of them at random off the street.

Dr. Ridges looks to his side. "Rex, let's kick things off with you."

Dr. Ridges reaches behind the screen to retrieve a glass jar with scraps of paper inside. Rex steps closer to him, happy to go first.

"Rex enjoys beating foes in Monopoly, cringy rom-coms, and pineapple on pizza—quite the controversial position to hold, I've heard," Dr. Ridges says like a game show host, swirling the jar in his hand. "If you're wearing the color Rex selects, he'll be your Mentor for the week."

Oh no.

Please don't draw blue, please, please, please, not blue . . .

Rex reaches for a scrap piece of paper like a kindergartner diving into a cookie jar, his face glowing in delight. He glances down at the paper in his palm and grins. "Green."

Crisis averted.

In front of me, Mavis leans to her side and nudges Goldie. "You got this."

I catch the subtle but distinct scent of fresh laundry and art supplies, which I associate with Mavis and her bedroom. We've inadvertently crossed paths in the hallway, but I haven't sat this close to her in over a year. And between the piano, that smell, and the warmness she just showed toward Goldie, I feel a quick but powerful tug of nostalgia for what our friendship used to be.

"You're up next, Jade," Dr. Ridges says, pulling my focus to the front again.

As Jade reaches inside the jar, batting the scraps of paper around with her fingertips, Dr. Ridges adds, "Jade is a master of languages. Aside from English, she's fluent in German, Portuguese, and . . . which one am I forgetting? Ah, Spanish, of course."

Jade lifts her hand out of the jar. "Orange!" she squeals.

"A magical color," Dr. Ridges says. "Oranges, you're with Jade. Dorian?"

The muscly Mentor moves forward. He sucks his teeth excitedly, his thick wrist hardly able to fit into the jar far enough to secure either of the two remaining colors.

"When he's not lifting weights in the gym, Dorian is lifting baking trays in his kitchen," Dr. Ridges says. He begins to explain what makes Dorian's blondies so uniquely satisfying, but I'm distracted by Jacob muttering, "C'mon, Red . . ."

"So your vocal cords *do* work," I whisper at him with a grin to show I'm only poking fun.

But Jacob sneers.

It's not like I expected us to hit it off, but I'm surprised at how cold Jacob's being toward me. Normally, I wouldn't care—likability has never been a quality worth pursuing, in my opinion—but when my fate rests in his hands, it's a different story. Dylan and Jacob may have been friendly, but they were hardly friends. Did the mustache really piss him off *that* much?

"Why do you want to be with Dorian?" I ask. "Besides the fact he's extremely hot."

"Hot or not," Jacob answers, "that's irrelevant."

A response more than three syllables. *Finally*. "Well, what *is* relevant, then?"

"If I have to trust any of them up there, I'd prefer it be the only other Black guy in the room."

I glance around and notice his observation is correct. "Fair point."

Then it hits me: if Dorian is Red, then Nora will have the Blues. I'm not exactly sure what being a Mentor entails, but I can't imagine Nora being mine could be a bad thing.

Dorian struggles to take his meaty hand out of the jar—I'm pretty sure even his fingers have six-packs—but when he does, Jacob and I both get our wish. "Red."

I keep a great poker face but see Jacob's lips briefly curl up into his cheeks.

"That means Nora"—Dr. Ridges points at her—"has the Blues. And Blue, I must say, is quite the fitting color for a Wolverine. Nora grew up just a town or two away, and her current research on pubescent neurotransmitter behavior at the University of Michigan has been nothing short of groundbreaking. I think I speak for Jade, Rex, and Dorian when I say that Nora is the *brains* of our group." He smirks at his own joke.

Nora waves at us, taking stock of those wearing navy. I may be imagining it, but I think her eyes light up when she spots that I'm a Blue.

"All of you will receive your daily schedules for the week shortly," Dr. Ridges says. "But before we move on, let's pause for questions."

In a room filled with teens who are either shy, sad, socially awkward, or all of the above, it's unsurprising that no one wants to speak first. Finally, Biggs raises her hand into the air.

"Yes, Alex?" Dr. Ridges says, pointing at her.

She stands proudly. "I prefer to go by my last name, doc."

Dr. Ridges grins like he's amused by her. "The floor is yours, Biggs."

She turns to face the other nineteen of us. Biggs has high cheekbones, glittery eyebrows, and long, black braids with subtle streaks of teal that work well with her navy shirt. "Anyone want to unionize to get our phones back?"

I'm relieved to have a moment of levity, until I realize Biggs is being 100 percent serious. I expect one of the adults to shut down the conversation immediately, but Dr. Ridges looks on excitedly, apparently curious to see how we'll react.

Biggs scans our faces for hints of interest. "No?"

After it's clear Biggs's plan to rally us behind a common cause has fallen short, Dr. Ridges motions for her to take a seat. She does, but begrudgingly. "I'm sorry, Biggs, but for the good of the study there's no compromising on our no-phones rule. Marcus?"

He nods at another hand in the second row.

Marcus, who I notice is a Green, bends his raised arm to point at one of the cameras in the corner. "So, uh . . . is that thing already recording us?"

Dr. Ridges's eyes follow Marcus's finger. "Aha, thanks for the reminder. As your consent form noted, participants should assume they're being filmed everywhere in the E-Wing at all times, except for the bathrooms and locker rooms. All footage is being collected for research purposes only. Affinity will review it after the trial ends. I encourage you to read more on how we safeguard this in the packets your Mentor will provide to you." He turns to another raised hand, this one in the back row with us, two seats down from Jacob. "Oaklyn?"

I lean forward and see that Dr. Ridges is pointing at a jittery girl I don't recognize with a long ponytail, thin lips, and intense light eyes. She's also a Blue.

"I met her in the lobby," I hear a Red in the row ahead of us whisper. "She just moved here from Wisconsin."

"Hi," Oaklyn says slowly, her voice trembling with nerves. "May I ask . . . why should we trust anything you're saying?"

The whole room turns toward her in stunned silence. Nora's eyes open wide, and I catch her sneakily mouthing *fucking awkward* at Dorian.

Dr. Ridges laughs. "Can you clarify your question?"

Oaklyn pauses to think. "It's just . . . as subjects of the study, we can't know what you're *actually* researching . . . right?"

Dr. Ridges nods thoughtfully. "Go on."

Oaklyn starts speaking faster. "Because if we *did* know the full extent of what you're studying, there's a good chance we'd modify our behavior throughout the next week, in both intentional and subconscious ways, which would alter the results and reduce the quality of your learnings."

A smirk creeps onto Dr. Ridges's face. "Yes . . ."

"You know all this, obviously," Oaklyn says, visibly more nervous, as her words come firing out of her mouth, "and I assume you know that many of us realize this, too, so, no offense, but I can only assume that you're not telling us the truth—or, at the very least, you're not telling us the *whole* truth, and . . ." Oaklyn forces herself to pause, closing her eyes and catching her breath. Her cheeks are bright red and her forehead is glistening with sweat. "I guess that brings me back to my question," she says more slowly, opening her eyes. "Why should we trust anything you tell us?"

Dr. Ridges is beaming at her now. "You're absolutely right to be asking that question, Oaklyn," he finally says, "because you *can't* trust anything I'm telling you."

15

RIVER

I don't think I've ever been in a room as tense as this one just got.

Every participant is staring at Dr. Ridges, some with dropped jaws, and every Mentor seems irked by Oaklyn's question, except for Nora, who looks both a bit entertained and impressed by the transfer student.

"That's enough questions for now," Dr. Ridges concludes without further explanation, bending behind the screen again, his grin still intact.

Whispers break out across the room. Apparently, I'm not the only participant surprised by his abrupt change of topic after throwing gasoline on a fire.

I lean toward Jacob. "That was . . . weird. Right?"

He nods, craning his neck in an attempt to see Dr. Ridges behind the screen.

A moment later, Dr. Ridges reemerges with both hands full, balancing papers on one palm and what looks to be four mini, metallic briefcases stacked on the other. He hands out the papers to each Mentor along with a briefcase. "Green for Rex, Red for Dorian, Blue for Nora, Orange for Jade—"

"Seriously?" Goldie scoffs. "You're ending our Q and A after *that* answer?"

As if he didn't hear her, Dr. Ridges pivots on his heels and heads for the exit. "Additional questions can be directed toward your

Mentors, who you should meet with now for further instructions."
He disappears out the door.

The whispers get louder.

"Hey, *hey*!" Rex shouts, trying to gain everyone's attention.
"You heard the doctor. Huddle up with your respective Mentor."

Nora steps forward, accurately sensing that what the group
doesn't need right now is to be shouted at. "Hey, guys," she says,
smiling, "Dr. Ridges can be a bit dramatic, but he truly is harmless,
I swear. Blues, meet me in the front right corner."

Her words help calm the room's jitters a fraction as we break off
into the four groups.

"Godspeed," I mutter to Jacob.

"Ditto," he says, to my surprise, as we separate.

Jacob still may not like me, but I think he dislikes me a smidge
less than he did when I walked into Headquarters. I'll take it.

I walk to the front right corner of the room and stand next
to Nora, who's holding the papers and a tiny briefcase, which I
can now see has several locks keeping whatever's inside secure.
She nudges me with her shoulder but keeps her eyes on the room.
"Glad to see you here, River."

She seems to genuinely mean it, which lifts my spirits a bit.
The four other Blues—Brady, Biggs, Oaklyn, and Mavis—join us.
Mavis, unsurprisingly, stands the farthest away from me.

"My Blues!" Nora addresses us excitedly. "Do you all know one
another?"

Each one of us glances around the circle we've formed, but
none of us answer.

"Don't all talk at once," Nora quips. "I detest icebreakers, so I'll
leave it up to each of you to introduce yourself on your own time.
On to our first point of business." She hands out the papers. "Here
are your schedules."

Mavis raises her hand.

"Yes?" Nora nods at her.

"Can we talk about Dr. Ridges's answer to Oaklyn's question first?" Mavis asks.

I'm not surprised that she's the one to bring it up again. Mavis has always preferred operating under structure and clear rules, so Dr. Ridges's answer can't be sitting well with her.

"Look," Nora says gently to the group, "are there aspects of the trials we're not telling you? As Oaklyn alluded to in her question—which was excellent, by the way—sure there are. But it's not malicious and there's nothing to be fearful of, okay?"

"So there really *aren't* cameras in the bathroom?" Brady asks, a worried expression draped across his face. "Because I'm lactose intolerant and—"

"I'll stop you right there." Nora raises her palm and holds back a laugh. "I promise, Brady, there are no cameras in the bathrooms."

"And the video footage taken of us in *here* will never be shared out *there*?" Biggs follows up, gesturing to the world beyond the E-Wing. "Because, not to sound like that person, but I have somewhat of a public profile, and if an embarrassing clip of me like, picking a wedgie goes viral . . ." Biggs's eyes grow wide.

Nora shakes her head. "You have nothing to worry about, you internet icon." She winks at Biggs before looking my way, expecting me to have a question, too.

But I stay silent. There are too many thoughts fighting for my attention already—the piano and "Dylan's Song," the dynamics between me and Jacob, the eggshells I'll be walking on with Mavis around—and I can't cram it with more right now.

"I know this must be a strange experience for you all," she says to us sympathetically, "but keep in mind that, stipend money aside, there's a lot to be gained by your being here. We mean it when we say that we believe these trials will benefit participants immensely—especially those of you who are going through a rough time."

I catch Biggs and Brady glancing at me and Mavis but keep my eyes on Nora. The trials may feel light-years away from a typical school day at Teawood High, but it's a sad reminder that, in this building, in this town, I'm still the best friend—and Mavis is the girlfriend—of the dead kid.

"Okay, so"—Nora nods at the papers in our hands—"let's talk schedules."

BLUE SCHEDULE | D3

8 A.M. WAKE-UP KNOCK from MENTOR

9–9:50 A.M. BREAKFAST at HEADQUARTERS

10–10:50 A.M. FITNESS with GREENS

11–11:50 A.M. ART with REDS

12–12:50 P.M. LUNCH at HEADQUARTERS

1–1:55 P.M. MENTOR CHECK-INS

1:00–1:11 | D1

1:11–1:22 | D2

1:22–1:33 | D3

1:33–1:44 | D4

1:44–1:55 | D5

2–2:50 P.M. GAMING with ORANGES

3–3:50 P.M. MEDITATION

4–4:50 P.M. GROUP TALK

5–6:50 P.M. FREE TIME

7–7:50 P.M. DINNER at HEADQUARTERS

8–8:50 P.M. QUIET HOUR

9 P.M. LIGHTS OUT

"As you can see, Fitness, Art, and Gaming will all be shared time with one of the other three color groups," Nora explains as we read over our schedules. "All your meals will be provided here at Headquarters, and I'll have individual Check-Ins with each of you following lunch. We'll meditate every afternoon—don't roll your eyes, Biggs, you'll end up enjoying it, I swear—followed by Group Talk with the whole Blue crew." She pauses, looking up at us. "The Blue Crew . . . I kind of love that."

She looks down again.

"Anyway. The rest is pretty self-explanatory. Now"—Nora gives us each a brochure, which I hadn't noticed her holding on to beneath the schedules—"I highly encourage you to read these Affinity Mind and Body information packets at some point today to better understand the trials and how badass it is that you're each a part of it." She pauses again. "Is *badass* a curse word?"

"No," Brady says, right as his stomach lets out another gargantuan gurgle.

Nora leans away from him, startled, while Oaklyn's eyes bulge in surprise.

"All good," Brady tries assuring us. "Went a little hard on some ice cream."

"Didn't you just say you're lactose intolerant?" Biggs asks, eyeing his belly.

He nods with a confidence I don't share. "I took my pill this morning, though."

Nora looks at him hesitantly before turning her attention back to the group. "What else do I need to tell you. . . . Oh, please keep in mind that while I'll almost always be available for each of you to chat, even outside of our Check-Ins, there won't be Mentors overseeing the activities you'll share with the other color groups—like Fitness with the Greens or Art with the Reds."

I look up from my schedule. "We're on our own? No Dr. Ridges?"

"Or Harry?" Brady asks.

Nora shakes her head. "No researchers, custodians, or adults of any kind."

That's another curveball for Mavis. "Why not?" she asks, even more on edge.

"Dr. Ridges said camera footage will be referenced after the trials are done," Biggs begins suspiciously, "so if you're not watching us in real time through those"—she nods at the closest camera—"are we safe to assume *no one* is watching us during activities?"

Nora grins at us, seemingly happy with our curiosity. "All I'll say is, remember that we're studying social dynamics between *you* all . . . the participants." She pauses.

The five of us stare, waiting for her to finish answering, when Jade begins leading the Oranges out of Headquarters. It prompts Nora to check the time. She cringes at the clock and then turns back to us with an added sparkle in her dark brown eyes.

"Let's talk Disks," she says.

Brady's face falls into confusion. "Disks?"

Nora flips the many clasps keeping the small briefcase in her palm shut, and it pops open. "*Disks.*"

We take a step closer to look inside.

Five thin, navy blue circles about the width and thickness of dimes are on display against black felt. Brady goes to grab one, but Nora pulls the briefcase out of his reach.

"Hold your horses," she says with a wink. "These may look like flimsy pieces of plastic, but they're anything but."

"What are they?" Oaklyn asks, staring into the briefcase anxiously.

"You'll stick them to your left temple"—Nora points to the side of her head—"where they'll stay throughout the trial. Once they're on, we can monitor what's happening in your brain in real time."

My stomach churns, but for the first time since arriving, it's due to excitement, not fear or dread. "Like what the Neuro could do," I say.

Nora looks at me. "Exactly."

"Can it like . . ." Brady trails off. ". . . read our minds?"

Mavis drops her chin to her chest to stop herself from laughing. Even with things the way they are, I'm glad to see a glimmer of joy come out of her.

Biggs, on the other hand, is less subtle with her reaction. "Babe, are you for real?"

"Hey, be nice," Nora says. "No, we won't be able to read your thoughts, Brady, but check back with Affinity in a century. Maybe then, science will allow for it." She smiles at him. "We can, however, see which parts of your brain are active in very great detail. We think these little guys"—she nods down at the Disks—"could be revolutionary."

"So, considering what this study is all about," I say, leaning closer to get a better look at the blue Disks, "I assume Affinity will be monitoring how our brain activity changes as we interact with one another?"

The five of us look at Nora.

She tilts her head back and forth, thinking about her response. "More or less, yes."

"Remember, guys," Oaklyn pipes in, "just like with Dr. Ridges, we can't trust everything she tells us, though." She glances at Nora nervously, turning red. "No offense."

Nora laughs. "None taken." She smirks at Oaklyn. "Because you're not wrong. Now," Nora says, turning back to the center, "you'll have to wear them all the time."

"*All* the time?" Biggs asks. "That seems excessive."

"I promise, you'll forget they're even there," Nora says. "Who wants to go first?"

Brady's hand shoots into the air.

"That's the spirit," Nora says, carefully lifting one of the five Disks between her fingertips. "River, do you mind?"

She holds the miniature briefcase in front of me. I take it from her, and my stomach does a somersault thinking about how much debt I'd be in if my fingers slip and Affinity has a *you break it, you buy it* policy with their products.

Using her fingernail, Nora slowly peels back the bottom side of the Disk and cautiously sticks it to Brady's left temple.

"There," she says. "Not so bad, right?"

Brady waits a moment, then nods. "Yeah. I don't even feel—"

He starts convulsing.

My heart stops. Oaklyn gasps. Mavis cups her hands over her mouth.

But just as suddenly, Brady freezes in place, a grin appearing on his face. "Just kidding. I can't even tell it's there."

Biggs groans with her hand over her heart.

"I swear to God, Brady," Nora sighs, "if I liked you any less, I would be kicking your ass—*butt* out of here right about now." She rubs her temples and takes a moment to collect herself. "Anyway.

The Disks weigh next to nothing, they're waterproof—so you don't have to worry about taking them off when you shower—and the adhesive we use is especially strong *and* nontoxic to the skin, if that's a concern for any of you beauty influencers." Nora grins at Biggs. "We'll pop 'em off your faces when the trial is over at the end of the week. Who's up now?"

Biggs steps forward. Nora carefully grabs another Disk from the briefcase in my shaking palms—I'm lucky I didn't throw them in the air after being scared by Brady—and sticks it to Biggs's temple.

"So?" Nora asks once she's finished. "What do you think?"

Biggs takes a moment to consider the question, shaking her head from side to side to see if it affects how the Disk feels. "Damn, it's like it's not even there."

Nora places Disks on Mavis's and Oaklyn's temples next, then on mine. Like Biggs and Brady said, it's so lightweight that I have to double-check with my own fingers that it didn't fall off. The adhesive isn't itchy, either.

The science nerd in me is fascinated at the potential of the Disks. It sounds like they could be the new and improved EEG, which would make diagnosing brain abnormalities easier, faster, and more accurate, for starters. But the skeptic in me questions just how revolutionary the tiny, practically weightless sticker on the side of my head truly is—especially after Dr. Ridges implied nothing we're told for the next week could be true. Could they end up being a placebo of sorts? Or maybe used as a distraction from what Affinity is actually studying?

And if it's the latter, what are they distracting us *from*?

Nora takes the empty briefcase from me, closes it shut, and looks at the five of us. "Ready?"

"For what?" Biggs asks.

"The Affinity tour," Nora says, spinning on her heels and

heading for the door. The five of us follow behind her.

The Reds wandered out behind Dorian after the Oranges, so we're the third group to leave Headquarters. I spot Mavis and Goldie exchanging weak, apprehensive smiles before Mavis disappears into the hallway ahead of me, and even though I feel bad for Mavis, too, a wave of jealousy ripples through my middle. The trials would be so much better if I had my best friend here with me, same color or not. Dylan would probably find a way to make them *fun*.

But if Dylan were still here, I wouldn't have signed up in the first place.

Nora spins around in front of us and begins to walk backward down the hallway like a museum tour guide. "Your Free Time can only be spent in your individual rooms—yeah, I know, it sucks—and you need to be in there by yourselves. The only justifications for leaving your room during Free Time are to use the bathroom or locker room, which you can use to shower and change in privacy."

"Free Time doesn't sound so *free*," Biggs whispers at me.

I grin in agreement.

"On your right, as you all know, is the school's courtyard," Nora says, gesturing to her left, "where you'll be doing some of your Fitness activities with the Greens."

I look outside. The courtyard has never been anything to write home about—the sidewalks are cracked and the grass is overgrown—but it looks more tempting than ever now that I realize it's the only place I'll be able to get fresh air during the trials.

We turn a corner, and another growl rumbles from Brady's stomach like it was manufactured as an effect in a horror film, not a noise produced by the human body. He's walking several steps behind everyone else except me, though, and I think I'm the only one who heard because no one else reacts.

"Here, as you probably know, are the aforementioned girls' and boys' locker rooms," Nora says, motioning to two doors on our left, "which is where you'll shower, brush your teeth, and do all the other things you need to do to avoid being the smelly kid." She lights up, remembering something. "It's critical that you all use the locker rooms during your Free Time and *only* during your Free Time. Boys, that rule is especially important for you."

"Why?" Brady asks.

"The football campers will be using the boys' locker room this week, too," Nora explains, "but Dr. Ridges spoke with the coaches and figured out a schedule so that none of the players will be in there during your Free Time. That's because, as you all should know by now, none of you should engage non-participants while the trial is occurring. That shouldn't be an issue, given our security guards will keep non-participants from entering the E-Wing, but the potential to break that rule is there if you use the locker room outside Free Time. Oh, and you'll see Harry the custodian around, too. He's been approved by Affinity to be in the E-Wing, but technically, he's not part of the trial, so refrain from interacting with him beyond a polite hello."

"Is this football camp a big deal or something?" Oaklyn asks. "I saw reporters interviewing players on my walk in."

Nora nods. "Many top recruits across the state attend, and some of them will commit to their preferred colleges while they're here."

"Not to stereotype," Biggs says, "but you don't strike me as someone who'd know much about the significance of a high school football camp, Nora."

Nora laughs. "You're not wrong, Biggs. But I've been force-fed football culture the past decade because my brother plays. Funnily enough, he's playing at the camp this week." She shakes her head, both amused and annoyed at the irony, as we approach another corner. "I know, I know, *how can someone who studies neurology be okay with their sibling smashing their skull into smithereens?* Believe me, I wish my dad had gotten him a chessboard for his fifth birthday and not a football." Nora sighs as we approach a corner.

"Where are our rooms?" Mavis asks.

"Perfect timing, Mavis," she says as we turn left.

The hallway we enter is lined with streamers. For a second, I'm taken aback, as it reminds me of the main hallway during Summer Sign-Ups. But I quickly realize the streamers aren't Timber Wolf blue, they're navy.

"This is Blue Sleeping Quarters," Nora announces. "Home sweet home. There are six classrooms in our hall for us. Think of them like make-believe dorm rooms. It'll be cute."

"Six?" Biggs says, eyebrow arched in surprise. "Are you sleeping here, too?"

Nora nods. "You're stuck with me." She motions at the first classroom door we pass. "I'll show each of you which classroom is yours after the tour and make sure you have everything you need to settle in comfortably."

We walk a bit farther and hang a right.

"And *this*, ladies and gentlemen," Nora says, "is the Gaming space."

She swings open the door to the old woodshop room.

"This is *not* how I remember this place looking," Biggs says, pleasantly surprised.

The room has been turned into a lounge, with several plush sofas, sets of tables and chairs, and beanbags scattered throughout. A large, flat-screen TV is perched on the wall, too.

"There are preselected video games you can choose to play or watch, but they're all family-friendly and Dr. Ridges–approved, so don't get too excited," Nora says, pointing to the entertainment center. "Board games are over there. . . . Oh, and my personal favorite perk about this room is easily the snacks." She points to a table covered in bags of chips, bowls of candy, and rows of canned drinks. "Not bad, huh?"

After giving us a minute to wander around, Nora stands by the exit and clears her throat to get our attention. "Let's keep it moving, Blues."

"Can I, uh . . . take a break?" Brady asks, his voice strained.

We all turn to find him lying on one of the sofas, his face significantly paler and sweatier than it had been just moments ago.

Nora hurries to his side. "What's wrong?"

"There's a fifty-fifty chance that boy's gonna hurl," Biggs mutters, eyeing him from afar. "Maybe sixty-forty."

I sit near Brady's feet on the sofa, while Nora squats down by his head.

"Do you feel sick?" she asks him.

He moans in pain.

"Can one of you go find Dr. Ridges?" Nora asks the four of us.

Mavis nods and leaves.

But then Brady bolts upright and freezes in place, a big smile spread back across his face. "I know what happened!"

"What?" Nora asks.

"I was wrong," he says, looking at me, relieved to have figured it out. "I took an *Advil*—not my lactose intolerant pill this morning."

Nora groans. "Brady—"

But she's interrupted by a bucketful of chunky beige liquid jetting out of Brady's mouth . . . right onto me. Everyone gasps and then falls into stunned silence.

The smell is so atrocious, I'm about to hurl myself.

"Well," Biggs says, hovering behind the sofa, "make that a hundred percent chance."

16

"I read that your grandpa's getting honored at U of M's Homecoming game this fall." Mr. Meyers says to Goldie, resetting the energy at the table, and not a moment too soon.

The rest of Saturday dinner trudges on awkwardly without me or Mavis speaking again. After everyone finishes their second—or, if you're Ari and Ryan, third—helpings, Mr. and Mrs. Meyers start collecting plates, signaling the end of the meal. Thank God.

As I help Mr. Meyers load the dishwasher, I see Mavis and Goldie disappear up the stairs together quietly. Surely, I wouldn't enjoy whatever conversation they're about to have concerning me.

I feel a hand gently land on my back. It's Mrs. Meyers.

"You two okay?" she whispers with a soft smile.

I exhale, having no idea what to say.

Mrs. Meyers sees me struggling to answer. "Why don't you invite River over? Things tend to take a turn for the better whenever the three of you are together."

It's not a bad idea, seeing as River wanted to hang out today anyway. But I doubt Mrs. Meyers knows just how badly Goldie can get under his skin, and I don't think me or Mavis can handle any more potentially combative conversations tonight.

"It'll work itself out," Mr. Meyers says with a snort, taking the plate in my hand and slipping it into the dishwasher. "I've been in your shoes, too, big guy. *Many* times."

Shit.

How can I follow through with the breakup after Goldie's melt-down, Mavis being peeved at me, and Mr. and Mrs. Meyers treating me like their fifth kid? It feels like a mistake to put off the inevitable and avoid ending it, but it feels like a worse mistake to do it like this.

Once the table is clear and the dishwasher is full, I head upstairs with a pit in my stomach and see that Mavis's door is shut. Message received: she wants to keep me out.

I've never been a nosy boyfriend, but my curiosity gets the best of me and I press my ear against the door. Their voices are hushed and distant, though—it sounds like they're whispering something to me from ten feet underwater—and I can't make out anything.

I'm startled by the pitter-patter of footsteps coming up the carpeted staircase and I don't want anyone in the Meyers family to see me eavesdropping, so I knock on the door before I'm spotted.

"Hey," I say as Ari passes behind me toward her room. The room goes quiet. "Can I come in?"

There's a short but telling pause before Mavis answers, "Yeah."

I open the door just enough to stick my head in. Mavis and Goldie are sitting cross-legged on the bed facing each other with pillows on their laps.

"What's up?" I ask.

Another pause.

I can sense Mavis's brain beginning to scramble. She's a terrible liar.

But Goldie isn't as bad. "We're crafting a plan to get revenge on Greg," she says quickly with a nasty, fake grin. She looks to Mavis, who nods in agreement.

My chest tightens. Mavis doesn't lie to me—not that I know of, at least—but the mood of the room suggests that whatever they've been saying about me in there feels heavier and more secretive than I expected.

"Okay, well . . ." I think fast, needing an excuse to not be hovering in the doorway when I'm clearly not welcome. "I'll let you two plot your revenge. I'll see what River is up to."

Mavis sits up straighter and stares at me. "Are you coming back?" she asks, her tone telling me she'd like me to.

It surprises me and I hesitate.

"I didn't plan to get snarky at dinner," she adds, a small, regretful smile appearing on her face. "I'm sorry. Maybe we can talk about it once you're back?"

I exhale and return the smile. "Yeah, sounds good."

I close the door quietly and head downstairs. As I slip on my shoes, my phone buzzes and I glance at the screen.

Fuck. It's my dad.

I don't want to open the message because I already know it'll just be him scolding me for forgetting to touch base earlier. So instead of reading it, I call River.

"Yo," he answers immediately as I hop into my car. "Let me guess, the screaming twins ruined your faith in humanity, and you need me to restore it?"

"Still want to hang out?" I ask, backing out of the Meyerses' driveway.

"Can't, I'm watching Dr. Skelemont's livestream on white dwarfs and . . ." He trails off. "I heard the words that just left my mouth, and it was the nerdiest sentence I've ever—"

"Seriously, are you free?"

He pauses, then laughs. "Wow, the Meyers must really be getting on your last nerve."

I turn out of Mavis's neighborhood and onto a busier street. "Pretty much. Our spot? Ten minutes?"

"Our spot?"

"Yeah."

A pause. I knew that'd get his attention.

"It's Saturday," River says. "How would we even get into the gym?"

"Principal Fyres gave me a set of keys for Summer Sign-Ups prep, and I don't have to give them back until Monday," I say, surprised to hear my own willingness to bend the rules. "No one will catch us, but even if they do, I can just say you were helping me get ready for next week."

There's another pause on the other end of the line, this one longer than his first. He has to know something's up. Yeah, I could go to his place, or he could come to mine, but I don't want to be around my dad, and while Mr. and Mrs. Lang are chill, after the day I've had, I want it to be just us.

"Sweet," he finally says. "Give me ten minutes."

I hang up and make a right toward the high school.

Thankfully, the parking lot is empty when I arrive, but I take a spot in the distant corner anyway, where the limbs of an old tree help to hide my car, just in case a teacher or Harry is around. I search for the key to the front entrance on my walk up the sloping lawn to the doors. It takes me a minute to do so—the set Principal Fyres gave me opens way more doors than I need for the sign-ups, which was probably a mistake, knowing him—and I let myself in. I remember that the doors automatically lock when closed, so I leave the keys there for River to get in, too.

I've never been inside the school alone like this. The quiet is unsettling. Although it's still light out, the setting sun is low enough that big chunks of the main hallway are blanketed in darkness. I walk past my school photo in the display case again on the way to the E-Wing, but this time I'm thankful it's too dark to make out my crooked smile.

After a few twists and turns toward the center of the school, I pull open a door to the gym. It creaks loudly, or at least it *sounds* loud, then I walk inside and flip on a single switch. I don't want to turn them all on—the high school gym fully aglow on a Saturday evening for no scheduled reason could attract unwanted attention—but I want to at least be able to see where I'm walking. Just two lights come on—one above each basketball hoop—and their buzzing fluorescent bulbs illuminate enough of the hardwood for me to navigate to center court.

I lie down on my back, staring up at the ceiling as I wait for River to join me. Anxious questions start swirling through my head—what Mavis and Goldie were talking about in the bedroom; when I'll break up with Mavis if I'm not doing it tonight; just how angry my dad is at me right now for not touching base—until I hear the gym door creak open again.

It's hard to make out anything in the low lighting at first, but I know it's him just from the vague silhouette in the doorway. Immediately, the noise in my head quiets down.

River comes striding across the hardwood and into view. I make out his ripped, light blue jeans and tank top first. My heart starts pounding hard, but not in a frenzied, anxious way, like it's been doing due to dreading the breakup. It's pumping in . . . a different way. It's strange, having such an intense reaction to seeing someone I hang out with just as much as Mavis. I must have been even more stressed today than I thought I was.

The buzzing light finally illuminates one side of River's face and the short strands of his blond buzz cut as he approaches me.

His blue eyes are somehow even more vivid in the dimly lit gym, and it makes my pulse quicken even more.

What's happening?

I've been so out of whack today, it's hard to make sense of it.

"Chicken enchiladas?" River offers. Only then do I realize he's carrying a Tupperware container, two plastic sporks, and a handful of napkins.

"Thanks, but I'm good," I say, desperately trying to get a handle on this surge of weird feelings, whatever they are. "I had Saturday dinner at the Meyerses."

"Yeah, thanks for the invite," he jabs, sitting down on the hardwood next to me.

I open my mouth to respond.

"I'm just kidding," he says with a smirk. "I know you two wanted some quality time before she's gone for the month." He tosses Principal Fyres's keys onto the floor next to me, sending a jingling echo throughout the gym. "I think there are more keys on that ring than there are doors in all of Teawood."

I smile. "Just the C-, D-, and E-Wing doors, but point taken."

River cracks the lid of the container open. And despite what I just said, the sight and smell of Mrs. Lang's most beloved home-cooked meal wins me over.

I grab a spork, River grins, and we both dig in.

At first, neither of us says much. Maybe it's because our mouths are so full, or maybe it's because he's not exactly sure why we're here on a Saturday night, and I don't know, either. But the quiet is nice.

Once we've each gotten our fair share of the enchiladas, River joins me on his back, his palm cushioning his head against the floor, and we stare up at . . . the worst-executed construction job in Teawood High School history.

"Beautiful, isn't it?" he says sarcastically.

I smirk. "Stunning."

The gym's new skylight was supposed to be completed our freshman year, but two and a half years later, River and I are still staring up at a massive tarp covering a hole in the ceiling instead. Maybe it shouldn't be surprising that the same principal who accidentally gave a student keys to half the school can't be trusted to competently plan a building renovation.

"Do you think they'll finish it before we graduate?" I ask River.

"Probably not," River says, waiting a moment before continuing, "but more importantly, is everything all right with you?"

I take a deep breath.

"Because it didn't seem like it on the phone," he adds quietly.

Clearly, everything's *not* all right with me, but it's difficult to create a coherent response out of the mess in my head.

So I decide to just start talking. "Harry saw me setting up this morning and told me I needed to slow down."

River looks confused. "Did the streamers look sloppy or something?"

"No, not like that. Slow down, as in, I work too hard."

"Well . . . yeah," River says with a grin, "you do. I've been telling you that the past two years—and to Mavis the past *ten*." He laughs.

"I know you have. I guess I started wondering if I'd be so overwhelmed if I were doing things that make me feel good, that make me feel more . . . me."

I feel myself blush, surprised that I allowed myself to be earnest, and am grateful the darkness will hide the color in my cheeks—which River would call out playfully, without a doubt, if he could see it.

"This is what I've been saying." River sits up and curls his feet inward, cross-legged. "Less practicing free throws, more planetarium trips."

"Exactly," I say, feeling tingly at the thought of it, "or signing up for actual piano lessons, too, instead of relying on terrible tutorials online."

River nods supportively. "I approve of this message."

"So there's that," I continue, "and then my dad was pissed about one of my final grades."

He rolls his eyes. "What's new?"

"And me and Mavis got into it a bit, too. Nothing big, but I don't feel great about it."

"What happened?"

I'd tell River about the whole interaction if it hadn't been the runway leading into the breakup conversation I'd intended to have. I pause and decide to shift gears instead, wanting to keep him out of it.

"It was dumb," I exhale, "just stupid post-graduation stuff."

"Do you want to talk about it?"

I shake my head. "It's fine, really. I'm going back to her house later. We'll be good."

River waits a moment. "You know you can always vent to me about shit."

"I know."

"Really, though. You keep a lot in sometimes. School, basketball, Mavis stuff, your dad . . ." He trails off, but keeps his eyes on me. "Anything you want to talk about, I got you."

I get butterflies.

What is going on?

"You know what I was thinking about during Skelemont's livestream?" River continues. "Why don't we pay more attention to the fact that the universe is just as *small* as it is *big*?"

I try not to get distracted by the unexpected flapping in my stomach. "Huh?"

He scooches closer toward me and the butterflies' wings start working even harder.

"There's some gargantuan star one hundred million light-years away from us right now," he says, "and to that star, we're so far and so incredibly minuscule, we might as well be nothing, right? But we *do* exist, and we're *not* nothing."

I let his words sink in. "Okay. . . ."

"Then on the other hand we're probably that gargantuan star to a tiny, microscopic . . . *something* that we'll never even know exists," he explains. "Do you know what I mean? Just as everything out *there* is infinitely big, everything down *here*"—he nods at the hardwood—"is infinitely small."

"So how many microscopic life-forms do you think are looking up at us right now through whatever their version of a telescope is?"

"Life-forms?" He sucks his teeth. "It's debatable how small is too small for something to be considered life—or at least, the most widely accepted human definition of life."

"Okay, then," I say, reworking my question patiently, "how many microscopic *things* are looking at us right now through whatever their version of a telescope is?"

"Well, if they have enough awareness to be curious about us, then I'd argue you were probably right to classify them as life, but—"

"Never mind, River," I say with a sigh, acting like I'm more annoyed than amused as he spirals into his own black hole of astronomical theories. But the opposite is true. I'd listen to him talk about intelligent life, whether it's infinitely big or infinitely small, for as long as I'd sit there quietly watching Mavis sketch her comics when we first started dating—

That's it. That's the difference.

I've known something's been off between me and Mavis, something beyond the fact she's been leaning in to her ambition while I've been leaning away from mine. But the insistent butterflies, the fluttering heart, the fascination with every word that leaves her lips—that's what's been missing. The spark.

But even though I've known about that difference for a while, I didn't *feel* the difference until now.

When I felt the spark for someone else.

For River.

He pulls out his phone. "We've got to take a pic."

"Really?" I say in surprise, glancing around the dark gym, then up at the construction site. "In here, of all places?"

He smirks, shaking his head. "You clearly don't see what I see," he says, nodding his head back. "Look."

I glance behind us at a wall of bleachers that look exactly like always. "So?"

"No. Look *up.*"

I do.

The sun, now nearly set, is casting thin beams of dark reds and deep pinks across the rafters above. It's turned one side of the ceiling into a sunset-colored kaleidoscope.

"See what I'm talking about?" River asks, swirling around on his butt to face the opposite direction. The reflections light up his face in a magical glow.

"Yeah," I say, following his lead.

He's right; the sunset is beautiful. But as gorgeous as it is, I want to capture this moment, *this feeling*, more than I want to document the reds and pinks bouncing off the gym ceiling.

He holds his phone out in front of us, the rich colors turning our faces into golden orbs on-screen.

"Don't stress it," River says with a laugh, as I tousle my hair back into place. "You look good."

You look good.

My heart thuds.

River starts snapping away. We tweak our smiles and expressions to get a good variety. Then he turns and faces me—his lips are just inches from my ear—and peeks out of the corner of his eye to see what his profile looks like on the phone.

"*Ooo*, this looks sweet," he says. "You should do it, too."

Is he . . . flirting? Or is it wishful thinking? River's never had a boyfriend. So for as well as I know him, I don't know what River's like around a guy he's into. Flirting or not, I might crack a rib, though, my heart is pounding so hard.

I turn toward him slowly. "Like this?"

Our eyes lock together. And it's like something deep inside me clicks into place.

I lean forward, pressing my lips into his—

He pulls away at once and I lean back quickly, too.

"*Whoa.*"

We stare at each other, stunned.

Barely a second goes by before laughter erupts from my mouth, my nervous energy finally having an excuse to burst across the gym.

He keeps staring at me, like he's still a bit rattled, until his face melts into a smile, too. "What was that?"

"Sorry," I say, backing away. "I thought it'd be funny to catch your reaction in the photo."

Shit.

Whatever clicked in my head urging me to lean forward clearly wasn't clicking in his.

"You're a weirdo." River shakes his head and opens his photos. His eyes double in size. "Oh my God."

"What?"

He shows me the last image: a perfectly timed snapshot of our *not-really-a-kiss* kiss, which, despite my bad acting, definitely wasn't just a joke to me. And it doesn't look like it was just a joke on the screen, either.

"Your timing was just—" He makes a chef's kiss with his hand against his lips, then follows it up with a question I don't hear because I'm too distracted by what I just did.

I can't believe I didn't realize it earlier but . . . I like River. I really, *really* do. After the reaction he just had to my lips against his, though, I doubt the feeling is mutual.

River tilts his head to the side and stares off in thought for a moment.

"What is it?" I ask him.

"Do you hear that?" he whispers back.

We both go silent.

"No," I reply, "why, what do you—"

But a melody hits my eardrums. A song is playing softly—barely audible, really—from somewhere nearby. It's . . . *my song.*

My jaw drops and my eyes almost bulge out of their sockets. "Where's it coming from?"

"I don't know." River looks around, but it sounds too distant to be playing over the gym's sound system. "C'mon."

We get up and creep toward the exit. River opens the door slowly—thankfully, it doesn't creak as loudly as it did earlier—and we pop our heads just far enough outside to see down the hallway and spot—

"Harry?" River whispers at me in surprise. "*He's* playing your song?"

I stifle a laugh, realizing the song is coming from Harry's phone. The custodian is humming along as he ties up the top of a garbage bag. I'm as flattered as I am amused to know my piano playing made an impression on him this morning.

River bumps the door, and it creaks just loudly enough to get Harry's attention.

"Hey!" he shouts down the hallway, squinting into the darkness toward us. "Who's there?"

"*Run*," River says, taking off down the hallway.

I panic, looking right and left before following in his footsteps down the dark hallway. River starts laughing, clearly getting a kick out of the chaos, but I'm much more concerned that Harry is chasing after us, zigging and zagging through the E-Wing. He's surprisingly fast, too.

"The keys are too loud!" River hisses, rounding a corner and looking over his shoulder at me. "He can hear where we're going!"

He's not wrong. Principal Fyres's keys are tapping against each other like cymbals in a marching band, giving away our every move.

River pauses, grabs the set out of my hand, and throws them into the air. Instead of clattering to the ground, however, the keys land on top of the athletic department's awards display case—a good seven or eight feet above the floor.

"River!" I shout in shock, my jaw dropped. "I have to give those back to Principal Fyres on Monday—"

"Good," River says, as he grabs my wrist and pulls me forward, "you have all day tomorrow to worry about how you'll get them back."

We bolt out of the school, laughing as hard as we are panting, and beeline in separate directions to our cars. I glance backward at him as my feet hit the asphalt just as he looks my way, too, both our faces beaming in the starlight.

17

RIVER

I pull on a fresh navy blue shirt from my duffel bag and stare at my reflection in the mirror, still in a state of shock that lactose intolerant Brady Potts just spewed his half-digested ice cream all over me. I spot the blue Disk on my temple.

Nora said they're waterproof. Hopefully they're puke-proof, too.

I hear the bathroom door squeak open around the corner. "You doing okay in there?"

It's Nora's voice.

"As okay as I can be trying to scrub Brady's stomach stench off of me."

She makes a hurling noise in disgust. "Take as long as you need. Also, please never say the words *stomach stench* ever again."

I smile to myself as I hear the door close.

In ordinary circumstances, I would have sprinted to the nearest shower and washed Brady's vomit off my skin until I felt like a new person. But because Principal Fyres forgot what a calendar is and double-booked the building with the football campers, who are in the locker room now, I've been forced to get clean using a bar of cheap soap in one of the E-Wing bathrooms with faucets that hardly drip water.

I hesitantly sniff the back of my hand—finally, I can't smell Brady's barf—and adjust the fit of my fresh shirt around my shoulders before walking out with my duffel bag. Nora is waiting for me in the hallway, her shoulder leaning against a row of lockers.

"So?" she says, eyeing me cautiously. "Feeling fresh?"

"Fresh enough, I guess."

She nods down the hallway. "Dinner is happening at Headquarters if you're hungry."

I shake my head adamantly. "I may never get my appetite back after this."

Nora pulls her hand out from behind her back and tosses a banana and bag of chips at my chest. "I had a feeling you'd say that. In case you get hungry later."

I smile at her appreciatively. "Can I just go lie down?"

I want some alone time after such a weird day.

She pushes herself off the lockers and the clicking of her heels leads the way toward Blue Sleeping Quarters. "I'll be a little lenient for any participant who gets puked on their first day. But it's lights out at nine o'clock."

We make it to the Blue Sleeping Quarters hallway. Nora points out my room, then shares that she's taken the farthest classroom down the hallway. Mavis's room is next to hers, Brady's and Biggs's are on either side of mine, and Oaklyn's is the closest by foot, directly across the hall from me. She opens the door to my temporary pseudobedroom—it'll be weird sleeping where I once gave a presentation on Hitler's invasion of Poland—and I step inside.

Similar to what was once the band room, the classroom has been gutted. All the desks and chairs have been removed. There aren't any inspirational quotes above the board or world map posters anymore. The walls have been left fully bare. You'd think it'd feel empty and cold in here, but it doesn't.

A bed—it looks king-sized—is centered against the wall opposite the door and topped with a half dozen big pillows, all of which are in the same navy blue color. The fluorescent lights above are off and a floor lamp directly next to my bed makes the room surprisingly cozy.

I toss my duffel bag onto the bed.

"You can leave to use the bathroom at any time," Nora says, "but after lights-out, a security guard will have to escort you there."

"Got it."

"Any questions for me?"

"So, without a phone alarm, how do I wake up?"

"I'll come knocking at 8 a.m., sharp."

I nod.

Nora smiles on her way out. "Rest up, River."

Once the door closes, I jump onto my bed and sink deep into the mattress. The exhaustion from a surreal day starts to take over and I drift off.

My eyes pop open. For a moment, I'm not sure what woke me so suddenly, until the stench hits me again.

Damn it, Brady.

I sit up and groan, checking my skin for any regurgitated ice cream chunks I may have missed earlier. I passed out for a long time, I realize, seeing that the clock on the wall reads 8:42 p.m. I could really use a legitimate shower, but it's not Free Time and lights-out is in eighteen minutes. Would Nora be okay letting me go? She did say she'll be more lenient today with a participant who's been puked on. . . .

I hop out of bed, grab my duffel bag with toiletries inside, and slip out into the hall. I mouth *I'll be quick!* to the security guard who glances at the time before letting me pass, and jet off to the locker room.

As I'd hoped for, there's not a single jock in sight when I enter the boys' locker room. I do notice another security guard standing near the opposite exit, though, which leads to a C-Wing hallway that connects to the football field. I zip around the corner before he notices me and then toss my duffel bag aside before stripping down and hopping into a shower.

The water isn't so much hot as it is warm, but beggars can't be choosers. And with the remnants of Brady's stomach juices seeping into my skin, I absolutely admit to being a beggar. My fingers skim across my Disk as I wash my face, and I wonder if my brain activity is relaying to Affinity just how relieved I am to finally be having a proper shower.

As I finish washing off the suds, I hear a door swing open, followed by the unmistakable sounds of a group of guys.

"Fuck," I mutter, turning the water off.

The campers must have locker room access starting at nine. If that's the case, they're four minutes early, I realize, seeing a clock on the wall.

Nora warned all of us against interacting with any non-participants who are outside the study. I haven't even been here a full day, and I'm already dangerously close to breaking an Affinity rule. Is it possible that my Disk would alert them?

I snag a fresh towel that's folded near the entrance to the showers, dry off at record speed, and tiptoe back to my duffel bag. I see a flurry of blobs out of the corner of my eye headed to where I just was: the showers.

This . . . is not great.

I'm cornered in a section of the lockers where, should I attempt to run for the exit, one of the players will almost certainly spot me, creating the possibility for an encounter that could get me kicked out. If I wait here for all the players to finish up, though, I'll return to my room inexcusably late.

I see the clock: 8:58 p.m.

Shit.

As my mind races, trying to decide which option is less bad, I peek at a big group of football players standing near the showers, all of whom put the varsity Teawood team to shame. Even the smallest guy I see could break me in half, and every player's skin is glistening from practicing all day in the summer heat. A few of them drop their towels from their waists, which is even more of a distraction, but I don't have a second to waste ogling at guys with so much at stake. I need to make a decision.

I'll run for it.

The locker room is filling up with steam floating out from the showers, making it foggy and difficult to tell who's in here. Maybe I'll be mistaken as just another player at a distance. Besides, even if one of them does see me and knows I don't belong, that doesn't make it an *interaction*, right? I'll sprint out the locker room before a conversation can happen.

I grab my duffel bag and book it toward the E-Wing exit, but just when I'm steps from the door, I freeze like a deer in headlights.

My heart stops. I lose my breath.

"Dylan?" I mutter.

There he is, standing ten feet away in a shirt and jeans. The steam in the air distorts the details of his face, but it's him—*it's definitely him*—with his gentle eyes staring straight into mine above his crooked grin. Clearly, I'm imagining him again, as I'd feared after thinking I saw the billboard during my A-Test slide-show. But this sighting is different from any of the others, I realize, as my throat runs dry. This time, he's more real.

This time, he's . . . alive.

Dylan turns to his side and disappears down an adjacent aisle of lockers, headed in the opposite direction from where I need to go to get back to my room. But I don't have a choice. Not even with all I have at stake. I need to follow him. I sprint forward and turn the corner—

"*Oof.*"

I slam into a body and stumble backward.

"Whoa," the brick wall of a human says as I stand up straight. "You good?"

A shirtless football player is looking at me with concern, a white towel wrapped around his hips. His hair is messy and damp with sweat, with strands dangling in front of his forehead and touching the tops of his ears. His brown torso is glistening and muddied from practice, and his dark eyes, big and magnetic, look familiar, though I'm not sure why.

I stand on my toes to see over his shoulder, searching for Dylan, but only spot three other football players a few lockers away, huddled together and talking.

Of course he's not there. What did I expect?

"I'm fine," I finally answer him.

"Are you sure?"

I nod, visibly shaken.

He keeps his eyes on me. "Because you look like you saw a ghost."

I swallow hard.

"Hey"—one of the huddled players calls for his attention, looking over at us with a phone in his hand—"the video finally loaded."

The brick wall I just ran into glances backward and tells his teammate, "One second," before facing me again. "I'd slow down if I were you." He grins.

Slow down . . .

"What did you just say?"

"I said, you should slow down." He looks at me with even more worry. "You know . . . because these floors get slippery?"

"Oh." I close my eyes and nod. "Right."

"What school do you play for? I haven't seen you around." His eyes find the blue Disk on my temple and narrow with curiosity. "What is that?"

Shit.

It's 9:02 p.m., and not only am I late but this accidental run-in has now become a problematic interaction.

I throw my bag over my shoulder and dash off to Sleeping Quarters without saying goodbye. I'm scared what breaking two unforgivable Affinity rules may mean for me and my deal with Jacob, but I'm far more afraid that my wanting so badly for Dylan to be alive means he'll never stop haunting me.

18

RIVER

I wake up early the next morning before Nora's knock, anxious to know if my tardiness to bed last night and interaction with a football player were noticed. To distract my panicked brain and with time to kill before breakfast, I decide to finally read the information packet about Affinity that Nora gave us. I scan the front, which includes the same four colored dots and the researchers' tagline: *creating the future of friendship*.

The first page features an essay by Clarence Pedals, the thirty-something tech bro who launched Affinity Mind & Body a few years ago. The pasty Mark Zuckerberg–wannabe wrote that he wanted to launch "a twenty-first century research lab that solves twenty-second century problems." It makes me wonder what kinds of critical issues could possibly be solved by studying kids like me.

Then I flip to the next page and learn that Affinity's research is going far beyond one sleepy Michigan suburb. Sixty-four other high schools are holding trials this summer, all with their own Dr. Ridges and Mentors, too. The schools are all over the place, in big metropolises like Seattle, St. Louis, and New York, and smaller cities and towns I've never heard of—Logan, Utah; Jasper, Florida; Rosedore, Illinois. Teawood, Michigan, making the cut for this list gives me a surprising twinge of pride. *Could I be helping make history, like Dr. Ridges said?*

But then there's his answer to Oaklyn's question yesterday. I shouldn't assume everything—or *anything*—explained to me throughout the next week is truthful, including what I'm reading in this information packet.

"Wild," I mutter under my breath. Hearing my own voice in the quiet makes me feel silly but also suddenly aware that I might not be talking to just myself.

I forgot to check for cameras in my room last night, but neither Dr. Ridges nor Nora mentioned Sleeping Quarters being off-limits for filming. And, sure enough, I spot two small cameras on opposite corners of the room, both blinking red at me.

Feeling more like a lab rat than before, I flip to the section in the pamphlet that outlines Affinity's camera-recording policy. Beyond reiterating the basics, the packet specifies that Affinity will match our actions on tape with the brain activity collected by the Disks occurring at that time, allowing researchers to see how interactions with others affected our cognitive functions. It doesn't go into that great detail, but even just a small peek behind the curtain makes me feel like at least there's a legitimate purpose to being recorded almost all day, every day, throughout the next week.

A knock on the door startles me. I glance at the clock and see that it's 8 a.m. on the dot.

"Good morning, River!" It's Nora. "Can we talk?"

Talk?

My stomach drops. "Yeah, one sec," I say, climbing out of bed. I quickly throw on fresh navy clothes and crack the door open. "Hey."

She smiles. "If you're ready for the day, mind coming to my office?"

"Office?"

She leans closer. "I say office because I think it sounds creepy when Mentors invite participants to their rooms."

"Right. Okay."

I follow Nora into the hallway, my insides still churning with nerves. She doesn't say anything as we head to her room. It's only about a fifteen-second walk, but knowing how talkative Nora has been since meeting her, it's an unsettling fifteen seconds.

I can't imagine she knows about my interaction with the football player, seeing as there are no cameras in the locker room—unless my Disk somehow gave it away? But the security guard who spotted me returning to Blue Sleeping Quarters late could have told on me.

We enter Nora's room, and it's far homier than when me and Dylan took a CPR training in here our sophomore year. Nora's made bed in the corner is covered in fuzzy pillows and blankets. Just like in my room, the student desks and chairs are gone, along with all the signs on the walls and books on the shelves. But unlike my setup, Affinity kept the teacher's desk for Nora to use, along with a few chairs. I recognize her laptop on her desk from its assortment of colorful stickers, and I spot the Neuro I wore during my A-Test next to a collection of framed photos of Nora with who I assume are her loved ones.

"Good morning, River."

I jump at the sound of Dr. Ridges's voice. I hadn't noticed him standing against the wall next to the door. Predictably, he's wearing another tweed suit. Less predictably, he's *here*.

I must be toast.

"Is this about last night?" I blurt at the two of them. "Because the campers came into the locker room early, and I—"

Nora gestures for me to chill out and sit. "It's okay. Let's talk about it."

She closes the door as I take a seat across from her desk, then drops down into her own chair behind her laptop.

Dr. Ridges drifts over, hovering next to me like the grim reaper. My insides twist in knots, sensing the seriousness of the conversation we're about to have. How can I convince them to let me stay?

"So." Nora crosses her arms atop her desk. "As you're obviously aware, our security clocked you being out of bed past 9 p.m. last night."

Here it comes.

My mind goes into overdrive. How long do I have until Jacob starts telling people that I'm the one behind the mustache? I at least have the week, assuming he'll be stuck in here with no contact with the outside world. Surely I can find some other way to get a thousand bucks by the time he's out.

Nora must see how panicked I am. "River," she says gently, "you're not in trouble."

I look between Nora and Dr. Ridges as the knots in my stomach slowly untwine. "Really?"

Nora grins. "The head of the football camp, Coach Jones, notified Dr. Ridges last night that he forgot about the rules and mistakenly let some of his campers into the locker room early."

I feel a wave of relief. "I would have been back in bed by nine, but I had to hide from the players, knowing any interaction would have been against the rules."

"It's okay that you were late," Nora says, taking a sudden serious tone. "That's not why you're here."

Then . . . why else would I be in trouble?

"Have you felt . . ." Nora pauses, thinking through her words. ". . . different since last night?"

"Different?"

"Yes. Since you used the locker room to shower."

Their eyes feel like laser beams.

My insides start twisting in knots again. "No, not really."

"No headaches, lightheadedness, blurred vision?" Dr. Ridges follows up. "Nothing like that?"

I shake my head.

"Did anything out of the ordinary happen while you were in there?" Nora asks.

I guess seeing a vision of your dead best friend is pretty far from ordinary.

"You can be honest with us," Dr. Ridges says. I think he's trying to make me feel comfortable, but it comes out more like a warning than anything else. "It's important."

I swallow hard. "Out of the ordinary . . ." I mutter, trying to buy time to think about how I want to answer.

"It's okay if you talked to the players," Nora says in a much softer tone, countering Dr. Ridges's. "You won't be in trouble."

How detached from reality will they think I am if I tell them about seeing Dylan? Could imagining him disqualify me from the trials?

Sensing my stalling, Nora looks to Dr. Ridges as if for approval.

He hesitates, then nods. "You're not supposed to be seeing this," he says to me with a sigh, "so please keep this confidential from the other participants. Okay, River?"

I try to remain chill, but he's not making it easy. "All right."

Nora turns her laptop so that I can see the screen. "This will look confusing to you, but don't worry, we'll explain what you need to know."

She's right. Most of the screen is taken up by a chart that's covered in lines, and several small tables along the side are crammed with six-digit numbers and color gradients only making the data more overwhelming. I spot the title, *BLUE D3*, in the top corner, though, and recognize the letter-number combo from my schedule.

"Was this recorded by my Disk?" I ask, assuming the designation must mean the data is specific to me.

Nora nods.

I reach toward my temple and run my fingers across the Disk. Could something so small and forgettable retain that amount of information, or is it nothing more than a distraction tool—an Affinity prop?

"This, right here," Nora says, pointing at a section of the chart where a yellow line spikes before crashing down again, "isn't normal." She sees the look on my face. "Oh, no, not like that. From what we can tell, your brain is perfectly healthy."

Dr. Ridges steps closer. "That yellow line represents one of the key brain activities your Disk is responsible for tracking, and the sudden increase you're seeing on the screen is abnormally large."

I stare at the spike. "What does the yellow line track?"

Nora cringes regrettably. "I wish we could tell you that."

I look to Dr. Ridges.

"She's right. Affinity forbids us to disclose that information to participants," he confirms.

I squirm in my chair uncomfortably.

"I want to be clear," Nora says, "there's nothing wrong with you or your brain, River. We don't want to scare you."

"The increase may look alarming on a chart," Dr. Ridges adds, "but I assure you that it's not suggestive of an underlying health condition."

"It *is* an atypical data point for your Disk to record, though," Nora says, "and since there are no cameras in the locker room with footage we can reference, it'd be a big help if you could tell us about anything odd that happened that may explain the abnormality."

They fall silent, waiting for me to respond.

I rack my brain, contemplating how honest I should be. At the risk of sounding like the little boy in *The Sixth Sense*, I decide not to tell them about my Dylan sighting. A character who sees dead people may make for great horror, but in the real world, it could mean I'm too unwell to stay in the trial.

"I'm sorry," I finally say with a sigh, "but I don't know what it could've—" I pause as my eyes land on one of Nora's picture frames.

It's a photo of her taken several years ago. She's standing on the beach with her arm around a girl with big glasses and an even bigger smile. It's the boy her other arm is wrapped around, however, that gets my attention, with his big, brown, magnetic eyes that I'm almost certain I was staring into last night.

"Who is that?" I ask, pointing at the frame.

Nora seems happy to explain. "Ruthie." She pauses. "Actually, I may have mentioned her to you during your A-Test? My friend who moved to Ohio?"

"I'm talking about the boy—*oh*." It clicks. No wonder the football player's eyes looked familiar last night: they're identical to Nora's. "Is that your brother?"

I remember her mentioning during our tour of the E-Wing that he's at the football camp this week.

"How'd you . . . ?" Her face expands in surprise before making the connection. "Oh, I see. He had a late practice. You probably ran into him in the locker room, huh?"

Literally, yes.

I nod.

"*Hrm*," Dr. Ridges mutters in thought. Nora and I look at him, as his two pointer fingers press together against his bottom lip. "Did you two interact?"

I hesitate.

"Remember," he adds, "you won't be in trouble."

I take a deep breath. "I mean, briefly, yeah. But I'd barely even call it an interaction. We crossed paths and he asked which team I played for."

"What did you tell him?" Nora asks.

"Nothing. I ran to my room right after that."

"And you didn't talk to anyone else?"

I shake my head adamantly.

Dr. Ridges and Nora exchange looks, but I can't tell what they're thinking.

"I'm definitely not in trouble," I say, "right?"

"Definitely not," Nora answers. "We're grateful you told us everything and tried your best to not break the rules." She eyes the clock. "Doctor, do you have other questions for River?"

Dr. Ridges shakes his head. "You've been hugely helpful, Mr. Lang."

I look between them. "So . . . I can go?"

He nods, and I head to the door.

Before I walk out, Dr. Ridges speaks up. "Remember, though, it's critical that you keep everything we discussed to yourself. We've bent the rules ever-so-slightly just by showing you the chart, and we don't want the others thinking the same exception can be made for them."

I nod, feeling the weight of the secret pushing me into the floor, and leave.

19

DYLAN

I run to my car in the far corner of the parking lot with a smile on my face and adrenaline pumping through my veins. I hop behind the wheel and squint back at the school to see if Harry is still chasing us, which he doesn't appear to be. I take a deep breath to calm down and process everything that just happened, as the taillights of River's car disappear into the distance.

Somehow, it seems both embarrassingly obvious and downright shocking: I like River. I may even . . . *love him*? I cover my face with my hands and laugh into my palms, giddy from the last half hour, as the butterflies continue flapping away inside.

Why didn't I realize this sooner?

Other guys have crossed my mind before, but those thoughts and feelings were always so fleeting compared to how I felt about Mavis, I never gave them much thought. Or maybe I buried the idea of liking a boy without realizing I had, knowing how disappointed my dad would be to have a son who isn't straight. But meeting River in our spot, beneath the forever-under-construction skylight, made it crystal clear tonight. He's more than just a friend to me.

"I think I'm in love with River," I whisper aloud.

It's been a such a long time since I've had those same feelings for—

Mavis.

"Shit," I mutter as a wave of guilt washes away my elation.

That was hardly a kiss, let alone cheating . . . right? Or did I just fuck up a two-year relationship with an impromptu peck on the lips? Even if I had planned on breaking up with her today, we're still officially together *now*, and I'd hate for Mavis to ever believe my decision to end things was just because of him—just because of tonight.

My heart thunders away in my chest from the whirlwind of conflicting emotions bouncing around in my brain. I roll down my window, hoping the fresh air will help chill me out—it doesn't— and sweat begins collecting on my forehead.

I need to get back to the Meyerses' house, but I can't return this frazzled.

I remember the advice Mr. Babcock gave me once about battling overwhelming thoughts. *Pull them out of your brain and put them on a page*, I hear his voice in my head. *Don't overthink it. Just write*. So I find a pen in the glove compartment and then bend in every direction in search of something to write on.

I spot a small yellow notebook I don't recognize that has fallen between the seat belt and door. I flip it open and see *Brady Potts* scribbled on the top lefthand corner. It must have dropped out of his bag earlier.

There's only one page that's been written on, but it seems to be an important one:

Grandma and Brady's travel bucket list
  Grand Canyon
  Cinque Terre
  Paris
  Niagara Falls

My heart breaks a bit remembering his grandma waving at us earlier from the doorway of their house with an oxygen mask on. The list must be more aspirational than anything, but still, I can't forget to drop this off at his house tomorrow.

I turn to a fresh sheet and follow Mr. Babcock's advice to just go for it . . . *whatever comes to mind first . . .*

Dear M

I barely begin before a weather alert about an incoming thunderstorm vibrates my phone, and my unread messages light up on the screen beneath it. I can see the text my dad sent while I was leaving the Meyerses' house:

We're supposed to get a bad storm soon. Text me back.

20

RIVER

I walk to Headquarters for breakfast still a bit rattled from my meeting with Nora and Dr. Ridges. I know they said my brain is normal and the yellow-line surge isn't anything to be worried about, but I'm not that reassured, given that the data point was apparently so unprecedented that it not only prompted Nora to call a meeting with Dr. Ridges, but warranted breaking an Affinity rule to show me the Disk's chart.

Could imagining Dylan have caused it to happen—whatever *it* is?

When I walk into Headquarters, I see that chairs have been placed around several small, circular tables now scattered throughout the space, and a buffet of delicious-looking food has been laid out under the whiteboard. A couple Oranges are sitting together at one table, Goldie and another Green are at another, and Biggs and Oaklyn have taken spots at the table closest to the food. Jacob is sitting alone at the table farthest from the door.

I wander up to the food, where Dr. Ridges waves at me, as if our meeting earlier never happened. "How'd we sleep, River?"

I play along. "Fine."

"I heard about the unfortunate incident with Mr. Potts, by the way." He grimaces. "I'm sorry you missed dinner."

"Shit happens," I hear Goldie's voice answer for me. I glance backward and see her snagging a banana. "Or in your case, *vomit*." She spins away and back to her seat with a smirk.

I grab way more food than I normally would, having not had a legitimate meal since my dad dropped me off after lunch yesterday, and then scan Headquarters again, contemplating where to sit. Everyone seems to be separated by color, so my instinct is to just join Biggs and Oaklyn. I'll be with them all day, though, and my priority should really be to try again to get in Jacob's good graces. Hopefully then I'll learn why he decided to blackmail me in the first place.

And what he wants with half of my stipend money.

"We don't have to sit with our colors, right?" I ask Jacob, wondering if I missed an announcement about it at dinner yesterday.

"Nope."

I take the seat next to him. "I wonder if that's one of the things they're studying," I say, "if our color affects how we form our own social circles."

"If that's the case," he says, glancing at me, "it seems like you enjoy rebelling."

I smile.

"I didn't mean it as a compliment," he adds, lowering his voice, "Mr. Mustache."

My lips flatten, to his delight.

I dig into my food. "So," I begin through a mouthful, "why did you decide to sign up for the trials?"

He shrugs and bites into a strawberry.

"I mean, I assume it's for the money," I follow up.

He doesn't respond.

"Two thousand dollars isn't nothing," I continue.

Still, nothing. He's not budging.

Screw it.

"I guess what I'm getting at is," I say, leaning in closer, "why are you doing this to me?"

He stares at his plate, his lips curling into a small smile.

"Because if word gets out that I spray-painted Dylan's billboard, which, by the way, I'm *not* saying I did—"

"You did."

"—it could ruin my life. I'd probably get my scholarship revoked."

He scoffs. "So it'd be your scholarship getting revoked—not your supposed best friend's tragic death—that ruined your life?"

I tense up. "Okay, so maybe *ruin my life* is an exaggeration," I concede, "but it'd still be bad. My parents loved Dylan, too, and if they heard that I did it—"

"So, you're admitting it?"

Brady comes crashing down into a chair at our table, promptly shutting me up. "I'm so sorry about yesterday, River," he breathes, nearly knocking over his glass of chocolate milk. His mullet is a mess with bedhead, and I notice a bunch of crusties clinging to his eyelashes.

"It's okay, but"—I nod at his glass—"should you be drinking that?"

He nods. "I'm *positive* I took my pill this morning."

Jacob scans him up and down. "Dairy issues aside, are you okay?"

Brady examines himself, too. "Yeah, why?"

"You look exhausted," I say.

Brady exhales. "I had this really vivid dream that woke me up and I couldn't fall back to sleep."

"Hey, babes," Biggs greets us, taking a seat on the other side of Brady. "I'm glad this table is mixing colors, because I don't think I could handle three meals a day with Oaklyn." She glances over at the table she just left, where Oaklyn's now chatting with Jade. "I like her—truly, she's a sweetheart—but once she starts talking, that girl just doesn't stop."

"It's an anxiety disorder thing," Jacob says. "She told me and Brady about it at dinner."

Brady sips his chocolate milk. "The more nervous she gets, the more she says, and the faster she says it."

"Really?" Biggs cringes. "Great, now I feel like an asshole . . ." Her eyes almost burst out of their sockets, though, when she sees what Brady's drinking. "You're really gulping down whole-ass, chocolate-infused *cow milk* after what happened yesterday?"

I stifle a laugh.

"He took his pill," Jacob says, grinning.

"What?" Brady looks between the three of us. "I did!"

"I mess with people I like, babe," Biggs says, elbowing Brady gently. "Besides, I have sympathy for you. One of my favorite Tether friends is lactose intolerant, and I know her struggle is real."

"What's Tether again?" I say, assuming that's the app where Biggs is a big deal. "I heard you're a creator on there, but I'm not on it."

"Hardly any Americans are," Biggs says. "It's a newer social media app based out of the UK. They have great comment moderation, which is a big reason I love it. Way fewer racists, way more likes."

"It had user privacy issues last year," Jacob says to her, "right?"

"Yeah, but let's be real, what social site hasn't?" Biggs glances up at the camera in the nearest corner. "Speaking of privacy . . . what do you guys think they're *actually* studying about us? The colors have to mean something."

"Maybe, but maybe not," Jacob says. "The colors could just be a ruse to distract us."

"Distract us from what?" Brady asks.

"The real reason we're all here."

I spot Jade heading our way, her eyes sparkling with intrigue.

"Look at these Blues mingling with a Red," she says with a grin, breezing by. "The trial's first purple table."

Brady laughs, nearly choking on his chocolate milk. "Purple table."

Biggs considers the title. "I don't hate it?"

"Neither do I," Jacob says.

"That reminds me," Biggs says, laughing, "do you guys remember when Dylan Cooper parodied that political speech during the talent show last year? *There's no red Teawood or blue Teawood, just the United States of Teawood*—"

Brady clears his throat, getting Biggs's attention.

"What?" she asks, slightly offended, before realizing why he interrupted her. "Oh, fuck. I . . . sorry, River."

I feel myself turning the color of Jacob's shirt.

"It's fine," I tell them. "You can talk about him around me."

I appreciate Brady trying to protect my feelings, but I wish he wouldn't. Dylan would love that Biggs remembered that speech. *I* love that she remembered that speech and brought it up without mentioning the accident. Plus, she's right—it *was* funny.

Why does everyone feel beholden to the tragedy, as if remembering the good times degrades Dylan's legacy when just the opposite is true?

Biggs and Brady smile, but Jacob avoids my gaze. I wonder why he thinks I spray-painted the mustache. I'm sure he wouldn't get my reasoning for doing it, but he'd be far from alone in this town.

When breakfast ends, I head to Sleeping Quarters alongside the other Blues. Mavis, I notice, still keeps her distance from me.

We find Nora waiting for us.

"Hello, my Blues," she says as we approach. "Who's ready for their first Fitness activity?" None of us react. "*That's* the spirit."

I grin.

"Today, you have dodgeball," she continues. "So get your throwing arms ready and head on out to the courtyard." Nora turns and walks away in the wrong direction.

"Wait," Oaklyn speaks up, both alarmed and confused. "You're not coming with us?"

Nora smiles. "Like I said yesterday, you're on your own."

We walk to the courtyard and head outside. It's overcast and cooler than I expected it to be, but the fresh air is nice. Affinity has set up a small court for us to play on using traffic cones and rope. Five dodgeballs have been placed in the middle.

Biggs and I exchange looks.

"I hate dodgeball," she whispers.

"Same," I reply.

The doors swing open, and in walk the Greens. An iciness creeps across the courtyard as they take their spot opposite us on the court.

Goldie grins nastily at me before winking at Mavis. "Are there official rules displayed anywhere?" she asks.

"I don't think so," Mavis says, glancing around, then shrugging.

Once the teams have hashed out a few disagreements over the rules—and by *teams*, I mean a stubborn Biggs and arrogant Marcus—the match begins.

I mostly stay in the back and out of everyone's way. I'm not afraid of getting hit, I just don't care enough about winning to try.

But Goldie clearly does.

She gets a ball, pulls back, and launches it my way without hesitation. Her throw is so off, though, I don't even have to move. The ball just soars several feet to my right.

When I smirk, it infuriates her.

A few moments later, she gets the ball again. But instead of attacking a vulnerable Brady, who has tripped and fallen a few feet in front of her, Goldie rockets the ball at me yet again. This time, her throw comes closer. It isn't until her third attempt that I have to dive onto the dead grass to avoid contact. But Goldie is hell-bent on targeting me, and I start to get agitated when throw number four results in the ball whizzing dangerously close to my ear.

When a ball rolls toward me in the back of the court and no one seems to notice, I use the opportunity to sneak up and fire my shot back. I aim for her arm, but Goldie turns my way just as the ball leaves my hand, and it smashes into her face.

Everyone gasps, and a moment later, I see why.

Bright red blood is pouring out of Goldie's nostrils, covering her mouth and chin. All the Blues hesitate to help except for Mavis, who pushes through Marcus and another Green to be at Goldie's side.

"Way to go," Marcus scolds me from afar, glaring.

I'm not sure how to respond, so I stand in stunned silence.

"Relax, babe, injuries are part of the game," Biggs shouts at him. She turns to me and lowers her voice. "Don't feel bad."

But, as much as I dislike Goldie, I do.

I stride toward her, hoping to apologize, but Goldie shakes her head at me before I can get a word in, and I decide to respect her space. Mavis helps her to her feet, and they both head inside to get tissues.

A few awkward moments later, we decide to continue playing four-on-four, but the game is noticeably less heated, with gentler throws and less attention to who's winning, as everyone's fearful of causing another injury. When a pleasant twinkling noise comes over the school's PA system, it's momentarily confusing for all of us before we gather it's Affinity's way of signaling the end of the activity. We head back into the school, where the Blues and Greens break off in different directions.

Biggs, Brady, Oaklyn, and I meet Nora back in our Sleeping Quarters to get instructions for whatever Art entails. We find her waiting for us with Mavis at her side, clipboard in hand.

"Well, well, *well*," Nora says to me as we approach, an amused smile on her face, "if it isn't the dodgeball slayer."

No one laughs.

"*Oof*, too soon?" Nora cringes. "Tough crowd. I'm happy to report that Ms. Candles is doing just fine, aside from a possibly bruised ego."

I sigh in relief. I didn't intend for others to notice, but Mavis does. And she offers me a small, gracious smile before quickly looking away.

I was *not* expecting that.

"All right, Blue Crew," Nora says, "let's go."

I follow behind with a little pep in my step. Sure, it was just a smile—hardly something to celebrate—but after a year of glacial coldness between me and Mavis, I'll take it.

"You don't need to know how it went?" Oaklyn asks Nora as we trot down the hallway.

"How what went?"

"The game," Biggs says, similarly surprised. "We tied with Green. They won three matches, and so did we."

Nora considers the results and nods.

"Are you going to . . . write that down or something?" Oaklyn says with raised eyebrows, as if not documenting dodgeball results is a cardinal sin.

Nora grins. "I am not, Oaklyn." We round a corner and stop outside a classroom. "Unlike Fitness, you'll have Art in the same room every day. So moving forward, there's no need to find me before reporting here by eleven. Have fun, Blue Crew."

Nora turns and walks off before any of us can ask questions.

"Did that feel strange to anyone else?" Mavis asks, watching the back of Nora's head bob away. "It's like, not only did she not need to hear about how dodgeball went, she made a point not to care."

"Yeah," Brady mutters, deep in thought. "It feels like they're not telling us something."

Biggs sighs and pats his shoulder. "Oh, Brady."

She opens the door and we follow her in. The art room looks just like it did when I took an elective ceramics course last year, except for one notable difference: all the school's used and abused art tools in the back have been replaced with brand-new, top-notch supplies instead. There are blank canvases of various sizes, stacked crisp notebooks for drawing, and enough pencils, pens, paints, and brushes to resource an entire art school.

I see Mavis's eyes light up.

The Reds, who arrived shortly before us, are already calling dibs on their preferred seats. I see Jacob snag a canvas and claim a seat by the window.

Mavis, eager to get her hands on the new art supplies, is the first Blue to beeline to the back of the room, hardly able to contain her glee. She grabs a sketchbook and finds a quiet spot to work away from the other Blues and Reds.

I'm not the only one to notice.

"That's the most excited I've seen her in a *long* time," I overhear a girl I recognize from the volleyball team say quietly to a fellow Red. "Is she into painting or something?"

"I have no idea," the other replies, "but after the year she's had, she deserves to smile."

I agree.

"She loves drawing comics, actually," I chime in from behind. The two girls jump, not having realized I was standing there. "She's really good, too."

I scope out the art supplies, decide to grab a set of paint and a small canvas, and drop into the chair next to Jacob.

"I heard you were giving out bloody noses this morning," he says to me with a grin.

Finally, I don't have to think of some awkward, forced opening line to start the conversation. "It was one bloody nose," I clarify, "and it wasn't intentional."

But my luck stops there, as Biggs takes a seat close to me and Jacob.

I notice she didn't grab any supplies to work with. "Not the artsy type?"

"I am when it comes to beauty, hair, and makeup," she says with a sigh, looking around at what everyone else is working on, "but not *this*."

"That's your focus on Tether, right?" Jacob asks, mixing orange and gray paints.

Her face brightens. "Yep."

Biggs getting accepted into the trials is curious to me. She's one of the most outspoken, outgoing participants here, but I hardly ever saw her talking to other kids at school, and she's not involved in any sports or clubs that I know of. It makes me wonder how someone can be so influential on Tether without that success translating into real-world popularity. "How many followers do you have?"

"Just over eight hundred."

Jacob glances at her, hesitant. "You're considered an influencer with eight hundred followers?"

She shakes her head. "Sorry, eight hundred *thousand*."

Damn.

"So how can a popular Tether personality qualify for the Affinity Trials?" Jacob asks, voicing my thought aloud. "It doesn't seem like you meet the prerequisites—and I mean that as a compliment."

Biggs smiles. "Thanks, but tell that to my parents. They made me sign up. I didn't think I'd get in, but . . ."

"Why did they want you in the trials?" I ask, dabbing at my paints with a brush.

"I have lots of internet friends from all over the world. Good friends, too, who've had my back through thick and thin—well"— her face drops in disappointment—"most of them have, anyway. But they're not 'real-world friends,' as my dad says, and those have been much harder for me to come by. He doesn't get it, though."

"My dad's the same way," Jacob says. "I'm closer to my Marvel and gamer friends on Twitch than I am to anyone at school."

Biggs nods. "Right? Not having my phone this week is actually *killing* my social life, not helping it."

The more I learn about Biggs, the more I see how her attempt to rally participants yesterday to get our phones back wasn't just a funny way to get attention but an earnest plea to stay connected.

I mess around with random colors on my canvas for a while, hoping the blobs in front of me will eventually morph into something worth looking at. Despite the activity ending soon, Biggs finally bites the bullet and leaves for the back of the room to figure out what art supplies she wants to work with, giving me an opening to talk about the billboard with Jacob.

I turn toward him, but he's a step ahead of me.

"I'm surprised you're not painting a mustache," Jacob says, stroking his own canvas with the tip of his brush. "Why not?"

My heart skips a beat, and I glance around to make sure no one is listening to us.

"Can you please talk softer?" I whisper.

He smirks. "You'd like that, huh?"

"Why do you think I did it?"

"I don't," he says, eyes turning to me. "I *know* you did."

I exhale. "I'm doing what you asked. I signed up for the trials, I got in, and I actually showed up yesterday, prepared to be here for the next week."

"Good. So?"

"So I think it's only fair you fill me in a bit."

He pauses his painting and thinks for a moment. "Fine. What would you like to know?"

Finally, we're getting somewhere.

"How do you know it was me?" I ask.

"Well, the first red flag I noticed," he says, returning to his artwork, "was that you never posted anything online about the billboard using that hashtag the week it went up."

I almost laugh. "You mean, *hashtag Driving for Dylan*? That ridiculous thing?"

"That ridiculous thing practically the whole school joined in on except for Dylan's supposed best friend? Yeah, *that* thing."

I roll my eyes. "Whatever."

"I remember thinking, isn't it strange that River would opt out of doing something to honor Dylan?"

I shake my head. "First of all, Dylan hated performative hashtag activism, so I definitely don't see it as *honoring* him. And secondly, I can't believe *that's* what you're basing my guilt on—"

"Oh no. I didn't spend much time thinking about that. Then, for our Econ research paper last winter, you chose to cover how bloated the state's Department of Transportation's advertising budget is," Jacob continues, "which seemed both incredibly specific and suspiciously personal, given the circumstances. I thought it was a weird-as-hell choice."

Shit. My mom warned me that the topic would raise eyebrows for the same reason. I struggle to think of an adequate defense. I forgot Jacob was even *in* that class with me.

"Okay, but was I wrong?" I deflect. "How many potholes could have been fixed with the budget they spent on those keychains that read *Don't text and drive*? It's not all about the billboards."

"Still," Jacob continues, as my stomach moves into my throat, "I didn't know what to make of it. But then, on Monday, I saw your jeans."

I stare at him. "My jeans?"

"Yes. I noticed them because I have the same pair—except mine don't have a streak of black spray paint on the hem."

Mother. Fucker.

How could I have missed that? I inhale slowly, telling myself to keep it cool. *How could I have been so stupid?*

"To your credit, the streak does give the jeans a cool look," Jacob says, "and anyone else who noticed probably thought you bought them that way. But I knew better."

"I know this looks horrible," I whisper, scooching toward him, "but if you understood where I'm coming from, I think you'd—"

"Save your breath," Jacob says. "Just get through this week, give me my half of your stipend, and your secret stays safe with me."

"I swear, Dylan—"

"Was a great guy," Jacob says, "and he deserved a better best friend than what he got in you."

The twinkling noise comes over the PA system, ending Art. The Blues and Reds start cleaning up their workstations, but I sit there, stunned into silence, as Jacob walks away.

21

RIVER

Even when he showed up to blackmail me, I was much more confused than angry with Jacob, but that's over now. I'm pissed off.

He deserved a better best friend than what he got in you.

I may not have been a *perfect* friend to Dylan, because perfect friends don't exist, but I was certainly a much better friend than anyone who thinks Dylan would've been hurt by my aversion to posting a stupid hashtag. Jacob can suck a big, fat dick.

The last thing I want to do is eat lunch with him, but everyone seems to be sitting in the same seats as breakfast and I don't want the purple table thinking something's up between us.

So I stuff my face with more sandwich than I'm even hungry for just to get out of having to talk, avoid looking over at Goldie— she still has bloodied tissues crammed into her nostrils, which makes me think retaliation is a possibility—and then jet off to Blue's Mentor Check-Ins as soon as lunch ends.

Nora instructs us to wait in our rooms until it's our turn to speak with her one-on-one. I'm glad I get some alone time to cool off because once I'm able to think about Jacob's parting words with a more level head, my anger morphs into suspicion.

Sure, he'll get a thousand bucks out of blackmailing me, but did he even know about the trials when his suspicions made me the culprit? And if it was just about the money, he could be chill now that I'm here. I can tell he wanted those words to *sting*, and sting badly.

Why would a silly, spray-painted mustache offend him so deeply when he and Dylan weren't even really friends? This is exactly the problem. Everyone thinks they knew Dylan so well because he was always involved in everything and never said no when a favor was asked of him. But they didn't know him. Not really.

When it's time for my Check-In, I try my best to stay calm and push the Jacob incident onto my brain's back burner—I don't want any more weird Disk readings to draw attention to my chart—and knock on Nora's door. She calls for me to come in.

"Hey," she says, motioning for me to sit in the same chair I was in earlier.

She exhales, crossing her arms against her chest. "The first full day of the trials. How we doing?"

Beyond being blackmailed and hallucinating my dead best friend for the first time in months? "So far, so good," I fib, hoping the Disks can't act like lie detectors, too.

"During lunch, I was thinking more about our meeting with Dr. Ridges," she says, "and it occurred to me how fu—*freaking* bizarre that discussion for you must have been, especially on your first morning here. So thank you for rolling with it. Truly." Nora smiles and takes a sheet of paper off a nearby stack. "So, I'll make sure I live up to this session's name and check in with you on anything you want to talk about every time we meet one-on-one. Then you'll complete one of these."

I look down. It's another survey. Unlike the one I had to complete during my A-Test, there are only ten questions and they're all multiple choice.

"The questions will be the same every day," Nora says, pushing a pen to my side of the desk as well.

"What's the point of answering the same questions every day?" I ask.

"The survey focuses on your emotional connectedness. So even though the questions won't change, your answers to them could—though, not necessarily. Either way, we can track your responses to spot any insights, and then discuss them together."

I skim the page.

The questions seem simple enough, asking me things like *What's your current overall happiness level?* and *How are you feeling about your connections with—or aversions to—the other trial participants?*

"Making sense?" she asks.

"Yeah."

I begin breezing through the survey while Nora clicks away on her laptop. I push the paper and pen back across the desk to her once I'm finished.

"Terrific," she says, briefly looking it over and filing it away. "This establishes our baseline. With this being our first Check-In, though, I want to make space for you to bring up anything you'd like to discuss, especially after our meeting with Dr. Ridges this morning. What's on your mind?"

I think about my spiking yellow line. "Should I expect to get updates from you or Dr. Ridges about my Disk chart?"

"Yep. I have a meeting with him later, and we plan on discussing next steps. I'll be as transparent with you as I can be, moving forward." She pauses. "Anything else?"

I think. "I don't think so."

"You're sure?"

"Yeah."

She glances at her laptop, then back at me. "Then can I ask you about the gym?"

I swallow hard. "Uh . . . sure. What about it?"

"I read your A-Test survey responses," she says, "so I know it's been difficult for you to go in there this past year, which, to be clear, I completely understand." She smiles at me sadly.

I clear my throat. "Yeah."

Silence grips the room. Unlike the quiet between me and Nora during my A-Test, I suddenly feel strange and awkward. My cheeks get hot.

"Do you . . ." I trail off. ". . . have a question about it?" I laugh.

"Right." She purses her lips. "Would you be open to—"

"Nope." I smile. "I would not be open to going inside."

"Okay." She waits a beat, then bites her lower lip, grinning. "Can you at least walk me through why it's been so challenging to go inside the gym? Remember, I'm not here to judge."

My insides twist and turn.

I shrug. "I associate that place with Dylan, is all."

She stares at me and refuses to blink, wanting more.

I inhale, as memories from my final day with Dylan in there flash through my head like snapshots taken in a dream—the smell of the hardwood; eating my mom's enchiladas with sporks; hearing "Dylan's Song" playing in the hallway; listening to how he wants to do senior year right—do it better—by slowing down; running away from Harry into the parking lot.

Our kiss.

My eyes dart to the clock. "Isn't it time for me to go?"

Nora looks at the time, too, then back at me. "Yeah." She smiles. "Thanks, River."

I nod and leave the room before she can ask anything else.

That was exactly the sort of conversation I feared after Rex told me and Brady that the gym would be incorporated into the trials. I know why I mentioned it in one of my survey responses, I just wish I'd had the foresight to know my answer would come back to haunt me.

I head to the old woodshop room, hoping to distract myself from the surge of Dylan memories with some friendly competition.

The Blues and Oranges disperse across the lounge toward whatever games they'd like to play first. First I get trounced in an old-school boxing video game against a rising senior named Ollie, and then I'm demolished playing chess with an Orange who analyzes each move as if she were the lead in *The Queen's Gambit*. Again, we've gotten no instructions for what we should do here, so I don't take the losses all that personally and instead blame them on the trauma of having to sit on the same sofa where Pukegate took place just yesterday.

After Gaming, it's time for Meditation, which has me a little nervous because I've never tried it before. Nora leads us on a route I know all too well toward what students have dubbed the E-Suite: a collection of administrative offices on the other side of the E-Wing for people like Mr. Babcock whose jobs at the school are necessary but apparently not held in high enough regard to warrant prime main office space.

Biggs nods toward Mr. Babcock's office as we pass by. "So *that's* where he's been," she mutters at me. I turn, glimpsing Dr. Ridges working behind the desk, and recall that an annoyed Mr. Babcock mentioned the principal giving Affinity permission to use the space.

It's strange to see Dr. Ridges working across from the loveseat I spent every first period sitting on the past year, and stranger still that Mr. Babcock's archaic computer, dusty family photos, and pencil holders have been replaced by the doctor's thin tablet and a few neatly stacked white binders. It's as if one office belonged in 2010 while the other seems more suited for 2030.

When we get a few doors down from Mr. Babcock's, we learn that five of the E-Suite offices have been emptied out so there's one for each of us. In all five rooms, there's a yoga mat for us to sit on, an instruction card giving basic tips on meditation, and, of course, a blinking red camera recording our every move.

"I thought Affinity is here to study social dynamics," Mavis says, staring into the former teacher assistant office that she's now expected to meditate in. "Why are we being separated?"

"Calming the mind can affect how we open ourselves up to move through the world among other people, right?" Nora says, turning to the rest of us. "We all need space to recharge our social batteries. Don't be intimidated. There's no wrong way to do it! Just read the instruction card and try your best."

Mavis glances back at her hesitantly but walks in and the rest of us follow suit.

It takes me about thirty seconds to know that, contrary to Nora's take, there will *not* be any calming of my mind while I'm in here. The dead quiet creates the perfect amount of mental space for me to obsess over the questions that I've been trying to bury all day:

Now that yesterday's sighting happened, will I start seeing Dylan more frequently again?

Is Nora downplaying how odd my yellow-line surge is to protect me from the truth?

Is there something else motivating Jacob's blackmailing me beyond money?

If I hadn't sent that last text to Dylan, he'd still be around today, right?

After one of the longest hours of my life finally ticks to an end, I'm relieved to head back to Blue Sleeping Quarters for something on our schedules called Group Talk.

But on the walk there, out of nowhere, Mavis glances backward at me—*and smiles.*

It's not like her grin from this morning, which was lightning fast and an obvious reaction to my finding relief in learning Goldie was okay. This one is entirely unprompted, as she holds my gaze with a knowing sparkle in her eyes for several seconds.

Before I can process what's happening, Mavis has already turned back around. I look behind me and see Biggs and Oaklyn, who are bringing up the tail end of our group. She must have been smiling at them instead. Right?

"You good, babe?" Biggs asks, seeing the look on my face.

"Yeah," I say, shaking it off and facing forward.

Am I imagining smiles that aren't there, too?

A few minutes later we arrive at Nora's room to find the chairs have been placed in a tight circle near her desk. I take a seat between Biggs and Brady, while Nora sits directly across from me, Oaklyn and Mavis to her left and right. Between the smile I possibly got from Mavis and the room's sudden intimate energy, a surge of nerves fills my gut.

I have no idea what to expect out of this.

"Congratulations," Nora says pleasantly, crossing her legs. "You've made it through your first full day of the trials. . . . Well, almost." She scans our faces. "How are we feeling?"

As usual, no one speaks up first.

"C'mon." Nora smiles. "I know *someone* has to be feeling *something*."

Oaklyn mutters, "Anxious."

Nora nods. "Understandable."

"Tired," Brady says, still recovering from a terrible night's sleep. "I like what I'm working on in Art, though."

"Amazing. As long as it's not a painting of ice cream." She winks at him.

The room falls silent.

"Confused, I think?" Mavis admits. "But not in a bad way."

We all turn to her.

"Can you say more about that?" Nora encourages Mavis.

Mavis thinks through her words. "This doesn't feel like a normal social study—not that I even know what a normal one is like. I wasn't expecting this, I guess, and I'm glad my expectations were wrong."

"What did you expect?" Nora asks.

"I don't know." Mavis pauses again. "We get to play games and sketch whatever we want in Art. I expected the trials to be a lot more rigid and boring."

"Well, I'm glad to hear you've been pleasantly surprised," Nora says with glee. "Can I ask, though, are the trials meeting or missing your expectations when it comes to what you're experiencing on the inside?"

Mavis doesn't answer right away. "I'm . . . not sure what you mean."

"I guess what I'm getting at is," Nora says, looking around the room, "all of you are here for a reason, whether it be because you're lonely, anxious, grieving, or struggling in some other respect. Maybe it's all of the above." She directs her focus back on Mavis. "Aside from the trials being more fun and less boring, have you *felt* any differently today?"

Mavis moves uncomfortably in her seat and hesitates to respond.

"You also don't have to have an answer," Nora says softly. "We can—"

"No, it's okay," Mavis finally says. "Yeah, I think so. Today's been a good day."

There's something different about Mavis; a light in her eyes that's been missing the past year. Meditation must suit her well.

"River," Nora says, "how about you?"

I feel everyone's eyes turn toward me.

"Are the trials meeting my expectations?" I clarify her question, feeling my cheeks getting warmer. "Is that what I'm answering?"

"Sure," Nora says with a shrug. "It can but doesn't have to be. Anything else on your mind?"

A *lot* is on my mind. But most of it is things I either can't or don't want to talk about in front of the group. So I try to think fast.

"I mean . . . I don't know," I say, struggling. I look at Nora, and the warmth in her eyes helps me find one honest thing I can share. "It's not bad being around people more again, I guess."

It comes out way sadder than I meant it to.

"I mean," I laugh, "I've been around people, of course, but my senior year was tough for obvious reasons, and being here with you all has made it easier to feel connected again."

Brady smiles at me, and Biggs nudges my arm lovingly as my cheeks burn red-hot. I didn't mean to get all serious, but the words just slipped out. I guess it's not a bad thing that they did.

"What were the obvious reasons?" Oaklyn blurts out.

Brady's eyes widen, and Biggs sucks her teeth. Oaklyn clearly recognizes her words made an impact because she tries to backtrack fast.

"Wait, was that rude?" she says, cringing. "Ignore me. Don't answer that, River. I'm sorry, I'm new to Teawood, and I don't—"

"River and I were both close to someone who died last year," Mavis tells her. "His name was Dylan."

Oaklyn's jaw drops. "Oh," she says, "the boy on the billboard?" I nod.

"Wow," Oaklyn sighs, absorbing the information. "I assumed you two didn't even know each other before the trials."

I tense up.

I can't fault Oaklyn for assuming that to be the case, given we haven't exchanged a single word since arriving yesterday. Still, just because I can't fault her doesn't mean I want to talk about it now. It's only the first full day of the trials, after all.

Brady, however, doesn't mind going there for us. "Oh, Mavis and River go *way* back," he chimes in merrily, oblivious to the weightiness of the topic. "I was in Ms. O'Neal's fifth-grade class with them. They were inseparable."

"Is that when you two met?" Nora speaks up. Her eyes find mine before moving to Mavis. "Fifth grade?"

We're barely five minutes into our first Group Talk and already, me and Mavis's origin story has been thrust into the spotlight of a group discussion. It's exactly what I was afraid of when I saw her name on Dr. Ridges's clipboard during Summer Sign-Ups.

My gut churns with dread, unsure if I should speak first or just sit in silence praying Brady will vomit again soon, forcing an end to Group Talk.

"It was third grade, actually," Mavis answers.

I glance at her out of the corner of my eye and am shocked to see her not only smiling pleasantly, but perfectly content to be having the conversation.

She looks at me and lets out a small laugh. "We got paired up for the science fair. Remember?"

I'm speechless.

What happened to the Mavis who gave me the silent treatment for the past year? The one who blames me for Dylan's death?

I find my voice, finally. "Yeah," I say, trying to sound casual. "I remember. I couldn't make a compelling presentation on surface tension for the life of me."

"Well, I had no idea what surface tension even *was*." Mavis turns to Nora. "River's more left-brain and I'm more right-brain."

"That's sort of an antiquated way of thinking about—" Nora cuts herself off and shakes her head. "It doesn't matter. It sounds like you made a good team together."

"Can I ask," Oaklyn says, "how did you two know Dylan?"

"I was his girlfriend," Mavis says, "and River was his best friend."

Oaklyn seems startled by the answer. "Wait, really? That's strange, I . . ." She freezes mid-sentence, plunging the room into another awkward silence.

"What is it?" I ask.

"Nothing."

Biggs laughs. "That means it's definitely something."

Oaklyn presses her lips shut and shakes her head, like she's starting to suffocate under the weight of the room.

"Babe," Biggs says, smirking, "now you *have* to tell us."

"No, she doesn't," Nora says calmly, jumping in. "Oaklyn, you don't have to say anything you don't want to—"

"It's just, I haven't seen you two talk much, or maybe at all," Oaklyn exhales, her eyes darting between me and Mavis, "so it's surprising to hear that not only were you childhood friends, *you* were Dylan's girlfriend and *you* were Dylan's best friend."

I notice Oaklyn's words are pouring out of her mouth at an increasing rate, and recall what I learned at breakfast about her anxiety disorder.

"Because I'd assume that Dylan's girlfriend and Dylan's best friend would, at the very least, be friendly with each other," she carries on, seemingly uncontrollably, "if not eternally linked in a special way because of their shared loss—even if they weren't already friends, which was the point I was about to make before I stopped myself because I thought, well, if you're *not* friendly with each other, there's a good chance that something bad has happened between you two, and that would be an incredibly awkward thing to bring up with either of you *privately*, let alone in a group setting like this, which, *again*, is why I tried erring on the side of caution before saying all of this out loud like I'm doing right now, which, I know, is making this incredibly awkward thing *exponentially more awkward*—"

She gasps for breath, concluding her monologue, and I can't decide who had it worse: the other Blues, who seem to be dying of secondhand embarrassment, or me and Mavis, for having our messy history thrust into the spotlight. I want to run back to my Meditation room, lock the door, and never come out. Brady and Biggs are left speechless, and Nora doesn't seem to know how best to move on.

Before she can, Mavis stands. "May I go to the bathroom?"

"Of course."

Mavis leaves, and Oaklyn buries her head in her hands.

I've barely been in the trials for twenty-four hours, and already, all my fears are coming to pass.

22

RIVER

"I'm so, *so* sorry, River," Oaklyn whispers to me from across our circle. "When I get anxious, words just start pouring out of me without a filter, and I feel this irrational need to get them out as quickly as possible. It's fucked up, I know, *I'm* fucked up—"

"You're not fu—*screwed* up," Nora scolds her supportively.

Oaklyn barrels onward. "I have no idea what you've been through with Mavis, and I'm probably dead wrong—" She catches herself and cringes. "*Terrible* word choice. I'm probably very wrong about so many of the assumptions I make."

"You were pretty much spot-on," Brady chimes in nonchalantly. When he sees Nora glaring at him, he backtracks. "I mean, according to unconfirmed rumors about River and Mavis that've floated around school." He looks at me sheepishly and lowers his voice. "Sorry."

"It's okay, Oaklyn," I say, angry but empathetic. There's no doubt she's upset with herself, so I don't see the value in dogpiling. "Mistakes happen."

A few minutes later, Mavis returns from the bathroom with misty eyes and a wad of tissues in her hand. Nora rightly steers the rest of our conversations away from any potentially explosive topics, and we end our session halfheartedly debating the best *Star Wars* movies.

Ironically, Free Time is the least free part of my day, as Biggs points out, since Affinity requires us to stay put in our rooms without the company of other participants or any of our stuff. After what happened in Group Talk, though, I don't mind taking a break from the group *or* talking. I find some old geography magazines in a cupboard that Affinity either forgot to remove before the trials began or intentionally left behind to curb my boredom in times like this, and begin to flip through them. But either way, an essay written in 2015 about climates on the equator does little to distract me from the growing list of anxious thoughts in my head—most notably now the abrupt change in Mavis.

What could have prompted her to suddenly start smiling at me again and casually reminiscing about our third-grade science fair project in front of Nora and the other Blues?

I'm eager to get out of my head and room for dinner until I actually *get* to dinner and realize all the messy developments of our first full day together have now been forced into a single room.

For the second meal today, I have to avoid Goldie's glaring at me from across Headquarters—she's clearly still upset from my fastball to her face during Fitness—and also pretend I'm not incredibly pissed at Jacob at the purple table. I have no idea what version of Mavis I'm going to encounter, either, after Oaklyn's anxious word vomiting threw us under the bus in Group Talk.

The latter is answered quickly when Mavis and I accidentally arrive at the pasta bar in unison. The warm feelings she seemed to show toward me after Meditation have soured, thanks to the Teawood transfer, no doubt, as Mavis ladles marinara sauce onto her rigatoni and walks away without giving me a second thought.

To make matters worse, I arrive back at the table to Biggs and Brady bringing Jacob up to speed on Oaklyn's awkward fiasco during Group Talk—a conversation I'd rather not have with anyone, especially the guy who's blackmailing me. I wish I could complain about Oaklyn to them—just so that I could channel my emotions at *someone*—but even that's impossible to do, as we notice she's sitting alone and looking particularly miserable, probably still riddled with guilt.

"Poor babe," Biggs mutters, staring at Oaklyn, before realizing how I might take it. "I mean, I get why you'd be pissed at her, to be clear."

"I'm not, though," I sigh. "It's just . . . complicated."

"I'll go sit with her," Brady volunteers, standing with his plate of food.

Biggs watches Brady take a seat across from Oaklyn. "He may not be the brightest bulb at times, but tell me he's not the sweetest." After I don't respond, she looks at me. "Hey."

My eyes find hers.

"You win the award for worst first full day of the trials, hands down," Biggs says, nudging my shoulder in solidarity. If she only knew about the part where I was also accused of being an awful friend to Dylan by the same boy who blackmailed me into the trials.

Jacob and I exchange looks. I maybe spot a glimmer of sympathy in his eyes, but it's gone before I can know for sure.

"Not to silver-linings it, babe," Biggs continues, "but maybe it'll be a good thing that Oaklyn spilled the tea? It's difficult for dark things to fester once they're thrust into the light."

I head back to my room for Quiet Hour completely drained. Dinner didn't help in calming my racing mind, but thankfully my pillow does. I start drifting in and out of sleep for a while, until—

I hear the swing of a door, startling me. I shout, briefly disoriented, then I see the silhouette of a boy standing in the doorway.

"Brady?"

No, the silhouette is too tall for Brady.

Dylan?

My eyes adjust to the weak lighting of the room, and I realize it's the football player from the locker room. Nora's brother.

I turn on my bedside lamp, so relieved to not be hallucinating again that for a moment I forget he's not supposed to be in here. "Uh, what are you—"

"Hi," he says. "I'm Nash."

Nash has a shirt on this time, a gray tank top, and white mesh shorts. I can barely see his face above the mass of pillows, blankets, and an unidentifiable ball of bulky plastic he's carrying against his chest. He shuts the classroom door with his foot, drifts to the nearest corner, and drops everything into a giant heap on the floor.

I sit up in bed and realize that *I'm* the shirtless one now, so I yank the covers up until, at the very least, my belly button's not showing. "What are you doing in here?"

Nash pulls off an overstuffed bag I hadn't noticed was strapped to his back and tosses it onto the other items he lugged in. He slouches, a bit winded from carrying everything, and rests his hands against his hips.

Finally, he pauses long enough to read the confusion on my face. "Did . . . my sister not tell you?"

"Tell me what?"

"My sister—sorry, your Mentor—asked me to sleep in here tonight."

"What?"

The door swings open again, and Nora appears with a worried look on her face. "Are you okay? I heard shouting."

I point toward the corner at Nash, who's fluffing a pillow.

"You told your brother to sleep in here with me?" I ask, as Nora looks in his direction. "I thought we weren't even supposed to talk to the campers, let alone share a room with them."

"Ouch," Nash retorts with a smirk as he organizes his things. "You're not even supposed to *talk* to me. . . ."

Nora opens her mouth to respond, but just as she does, the three of us freeze at the sound of soft sobs nearby. It takes me a moment to realize the crying is coming from Oaklyn's room, directly across the hall.

Nora exhales. "River, hear me out."

"Yeah, River," Nash quips, grinning, "hear her out."

Nora ignores her little brother. "I meant to talk to you after my meeting with Dr. Ridges, but an urgent matter"—she tilts her head toward Oaklyn's room—"came up. Is it okay if he sleeps in here tonight and then we can talk about it first thing in the morning? You obviously won't be penalized."

Nash glances at me, tinkering with the pockets of his backpack, as he waits for my response.

I can't even be entirely sure this isn't a dream, and I don't have enough brain power to adequately compute the situation. But I don't feel like I have a choice.

"Sure?" I say, in a very unsure tone. "I guess?"

Nora mouths *thank you* at me and begins to back out of the room, glancing Nash's way one last time before closing the door behind her.

I look at Nash, who's pulling apart the folds of what I now realize is an air mattress.

"So . . ." I say, unsure where to even begin. "Can you tell me what's—"

But he turns on the mattress pump and a loud, rumbling noise makes having a conversation impossible. Once his bed has fully risen to life, Nash turns the pump off and begins neatly laying sheets and blankets across its surface.

"So," I try again, more agitated this time, "can you tell me why you're here, considering your sister didn't?"

Nash crashes down onto his mattress, and the material squeaks beneath his weight. "I know it has something to do with that blue dot on the side of your head."

My fingers find my temple. "My Disk?"

"Not to act like a dick," he continues, pulling the covers around him, "but I have to wake up crazy-early for practice and need to sleep. Can you . . . ?" He points at the lamp next to my bed, implying I should turn it off, and rolls away from me to face the opposite wall.

No way I'm just going to sleep after he mentioned that. "What do you know about my Disk?"

"Honestly, you should ask my sister," he says. "I don't know that much about it." It sounds like he's already drifting off to sleep even with the lamp still on.

He may not *want* to be, but Nora's brother *is*, in fact, acting like a dick.

I reach up, turn off the lamp, and try to get comfortable again under the covers. It's not an easy task, considering there's a non-participant sleeping a few feet away from me under the blinking red light of a camera recording us, and I haven't been given a reason as to why.

Also, his name . . .

Why does it feel like someone was just talking about a Nash—

My eyes pop open in the darkness as my dad's words from the car ride yesterday come storming back to me: *one of the best in the country* . . .

As if this day hasn't already been complicated enough, now I'm apparently sharing a room with a superstar quarterback, who just happens to be my Mentor's admittedly hot but total dick of a little brother.

23

DYLAN

"Thunderstorm?" I mutter, glancing out the window of my car and up toward the sky. I can't see a single star, so clouds must've rolled in at some point this evening, and I hadn't noticed how gusty the wind has gotten during my sprint across the parking lot away from Harry.

I finish writing down my thoughts in Brady's notebook taking Mr. Babcock's advice to just let the words flow out of me without overthinking it, then rip the page out and pocket it. Thank God I remembered to do so; I can't stomach the thought of Brady discovering it one day while he's flipping through the pages in search of his grandma's bucket list.

I type out a text to my dad to let him know I'll be fine—I'm still with Mavis, will be home later tonight. i'll be careful—and hit send before staring out the windshield in thought. I have no idea how the rest of my night with Mavis will go.

I can't break up with her right now, I decide. Even though journaling has helped me to relax, the tension between us earlier coupled with my River revelation has thrown my emotions into a blender. It's not ideal to wait until she's back from her family trip, but it'd be reckless of me to try to have such a charged conversation tonight, especially one that I need to get right.

Another incoming text pops up on my phone. I expect it to be a reply from my dad, but it's from River:

not to sound like your dad, but lmk when you make it home after you leave the Meyers.

Typing bubbles appear and the butterflies immediately come flapping back into my stomach. I grin and bite my lower lip, curious if he'll mention the kiss, before reading the new message from him that arrives:

I know you're good but just want to say again that I'm here if/ when you need to talk. ☺

I smile to myself and contemplate texting back, eager to keep the conversation flowing. But I want to give my response some thought, and I've been gone from Mavis for a while, so I decide to message him once I'm at the Meyerses' again. Unlike texts from my dad, I know I won't forget to respond to River, especially knowing his biggest pet peeve is being left on read.

I drive back to Mavis's house—it's getting windier, and I notice fewer cars on the road than a typical Saturday night—and park in the driveway.

As I walk up to the house, the front door swings open and Mavis steps outside. She's smiling at me, but it's a nervous smile— one that I've seen her use before to hide behind.

"Hey . . ." I say with concern. "Is everything okay with Goldie?"

"Yeah, I took her home," she replies, closing the door behind her. "Can we drive somewhere and talk?"

24

RIVER

I wake up to loud knocking.

"What?" I bark back groggily, my eyes still closed and my face buried into a pillow.

"It's me."

The *me* is Nora.

I remember I'm not in my own bed at home but in the classroom where I once bombed a pop quiz on Benito Mussolini.

"One second," I say, squinting around and pulling on my shirt. Nash has already left for practice, and all the bedding he brought into my room with him is gone.

I rub my eyes, stumble out of bed, and open the classroom door to find Nora in a floral purple top and snug blue jeans.

"Good morning, sleepy," she says.

"Morning," I croak back.

"I want to talk about last night before breakfast. Have a minute?"

I yawn.

"I have that update regarding your Disk chart, too," she says, sweetening the deal.

I perk up, recalling that Nash mentioned my Disk having something to do with why he slept in my room, and it's enough to make me follow Nora down the hallway and into her room. Thankfully, Dr. Ridges hasn't joined us today. He's harmless enough but still weirds me out.

"So," Nora begins, circling her desk as I take a seat. "How'd last night go?"

"With Nash?"

She nods.

"It was fine," I say. I decide that I probably shouldn't start things off by telling Nora her brother gave off major asshole energy.

"What all did he tell you?"

"Not much. Just that you wanted him to sleep in my room because it had something to do with this"—I point at my Disk—"and then he went to bed, claiming he had an early practice."

"Yeah, I think they want him out there on the field by five a.m.," Nora says. "Those coaches are nuts. Well, sorry again I wasn't able to ask your permission properly before he barged into your room. I told him to come get me beforehand, but my guess is he didn't listen—*shockingly*." Nora glances at younger Nash in the frame on her desk and rolls her eyes. "Though I guess I had my hands full anyway."

I remember the sobs I heard last night. "Is everything okay with Oaklyn?"

She nods.

"She was still upset about Group Talk, wasn't she?"

Nora pauses and lowers her voice. "I can't really get into other participants' personal stuff, but I wouldn't worry about her, River. Oaklyn will be fine. Now"—she turns her laptop so I can see the screen—"look familiar?"

The *D3* signifier and yellow-line spike in the same spot tells me it's the same chart I saw yesterday.

"Well," she continues. "I've got good news. Dr. Ridges and I decided it was worth notifying the Affinity bigwigs about your atypical spike, and they wanted to read your chart themselves. Out of sixty-odd trials happening across the country this summer and thousands of participants, it's wild that yours was extraordinary enough to get their attention." She pauses and clarifies, "Wild in a *good* way."

"Okay . . . ?" I squint at her inquisitively, unsure how excited I should be for having such a wildly atypical data point on my chart.

"They got back to us late last night and think it's best if we fill you in, and I agree. *But*"—she rolls her eyes, as if annoyed she has to say whatever comes next—"before I can utter another word, you've got to sign on the dotted line."

Nora flips open a manila folder and pushes a sheet of paper across the desk so I can read it more closely. "It's a lot of text, I know," she notes, "but it's basically just saying that everything I share with you during this meeting cannot be shared with anyone outside this meeting—forever, period, end of story."

NONDISCLOSURE AGREEMENT is typed in big, bold letters across the top. Similar to the consent form I signed in front of Dr. Ridges, it's crammed with legal jargon that goes right over my head.

"I barely know what any of this says," I admit, scanning the text.

She sighs, lowering her voice. "Honestly, same. This is the *not*-good news part." She leans back in her chair. "Because you're eighteen, you can sign all by yourself. But unlike with the initial consent form, we can't let you contact an outside resource—like a parent or lawyer—to get their input because of the rules of the trials."

I glance up at her from the form. "Because a parent or lawyer would be considered a non-participant?"

She nods reluctantly.

"And if I don't sign . . . ?" I ask.

"You wouldn't be penalized, of course," she says adamantly. "I just can't tell you what the yellow line and its spike mean for your chart." She shrugs. "Completely your call, River."

I stare down at the NDA.

My reluctance to have my parents help me understand the consent form bit me in the ass, I recall, thinking back to Rex man-handling me in the bathroom. But it was mostly just an inconvenience. And if this NDA only requires that I can't tell anyone what I'm about to learn, I can live with that. Plus, if my Disk really did pick up on something wild enough to warrant Affinity's leaders getting involved, I want to know more.

I sign and date the form.

Nora files it away behind her desk, then turns toward me and her laptop. "Now, your yellow line . . ." But she pauses as quickly as she began and takes a deep breath. "I have to say," she whispers, "it's a bit surreal for me to be telling an active participant about an Affinity secret, so bear with me if I get overly excited." She beams.

It makes me even more eager to learn about my spike.

Nora sits up and clears her throat, attempting to focus. "Okay. So. One of the many things Affinity is studying during the trials is the way our brains form friendships. Have you ever learned about the brain's prefrontal cortex?"

I'm insulted she'd even ask.

"Oh, right," she says, smiling at my offended expression. "I forgot that you said in your survey that you'd like to pursue neurology. So of course you know that the big chunk of our brains"—she points to her forehead—"right here in front does a *lot*: helps coordinate our thoughts and actions, express our personality, cues us in to social behaviors." She grins at me. "But it does even more than what we previously understood. And that's where your yellow line comes in."

I look at the spike on the screen.

Nora takes a breath. "Affinity researchers believe we've located a tiny, *tiny* spot in the prefrontal cortex that activates when at least one of an individual's five senses encounters someone else who they have a nonromantic *affinity* for." She grins. "In other words, it lights up when that person is around a friend. It's the area of your brain that your Disk is actively monitoring, *literally* as we speak. Your yellow-line data reflects how stimulated that spot is in real time."

What?

I grin at her skeptically. "But . . . how is that even possible?"

She tilts her head to the side, curiously.

I hesitate. "Not to mansplain to *you*—an actual neuroscientist," I begin, "but aren't our brains way more complex than that? We don't have, like . . ." I try to think of a comparable example. ". . . a *love* section that ignites when a spouse walks into the room, or a *hate* section that lights up when an enemy approaches."

"True."

"Love, hate, friendship—they're all social constructs that we've labeled to better understand our relationships. But in our brains, a billion different things are happening across many regions that result in us feeling what we consider love, hate, or friendliness, right?"

Nora nods, impressed. "Are you sure you haven't already gone to med school?"

I feel my cheeks get warm.

"You're right," she says, "which is why our research has the potential to be so ground-breaking." She lifts up the pen I used to sign my NDA. "See this?"

I look at her suspiciously, as if it's a trick question. "Yeah?"

"The spot in our brain I'm referring to—Affinity is calling it your Orbeus—is about the size of the tip of this pen," she explains. "It's a very small spot, River."

I study the chart on the screen, wondering why that matters. "Okay. So?"

"So, it's feasible—*likely*, really—that we haven't had the technology before now to pinpoint such minuscule specks in our gray matter that do such things since, like you said, so much brain activity is happening all at once. Friendship is a social construct, yes, but maybe not wholly apart from our neurological anatomy. Maybe we just didn't realize that our Orbeus has been operating under our noses—or behind our foreheads—all along."

I'm trying to be as excited as she is, but it's hard to buy in to the theory that a microscopic dot used to turn on in my head every time Dylan walked in. I can tell Nora is sensing that I'm struggling to understand how this could be possible, so she continues.

"We didn't see an Orbeus spike as significant as yours in any of the pretrial models we ran, though. Which is to say that, we thought a spike as large as yours was scientifically impossible—until you."

Scientifically impossible? What?

"There must have been an error with my Disk," I say. "Isn't that much more probable than me being a scientific impossibility?"

She shakes her head. "If there was an error with your Disk, it would have surfaced somewhere else in the data. Dr. Ridges and I combed through your chart. That wasn't the case."

I think for a moment. "Are you sure I shouldn't, like . . . go to the hospital?" I ask. "Because if the spot in my brain was activated to such a degree it caused my yellow line to spike that dramatically, how do you know something's not seriously wrong with me?"

"Because a dramatic activation of your Orbeus isn't harmful to your brain in any way," she says calmly. "A spike in activation, even like the one you had, doesn't affect blood pressure, hormone levels, executive functions, or anything like that. You weren't lying yesterday when you told Dr. Ridges you felt fine, right?"

"Right."

"See?"

I think some more.

Nora understands the brain much better than I do, obviously, and I should probably withhold my judgment before actually going to med school. But still. Everything I *do* know about the brain suggests that the notion of an Orbeus is complete—

Wait. *Of course.* I'm surprised it took me this long to realize what's happening here.

This is a cover story within the experiment. And for whatever reason, Nora is trying to sell me on it. That has to be the case. Right?

The spike had me worried yesterday, so maybe this is their attempt to calm me down. Affinity really expects me to believe I've redefined what's possible for the human brain not even forty-eight hours into the trials? I call bullshit. Who knows, maybe every Blue will soon be seeing their own unprecedented *spike* on their own Disk charts, too, and forced into secrecy via an NDA.

"Do you have any other comments or questions for me before we continue?" Nora asks, as I sit in silence, thinking.

I'm tempted to tell her that I think this is all a ruse but stop myself from doing so. Because maybe if I play along, I'll get a hint at whatever it is they're trying to direct my curiosity away from.

"I think I'm getting it thus far," I say slowly, looking up at her. "So . . . let's say my spike *was* accurate and my Orbeus went hay-wire in the locker room our first night here. What now?"

Nora lights up, pushing the laptop closer to me to ensure I can see it. "According to your chart, your Orbeus became activated somewhere between . . ." She leans closer. ". . . 8:59 and 9:02 p.m. That's when you ran into my brother, right?"

I nod.

"So, as weird as it is for me to say this," she exhales, "me, Dr. Ridges, and the Affinity bigwigs who saw your chart believe running into my brother is the most likely cause of your Orbeus going fu—*freaking* bananas."

I stop a laugh from escaping my mouth.

Nora believes that *Nash*—the dickhead who stormed into my room, didn't apologize for waking me up, and then promptly ordered me to turn off the light instead of having a conversation— caused my friendship-o-meter to surge?

"Well, no offense to you or your brother," I say, "but I didn't feel any connection to Nash."

"That's okay," Nora says. "There's no evidence to suggest Orbeus only activates when it's friends at first sight. Some Affinity researchers theorize that the Orbeus has detection we have yet to understand that identifies friends before our conscious minds can."

Could what Nora's telling me really be true? She has an answer ready for every one of my questions. So either she's an excellent performer or my Orbeus really did pinpoint Nash Mehta as BFF material before I could.

I mean, I guess there is a third option. *Dylan.*

The sighting happened just a few seconds before I ran into Nash, so the spike could have been in response to my imagining him and nothing to do with the quarterback. Plus, Nora did say that the Orbeus can activate if even just one of a person's five senses engages a friend. I may not have heard or smelled Dylan, but I definitely did see him. Or, at the very least, my grief tricked me into thinking I had.

But if seeing Dylan caused the spike . . .

"What about my chart from yesterday?" I ask. "If Nash activated my Orbeus in the locker room, he would have last night, too, right?"

Nora's eyes grow wide. "Exactly." She taps at her keyboard and a different but nearly identical chart appears. She points out the date to confirm it's my Disk recording from yesterday. "See?" she says, nodding at the yellow line. It shoots up just like the first spike had done. "Your Orbeus was activated by my brother again with a similarly sky-high surge, River." She shakes her head in stunned disbelief. "It's fu—*freaking* bonkers."

I don't know what to think about any of this.

I want to trust Nora—maybe the idea of an Orbeus isn't as outrageous as it seems—but I'm also not naive. I know she's a researcher and I'm her lab rat. But most of all, I want to believe the option that I now know is the least likely to be true: that Dylan sent my yellow line spiking off the charts. Because that would mean he's still a living, breathing person on this planet—at least, according to my Disk, he would be.

"River, I have a proposal," Nora says, tugging my thoughts back into the room.

"Yeah?"

She inhales slowly, like she's about to drop a bomb on me. "I'm suggesting Nash sleeps in your room from here on out in the trials."

My eyebrows shoot to the ceiling.

"Hear me out. Affinity can't approve a new Trial participant now that we've started," she continues, "and it's not like my brother would have joined anyway, with camp and all. So the next best thing is to allow the two of you to spend a controlled amount of time together."

"But you already have two spikes to back up your thinking," I argue. "Why do you need more?"

"Because the more data we can collect on your Orbeus's response to him, the more confident we can be about the data," she says. "We may be able to see how your spikes change throughout the trials as you get to know each other, too."

I spot Nash in the frame, younger, shorter, and significantly skinnier than the guy I saw in the locker room. "*Every* night, though? For the rest of the trials?"

Nora weighs the question. "No, not necessarily." She sees I'm not too pleased. "This is entirely up to you, River. You can say no. Really, I don't want to pressure you. Or you can say yes now and change your mind later." She studies my face. "I realize this wasn't part of the deal when you signed up and it'd be unfair for us to change the expectations of you now."

"Your brother can't be cool with this, though," I say, "can he?"

"Ah," she laughs, "you underestimate how much my brother prioritizes his sleep, especially during these hellish summer camps. Without commuting from my parents' house, he'll get an extra two hours a night, easy."

"Does he know"—I gesture at my chart—"about all of this?"

"*No*," Nora emphasizes, "and it's critical you don't tell him anything. Remember, Affinity's not messing around with these NDAs."

"Why does he think you asked him to sleep at the school, then?"

She cringes. "I told him the participant he ran into in the locker room is having trouble sleeping alone and could use the company," she says sheepishly.

I sigh. At least I'm not trying to impress Nash. "And Dr. Ridges is okay with all this, even though I'd be interacting with a non-participant?"

"This request comes from the top of the Affinity food chain." Nora folds her hands against the desk. "Even if Dr. Ridges wasn't on board, which he is, it wouldn't matter."

My chest rises as I take a deep breath.

"So," Nora says hesitantly, "what do you think?"

I exhale. "Okay. Nash can sleep in my room."

25

RIVER

I wish I could ask the purple table what their takes are on this whole Orbeus and Nash thing, I think as I walk to breakfast—what parts might be true or what it all really means. But after signing that NDA, I have a feeling spilling the beans would make the spray-painted mustache the least of my legal trouble.

Clearly, it's not worth the risk.

"Hey," I say, sitting down with Jacob, Biggs, and Brady.

I take a big bite of a donut, and a handful of sprinkles falls to the floor right as Harry happens to wander by. He pauses, pointedly eyeing the mess I made. "On it," I say, bending over at once and collecting the crumbs with a napkin as he walks off.

When I resurface, I notice Oaklyn sitting with Marcus at a table nearby, looking in better spirits. It's a welcome sight to see. Sure, her anxiety-ridden monologue was painfully awkward to be the subject of, but Oaklyn's been way harder on herself than she needed to be. Also, who knows? Biggs could be right—maybe it'll turn out to be a *good* thing that me and Mavis's dirty laundry got aired out in front of the group.

I'm about to mention this before realizing how uncharacteristically quiet Biggs is being. I don't think she's said a thing since I sat down. Then I notice a distracted smile on Brady's well-rested face and realize no one at the purple table is in a talkative mood this morning.

"Any vivid dreams last night?" I ask Brady, breaking the silence.

He jolts back to life. "I had a very surreal dream again, but it was . . . *incredible*, actually? The best I've ever had. I slept much better."

Jacob's head tugs backward in surprise. "The best dream you've had? *Ever?*"

"Yup. A girl was in it, and we—"

"Oh," Jacob says with a smirk, "so it was *that* sort of dream. Now it's making sense."

"No, not at all," Brady pushes back, looking disgusted at the thought. "I don't know who she was. We've never met in real life. We were just hanging out together, and . . ." But he gets lost in his thoughts again, relishing in the memory. "It was nice, is all."

I eye him suspiciously, having never had a dream anywhere near euphoric enough to leave me in such a state.

"How's your phone addiction going?" Jacob asks Biggs. "Are you still just as antsy to get yours back?"

No answer.

She doesn't seem to be in a happy trance, like Brady had been, but her mind is still a million miles away from Headquarters. I can sense her thoughts working overtime behind her eyes.

"Hello?" I say, nudging her foot with my own beneath the table. She snaps back to our conversation with a beaming smile. "Sorry, babe, got distracted."

"I asked if you're still missing your phone a ton?" Jacob says.

She rocks her head back and forth, and I'm surprised to see how torn she is. "Eh, yeah, sort of? But not as much as on day one." She stands and starts to drift away to the food table. "Anyone need anything? I'm getting another strawberry with sprinkles—they're *amazing.*"

I don't care how delicious they are; there's no way Biggs is in a mood as great as the one she's in due to donuts.

After breakfast wraps up, the Blues and Greens are sent to spend our Fitness hour in the longest hallway in the E-Wing, which has been set up for us to run relay races, and play cornhole and tug-o-war together.

If the Orbeus is in fact real, I wonder how our activities might affect their activation. Could that be something Affinity is documenting? If being artistic, or exercising, or playing mind games, or meditating impacts the Disk's reading?

Oaklyn takes me aside before the games begin to apologize again.

"I'm working with a therapist on controlling my intrusive thoughts. Sometimes they get turned into words that leave my mouth without my own consent," she explains nervously, "and it's not fair to people like you, who have to pay the price—"

"I'm not upset about it," I jump in, sensing she's on the verge of another anxious word dump. "Please don't beat yourself up."

Her face melts in relief. "Thanks. Do you think Mavis hates me, though?"

"Why, is she acting like she does?"

"No, but . . . she's hard to read."

Believe me, *I know.*

We rejoin the group as the games begin. We end up trouncing the Greens in the footraces, they demolish us in tug-o-war, and no one keeps score during cornhole because everyone hates it equally—especially Harry, who watches in real time as a tossed bag somehow gets punctured, scattering corn kernels as far as the eye can see. I keep my distance from Goldie, hoping to avoid any possibility I could cause her bodily harm for a second day in a row. Surprisingly, she seems to do the same for me.

Art could not pass by any more slowly. I try my best to ignore Jacob and fiddle around with my supplies instead, spending far more brain power imagining what my Disk is recording at any given moment than what I could be creating on the canvas.

I feel worse about my lack of effort after glancing over at Mavis working diligently in the corner on what I'm sure are beautiful comics and seeing Brady working on his painting with the focus of a heart surgeon in the operating room.

He seemed to be in such an opposite state of mind at breakfast, staring off dreamily and barely touching his donut, that it makes me wonder what he could possibly be creating to keep his eyes so glued to his art. I'm about to go check it out when I spot that even *Biggs* is hunched over her workspace in deep thought.

"Don't tell me you've left me all alone in the Apathetic Artist Club," I say, appearing at her side. "What are you working on?"

She glances up at me with a wide smile before her eyes quickly dash back down to the desk. "A storyboard for a new Tether video I want to make after the trials are over. I think it's going to be cool."

I have follow-up questions but don't want to distract her. So I slink back to my space.

During lunch, I'm surprised to be feeling more on edge about having to spend one-on-one time with Nora soon. During my A-Test and the first day of the trials, I felt so trusting of and comfortable around her. But my apprehension around the Nash and Orbeus situation—not to mention her insistence on wanting me to go into the gym—has soured my excitement for our Check-Ins a bit.

After I sit down across from her, Nora and I spend a few minutes chatting about how Fitness went (we agree on cornhole being terrible), then debate the quality of the fried chicken at lunch (she loved the spicy seasoning in the breading, while I wasn't a fan). It feels kind of pointless, but I appreciate her not wanting to jump right back into the thick of the conversation we started this morning.

After I convince her to try my favorite fried chicken spot in Teawood, she hands me another survey to complete. As promised, it's identical to the one from yesterday. My answers are nearly identical, too, except my response to the question gauging how connected I feel to the other participants. I decide to bump up my answer a smidge, from a five to a six, after feeling tighter with the Blues. Well, except for Mavis.

We'll see how the rest of the week pans out with her.

I push my completed survey back across the desk toward Nora just as time's up.

"Hey, before you go . . ." she begins. I brace myself for a heavier topic, like something involving her brother or my plans to enter the gym. "You know, you can always talk to me about the billboard if you want, River."

I wasn't expecting *that* topic, though.

"When Oaklyn mentioned it briefly in Group Talk yesterday, it reminded me of your A-Test," she continues, "when you asked if there was a photo of it included in your slideshow."

"Yeah," I say, "was there?"

She turns her laptop so I can see the screen. "My guess is, this is what you saw."

It is a photo of a billboard. But the ad features a boy who looks about thirteen, happily promoting an arcade in Detroit. Since I saw it for just a split second before, though, I guess it's possible I only imagined seeing Dylan.

"I spoke to Dr. Ridges about this," Nora says, "and he agreed that it's fine that I show this to you, now that you've signed the NDA."

I nod.

"I didn't know if you were still thinking about the possibility of Dylan's billboard being in the slideshow," she continues, turning her laptop away from me, "so I wanted to confirm with you either way."

"Thanks."

"But it did have me thinking . . ." Nora leans closer, dropping her voice. "I know the pain of losing a dear friend, too, River, and it's a lot. Like, a *lot*, a lot. Go easy on yourself. Okay?"

"Okay."

"No, I really mean it."

The sudden seriousness in her voice catches me off guard.

"All this crazy bullshit aside"—she gestures at the Affinity cameras and then grins at me without apologizing for the cursing—"know that I care about you. All right?"

I smile back. "All right."

I leave Check-In in a better mood than when I walked in.

After I beat Ollie in chess during Gaming, it's off to Meditation, where my mind gets significantly more crammed instead of cleared again. So I'm beyond relieved when the soft humming of the PA signifies Meditation is over and I can leave the E-Suite with the others. I'm hopeful today's Group Talk will be much less dramatic, but I'm already learning to expect the unexpected when it comes to the Blues.

On the walk to Nora's room, I feel a tap on my shoulder and turn, expecting it to be Biggs or Brady, but it's . . . Mavis.

Her cheeks are pink and her eyes are watery. I feel my stomach drop, thinking Oaklyn must have gone on another awkward tirade speculating about our friendship, or lack thereof, to her, until a smile spreads across Mavis's face.

"Thanks again," she says. "That meant a lot to me."

Huh?

I rack my brain, wondering what she could possibly be referring to, but before I can figure it out, Mavis picks up the pace down the hallway, leaving me disoriented in the dust.

26

RIVER

That meant a lot to me.

What could Mavis be talking about?

After a much lighter Group Talk where Brady updates us about the vivid dream girl who's clearly made quite the impression on him, I wonder what I've done to deserve a teary-eyed thank-you from Mavis. But nothing comes to mind.

I go back and forth about asking her directly at dinner but ultimately chicken out. Being in her good graces feels nice, and I don't want to risk being put back on her shit list for forgetting about this good deed I apparently did.

Later that night, during Quiet Hour, I decide to use the geography magazine to distract myself from the mystery. As I flip the page on an unexpectedly fascinating report on the most complex international borders in the world, my bedroom door opens, and I look up to see Nash walking in, carrying the same mass of blankets and pillows he had with him last night.

"Oh," I say, quickly sitting up in bed. "Hey." The Mavis mystery upended my evening so much, I forgot he's sleeping in my room again.

He can tell I'm surprised to see him. "You weren't expecting me?"

"No, I was," I say, tossing the magazine aside. "I just blanked on the time."

I notice at once that he's wearing a black T-shirt that reads

TO INFINITY in small white letters across the chest, which could mean one of three things: he's a *Toy Story* fan, he's a space nerd— either would win him points in my book—or Nora told her little brother accomplice to wear something related to the universe to further mess with my head.

Fearing it's the third one, I decide not to acknowledge it.

He drops his things onto the floor and exhales.

"You can keep all that stuff in here, you know," I say, nodding at the pile of pillows, "instead of having to haul it back here every night."

"I wish I could," he says, plugging in the air mattress and turning the pump on. He raises his voice so I can hear him over the noise. "My sister won't let me."

"Why not?"

"I guess she doesn't want any other kids seeing my stuff in here during the day?" he says, confused why that's apparently a rule. "Which, by the way, why aren't you guys . . ."

I can't make out what he's asking over the noise of the pump. "Huh?"

"I said"—he speaks even louder—"why aren't you guys supposed to talk to anyone outside the study?"

I shrug, unsure how forthright to be. I know I can't discuss the Orbeus with him, but it's less clear how much I can say about the trials themselves. "Affinity has strict rules."

He looks up at the camera in the corner, and I get the sense he's just as weirded out by it all as I am.

"What's my sister studying about you guys anyway?" he asks.

"You have a Mentor as a sister," I reply. "I'm sure you know way more about the trials than I do."

He laughs. "Not possible. I didn't even know the name of the place she worked was Affinity until yesterday."

"Really?"

"Really. She keeps her work-life shit top secret. I was shocked when she asked me to sleep in here with you."

I look at him disbelievingly.

The air pump gets louder as the mattress expands to its fullest size. Once Nash decides it's as big as it'll go without exploding, he turns it off and walks over to the side of my bed.

"I'm Nash," he says, extending his hand to shake.

I grin, not sure what game he's playing. But I play along anyway and give it a shake.

His hands are huge, I realize, which I guess makes sense. If you're going to be as great a quarterback as my dad claims *the* Nash Mehta is, genetics have to be working in your favor.

He doesn't explain why he's reintroducing himself to me, though. Did a day full of tackling give him amnesia? "You know we met last night, right?"

"Technically, we met the night *before* that, in the locker room," he answers, "but I say we pretend like this is the first."

My eyes narrow on his. "Why?"

"Well," he sighs, thinking, "*you* ran into me like a bank robber fleeing the scene that night, and then I was an asshole to you after an awful practice." He looks at me. "Sorry about that, by the way."

I wasn't expecting an apology—whether genuine *or* scripted by Affinity—and I wonder how my Orbeus might be responding to it this very moment.

If, of course, an Orbeus is even a real thing.

He returns to his corner and starts making up his bed, so I open the magazine again and dig back in. I find myself peeking at him every so often, though, searching for any hints that he's another Mehta on Affinity's payroll and not just a jock who appreciates his sleep.

Nash falls onto the mattress once it's made. Clearly, he's not as tired as he was after his practice last night, though, as he lies there with his eyes wide open, unsure what to do with himself.

"Your sister made you give up your phone in order to be here, I take it?" I ask.

He nods. "They say screen time before bed isn't good for sleep anyway, so I shouldn't complain. But for anyone who's *not* obsessed with getting eight hours a night"—he gestures around the room—"why would you sign up for something as insane as this?"

"They were looking for kids like me for the study," I say, deciding to go with the short and sweet version, not the one involving spray-paint vandalism and blackmail.

"Kids like you . . ." He trails off, tucking his legs under the covers. "What does that mean?"

"Kids who are"—I use air quotes—"'struggling socially.'" I roll my eyes. Even if this is a setup and Nash is an Affinity plant, I can't help feeling embarrassed saying it out loud.

He lies on his side facing my direction and props his head up using the palm of his hand, his bicep ballooning to twice its size.

"I don't think that's pathetic," he says. "Why are you"—he uses air quotes, too—"'struggling socially'?"

I turn on my side so that I'm facing his direction as well.

"My best friend died in a car accident a year ago," I explain with a shrug. "Everyone sees me as just the dead kid's best friend now. But losing him . . . it's messed with me a bunch."

Nash grimaces. "Fuck. That sucks." He pauses. "What was his name?"

"Dylan."

He nods solemnly. "Dylan. I've always loved that name."

Our conversation comes to a lull. I wouldn't mind staying up longer to chat, especially with someone who's not wearing a monochromatic blue, red, orange, or green uniform for a change. Besides, Nash is so much more pleasant tonight, he hardly seems like the same guy. But I see him let out a huge yawn, remember Nora's mention of his 5 a.m. practices, and decide to call it a night.

"I'll let you get on with your eight hours," I say, sinking lower into bed.

Nash nods and reaches over to the side of his mattress to plug in an old-school alarm clock. He struggles to set the time right, though, cursing under his breath—even his *shit*s and *fuck*s sound like his sister's, I notice—until he figures it out.

I flip my lamp off.

"G'night, Nash," I say in the darkness.

"Sleep tight, River."

27

RIVER

I awake to an empty room the next morning and hear the faint whispers of referee whistles coming from the football field. I don't know if Nash is out there still—5 a.m. to almost eight sounds agonizingly long for a practice—but either way, I'm impressed he can do this every day, even if it's just for camp.

I roll around in bed for a few minutes before Nora's knock lets me know what time it is.

"Hey," I call to her, "I'm up."

"Can I peek inside real quick?"

I cover my torso with a blanket. "Sure."

Nora cracks the door open and glances around the room, presumably looking for Nash.

"He's gone," I confirm.

"Just wanted to make sure. He hasn't woken you when he gets up for practice, right?"

"Nope. I must be a heavy sleeper. I haven't even heard him pack up the mattress."

She smiles. "That's because I'm an amazing Mentor and told him to drag it out of the room before deflating it. Those fu—*freaking* air mattresses are loud as hell."

Nora closes the door, and I climb out of bed. After putting on a clean navy blue shirt and pants, I head to breakfast.

I approach the purple table, where Brady is humming a song pleasantly while buttering his toast and Biggs is jotting down notes using the Affinity notebook and pen we got in our white duffel bags. Jacob, I notice, is at the food table talking to Mavis as she chooses a cereal. He's speaking animatedly, which is already throwing me because he's typically so reserved, and then lets out a hearty laugh. Are those two becoming friends? That can't be good for me.

"Morning," I say, taking a seat. "What's up with that?" I nod at Jacob and Mavis.

Brady pauses his humming and glances toward the food table. "What do you mean?"

"Jacob and Mavis," I say. "They, like . . . talk? To each other?"

"They have the whole comic books thing in common, babe," Biggs says while scribbling down bullet points, as if I should have known.

"They were nerding out over Ant-Man together at dinner the first night . . ." Brady pauses in thought. "Wait, how come you weren't here?"

Biggs chuckles. "It was the dinner he missed after you spewed your ice cream all over his face."

Brady nods sheepishly, turning red.

I recoil—not at the thought of Brady's vomit, although it's certainly deserving, but at the potential outcome of Mavis and Jacob getting close. I'd hate it if he were to tell her about the billboard just as she seems to be warming up to me again.

Sure, I still have no idea what I could have done to inspire Mavis's teary thank-you, but I'd rather not question it—at least not right now. If Jacob tells her that I'm the one who spray-painted the mustache, we'd definitely be back at square one again.

I turn to Biggs, aiming to distract myself from the worrying thought. "What are you writing? I haven't even opened my note-book yet."

She looks up at me with bright eyes. "I've been getting a bunch of ideas for new Tether content, like the storyboard you saw me working on in Art. I know myself; if I don't document the ideas while they're still fresh, they're gone forever."

Biggs is getting inspired? In *here*, of all places?

I can't think of a less creatively stimulating place than the E-Wing of Teawood High, which, come to think of it, will be the excuse I tell myself for being so unproductive in Art.

"I think it makes sense," Brady says through a mouthful of toast. "My brain feels most awake when I've been away from my Switch and phone for a while."

"Are you the same way?" I ask Biggs.

"*Eh*, I don't know," she says. "I finally reconnected with my old Tether friend, Frankie, right before the trials, and began to do some brainstorming. And a lot of those ideas are resurfacing now, but in more clever ways." She goes back to her notetaking. "I can't wait to update her on my ideas once we're out of here."

"What about you?" I say to Brady, realizing his great mood from yesterday seems to have persisted. "Another incredible night filled with blissful, vivid dreams?"

He sighs as the smile on his face expands. "Yep."

"Wait . . ." I say, "I was joking, Brady. Really?"

He nods. "With the same vivid dream girl, too. Well." He pauses and clarifies, "I guess it wasn't the same dream, *exactly*. We did different things together than the night before, hiking around the bottom of this enormous canyon and then spending the afternoon picnicking next to the Eiffel Tower."

I think. "Do you usually have reoccurring dreams like this?"

He shrugs. "No, not really."

Biggs perks up, and we exchange curious glances.

"Do you . . . ?" I begin.

". . . Think that's weird?" Biggs finishes my thought. "Yeah, I do." She looks at Brady. "You've had the same type of realistic dream every night we've been in here, huh?"

He nods.

Biggs looks at me again with one eyebrow arched. "Interesting."

It's definitely strange, without a doubt. But also, Brady *is* a little strange. Maybe we should expect that his dreams are too.

Out of the corner of my eye, I spot Mavis taking a seat with Goldie. I scan the room for Jacob and catch him headed left out of Headquarters, in the direction of the bathrooms.

"Be right back," I say, standing up and following in his footsteps.

I'm still pissed at him, but his budding new friendship with Mavis has relit my urgency to get to the bottom of the blackmailing. After the way he spoke to me in Art, I'm still convinced there's more to it than a thousand bucks.

Plus, the bathroom doesn't have cameras.

I enter and see Jacob standing at a urinal. Admittedly, this isn't the best way to have a private talk with him, but who knows when the next opportunity will come along?

"Hey," I say.

He glances at me before facing the wall again. "Hey."

I quickly bend over to see beneath the stalls—I don't spot any feet—and then join him, leaving a urinal between us, of course.

"Listen," I begin, "I really need to talk to you."

"While I'm peeing?" Jacob interjects, zipping up his pants. He flushes and walks to a sink.

I follow behind him. "I promise that I'm fully committed to being in these trials and getting you your half of my stipend."

He turns the faucet and rubs soap between his palms. "Great. I assumed so."

"But if I'm being honest," I say, nervous to broach the topic, "I've gotten the sense that it's . . . not just about the money to you."

He freezes, then turns and stares at me. "What's given you that sense?"

"Well, you seem legitimately upset about what I did, which I understand—"

"You mean the time you vandalized your dead friend's billboard that's aimed at preventing car fatalities?" he says. "Yeah, hopefully you *do* understand why I'd be angry about that."

I swallow hard and take a breath, reminding myself to keep it cool. "I get it, Jacob, I do. But it doesn't make sense to me why you'd be *that* outraged about it, considering you and Dylan weren't really . . . friends?" I say cautiously, hoping I'm not ruffling his feathers even more. "At least from what I could tell."

The bathroom door swings open, and Dorian comes marching in, biceps first.

"Gentlemen," he says, nodding at us. He starts whistling as he pees, effectively shutting down our conversation.

But as he dries his hands, Jacob mutters, barely above a whisper, "Maybe you didn't know everything there is to know about your friend, River." He tosses the paper towel in the trash and walks out before I can respond.

What is he even talking about?

Surely I didn't know *everything* about Dylan, but it seems as though Jacob's implying that I missed something . . . *big*. Something important. What does he know that I don't?

"Better get to your first activity, River," Dorian says, patting me on the back on his way out of the bathroom. I stumble forward into the sink. "Don't wanna be late."

• • •

Things start to feel more routine now that it's the third full day of the trials.

I head to Fitness, which is back out in the courtyard today. Five sets of Giant Jenga are waiting for us there for each Blue and Green to face off in what has to be the least fitness-oriented Fitness session thus far. Despite how little we have to move, the scorching heat alone is enough to zap each and every one of us, and we all end up finding patches of shade to cool off in with ten minutes left.

Art is as uncomfortable as I expect it to be, having to sit next to Jacob and act like everything's chill with Biggs nearby, working on her storyboard. Brady, I find out, has chosen to paint the girl from his dreams, which explains why he's been so laser focused on getting it right.

I'm helping myself to more chicken tenders at lunch when I feel a presence approaching from behind. I turn and find Mavis.

"Oh," I say, surprised to see her. I smile. "Hey."

She doesn't look happy, though. "Why didn't you come over in Art?"

I pause, trying to think of what she could mean. "Um . . . what?"

Mavis's jaw drops. "Seriously?"

I look around Headquarters, feeling like I'm being pranked. I see Goldie glaring at me, Jacob, Brady, and Biggs watching us curiously, and Nora glancing over from where she's eating with Jade. My heart starts to pound.

"Was I . . . supposed to come see you in Art?" I ask, beyond confused. "Because I never got that memo."

A dumbstruck smile starts to creep into her cheeks.

"What?" I push back, feeling increasingly gaslit by her. "Mavis, you're not making any sense—"

"Why are you messing with me?" she snaps. "Is it funny to you?"

"Huh?"

She shakes her head in disbelief, genuinely stunned by whatever it is she thinks I did—or apparently *didn't* do—to her.

"Whatever, River," she says. "Fuck you."

She beelines back to Goldie, who looks enraged at me once again. I take my plate of chicken tenders I'm no longer hungry for back to the purple table, shell-shocked.

"What was that about?" Biggs asks as I sit down.

"Mavis did *not* look happy," Brady says, stating the obvious.

I don't even know what to say. "So apparently Mavis is pissed off at me?"

Jacob bends his neck to see her across the room. "Why?"

"Maybe I should be asking you," I snap. It comes out more heated than I intended it to in front of Brady and Biggs.

Jacob looks at me. "What's that supposed to mean?"

"Nothing," I backtrack with a sigh. "Sorry, I'm just rattled. I know you two are friends. Has she said anything about me to you?"

Jacob thinks.

"I've never seen Mavis irate like that," Biggs says, turning to me. "What'd she say to you over there?"

"She's mad I didn't come over to see her during Art, I guess." The words sound even more childish leaving my mouth. "But I have no idea why she thought I was going to, or why she'd be so pissed off that I didn't."

"Well, you did tell her you'd stop by," Jacob says, as if it should be obvious.

My pulse is racing. "Huh?"

"When I was talking to Mavis at breakfast," Jacob continues, "she said you'd asked her about what she's been sketching and that she was excited to show you in Art."

I'm speechless. The three of them stare at me.

"I have no idea what she's talking about," I finally get out. "I never told her that. I mean, what you two just saw was the most me and Mavis have talked since the trials began. Actually, since Dylan died."

"Wait . . . really?" Brady says in disbelief.

"I thought I sensed you two warming up to each other, though," Biggs adds curiously. "She was being friendly toward you in our first Group Talk before Oaklyn ruined it."

"Yeah, but even that's been confusing to me," I admit. "She thanked me out of nowhere yesterday because apparently something I did meant a lot to her?" I shrug, bewildered. "I don't have a clue what she could've been talking about."

"She was probably thanking you for talking to her about Dylan during Meditation," Brady says, dunking his chicken tenders in ranch. "That seemed to mean a lot to her."

Biggs slowly turns to him. "What was that now?"

"Yeah," I say, thinking I must have misheard him. I lean closer. "Are you saying she told you that I talked to her about Dylan in Meditation?"

Brady turns red, realizing the weight of his words, and nods.

"She said the same thing to me," Jacob adds, looking at me with suspicion once again.

I look between both of them, trying to keep track of all the alleged conversations I've supposedly had with Mavis. "I've never talked to her during Meditation. We have to be in our own individual rooms anyway, so how could I?"

"I assumed you snuck into hers," Jacob says. "It's not like the Mentors stay with us to stop you."

Biggs looks at me with worry. "I believe you, River, but it doesn't seem like Mavis to make shit up about people, does it?"

My stomach twists and turns anxiously, trying to make sense of it. As cold as she's been to me the past year, Biggs is right—Mavis isn't one to lie like that. "No."

"Maybe you should go talk to her," Brady suggests. "I'm sure there's an explanation."

"He can't," Jacob says, nodding toward the exit, "at least not right now."

I look over and see Nora, a worried expression on her face, accompanying Mavis out of Headquarters, and a sinking feeling fills my gut.

28

RIVER

I'm nervous when I step into Nora's room for my Check-In, clueless what to expect other than an uncomfortable conversation involving Mavis.

"Hey, you," she says pleasantly, "take a seat."

At least it seems like Nora's not mad at me for some unexplainable reason, too. I cross the room and sit in front of her desk.

"I have something I want to talk to you about," she says, "but I want to make sure you have enough time for your survey, so let's knock that out first."

She pushes the sheet of paper and a pen my way, and I fill it out, beginning to get annoyed at the tedious nature of these things. Between the identical surveys, our monochromatic wardrobes, and unchanging schedules, I start to wonder if Affinity could also be researching how long teenagers can keep their sanity while being stuck in a repeating Groundhog Day.

My answers all stay the same except for the one asking about my "overall happiness level"—I go with five, when it had inched up to seven yesterday—and the question gauging my connectedness to the other participants, which I drop down to a four. This baffling situation with Mavis coupled with my conversation with Jacob after breakfast really has put me in a mood, I realize. I hand the survey back to her.

"Thanks," Nora says, taking it. I notice she doesn't scan my answers to make sure it's completed like she typically does before she tosses it aside. "I'm sure you've been anxious to talk to me, River . . ."

Here it comes. What other make-believe things has Mavis claimed to Nora I said or did?

". . . but don't fret, the good news continues."

I stare at her. "Huh?"

Now *Nora* is the one who looks confused, as she turns her laptop to face me. "Your Disk chart?"

"Oh." I exhale, relieved. "Right. Of course."

"I wanted to tell you that your Orbeus experienced a similarly large burst in activation last night when you were with Nash, further confirming the phenomena," she explains. "Why, what did you think I—*ah.*" She pauses, then nods knowingly. "Mavis."

I breathe out. "Yep."

"I should have known." Nora purses her lips, thinking through her words before saying them out loud. "Unfortunately, River, Mavis is no longer on the Blue Crew."

"What?" My stomach drops. "Why?"

"I plan to give you all a proper update in Group Talk."

There's a knock on the door.

"Hello!" It's Brady, whose Check-In follows mine.

"You're early," Nora calls out to him, glancing at the clock. "Give us another minute, Brady."

"Did Mavis tell you why she's saying those things about me?" I ask. "Because the other Blues told me she's claiming I've told her things that I haven't. I don't get it."

Nora waits a beat. "The trials are harder on some participants than others, I think, River. Dr. Ridges, me, and the other Mentors want a good understanding of the situation before we reshuffle the groups."

Reshuffle? "You're replacing Mavis?"

"I—"

"Who's going to take her place?"

"River—"

"Because I'm—"

"*River.*" Nora smiles at me through her frustration.

"Sorry," I say, turning pink.

"I don't want to eat into Brady's Check-In time," Nora says calmly. "I'll see you in Group Talk, where I'll have more updates to share. Okay?"

I nod, stand, and head for the exit.

I remember Rex telling me and Brady on day one that changing colors was strictly forbidden. So if that's the case and Affinity's making an exception for Mavis, what could possibly be happening with her for the Mentors to justify a swap?

29

RIVER

I sit on the edge of my bed, my foot tapping the floor anxiously, as I wait for the Blues to finish up our Check-Ins and recap what I just learned from Nora.

I expected to get angry during our one-on-one, assuming I'd be unfairly implicated in Mavis's lying about me, but now that I know I'm not in trouble and Mavis has been booted off Blue, I'm more worried than I am upset with her. Because Biggs was right; Mavis isn't the type to spread lies about made-up conversations—even about a former best friend she no longer speaks to. I get this sinking feeling, like there's something strange happening.

Could Mavis's Disk have something to do with it?

If Nora's telling me the truth, Affinity is using us to test prototypes, and it's feasible, if not expected, for prototypes to have errors. Could Mavis's Disk somehow be affecting her Orbeus? And could that be impacting her social connections—*and* her grip on reality?

"Chill out," I scold myself under my breath. It's pointless to dwell on what could be happening when I don't have all the facts.

Even though there are only a few more minutes left before Gaming, I don't want to fixate on Mavis. So I open another one of Ms. Benson's cupboards to look for other ancient magazines to distract myself. While squinting inside, I spot a dark rectangular object in the far back corner. I reach back and pull out something

Affinity clearly missed while clearing out Blue Sleeping Quarters: Ms. Benson's infamous black box.

I forgot just how much my former social studies teacher enjoyed taking any and all items distracting students in class. I open the lid excitedly, hoping there's something more entertaining inside than geography magazines to keep me occupied. There are no phones, of course—what student would be stupid enough to forget to get theirs back before summer break?—just entangled white headphone wires, purple lipstick, a few Pokémon cards, and a—

"Polaroid camera?"

I wander back to my bed with it. The top is dusty and scratched, so who knows how long it's been hidden away in the cupboard. There's no chance it still works, though—

Ka-churr.

The shutter startles me as the camera proves me wrong and spits out a square, dark image that will soon develop into a terrible photo of my blankets. Maybe boredom will push me to find something worth capturing in this dull, empty classroom.

"River?" Brady asks outside my door. "You coming?"

I set the camera down next to my bed and leave for Gaming with the other Blues, minus Mavis. It's strange. Even though me and Mavis didn't exchange a single word in an activity, her absence still looms large. And I'm not the only one who feels it.

"It's sort of weird without her," Oaklyn says, hopping my checker with her own on the board in front of us, "isn't it?"

"Yeah," I reply, glancing around the old woodshop room, "it is."

Oaklyn suddenly looks nervous. "It's okay that I brought her up in front of you," she says cautiously, "right?"

I nod and try to smile. "Yes."

During our walk to Meditation, Biggs and Brady seem just as

puzzled about the Mavis situation as I am, and they discuss theories about what could be going on behind the scenes.

"Do you think Nora kicked her out of the trials but just didn't tell us yet?" Brady asks.

Biggs scoffs. "There's no way. I mean, at least I wouldn't *think* so . . ."

I hang back to remove myself from their conversation, deciding that no good can come from adding to the carousel of unanswered questions looping my brain right before sitting in a room alone with my thoughts for an hour.

During Meditation, I'm surprisingly successful at distracting myself from the Mavis situation by focusing instead on my favorite videos by Dr. Skelemont that I've memorized. It's impossible *not* to be reminded of Dylan doing so, but I don't mind for once. I actually enjoy thinking about him when it involves astronomy and not his blown-up grayscale photo on a billboard.

Afterward, the Blues head to Nora's room for Group Talk. I'm eager to learn more about Mavis but also dreading the discussion that will ensue, knowing that I'll inevitably be at the center of it. When we walk in, Nora is sitting behind her desk.

And Ollie is in one of the chairs . . . wearing navy blue.

"Hi," they say with a hesitant smile, unsure of how we'll react.

The four of us quickly suppress our surprise and welcome Ollie with waves and hellos. Brady even hugs them excitedly and whispers gleefully, "I'm glad it's you!"

Ollie beams as their face turns bright red.

Once everyone's settled, Nora commands the attention of the room. "So, let's state the obvious," she says to everyone before turning toward Ollie. "Ollie generously volunteered to switch colors after it became known that our group wasn't a good fit for Mavis. I'm sure everyone's already gotten to know each other in

Gaming, but it might be nice for you to share a little about yourself, Ollie."

Ollie clears their throat and tucks their auburn hair behind one ear. "Hey, you guys. So, I'm Ollie, *obviously*. Um . . . what can I share . . . I was born in Anchorage, Alaska, which not a lot of people know about me. . . . I love all things football, which surprises a lot of people because, *yes*, nonbinary people can be annoying sports bros, too."

The original Blues laugh.

"Oh! Also, I'm the proud human of a cat named Purris Hilton," they conclude.

"That was *purr*-fection," Nora says. "Thank you, Ollie. Yes, Biggs?"

I turn to Biggs, who lowers her raised hand and looks at Ollie. "Love having you in the Blue Crew, babe, welcome! But, um . . ." She pauses, pushes her lips in and out, and turns to Nora. "What the heck happened to Mavis?"

The room goes silent except for the humming, overworked laptop on Nora's desk.

"I need to respect her privacy, so I can't comment on any personal details," she explains, "but suffice to say there were certain group dynamics that were challenging for her. It's okay, though!" Nora attempts to squash the worry in the room with a wide smile. "Me, Dr. Ridges, the other Mentors—none of us expected to get through the week without a few bumps in the road."

Bumps in the road?

I clear my throat. "Isn't it a really big deal for participants to switch colors mid-trials, though?"

"Yeah," Brady chimes in, and I'm grateful for it. "Rex made it seem like it's basically out of the question."

Nora sighs dismissively. "Sometimes Rex can just be . . . *Rex*.

It's definitely not ideal, no, but sometimes unforeseen factors crop up and we have to make do."

"Oh no," Oaklyn breathes. I see that panic has taken her face hostage. "This is because of me, isn't it?"

"What? No." Nora shakes her head. "Why would it be?"

"Because of what I said in our first Group Talk," she answers. I sense one of her spirals about to begin. "Right?"

Ollie glances around at us, both curious and confused.

Oaklyn barrels onward. "I'm not sure we ever recovered as a group after I brought up the fact that she and River had been good friends at one point and now they aren't—"

"Oaklyn." Nora nips it in the bud—more intensely than I'd expect her to. "It had nothing to do with that. It had nothing to do with *you*. All right?"

Oaklyn wants to keep talking, I can tell, but the severity in Nora's tone is enough to keep her mouth shut.

"So, is Mavis an Orange now?" Biggs asks.

Nora nods. "She took the rest of today off from activities, but you'll see her during Gaming tomorrow."

"And we can still, like . . . talk to her, right?" Brady asks mournfully.

"Of course," Nora says with a laugh, as if it's a preposterous question. She pauses to scan our faces. "If no one else has any questions, let's move on to today's topic. Now, I know—"

"Wait," I blurt. "That's it?"

The room turns toward me.

Nora gestures for me to go on. "Do you have a question, River?"

"Well, yeah. I mean, you didn't tell us why she got swapped."

Everyone's eyes shift to Nora.

"Like I said," Nora says calmly, "certain aspects on the Blue Crew were a challenge for her, so we decided it'd be best if she left."

We lock eyes. And she must be able to tell I'm not satisfied with her redundant answer.

What is she not telling us?

"Unfortunately, I can't say much more beyond that, River," Nora continues, "but if you'd like, we can revisit during our next Check-In?"

I nod, not too pleased as she steers Group Talk in a different direction. I'm too distracted thinking about Mavis to stay all that engaged the rest of the hour, but I do tune in while Brady's noting how difficult it's been losing his grandma, whom he considered a friend, and listen to Biggs explaining to Ollie a new video idea she came up with alongside her Tether friend Frankie. But I hardly chime in myself.

"Hey, River?" Nora calls to me as the Blues leave her room. "A quick chat?"

Is she frustrated with my stubbornness earlier or something?

I hang back near the doorway.

Once the other four are gone, Nora walks over to me and lowers her voice with a regretful expression on her face. "So, I spoke to Dr. Ridges, and we think it's best if you avoid interacting with Mavis, and that she does the same with you."

What?

My eyes narrow on hers. "How come?"

Nora sighs. "It's complicated and I wish I could say more, especially because I know you two used to be close. But . . . can you do this for me?"

30

RIVER

It seems that any chance I had of making amends with Mavis during the trials has gone out the window. Now, we're back to square one: avoiding each other. I understand Nora has to respect Mavis's privacy, but surely if I'm trustworthy enough to learn about the Orbeus and sneak her own brother into my room to sleep each night, I can know at least a *bit* more information about a scandal that directly involves me?

After an uneventful Free Time and dinner—Mavis seems fine ignoring me while eating tacos with Goldie, and the purple table catches Jacob up on the Ollie-Mavis swap—I'm surprised to find myself weirdly looking forward to seeing Nash. It'll be a nice break to talk to someone who's removed from all things Affinity.

When he comes striding in after his practice, I'm reminded why he's *the* Nash Mehta of local high school football fame and not just my Mentor's younger brother. Above his short shorts and grass-stained sneakers, several medals are hanging from around his neck, most of them gold.

"Wow," I say, as he puts his things down. "It looks like someone had a good day at camp."

"*Meh*," he replies, lacking the enthusiasm I'd expect from some-one who appears to have won the entire Olympics. "Why do you say that?"

I nod at his chest.

He glances down, seeming to have forgotten what's dangling there. "Oh, yeah. Thanks."

Nash plugs his air mattress in, and once again I wait for the obnoxious noise to finish, then ask, "What did you do to win all those?"

He tosses the medals onto the foot of his bed as if they're nothing more than dirty laundry. I spot a few flashes of silver in the mix, too, proving he's not a robot created for football greatness. "They time us doing things for recruiting purposes—sprints, jumps, throws, tackles—and top performers get them."

I'm clueless as to what even qualifies as a good sprint, jump, throw, or tackle. "Well, it looks like you dominated almost every category."

He glances at me and smirks a little. "Almost."

Nash puts his pillows into place with notably more care than he'd handled the medals and collapses onto the mattress in a level of physical exhaustion I've never come close to experiencing myself. It reminds me of the time Dylan lay almost entirely flat in my passenger seat, hardly able to move a muscle after I picked him up from a basketball tournament. He'd spent the day sprinting up and down hardwood while I'd spent the day binging Dr. Skelemont videos in bed, eating popsicles.

He may be spent but he doesn't seem sleepy, so I strike up a conversation, hoping—and maybe a bit desperate—to get my mind off the trials.

"So," I say, "no offense, but I didn't know who you were before my dad mentioned you."

"You and about eight billion other people," he says, his voice muffled through the pillow his face is buried in. "No offense taken."

"Word on the street is, you're sort of a big deal."

"I appreciate that, but objectively, I am not." He pauses. "The Webb Telescope just discovered another rocky planet in its star's habitable zone—the nearest one to Earth yet. *That's* a big deal. Not me."

I'm glad he's face down in bed and doesn't notice the surprise on my face.

For a split second, I question how I wouldn't have heard this news—I have push notifications set for NASA's posts, after all—before remembering Rex locking my phone away days ago. The entire West Coast could have broken off in an earthquake, and I'd have no way of knowing in here.

Nearly a hundred follow-up questions about the planet bombard my brain, but before I start firing them off, I realize what an opportunity this is. If Nash is, in fact, a true space nerd like me and didn't memorize some astronomy terms last night to help pull off Affinity's experiment, surely, I could suss it out now.

"What's a habitable zone?" I ask, playing dumb.

"The distance from a star where water can exist in liquid form," he says at once, his face still submerged in the pillow like a rock.

"So . . . why is that a big deal?" I follow up.

His head turns to the side subtly, and I spot one of his deep brown eyes peeking out at me above the pillowcase. "If the temperature allows for liquid water to exist there, that means so could life. At least, potentially."

Throw him off, my question did *not*. If anything, he seemed bored having to explain a simple concept to an outer space amateur.

So I decide to step it up.

"It's the closest planet to Earth that could sustain life, huh?" I say. "How far away is it?"

The nearest habitable planet that we know of—at least before I gave my phone over to Rex—was 4.22 light-years away. I doubt Nash can stick the landing on this one.

"Three-point-nine light-years," he answers without missing a beat, "which is *right* next door, relatively speaking. The planet that just got dethroned is Proxima Centauri b, and that was just over four light-years away, if I'm not mistaken."

Holy shit. Either Nash truly does love space or Nora *really* forced her brother to do his homework before putting him on Affinity's payroll.

"I heard you're having trouble sleeping alone," he says, changing gears.

I almost make a bewildered face but catch myself, remembering that that's the story I was told to run with. "Yeah. Thanks for agreeing to be here."

"It works better for both of us. You rest easier, and I get away from my mom."

His mom?

I thought he agreed to be here to get more sleep without the daily commutes to camp?

"Besides," he continues, "I can only imagine."

I pause. "You can only imagine . . . what?"

"Losing my best friend." His face melts with regret the second the words leave his mouth. "Shit. I probably shouldn't have said that, sorry."

"It's okay."

"My sister barely told me anything about you. But she did mention that you get insomnia when you have to sleep alone, and that she thought it was probably because you're still grieving. Maybe I wasn't supposed to know all that, though."

I smile. "Seriously, it's cool."

He sits up to see me better. "You don't mind talking about Dylan?"

"Not at all," I say. "I mean, sure, it makes me sad, and I hate when people focus on the spectacle of the tragedy, which they tend to do a lot in Teawood. But I want to remember the Dylan who lived, not the Dylan who died, and I want other people to remember him that way, too."

Nash curls his knees up to his chest beneath the covers and nestles further into the mattress. "So, let's do it then."

"Do what?"

"Remember the Dylan who lived," he says. "What was your favorite thing about him?"

I laugh as my cheeks get hot. "I don't know."

"There had to be something."

It's tough to narrow down a favorite.

I liked that he was kind to everyone—not just nice. How little he cared about popularity, even though he was Mr. Popular. I liked how he sneakily kept learning piano just because he liked it, even though his dad didn't want him to.

I liked the expression he wore whenever he stared at the night sky, clocking constellations, with his eyes big and unblinking, and his mouth hanging open. I liked how he was the furthest thing from a jock, but a spectacular athlete. I liked his laugh. I liked his smile.

There are infinite things to choose from.

Which is why I'm surprised at the answer that rolls off my tongue first: "I liked that he trusted me."

Nash stares, trying to make sense of my response. "Trusted you?"

"It's hard to explain," I say, pausing a moment to think because I've never said this out loud before. "I knew Dylan better than anyone else. He always seemed so open, even if he just met you, but when we became friends, I saw there was a lot he kept close to his chest."

"Yeah?"

"Yeah. Like, there was more to his story that nobody knew about, or maybe that he hadn't quite figured out himself. . . . I don't know, it's like I was the only one he trusted to read his story as he wrote it, like I was on chapter twenty when he let the rest of the world only read through chapter ten."

My throat narrows.

I always knew that—how much he trusted me to see the real him—but finding the right words and saying them out loud clarifies the truth in a way I hadn't appreciated until now.

But then there's Jacob.

I recall what he told me in the bathroom after Dorian interrupted us—how maybe I didn't know Dylan as well as I thought I did. Could others have been further along reading Dylan's book than I realized?

Quiet settles into the room, and I question if I went too personal.

"Sorry," I say with a sheepish laugh. "Shit just got heavy."

Nash smiles. "I like heavy. So, what was your favorite scene?"

"What do you mean?"

"Your favorite scene in the book of Dylan."

I clear my throat and try to choose an answer.

Affinity undercover agent or not, I'm glad that I have someone an air mattress away wanting to know more about the real Dylan, not the billboard one.

The Dylan who lived.

31

RIVER

I didn't need Nash to get a good night's sleep in the trials like his sister's cover story said, but his being there definitely didn't hurt after our talk. When I wake up to Nora's knocking, I'm smiling, well rested, and actually excited for the trials in a way I wouldn't have expected last night.

At Headquarters, I grab a banana and bagel and sit down next to Biggs, who's captivated by whatever Brady is telling her from where he's seated across our table.

"Don't get me wrong, babe," she says. "I'm happy if you're happy, but you can't tell me that it's not weird."

"What's weird?" I say, peeling open my banana.

Biggs gives me a knowing look. "Take a guess."

I glance at Brady, whose blissful grin has become a permanent fixture on his face every morning. "Again?"

He nods.

"With the *same* dream girl in it, too," Biggs adds.

"The dream got even more real, too," Brady says quietly, as if it's a secret.

I scrunch my face. "What does that mean, exactly, for a dream to get more real?"

"I also would like to know," Biggs says, spooning cereal into her mouth.

"It felt almost like . . . virtual reality?" he replies. "Like there was still a difference between the dreamworld and real world, but not much."

Biggs crunches down on her sugary flakes before discreetly gesturing at her Disk. "You don't think it could have something to do with these freaky-ass things?"

Brady shrugs.

They both turn to me.

"I mean, maybe?" I respond.

But the truth is, I have no idea how there could be a link between Brady's Orbeus, Disk, and vivid dreams.

"Have your dreams felt off during the trials?" I ask Biggs.

She thinks for a moment, then shakes her head.

"Neither have mine." I look at Brady. "Have you brought up the dreams with Nora during your Check-Ins?"

"Yes," he says, "and she thinks it's cool."

"Well then, if Nora isn't concerned and you're enjoying them," I say with a shrug, "I say dream on."

Biggs sighs. "For the record, I *don't* say dream on." She bends closer to us and softens her voice. "*You're* having these euphoric dreams, Mavis is imagining whole-ass conversations with *you*." She shakes her head. "Something's up."

"The trials are affecting different people in different ways," Brady says cheerily. "So what? It's not like you haven't changed since arriving. . . ."

Biggs looks offended. "In what ways have I changed?"

Brady eyes the notebook in front of her, which is covered in notes.

She rolls her eyes. "So I've gotten some good video ideas for Tether. At least I'm not having VR sex dreams with the same person every night—"

"I told you, they're *not* sex dreams," Brady pushes back, both irked and humored by Biggs's roast. "Dream Girl is my friend. It's purely platonic!"

The two get swept up in a playful back-and-forth. But when it starts to get heated, I jump in to prevent an actual fight from ensuing.

"Where's our Red?" I ask, scanning Headquarters. He's usually one of the first participants at breakfast.

"Getting cozy with the newest Orange," Brady says.

"What?"

"Be subtle," Biggs says, "but check your six o'clock."

I pretend to crack my back by twisting my torso to the side, glancing directly behind me. A smiley Mavis, now dressed in Orange, is leaning against the wall, chatting with a noticeably close Jacob, identical granola bars in their hands.

I turn back to the purple table, which I guess is just a Blue table at this point.

"I sense some sparks flying," Brady says, smirking while staring at them.

"You okay, babe?" asks Biggs, who, unlike an oblivious Brady, remembers yesterday's disaster with Mavis.

"Sorry." Brady's smirk vanishes as he looks at me. "How does that make you feel?"

I sigh. "It's fine, I guess?"

But my most honest answer is that it's complicated. I was worried about Mavis more than anything after learning she got bumped off Blue, because it's difficult to be angry knowing Nora isn't faulting me for what happened and having Biggs and Brady believe that I wasn't lying about the fabricated conversations.

It's strange, though. Even if Mavis still blames me, at least in part, for Dylan's death, and we haven't had a legitimate conversation in over a year, it's impossible not to feel a little bit relieved to see her smiling again—even if it's because of my blackmailer.

"Did you ever figure out why she was telling people you snuck into her Meditation room to talk?" Biggs asks.

"Not yet," I say, "but I'm bugging Nora about it some more in my Check-In. Mavis and I spent a year avoiding each other, so a week in here shouldn't have been a problem. Something else has to be going on."

"Do you want us to ask Mavis about it?" Brady says. "We could, you know, and report back to you."

I pause to think it through.

To the best of my knowledge, Mavis hasn't told anyone that I'm the one Dylan was texting when they crashed—apart from, in all likelihood, Goldie. But I've never seen her as livid with me as she was yesterday, and I'm not confident she wouldn't tell Biggs and Brady if they get more involved in our situation—especially if she gets the sense that they're more loyal to me than to her. Come to think of it, I'm surprised she hasn't told Jacob already, knowing how close they've gotten—*wait*.

Could *that* be why Jacob's blackmailing me?

Biggs and Brady said they were talking at dinner the first night of the trials, which means they could've already been friends coming in. If that's the case, it may explain why Jacob's been so fired up over the mustache. Maybe he's not only blaming me for Dylan's death, but doing so in defense of Mavis, too.

And . . . if Jacob figured out that I spray-painted the mustache, and he and Mavis were already friends before the trials, could he have told Mavis—and, by proxy, Goldie as well? Is that why she cornered me on the steps on the deathiversary, suspicious that I'd done it?

"Yo," Biggs says, nudging my tray. "You good?"

I get pulled back down to earth. "Yeah, sorry," I say, clearing my throat and refocusing on Brady's question. "Nah, don't worry about asking Mavis. I don't want you two getting involved in the mess on my behalf."

Biggs nods in thought, tapping her pen against the table. "Well, in the meantime"—she uses the pen to flick a Froot Loop onto my lap—"you got us, babe."

I smile.

With the usual exception of Goldie giving me the stink eye, Fitness in the courtyard goes smoothly, as both the Blues and Greens have a good time without trying to kill each other. I spend the bulk of Art distracting a giggly Biggs from her storyboard by painting dicks and boobs on my canvas.

Inspired by my good morning, I rethink bringing up the Mavis ordeal with Nora by the time Check-In rolls around. I don't want a stressful conversation to sour my rare good mood. Billboard and blackmail worries aside, seeing Mavis happy with Jacob eases my concerns that she's not doing well, which was the main reason I wanted more answers. Besides, it seems like Nora already told me everything she's willing to share on the matter.

"You seem surprisingly chipper today," Nora says, almost suspiciously, as she takes my survey. I'm almost disappointed that she tosses it aside without reading it over, as my response to each question moved in a positive direction. "What gives?"

I shrug. "I don't know. Just feeling good, I guess."

"Yeah?" She looks me up and down. "And last night with my brother went okay? Your Disk chart data continues to say so."

I nod. "You never mentioned he's a space nerd, like me."

She grins. "Didn't I?"

I don't tell Nora this, but I think I can credit my good mood mostly to him.

Because really, none of the anxiety-inducing problems swirling around me during the trials have been solved. If anything, they've gotten *worse*. But I've felt much lighter after talking to him last night. Could Nora be right?

Could the yellow spikes on my chart really reflect my Orbeus's affinity for her brother?

The more I think about our conversation, the more I realize just how much I needed it. Who knew discussing habitable zones and reminiscing about Dylan in my old social studies classroom would work like a defibrillator on my spirit?

Mavis and I enjoy our first Gaming hour together without it being awkward—she plays Scrabble with Ollie on the opposite side of the lounge while I go undefeated against Oaklyn in chess— and even Meditation isn't so bad. I decide to think through old Skelemont videos again but my thoughts keep wandering back to Nash. I don't mind it either way.

I head to dinner later with a spring in my step, hoping the rumors are true and Affinity created a sundae bar for dessert. But Jacob scoops me up before I can walk into Headquarters. "Bathroom," he says, gripping my forearm and tugging me in the opposite direction, "now."

I stumble in surprise. "What's going on?" I ask, reluctantly following in his footsteps.

Jacob doesn't respond.

I can already feel my good mood slipping away, assuming this has to do with the billboard, and similarly to my Check-In with Nora, I'd rather save my many stressors for another day. But what choice do I have? Jacob holds the power until I can get home and destroy the evidence.

We walk into the bathroom, and I pause at a sink. "What's going on?"

But Jacob heads to the last stall in the row and swings the

door open before gesturing for me to join him inside.

"Okay . . . ?"

I peek in and see Brady sitting on the lid of the toilet seat with his knees pressed to his chest to keep his shoes from touching the floor.

"Come on." Jacob urges me to cram into the stall as well. "We have to be quick—"

"Jacob?" I hear a girl's hushed voice come through the large vent in the wall. "What the hell is going on, babe?"

"Biggs?" I ask.

"*Shhh*," Jacob scolds us. He locks the stall door and crouches down next to the vent to better communicate with Biggs. "We're all here."

Someone else clears their throat in the girls' bathroom. "Okay, everyone, listen the fuck up," Goldie says sternly. "We need to talk about Mavis."

32

DYLAN

I tense up. "Sure," I say slowly, looking at Mavis on her doorstep. "Where do you want to go?"

She looks past me in thought, then shrugs. "I don't care. Let's just go for a drive."

Mavis walks toward my car. I follow behind, my body slowly becoming a big ball of nerves. What does she want to talk about?

Yeah, I got under her skin this morning with the art stuff and she fired back during Saturday dinner. She seemed apologetic before I left to see River, though, and the tone she's striking now makes me feel like this is about something more.

Does she want to talk about Goldie?

We hop into my car, and I back out of the driveway. I hesitate for a moment, unsure which direction to go in, before deciding to drive back into town. If that weather alert was accurate, the storm should be arriving soon, and I'd rather not be in the boonies when it does.

"Whose is this?" Mavis asks.

I look to my right and see that she's holding the notebook. "I took Brady Potts home earlier. He left it in my car. You can just"—I lean to the side and pop open the glove compartment—"throw it in there."

She tries to, but it's already overflowing with stuff. "You still haven't cleaned this out yet, huh?" she says with a grin, glancing at me.

I'm relieved to see her smile. "It's on my to-do list."

Mavis tries to make room for Brady's notebook, but the sports section of a newspaper falls onto her lap before she can. "I thought the *Daily Timber Wolf* went digital," she says, scanning the front page.

"They print quarterly issues. My dad asked me to pick that one up because it compares my stats to other college recruits in the area."

"'Number One Nash,'" she reads the bold headline of the cover story. "Do you think this quarterback at Pioneer deserves all the hype?"

She's trying to buy time, I can tell, which means she's avoiding whatever it is she wanted to talk about. And that doesn't feel good.

"I think so," I answer with a lump in my throat.

"*Piano for Beginners*," Mavis says, and I see that she's reading the cover of the guidebook I bought when I decided I wanted to learn. "You know I love that you play, right?"

"Of course."

"Because I used piano as an example at dinner to make my point—not because I wanted to make fun of you," she clarifies. "'Dylan's Song' is on a playlist Ari listens to all the time, by the way. It reminds me of you every time it comes on."

I smile. "Yeah? I bet Ari would learn the chorus faster than I currently am."

Mavis carefully fits the newspaper, Brady's notebook, and piano guide back into the glove compartment without bending any of their edges, then we drive in silence. My anxiety begins to climb, and just before I'm about to ask what she wanted to talk about—

"So," she sighs heavily, "Dylan . . ."

Dylan.

There's something about the way she says my name that makes

it crystal clear: I'm not going to break up with Mavis, she's about to break up with *me*.

For a split second, I'm overcome with relief. If we're on the same page with why we're no longer working as a couple, there won't be any hurt feelings. We can move on together, as the friends we were always meant to be.

But . . . what if Mavis *doesn't* want to be friends? What if she planned a different kind of breakup conversation, one that ends with wanting an indefinite amount of space or going our separate ways senior year? And even if we are on the same page, will that change if she ever finds out about my crush on River?

I panic and take my foot off the gas.

"Actually," I say, gently pressing the brake, "can you hold that thought? I'm craving something sweet." I'm already taking a left before she responds.

"Sure, but here?" Mavis says, looking out at the gas station as I park. "They basically just have stale donuts."

"Do you want anything?" I say, unbuckling my belt and hopping out of the car in a hurry.

Mavis stares, confused at how rushed I suddenly seem. "Uh, no? I guess not . . ."

I dash across the parking lot as raindrops begin to fall and splatter on the pavement.

Fortunately, the gas station is empty except for the one worker at the register. Unfortunately, that one worker is Roy, who grew up down the street from me and will definitely want to talk if he spots me in here. I creep into the back aisle—rows of chips on my left, rows of candy bars are on my right—and stop to collect my thoughts when I know no one else is around.

I close my eyes and exhale, trying to process this moment. Trying to process this *day*.

I wanted to break up with Mavis on my own, but I don't want to be the one who's broken up with on my own. I panic and decide to call River.

He answers at once. "You want more of my mom's chicken enchiladas, don't you?"

A tear leaks from my eye just hearing his voice. Why is so much hitting me so hard and so fast?

"I hate to tell you this," he continues, "but my dad ate the rest of the leftovers."

I can't say anything or he'll hear that I'm crying.

"You there?" he follows up.

I cough, clearing my voice. "Hey, yeah. You broke up."

A pause.

"Where are you?" he asks. Another pause. "Is everything okay?"

"Yeah, yeah, I'm just . . ." I lick my lips and start pacing the aisle, wondering what I want to say, wondering where to even begin. "Mavis wants . . ."

I trail off.

"Mavis wants . . ." he replies, "what?"

What am I doing? I can't get ahead of myself.

"Mavis wants Doritos," I say, staring at the row of junk food in front of me. "Is she more Nacho Cheese or Cool Ranch?"

Really? Chip flavors?

"Cool Ranch, duh. How did you not know this?" He pauses, and I can hear his suspicion in the silence. "You actually called to ask about Mavis's Doritos preference? Aren't you with her right now?"

I force a fake laugh. "Yeah. I'm at the gas station on the corner of Third. She's in the car."

"You're close. You two should stop by." More silence. "I'm still not convinced something else isn't on your mind."

I look out the window and see Mavis's silhouette in my car as the rain continues to pick up. "I think we'll just lie low at her place tonight."

I can tell he's still trying to figure me out. "You swear you're good?"

I don't respond, fearful my voice will crack when I talk again. "Dylan?"

"Sorry, my reception is terrible," I lie, thankful my voice stays intact. I hold the phone away from my face for a moment and collect myself. "What did you say?"

I'm not sure he buys my reception excuse. "Are Summer Sign-Ups still stressing you out? Or is it something else?"

I swallow hard.

He sighs gently into the phone. "Whenever a human problem feels too big, just remember what our guy had to say about it."

I smile. Because I was *just* thinking about this a little bit ago. Can he read my mind?

River and I didn't mean to memorize every line of Dr. Skelemont's video "The Awesomeness and Purposelessness of Our Existence," but it just sort of happened after rewatching his six-minute explainer about five hundred times the summer before our junior year.

"'The catastrophic thought pestering you was born from a series of electrical reactions contained in a three-pound sponge of flesh floating between your ears,'" River begins, quoting the video. He deepens his voice to sound like Skelemont, which he knows makes me laugh. It's probably why he's doing it again now. "'That three-pound sponge of flesh floating between your ears lives in your one, singular body.'"

"'And your one, singular body,'" I chime in, "'is just one tiny dot, surrounded by billions of other tiny dots, all clinging to a pebble spinning through space.'"

I close my eyes again and feel drips trickle down my cheeks.

I bend at my knees and sink toward the floor until my butt lands on the backs of my sneakers. I know I'll look like an idiot if Roy or Mavis or anyone else sees me like this, but in this moment, for once, I don't care. Even with all my emotions burying me at once, it feels good not to care.

"'That spinning pebble is circling a bigger, fiery speck,'" I say, continuing Dr. Skelemont's monologue, "'that's clustered together with billions of other bigger, fiery specks. And that cluster of bigger, fiery specks is just one of *billions* of clusters of bigger, fiery specks suspended throughout infinity.'"

I feel my smallness as the words leave my mouth, but that's the whole point, weirdly enough. It's a good kind of smallness.

"'So when that catastrophic thought tries to convince your three-pound sponge of flesh that the fate of the universe rests on your shoulders,'" River says, "'remember that you're just that one tiny dot clinging to that one spinning pebble.'"

"'And marvel at the fact that, of all the pebbles spinning around all the fiery specks,'" I say, "'you get to share this pebble with these dots at this exact moment within infinity.'"

A bolt of lightning rips through the nearby sky, and a loud clap of thunder quickly follows. I look outside and see the rain picking up.

"You better get out of that gas station," River says, "unless you have faith in Roy to handle the power going out."

"That, I do not have," I whisper, glancing around.

We've run through Dr. Skelemont's lines in that video countless times before, but this time felt different. I breathe in and out much easier, happy I decided to make the call.

"Are you two having a movie night?" River asks. "Is that what the Doritos are for?"

I get tugged back down to earth and am suddenly aware of how long I've been keeping Mavis waiting outside.

"I'm not sure yet," I say, slipping out of the gas station without Roy noticing. "Me and Mavis are just driving around right now."

"Okay," River says. His deep breath out muffles the speaker.

I pause, standing in the rain. The droplets splatter the pavement around me and trickle down my forehead. The cooler storm air fills my lungs, and I'm filled with the sudden urge to tell him everything—that I *meant* that kiss earlier, that Mavis is ending things with me tonight, that both of those realities are downright terrifying, and that I have no idea where all of it leaves the three of us.

But before I decide to speak up or not, River decides for me. "Bye, Dylan."

I hesitate, not wanting to hang up. *Not yet.*

"Bye, River."

I step into my car and toss my phone into the cupholder.

"You didn't buy anything?" Mavis says, noticing that I'm empty-handed as she buckles her seat belt.

"You were right," I answer. "Not too many good options."

"What were you doing in there for so long then?" she asks.

I hope she can't tell that I was crying. "I had to call River about something."

I put my car into drive and pull out of the gas station as my headlights illuminate the falling droplets ahead. Another bolt of lightning flashes above.

"Dylan," Mavis says softly, as a wave of thunder rolls across town, "I think we need to break up."

33

RIVER

"Can you guys hear me?" Goldie's voice drifts through the vent after none of us react. "*Hello? Mavis Meyers? Ever heard of her?*"

"Y-yeah, sorry," Brady stammers, seemingly even more confused than I am as to what's going on. "We know Mavis Meyers."

Goldie groans. "Yeah, no shit, Sherlock, it was—"

"Don't talk to him like that, babe," Biggs snaps at her.

"Don't call me *babe*, babe."

The two of them start bickering.

"*Hey!*" Jacob hisses, his lips inches from the vent. "We don't have much time before the Mentors notice we're all late to dinner. Goldie, go."

I step closer to the vent so I can hear better, but it's difficult for me to focus on anything other than the absurdity that I've been bum-rushed into a bathroom stall to apparently get some intel from Goldie through a vent in the wall.

"Long story short," Goldie says, "Mavis was certain she talked to you during two of your Meditation sessions, River."

Jacob and Brady look at me to see how I'll react.

"Okay, well, she's mistaken, then," I push back, trying to be assertive without sounding angry, "because I never talked to her during Meditation, Gold—"

"Emphasis on *was*," Goldie cuts in. "Mavis definitely *believed* that you two talked, but now she's starting to think that something weird is going on. You know her just as well as I do, River—well, you used to anyway. Mavis isn't a liar." Goldie pauses. "Do you have a scar on your hand?"

Brady and Jacob look at me again.

"A scar?" I say, pausing to look down and confirm. "No, why?"

"Are you sure?" Goldie presses. "From an accident when you were younger. Mavis said you'd know what I'm talking about. . . ."

"Why isn't she here instead of you, then?" I ask, frustrated to be in the spotlight of the situation.

"Mavis is at Headquarters trying to distract Nora to buy us more time," Jacob answers pointedly, "or else she would be."

"Really think about it," Goldie urges. "It had something to do with a class project."

A class project?

I can't remember the last time I had a class project with Mavis. Maybe at some point in middle school? But it's difficult to remember anything specific now, especially being put on the spot like this. In fact, the only class project that comes to mind now was the one we were just discussing in Group Talk—

"Oh, the one on surface tension?" I say, as the memory comes storming back. "I cut my hand using scissors and almost had to get stitches."

"That must be it," Goldie says, excited.

"Our parents thought it might leave a scar after the stitches"—I glance down at the spot where it happened—"but it didn't. So how is that relevant?"

"It's how she realized something weird was happening," Jacob says. "When you were talking to her during Meditation, there was a scar on your hand. She was surprised she'd never noticed it before."

"But then, when she walked by you in Gaming," Goldie adds, "she saw that you didn't have the scar anymore."

"What?" I squint in confusion and turn to Brady to see if he's following. "I don't get it."

"Neither do I," Biggs whispers. "Did you sneak weed in here? Because you sound stoned."

Goldie ignores her. "We think her Disk is screwing with her when she meditates, creating, like . . . daydreams, or whatever. But like, *really vivid* daydreams. Daydreams so real, Mavis thought they were actually happening."

"That would explain why she thought you were in her Meditation room with her when you weren't," Jacob says.

My chest tightens.

I had the same thought regarding Mavis's Orbeus, but I can't tell them that.

"But does that mean . . . ?" Brady mutters, white in the face.

"Yeah," Jacob says. "When Mavis told me, I thought about the dreams you've been having with the same girl. It sounds very similar." He looks at me. "I haven't experienced any weird dreams like that, though, have you?"

I shake my head.

"Nope," Goldie says.

"I haven't, either," Biggs says. "I mean, I robbed a bank in a snowman costume a couple nights ago, and then made out with Shawn Mendes, but that's standard for me."

There's silence on the other end of the vent as we all struggle to connect the dots before Goldie speaks up. "Does anyone else feel like there's just something . . . *off* with Affinity?"

I can hear the fear in Goldie's voice, and it throws me. I've never heard her sound like this before.

"I do," Jacob says, surprising me.

"What do you mean by *off*?" I ask them.

"Like, I get why we can't know *everything* about what they're studying," Goldie says, "but I can't make sense of anything they ask us to do. These activities? These pointless Mentor Check-Ins? None of it adds up."

"I will say," Biggs chimes in, "I think it's strange how much alone time they force onto us for researchers examining social dynamics and friendship."

"Right?" Goldie says. "What's up with that?"

"They also don't seem to care about the surveys they require us to fill out every day, even though Dorian emphasized how important they were on day one," Jacob adds. "You guys have to take those, too, right?"

Brady and I nod, and I think about how Nora barely even glanced at mine the past couple days before she tossed them aside.

"Nora accidentally threw mine in the trash, I think," Brady says.

"See, this is what we're saying," Jacob says, and similar to Goldie's fear, there's an urgency in his voice I haven't heard before. "They say these surveys are critical, but they're not acting like they are. So what are they trying to hide by making us do them?"

Jacob pauses, staring at the floor in thought.

"Goldie," he says, now more subdued. "What do you think?"

Silence follows for a beat.

"I think we do it," she answers through the vent.

Jacob looks at me and Brady, and I can tell that he's nervous. "Goldie and I want to break into Dr. Ridges's office to try to find some answers."

My throat dries up.

Brady's eyes bulge out of their sockets.

"Well, damn," Biggs says. "How, exactly?"

"They have cameras everywhere," Brady says.

"But they told us the cameras aren't live feeds," Goldie notes.

"And, yes, we know that's a risky bet," Jacob cuts in before Biggs can make that point. "They could be lying to us about that, too. And maybe we're naive for thinking they might *not* be. But if that is the case, Affinity wouldn't see that footage until after the trial ends—or they'd never see it at all. Who's going to watch all these hours of tape when we're supposed to be in bed?"

"Dr. Ridges's office has to be locked at night, though," I say. "There's no way Affinity would just leave it open. Plus, the twenty-four seven security guards. How are you going to avoid them?"

"Harry told me that he's noticed a fifteen-minute window, from about 4:15 to 4:30 a.m., where the guards whose shifts are ending and the guards just arriving to work meet briefly near Headquarters. It's a decent distance away from the E-Suite, where Dr. Ridges's office is."

"We plan to go then," Goldie says.

"Harry . . ." I say, "the custodian Harry?"

"He *hates* Affinity," Goldie says. "He overheard Mavis and Nora talking, and he got a bad feeling. So he's been happy to share info and help us out."

"But not *so* happy that he's willing to give us the key to Dr. Ridges's office," Jacob adds. "We already asked."

"That's our final roadblock," Goldie says, "finding a way to sneak in without busting down the door."

Harry . . . the keys to Dr. Ridges's office . . .

A memory from Dylan's last day comes storming back into my head. As is usually the case when that happens, the memory is quickly followed by a wave of guilt and sadness, but I try to bury it as fast as I can.

"I think I know a way we can get in there," I say quietly.

Goldie gasps. "How?"

"Don't ask me how I know this, but I think there's a set of Principal Fyres's keys on top of the display case outside the gym," I say. "It should have a key to Mr. Babcock's office."

"Really?" Brady asks in shock.

"I'll see if I can find it on the way to my room later," Jacob says. "If I can, let's do it tonight."

"Tonight?" Biggs asks in surprise. "That's quick."

"We need some answers fast," Goldie argues. "Because if these Disks really are fucking with our brains, I'd rather know sooner than later."

I'm tempted to tell them about the Orbeus, but not *break-my-NDA*-level tempted.

After all, the whole point of my being here is to make sure I can still go to Cascara in the fall, which might be tough to do if I'm stuck in a jail cell.

"Let's bring our notebooks and pens that they gave us in our bags," Goldie says, "so we can take notes on anything we find in Dr. Ridges's office that seems important. We can't steal anything and risk Dr. Ridges noticing."

Jacob cranes his neck to see the clock on the wall. "We have to go. Are you guys in for tonight?" His eyes dart between me and Brady. "We could use the extra hands taking notes."

Brady and I exchange worried looks, but he gulps and nods. "Sure."

"Same, babes," Biggs says. "I'll be there."

"Great. Let's all meet outside Dr. Ridges's office at 4:15—and *don't* oversleep." Jacob turns to me. "What about you?"

My mind is spinning, trying to absorb everything I just learned.

I can't trust that Jacob or Goldie have my best interests at heart, but their motives seem like they have much more to do with supporting Mavis and finding answers than anything to do with me. Dr. Ridges's office could hold more info on Orbeus and our Disk charts, too, including what my yellow spikes could mean for me and Nash.

"Okay." I take a deep breath. "Count me in."

34

RIVER

I try to unpack the madness of our bathroom meeting during my Free Time, wondering if I made the right call in agreeing to join them with the early-morning break-in. Because I have an extra complication that they don't: Nash. I can't tell him about our plans to sneak into the office, but if his practice starts at five, he might be getting up around the time I'm getting back.

I'm relieved Mavis has acknowledged the conversations between us never happened, but the more I think about it, the more far-fetched the dream theory that she, Goldie, and Jacob discussed feels to me.

After all, Brady's brought up his vivid dreams more than once in Group Talk. If they're being caused by the Disk in some nefarious way, wouldn't Nora have stopped him from telling us about them? If anything, she's seemed just as amused and curious about them as the rest of the Blues. And besides, if his intense dreams are somehow associated with his Disk and Orbeus, wouldn't Nora have mentioned that to me during our Check-Ins after I signed my NDA?

Nash comes striding into my room with his things, yanking my thoughts back to the ground. "Hey," I say, sitting up in bed and running my fingers over my Disk, "how do you know if you're dreaming?"

He gives me a quizzical look. "What do you mean?"

I sigh and fall back onto my mattress. "Never mind, it's stupid."

"Try me."

I choose my words carefully. "A kid in this study keeps having dreams that feel so real, they're almost lifelike. It just made me wonder."

"Wonder . . ." He pauses and smirks. ". . . if you could be dreaming this very second?"

I think about it, then smile. "Well, yeah. Who's to say I'm not in a REM cycle right now?"

"Or, better yet," he says, setting up his bed, "have you ever thought about the fact you could be stuck in a simulation and not even know it?"

"And my actual body is fast asleep in a capsule somewhere in Siberia?"

"Or on *Mars*?"

We exchange grins.

"There's a more reliable way to test if you're asleep, you know," he says. I hear the sudden squeakiness of his sneakers against the floor and sit up to see what he's doing—

"*Agh!*" I yell in surprise as his body crushes mine, pushing me back into a mound of pillows. He lingers on top of me for a half second, his partially zipped backpack hanging loosely off one shoulder, before rolling to the side. "Getting tackled. So?"

"So what?"

"Are you still here?" He waves his hands inches from my eyes like I'm waking up from a coma.

I laugh. "Yes."

"Then it's confirmed," he says. "You are officially not dreaming. I repeat: *not* dreaming."

I expect him to bounce right back up again and return to his corner, but he slips his backpack off and stays put right next to me.

I don't hate it.

"Tell me," he says, getting comfortable. "Why would you be stuck in a dream right now and not know it?"

"It's a long story, Nash."

"I've got time, River."

"It involves . . ." I nod at the camera in the corner. "So I probably shouldn't."

He glances up to where I gestured. "Oh." He smiles. "So *that's* what this whole thing is. A sleep study."

I open my mouth, unsure how to respond.

"Wait," he follows up, "a sleep study . . . specifically for kids who are struggling socially?"

I still don't know how to answer him.

"Hold on." He lifts his pointer finger up. "A sleep study specifically for kids who are struggling socially *and* have super blue eyes?" He leans closer and squints at me like a scientist looking through a microscope. "Seriously, they're like the waters off a tropical beach."

My cheeks burn red as I smile and look away bashfully.

Is Nash . . . into me? Because his behavior the past few minutes isn't screaming *straight guy*. But the other question feels even more difficult to answer: Do I *want* him to be?

Before I can think on it more, Nash's jaw opens so wide to inhale a yawn. It reminds me of one of those massive jungle snakes who swallow entire animals whole. "Tonight's drills ruined me. I'm drained."

"Do you want to sleep here?" The question comes out having bypassed my brain entirely. "I mean, only if you'd appreciate not having to blow up your bed again."

He looks at me and pauses. "You wouldn't mind?"

My heart flutters as I shake my head.

Nash stares up at the ceiling again. "I guess this *is* a king."

"A king that has to be more comfortable than that loud piece of shit that you haul in here every night."

He thinks some more, then smiles. "Okay."

I take a breath, suddenly nervous. But it's a good kind of nervous, when the butterflies spread from my stomach to every limb on my body, fluttering in anticipation. I felt it in the gym on Dylan's last day, actually . . . but that was different. *Way* different.

I wasn't nervous to be sitting next to a hot guy; I was nervous because we'd sneaked into the school together. I was giddy to be with my best friend in our spot taking in a cool sunset. So no, it couldn't have been the *same* good kind of nervous that I'm feeling now.

Right?

Nash sits up, swings his legs over the side of the bed, and slips off his tank top. I take a peek at his protruding back muscles and get a whiff of the same shower gel I smelled the first night I met him in the locker room. Then he lifts his backpack off the mattress to place onto the floor, but doesn't notice that a wrinkled sticky note escapes through the unzipped pocket.

I look down and read what I assume is Nash's handwriting:

> **Death isn't the end but a conclusion to a single chapter within the infinite story of us—a cosmic transfer when our essence merges with the skies above. In death, we return to stardust, forever woven into the celestial tapestry of a universe that cannot be anything but immortal.**

My heart thuds wildly.

"What's this?" I ask Nash, although I already know the answer.

He turns, and when he sees what I'm referencing, his expression immediately melts in embarrassment. He snags the sticky note out of my reach. "It's nothing."

"It's a quote from Dr. Skelemont."

He stares at me, surprised. "You know him?"

"Know him? I've watched every one of his videos—most of them at least a dozen times," I say. "Why do you look so surprised?"

He closes his jaw. "I guess I just assumed a Dr. Skelemont fan would know what the habitable zone is."

I grin. "Fair point. I was . . . sort of testing you."

He bites his lower lip and stares down at the bed. "When you were talking about Dylan trusting you last night—how he let you read the furthest into his story—it reminded me of this quote; how death isn't *the* end but just *an* end within our infinite stories." He shrugs. "I don't necessarily believe in heaven, but I think I believe in that. I wanted to share it with you." He looks at me, and I think he's unsure if it's okay for him to be this open. "But then I thought about how we just met, and that it might be sort of a heavy thing to share with someone I barely know—"

"Nash," I cut in, swallowing a round of tears. "I like heavy, too."

He lets out a small laugh, relieved. "Cool."

"Cool."

I slip off my socks and nestle into my side of the bed. Nash fluffs his pillow, and he's still looking at me when I turn off the lamp.

"Good night, Nash," I whisper through the darkness.

"Sleep tight, River," he says back.

35

RIVER

I wake up in a panic.

Dr. Ridges's office.

I was so distracted by Nash's agreeing to sleep in my bed that I totally forgot about the purple table's plans to break in to Dr. Ridges's office overnight. Well, the purple table *plus Goldie's* plans. I wait a minute for my eyes to adjust to the darkness of my room, then squint at the clock on the wall. It's 4:03 a.m.

I didn't oversleep. *Thank God.*

I don't trust myself to drift off again so I lie on my side until it's time to leave. At 4:13 a.m., I slide out of bed as delicately as possible, grab my notebook and pen off the ground, and tiptoe to the door. I glance back at Nash to make sure I didn't wake him. It's too dark to be certain, but I don't hear anything and the mass of blankets doesn't appear to be moving, so I quietly open the door.

I peek down the hallway, where the security guard in Blue Sleeping Quarters is usually stationed. Harry was right, I don't see a soul. So I slip out in the hallway and close the door gently behind me.

A moment later, Biggs's door opens and she appears.

"Hey, babe," she whispers groggily, squinting at me. "Can I be honest?"

I nod at her.

"It's too early for this shit."

Brady emerges from his room as well with an uncharacteristically grumpy expression planted on his face. Then the three of us take off to the E-Suite, praying the hallway cameras are not, in fact, being livestreamed to an Affinity worker who will come wring our necks.

"What's got you all fussy?" Biggs asks Brady quietly as she peeks around the corner, checking to make sure the coast remains clear.

"Nothing," Brady bites back.

"*Whoa,*" Biggs says.

"Sorry," he says, lowering his voice. "I forced myself to stay awake all night. I even did jumping jacks to avoid passing out. I'm tired, is all."

"Or is it that you missed out on seeing your dream girl?" I ask.

He hesitates to answer. "Maybe that's part of it, too."

Biggs and I exchange grins.

The school is dead quiet and eerily dark—recessed bulbs in the ceiling near the fire exit signs are the only sources of light—and it's easy for my imagination to concoct all the people, creatures, and things that could be hiding in the shadows. It reminds me of my last night with Dylan, when we met up together in the gym. The building was just as creepy then, but as much as I'm starting to love Biggs and Brady, the company was better.

We round the final corner to the E-Suite offices. I spot blobs of red and green ahead approaching from the opposite direction. There's an Orange, though, too.

I didn't know Mavis was joining.

"Thanks for letting us know about these keys, River," Jacob says, showing me Principal Fyres's set in the palm of his hand. "Someday I want to know how you knew they were up there."

I smile at him as my insides crumple, realizing Dylan was the last person to carry those keys before tonight.

"We have to be lightning quick," he continues, stepping further into the leadership role he embraced in the bathroom. He looks at the clock. "It's 4:18 and we need to be back in our rooms by 4:30, which means we only have about ten minutes tops, starting now. Okay?"

We nod in silence. I can feel the nervous energy bubbling between the six of us.

"Remember," Goldie adds as Jacob starts testing out keys in Mr. Babcock's door to see which one works, "don't take *anything* with you. And move everything you touch—even if it's a slight bump or nudge—back to its original location."

Brady raises his hand. "What are we looking for again, exactly?"

"I . . . don't know," Goldie says. "Just take note of anything you see about the Disks."

"Come the *fuck* on," Jacob mutters, quickly testing key after key with no success.

I look at Mavis, who's watching anxiously the farthest from the door.

Maybe I'm too exhausted to be thinking critically, or maybe sleeping in the same bed as Nash last night lifted my spirits and I'm still riding high, but I want to go talk to her. She admitted to Jacob and Goldie that I hadn't had those conversations with her, after all, which I appreciated. And now that I think about it, Mavis was so smiley after Meditation when she *did* believe we'd actually spoken, it gives me confidence that she might want to talk in real life.

I discreetly float her way. "Hey."

"Hi." She doesn't look at me, but her tone is gentle enough that it feels like a green light.

"Thanks for telling Goldie and Jacob that I wasn't lying about those conversations," I say. "I'm sure that was difficult to do."

She keeps her eyes glued on Jacob.

For a moment, I feel like she might ice me out again, so I prepare to step away. But she glances at me before I do. "I got too worked up at Headquarters when I yelled at you. I was confused—*am* confused—by what exactly happened. But now I know you didn't deserve that. I'm sorry."

My heart thuds.

It's been so long since me and Mavis have spoken like this, I don't want to screw it up.

"It's okay. After my . . . text, I assumed you never wanted to talk to me again. But now I know that's not the case."

I smile.

She looks at me, confused. "Your text?"

"Yeah. My text the night of . . ." I hesitate. "Last June third?"

She stares at me.

What?

"*Finally*," Jacob breathes.

I hear the lock click and turn to see him swinging the door open. "We're down to seven minutes now. Let's hustle—"

"Someone should stay at the door to watch for security," Goldie says.

"Good idea." Jacob looks to the group. "Any volunteers?"

Brady raises his hand. "I'm a slow notetaker, so maybe I should?"

"Great."

It's surreal to be on the hunt for top secret info in the dead of night in the same room where I spent every first period fighting the urge to fall asleep.

"Let's each focus on one area," Biggs proposes.

Biggs, Goldie, and I each claim one of the three binders on Dr. Ridges's desk while Jacob snags a pile of manila folders.

Mavis boldly steps in front of his tablet. "Okay," she exhales, long and hard, rubbing her hands together and staring at the screen. "If I were Dr. Ridges's password, what would I be . . . ?"

I start quickly but carefully flipping through my binder. The first few pages are densely packed with small print that reminds me of the NDA that I signed. I have no way of knowing if it's important information, seeing as I can't read more than a paragraph of legal jargon in eight-point font without my head exploding, so I move on.

"Damn it," Mavis breathes, struggling to sign in to the tablet.

"Save your energy, babe," Biggs says, hunched over her binder. "What are the chances you'll randomly choose the correct—"

"Holy shit," Mavis breathes, "I'm in."

Goldie gasps. "What was the password?"

"Pickeball," Mavis answers, just as shocked as we are. She looks at us. "He's mentioned it's his favorite sport at least three times."

Buoyed by Mavis's good luck, I refocus on my binder, even more determined to find something worthwhile. After skimming through another few pages, I land on one that reads *LOCATIONS: SETTING REQUIREMENT,* and read the paragraph that follows:

> *At this stage of the product's development, we know there's a strong correlation between setting and the Disks' ability to operate effectively. Participants need to be in a familiar environment that's conducive to social bonding with peers, pretrial research suggests. This makes the school in which they attend or recently attended an ideal location. If this requirement is not met, a participant's Disk will likely fail to engage their Orbeus.*

Damn. Nora wasn't full of shit; our Orbeuses *are* real.

But I have no idea why the Disk would work better or worse recording my Orbeus's activation depending on where I am. . . .

"Has anyone come across something that mentions dreams?" Jacob asks. "Daydreaming . . . lucid dreaming . . . maybe even something on sleep?"

"Or anything related to our Meditation sessions," Mavis adds, staring eagle-eyed at the tablet as she scrolls.

Biggs, Goldie, and I murmur variations of no.

I start jotting down a summary of page 7 in my notes but pause before I get "Orbeus" on the page, as it dawns on me: If I get caught with any information about it or my Disk chart, I'd be breaking my NDA. It wouldn't matter that I read about it *now*, along with other participants who've broken into the office too; I'm the one who already signed on the dotted line.

"We've got to go," Jacob says, looking at the time. "Wrap up whatever you're writing down now. We probably should have left a minute ago—"

"I hear something!" Brady squeals at us, peeking back into the office.

My pulse skyrockets. Biggs, Jacob, Goldie, and I make sure to grab our notebooks and pens, straighten the piles of paperwork that got bumped out of place, and run out into the hallway. Thankfully, no security guards are in sight—yet.

Goldie, Mavis, and Jacob turn right toward the other Sleeping Quarters, while me, Biggs, and Brady break left. We sprint as quickly as possible without being noisy, and then veer left into Blue Sleeping Quarters—

"*Shit*," Biggs says, coming to a halt.

Oaklyn is standing in the middle of our hallway outside her room, arms crossed angrily against her chest. It's impossible to tell from her expression if she's pissed that we left her out or upset that we sneaked out at all. There's little time left to wonder, though, as she storms back into her room, and the rest of us disperse before a guard appears.

I close the door behind me and sigh loudly, relieved to be in the safety of my room, before remembering: *Nash.* I cover my mouth and squint through the darkness until I realize his backpack and pile of bedding have disappeared from the floor. He's already left to get ready for practice. Did he notice I was gone?

I toss my notebook onto my duffel bag and fall into a heap of blankets. I won't be able to sleep, as adrenaline has flooded my veins, but I shut my eyes anyway and think back to what I read in the binder. So the Orbeus *is* a real thing—but what does its existence mean for Brady's dream girl and Mavis's Meditation sessions?

36

RIVER

I awake to knocking and sit up in bed with a yawn, wishing I had another five hours of sleep, preferably with Nash cuddled up next to me. I smile to myself, recalling the Dr. Skelemont quote that he said reminded him of Dylan's story. It's funny how I was so reluctant to have him stay and now I can't wait to see him again tonight.

"Good morning, sunshine," Nora says.

The pleasant greeting is a great sign that Mission: Dr. Ridges's Office miraculously flew under Affinity's radar.

"Morning," I croak in return.

I grab fresh navy blue attire and start to get ready for the day when another knock on my door—this one far fainter—startles me.

"Nora?" I say, confused.

No one responds.

I slip on my flip-flops, cross the room, and crack open the door to Oaklyn. Unsurprisingly, she looks one stressor away from a nervous breakdown.

"Oh," I say, trying to appear unsuspicious, "hey, Oak—"

"Where did you guys go last night?" she fires at me immediately.

I expected to deal with this today, just not seconds after waking up.

I struggle to answer.

"Whatever it was, it had something to do with me," she says on the verge of tears, "didn't it?"

"What? Of course not."

"Then why were all the other Blues included except for me?"

"Ollie wasn't with us."

"All the other *original* Blues."

It really wasn't personal. Oaklyn just hasn't sat at the purple table, and Mission: Dr. Ridges's Office would've been an excruciating ten minutes for her anxiety anyway.

She swallows hard, glancing up and down the hallway. Nora is nowhere in sight. "What's going on that I don't know about?"

"Nothing."

She stares at me. "Really?"

I sigh. "Have you talked to Brady or Biggs yet?"

She shakes her head, so I think on the fly.

"We were trying to play a practical joke on Jacob, is all," I say. "Did you see that we all had our Affinity notebooks with us?"

She pauses, then nods.

"We wanted to slip some notes underneath his door as if they were fake love letters from Dorian," I say nonchalantly. "Jacob always rips on me and Biggs for thinking he's hot, so we thought it'd be funny. Seriously, it was no big deal."

She stares at me, unconvinced. "You risked getting caught by the security guards and maybe even losing your stipend just for that?"

I swallow. "We heard a rumor that there's no security on duty around 4:15. As you probably could tell by us sprinting back to our rooms, obviously we were wrong." I shrug. "No one saw us, but it was close."

"Then why did Biggs say *shit* when she saw me?"

I decide to play dumb. "What do you mean?"

"If you three were just trying to pull some innocent prank on Jacob," she says, "why would Biggs be upset that I saw you sneaking back in?" She stares at the floor, seemingly hurt.

I shake my head. "I promise you, it's nothing like that. I think you probably just startled her because we weren't expecting to see you standing there."

I can tell that she's still not buying it.

Oaklyn steps toward me, even more on edge, and whispers, "Then why was there a boy in your room last night? Did *he* play a role in the practical joke?"

Fuck.

I furrow my brow in apparent confusion. "A boy?"

"I heard you shout," she says, "and it seemed like something was wrong. So I rushed over to make sure you were okay."

She heard me shout?

It must have been the yell I let out when Nash tackled me.

"But before I knocked," she continues, "I heard guys' voices coming from inside your room—voices, as in *two*."

My throat narrows with nerves. "I don't know what to tell you, Oaklyn. There wasn't a boy in my room last night."

"You're sure?"

I nod.

"Okay." She takes a step back, unsatisfied—and maybe even angry. "Never mind, then. See you at breakfast."

I close my door as a wave of guilt swirls around in my gut. I hate lying like that, but I didn't have a choice.

I make sure to catch Brady and Biggs in their rooms so we can get on the same page before Oaklyn can question them about last night, then walk to Headquarters. We get food and sit next to Jacob. Goldie and Mavis are eating nearby, but everyone seems to understand why the two tables should avoid interacting and raising suspicion, as Nora and Rex are hovering a few feet away, chatting with canned coffees in hand. Technically, I'm supposed to be keeping a safe distance from Mavis anyway.

Biggs sits next to Jacob and crunches down on an apple. "Guess who caught us sneaking back into Blue Sleeping Quarters," she says softly.

"Oh, don't worry," he replies, forcing a fake smile. "Oaklyn was over here a minute ago telling me all about it."

I spot Oaklyn helping herself to juice at the drinks station.

"What's her problem?" Biggs snaps. "I've tried being patient with her knowing how bad her anxiety can get—and I don't fault her for that—but now she's *really* testing me."

"Don't worry. I put two and two together and played along. What I couldn't explain to Oaklyn, however . . ." He turns and stares at me.

My heart skips a beat.

Did she tell him that she heard a boy in my room last night?

". . . is why you'd think I'd make fun of you guys for thinking Dorian is hot," he says with a slight grin. "Dorian *is* hot."

I breathe easy again.

"Hey, losers."

I've never been more relieved to hear Goldie's voice insulting me than right now, as we turn our attention away from Oaklyn's nosiness.

"Biggs," Goldie says, approaching the purple table. Her eyes are darting between our table and Nora and Rex, who are standing likely within earshot. "In Fitness, I will give you my and Mavis's ideas for the Tether video you brought up yesterday. Is that cool?"

Biggs sees what she's doing. "Yeah, sure."

Goldie returns to her table.

"Huh?" Brady says, completely lost. "You were looking for Tether video ideas?"

"Yeah," I say, "don't you remember when we discussed it *last night*?"

He's still confused.

Biggs sighs. She glances at Nora and Rex to make sure they're caught up in their own conversation before leaning toward him and whispering, "Babe, we'll get updates from Goldie in Fitness about what she and Mavis discovered."

"*Oh.*" He nods.

"Speaking of last night," Jacob says, "let's discuss now."

"Right now?" Brady whispers nervously. "Isn't it risky with the Mentors being here?"

"Yes, but I'd argue the Art room is even riskier, given it's way smaller and quieter when everyone's working on their projects," Jacob says. "It'd be impossible for Oaklyn and the other Reds not to hear what we're saying."

"Agreed," Biggs says, "and for the record, I'm done communicating through bathroom vents from now on. I have standards."

I can tell Brady's still on edge. "It'll be okay," I say. "Let's just keep eating like normal, make sure we don't overreact to anything anyone says about what they saw, and"—I glance at Nora and Rex, who still feel too close for comfort—"maybe talk especially soft."

Jacob pulls apart his string cheese. "River, you go first."

I quickly mull over exactly what I should say and how I should say it. I can't tell them about the Orbeus because, assuming word won't get out about our office break-in, I'll be immediately blamed if Nora or Dr. Ridges were to catch wind of other participants knowing about its connection to our Disks.

"I mostly skimmed through boring contracts that didn't look noteworthy," I say, "except for a sheet explaining why the trials need to take place in high schools. Our Disks apparently don't work if we're not in a place that feels familiar to us and can be . . ." I try to remember the exact language I read, "quote, unquote, 'conducive to social bonding.'"

"They won't *work*?" Biggs yanks her head back in surprised confusion before remembering to keep it subtle. Her expression fades back to normal. "Why would it matter where we are physically for the Disks to monitor our brains?"

"If a place feels familiar, we're more likely to be comfortable there," Jacob says slowly, thinking aloud, "so maybe it's important that we're not overwhelmed or stressed for the Disks to be able to monitor our brain activity?"

I guess it makes sense that the Orbeus would be more likely to activate if I'm in a familiar, friendly place, although I'm not sure why the Disk wouldn't work at *all* if I'm not. People make friends in shitty places all the time. And a lot of kids who struggle socially wouldn't find school to be that welcoming a place. Something still isn't adding up.

Our table falls silent, as no one else has input on my discovery.

Biggs spoons some peanut butter on her final bites of apple. "What'd you discover, babe?" she asks Jacob.

"I found a bunch of paperwork on Neuro Scores," he says, looking at us. "Has anyone heard that term before?"

We shake our heads.

"The Neuro is what we wore during our A-Tests, right?" Brady asks.

"Yeah," Biggs says, "so the scores must have something to do with getting accepted into the trials."

"That's what it sounded like," Jacob says, nodding, "and the higher a participant's score, the more likely they're a good candidate. But the language was so scientific and dense, I can't be positive."

I notice that time is running short. "Biggs, what'd you find?"

"Okay, so . . ." she begins, "similar to your binder, River, there was a lot of paperwork that I did not have the time nor patience to sift through. But I found a section that pointed out which variables Affinity is testing in each of the sixty-five schools."

"Variables, like . . ." Brady trails off, unsure of what she means.

"Different factors that could affect the study's results," I answer.

"Holy *shit*," Jacob says, glancing at Nora and Rex, "I mean . . . that's cool." He gets quiet. "Big."

"What can I say," she continues, "my last name is fitting."

"I didn't consider the fact they could be studying something different at each school," I note, wondering how that's relevant to how the Disks operate in conjunction with our Orbeuses. If it's important that we're in a familiar place, could geographic location play a role as well?

Biggs reaches into her pocket and discreetly pulls out her notes. "Sorry for my shitty handwriting. I was trying to get it all down as fast as I could."

She checks to make sure the Mentors aren't looking, then pushes a sheet from her notebook into the middle of the table for us to see:

TEST SCHOOL   VARIABLE A   VARIABLE B
Teawood, MI circadian interruptions bereavement

"Bereavement?" Brady whispers, looking up from Biggs's notes.

I feel myself sinking into the floor as an awkward silence grips our table.

"It's like grief," Biggs says. Her eyes find mine and she smiles sadly. "It's what you experience after losing someone you loved."

37

RIVER

Before we have a chance to discuss *circadian interruptions* or *bereavement* more, Nora appears behind Brady. "How's my purple table doing?"

Brady jolts and his glass of orange juice spills everywhere. Biggs quickly scoops up her notes from the middle of the table before the liquid—or Nora's eyes—can get to them.

"I'm sorry!" Nora says, helping him dab at the spill with napkins. "I didn't mean to startle you."

For once, I'm grateful for Brady's clumsiness. By the time the mess is cleaned up, it's time for Fitness.

On my walk to the courtyard, I think through how everything could possibly be related—the Orbeuses and Disks, Mavis's daydreams and Brady's dream girl, Neuro Scores and the importance of our trials' location, circadian interruptions and bereavement. Could Dylan's death be the reason why Affinity wants to study Teawood kids—and, specifically, *me*?

When we arrive, Marcus and Ollie are firing water balloons at each other as the only Green and Blue willing to get wet on such a surprisingly chilly day. Brady, who probably feels guilty about Oaklyn feeling left out last night, goes out of his way to talk to her by the picnic table.

"Damn," a stunned Goldie mutters after Biggs updates her with what we discovered in Dr. Ridges's office. "Circadian interruptions . . . does that mean they're, like . . . fucking with our sleep?"

Biggs shrugs. "Maybe?"

"I've been sleeping great, though," Goldie says, examining her fingernails, "which is surprising, seeing as I'm in Mr. Wellingford's classroom. I basically have PTSD from flunking Algebra Two in there."

"Have you heard of any Greens, Reds, or Oranges who haven't been sleeping well?" I ask.

She thinks. "Not that I know of."

We fall silent.

"Then there's the bereavement thing, which feels . . ." Biggs pauses, her eyes darting between me and Goldie. ". . . pretty intentional."

"Right?" Goldie says, squinting in thought. "Like, if Affinity was looking for teenagers in mourning for a study, look no further than Teawood, Michigan."

She's not wrong, but Goldie's assertion still rubs me the wrong way. Because if that's the case, it feels like another outsider storming into town to exploit a local teen's death for their own gain. First it was Michigan's Department of Transportation, now it's Affinity Mind & Body.

Goldie's eyes open wide as she remembers something. "That might explain it, then . . ."

"What?" Biggs asks.

She steps closer to us. "I wanted Mavis to sign up for the trials, thinking she needed something to shake her out of her rut, but she didn't want to," Goldie explains. "I remember thinking Dr. Ridges seemed weirdly determined to get Mavis to take an A-Test after he found out Dylan was her ex. I just assumed he was an overeager salesman type, but this bereavement thing makes me wonder . . ."

"Why'd you sign up, by the way?" Biggs asks. "I don't think of you as someone who's struggling socially. I'm surprised you got in."

Goldie scoffs. "So am I, to be honest. I only did it to be supportive of Mavis."

I bet that's the reason why Affinity let Goldie in. Dr. Ridges had a hunch that accepting her into the trials would incentivize Mavis to come, too.

"What about you?" Biggs asks her. "What'd you and Mavis find in the office?"

"I didn't find jack shit," Goldie says before her eyes light up, "but Mavis did. On Dr. Ridges's tablet, she saw an open doc labeled 'Teawood,' and it had these bullet points. She said they read like a to-do list, or reminders. None of them stood out as important or telling, though, except for one, which said . . ." Goldie stares at the sky in thought before saying slowly, "'Big reveal final night of trials, no PF.'"

"'Big reveal final night of trials, no PF' . . . ?" Biggs repeats, turning to me. "What could PF stand for?"

I rack my brain. *PF . . .* "I have no idea."

"Well, whatever it means," Goldie says, looking between us, "it sounds like it'll be related to a *big reveal* tomorrow night—"

"Will you help me out here?" Marcus pleads to Goldie from across the courtyard, absolutely drenched. Another water balloon smashes into his head and a practically bone-dry Ollie cackles nearby, pleased with their aim.

Goldie rolls her eyes. "I guess I'll go freeze to death in the name of beating the Blues. For what it's worth, River"—she begins to back away—"Mavis really did want you to see what she's sketching in Art. That conversation may have been fake to you, but it was real to her. Top drawer at her workstation. Check it out." Goldie grins and takes off.

"Did Goldie Candles just smile at you—and it wasn't sarcasm?" Biggs says. "This study really *is* fucking with our heads."

It's a nice gesture, especially after the disorienting morning we've all had, but it makes me nervous heading to Art. What could Mavis be working on that would mean something to me?

As I walk to Mavis's workstation, I pass by Brady and get a glimpse of his canvas.

My jaw drops. "Brady." I pause. "This is amazing. Is this your . . . ?"

"Dream girl," he says, "yeah."

He may not be winning an art award anytime soon, but what his painting lacks in execution, it makes up for in adorableness. Brady's freckly dream girl, who looks about our age, is displayed front and center, her brown bob blowing in the breeze. Behind her in each quadrant of the canvas are various locations that I assume Brady visited with her in his dreams, like the bottom of a big waterfall and coastal beach town.

He doesn't appear that pleased with it anymore, though.

"What's wrong?" I ask.

He exhales. "My dreams with her have felt like . . . whatever the exact opposite is from the worst nightmare of your life. I feel like we've become legitimate . . . friends? I know that sounds bonkers."

I shake my head. "It doesn't."

"She feels like a sister to me," he says, "but it bums me out, now that I know this thing"—he points at his Disk—"probably created her. And she'll be gone once the trials are over."

He swallows, staring into her blue acrylic eyes.

"Hey," I whisper to him, "fuck these things." He looks at me as I point at my own Disk. "Who cares if these are somehow responsible for your dream girl? She's still in *your* brain; she lives in *your* mind." I nudge him with my shoulder. "Don't let Affinity take her away from you."

His lips slowly bend into a grin.

"Besides, this is fantastic, Brady," I say, realizing that one of the locations behind Dream Girl looks very familiar. "Wait, is this Teawood?"

He nods.

I laugh. "I Scream, Janet's Dry Cleaners, the Timber Wolf Cafe—" I pause, hating what I see next. "And Dylan's billboard."

It's a small and blurry rectangle in the distance—easy to miss if it hasn't seared itself into your mind like it has in mine. But it's unmistakably my grayscale friend, confirming, once again, just how much Billboard Dylan has become a staple in this town.

"Does that make you sad?" Brady asks.

I look at him. "I guess I have a different relationship with the billboard than most."

"Why?"

I almost skirt the question. But then I think about how open Brady was just now, talking about his dream girl, and I'm inspired to reciprocate the vulnerability. "I drive by Dylan's face every single day. It's hard."

"I bet."

"And I get that it's promoting safe driving—cool, that's great— but sometimes I wish I could just give my brain a break from the tragedy. You know?"

"Definitely."

"And on top of that, it's not . . ." I pause. "It's not really *him*. Right? The billboard's reduced him down into this statistic—this cautionary tale for teen drivers. And that's how we're choosing to remember him: the kid who screwed up and lost his life."

My heart sinks in my chest as I remember the last text I sent him. Because the screwup wasn't even entirely his fault.

My gaze shifts off the canvas and onto a teary-eyed Brady, who says, "I never thought about it like that."

"Neither did I," a voice says from behind me.

I turn in surprise and find Jacob. "Oh. Hey."

Jacob's eyes leave mine to scan Brady's painting. "That's a good point, River. A really good point." He slaps Brady on the back, propelling him forward, almost spilling his paints. "You should paint more, Brady. You're not half bad."

Jacob heads to the art supply area, but I stay rooted there in shock. I've been trying this whole time to find a way out of this and to get Jacob to understand my motivation behind spray-painting Dylan's mustache—and I did it on accident.

Part of me wishes I would've said all that out loud since the billboard first appeared. Because if Brady and Jacob had never thought about it from my perspective, I bet lots of others haven't, either. Maybe if I had put more faith in people and been upfront, they would've understood my "strange" or "inappropriate" reactions to their comments about Dylan and his billboard. Who knows? Maybe I never would've wanted to give the billboard a mustached upgrade in the first place.

I walk over to Mavis's corner, find her sketchbook in the drawer, and flip it open to a comic strip that makes my heart tighten.

She hasn't quite finished, but enough of it is completed for me to understand the story she's trying to tell.

The first scene is Mavis and Dylan smiling next to each other on Mavis's bed, her cat, Albert, curled up between them. The second is Mavis, Dylan, and Goldie happily licking scoops of ice cream together on the sidewalk outside I Scream. The third is dinner at her family's house with everyone gathered around, laughing, smiling, and stuffing their faces happily.

And in the fourth scene, there's Mavis, Dylan—

And me.

We're on a picnic blanket spread out in a grassy area of Mount Marigold. The sun is nearly set and we're staring up at the purply, starry sky above.

Only then do I realize she's titled the comic strip, too.

The Day I Wish We Had.

38

RIVER

Everyone stays hard at work during lunch theorizing how *bereavement* and *circadian interruptions* and *dream girls* could be woven into the purpose of the trials, but all I can think about is Mavis and her sketchbook. I want to go tell her how much I love the comic she's creating, and I hate that I'm not allowed to do it.

"River." Biggs's hushed voice brings me back to the purple table. "You still with us?"

"Yeah," I say, pretending I never left. "What's up?"

"Did any ideas come to mind on what the hell PF could stand for? Because I, for one, don't even like surprises when it comes to *birthdays*, let alone social science studies."

I shake my head and quickly get distracted again remembering each scene in *The Day I Wish We Had*. I wonder what life would be like right now if Dylan hadn't been overwhelmed with anxious thoughts that day. If he and Mavis never took that drive and stopped at the gas station. If Dylan never felt pressured to text me from behind the wheel.

I go to my Check-In feeling a lot of different things and blow through my survey without even paying attention to my own answers. Unsurprisingly, it doesn't seem to faze Nora, though, as she casually tosses the sheet of paper somewhere behind her desk—maybe even into the trash, like Brady's—and moves on.

"Day six of the trials," she says. "How are you?"

"Fine."

Ugh. I feel like I'm in first period with Mr. Babcock again.

"You sure?" she says, looking skeptical.

I nod. "Yeah."

She waits a moment. "Okay. Well, as always, you know I'm here if you'd like to talk about anything. In the meantime, I'd like to ask about the boy in your room last night."

I tense up. "Nash?"

"Yes," she says, "but Oaklyn doesn't know that. She mentioned she heard voices."

Damn it, Oaklyn.

"I'm sorry," I say. "She came to my door to check on me because I shouted when your brother tackled me in bed—"

"He what?"

"Oh, no, it wasn't anything like that." My cheeks get warm. "We were messing around."

"Messing around . . . in your bed?" One of her eyebrows arches upward.

I exhale. "Yeah, but it was . . . he was making a joke about—"

"Actually"—she cuts me off, raising her palm between us—"I don't need to know. In this room, I am *your* Mentor, not Nash's sister. I'll reference your chart later to see if any tackling or messing around that may or may not have happened made any difference to your Orbeus." She smiles.

My eyes drop to her desk awkwardly.

"I only bring it up to say," she continues, "you have to be careful, River. You know how important the rules are, and how big a deal it is that we're making an exception for you because of this . . ." She struggles to find the words. ". . . *extraordinary* connection you have with my brother. All right?"

I nod.

"Speaking of extraordinary connections," Nora says, keeping with her serious tone. Her eyes dance across her computer screen before shifting over to me. "When did you last speak to Mavis before the trials began?"

I tense up, not having expected the question. "Why?"

"I guess I hadn't realized just how abruptly your friendship . . . shifted after Dylan's death," she explains. "Was it difficult having her on the Blue Crew?"

I'm not sure how to respond.

Because of course it had been hard. The idea of spending a week together almost prevented me from signing up. But after our brief but meaningful interaction outside Dr. Ridges's office and then seeing her comic strip earlier, things feel different. Or, at the very least, I'm more hopeful than ever before that they *can* be different. Someday.

"I don't mean to be nosy, River, I swear," she continues. "I only ask to be helpful."

I take a deep breath. "We hadn't really talked since Dylan died."

"And why is that?"

"It's . . ." I struggle to find the right word. ". . . messy."

She nods slowly in thought. "River, can I ask a more personal question?"

I swallow hard. "Sure."

"Did you have feelings for Dylan?"

"Feelings . . ." I mutter, wanting her to clarify in case I misunderstood. "You mean, as in . . . did I like him more than a friend?"

"Yes."

I breathe in, feeling my skin tingling. Where did *that* come from? "Did I ever have feelings for Dylan . . ." I repeat the question just to fill the silence.

"It's possible I'm off base here," she says. "I know he was your best friend, and close friendships can appear like romantic ones, especially to an outsider—"

"No," I say quickly, as the question settles into my head. *Of course not.*

"Okay."

"I didn't like Dylan like that."

"All right. I believe you." She checks the time. "We have a few minutes left, if you'd like to go over your chart from—"

"Why would you ask me that?" I say, as her question becomes more and more puzzling. "We haven't talked about Dylan all that much."

Nora puts her elbows on her desk and leans in. "True, we haven't. But after analyzing your A-Test survey responses, learning more about the dynamics between you, Mavis, and Dylan, and knowing how strongly you've felt about the billboard . . ." She shrugs. "I just wondered if that was a possibility."

I try to absorb everything she's saying. I mean, I *did* feel the good kind of nervous that night in the gym together . . . and I have at times wondered about that kiss but . . .

"Why have you wondered?" I say. "What would it change if I *had* had feelings for Dylan?"

She sighs in thought. "It's possible the grief you're experiencing may be associated with something other than platonic love. And that disconnect may have contributed to some of the challenges you've faced this past year while grieving."

Is this part of the *bereavement* portion of the study? Why is she asking such an enormous question right here, right now, toward the end of my Check-In?

"The tears you cried during your A-Test," Nora continues, "the way in which you talk about him . . ." She trails off. "It makes me think there may be more at play there."

"Okay." I say.

It's all I *can* say.

"All I'm suggesting, River," she says, "is that if you haven't explored any feelings you might have had, maybe you should."

I've never been as lost for words as I am right now. Silence steamrolls the room, and this time, it flattens me.

"River?" Nora says, bringing me back.

"Yeah?"

She stares at me for a moment, concerned. "I said, we're about a minute over. Brady's waiting outside for his Check-In."

I jump out of my seat and head straight to the door.

"Are you sure you're all right?" she asks.

"Yes." I turn the doorknob and step out. "I'm fine."

39

RIVER

The rest of the afternoon passes by in a haze, as Nora's question continues to haunt my thoughts. I'm not sure why it's messing with me so badly. I've only ever thought of Dylan as a friend . . . *haven't I?* We never had that type of connection . . . *did we?*

Sure, I always thought he was handsome, but that was practically seen as objective truth at Teawood. Even the straightest straight guys on his basketball team would routinely joke about his hotness. Besides, there's a lot more to liking someone than looks alone.

And yeah, we'd nerd out over astronomy together, and constantly make each other laugh, and wanted to road-trip over the summer together before going to the same college, but . . .

Dylan didn't like guys. He liked Mavis.

And that reality was baked into our friendship's DNA since we met.

Wasn't it?

I'm relieved to not be alone with these thoughts any longer when Nash arrives after his practice. He's dressed in uncharacteristically warm clothing—a purple Ann Arbor Pioneer hoodie and thick blue sweatpants—and I'm reminded of how frigid Marcus looked getting blasted in the face with water balloons earlier.

He dumps his things on the floor with a smiley sigh. "Hey."

But he doesn't make a move to inflate his mattress. Instead,

Nash strides across the room, sits on the corner of my bed, and brings a bended knee up to rest on my comforter. I'm surprised at his boldness, but I'm not complaining about it.

"I just realized," he says, "this is our second to last night together. What are you going to do without me?"

"Be grateful I don't have to hear that air mattress get blown up every night." I grin.

He smiles back. "Touché."

"Your little stunt got me in trouble with your sister today, by the way."

"What?" He looks at me disbelievingly. "No. Why?" His eyes quickly travel up and down my exposed arms, which makes me feel tingly. "It didn't leave a bruise, did it?"

"Relax," I say with a laugh, "you're not *that* strong. Another participant who—"

"Participant?"

"Another girl in the trial who sleeps across the hall heard me yell when you body-slammed me. She came to see if I was all right and heard us talking outside the door."

"And then tattled?"

I nod.

"Well, first of all, I hardly *body-slammed* you," he says, "and secondly, I don't get it. Why is it such a big deal if other kids here know I'm sleeping in your room?"

"It's an Affinity rule. We're not supposed to interact with outsiders."

"I know that part, but I still don't get the reasoning behind it."

I shrug.

Of course it makes sense to keep the E-Wing a controlled environment without non-participants coming and going, complicating our Disk recordings. But I can't tell him that.

Nash slides off my bed and starts organizing his things. I lie flat on the mattress and stare up at the ceiling. It takes all of half a second of quiet for my mind to wander directly back to Nora's question about Dylan.

"So how many brothers and sisters do you have?" I ask, desperate to distract myself. I try to remember the various faces in the photos on her desk. "Is it just you and Nora?"

He laughs. "Why do I feel like I'm on a first date?"

I get embarrassed. "What do you mean? It's just a question."

"It's definitely a first-date type of question," he says with a shiver, cupping his hands over his mouth for a moment to keep them warm.

"Fine," I say. "I retract it. What *non*-first-date question would you like to answer?"

"I didn't say I mind feeling that way," he pushes back, eyes on his backpack as he sorts through clothes.

My stomach flips as he snags a pair of socks and pulls them over the ones he's already got on. That wasn't so much an indication as a bold declaration that, yes, Nash is into me. And from the somersaults my stomach is still doing, I can confidently say that, yes, I feel the same.

"But to answer your question, it's just me and Nora." He springs up and lands back on my bed. "Well, unless you count Ruthie. She's basically like another sibling."

"Your sister's friend?" I say. "Nora's mentioned her a few times."

"Yep," Nash says, climbing up to the head of the bed next to me. "But in terms of *blood*, my mom and dad got stuck with just me and Nora."

Now that he's mentioned her and since we've gotten closer, I think it's okay to voice my curiosity. "I remember you mentioning that you wanted to get away from her."

"Who?"

"Your mom."

His silence makes me think I overstepped.

"We don't have to talk about it," I say quickly.

"But we can," he says, adjusting the pillows behind his back. "Our relationship's gotten rocky lately. It's mostly related to football."

"Football." I joke, "Sorry, can't relate."

"I'm jealous you can't."

"Really?" I look at him, surprised. "You don't love the sport you're amazing at, Mr. All-American First-Team Gold-Medal Whatever Champion?"

He smiles. "No. Well, yes, I love the game. But I don't love all the bullshit that's come with it. And lately, there's been a lot more bullshit."

"What kind of bullshit?"

"Just . . . everything." He sighs. "The team politics, the college recruiters to impress, the grades I need to keep up, which stats I need to improve if I'm going to make *that* team or *that* one. I'll be a senior. I just want to have fun this year, but it's getting impossible. And now, my mom's gotten all swept up in the bullshit, too. She doesn't understand the pressure she puts me under—the perfection she's grown to expect out of me."

Nash rolls onto his side, facing me. I get goose bumps.

"I guess it's sort of my fault, too," he says.

"What is?"

"The change in our relationship," he says. "I've sort of enabled it, wanting to make her proud." He shrugs. "Oh well."

"You remind me of Dylan."

He beams unexpectedly. "Really?"

"Yeah." The words slipped out almost unconsciously, but I

pause to think about that. "Actually, yeah . . . you really do. Like, a *lot*."

There are several similarities—the space nerd stuff, the athleticism—but the parental pressure especially hits home. Because it weighed on Dylan through his last day.

I pause because Nora's question weasels its way into my mind again. Maybe it'd be good for me to talk it through, to help my mind make sense of my feelings.

Nash smirks.

"What?" I ask.

"I can see the wheels spinning in your head," he says. "What's getting tossed around up there?"

I take it as a sign.

"Your sister asked me a question earlier, and . . ." I pause and laugh, feeling like it's absurd to say aloud. "She asked if I'd had feelings for Dylan."

"Did you?" Nash asks, like he doesn't find it absurd at all.

"Um . . ."

"Or *do* you?"

"I mean . . . no?"

He grins. "You don't sound so sure."

"It's confusing," I admit, "because I loved Dylan—I still do—and I'll probably always be at least a little bit broken no matter what without him. Is it normal to feel that way about someone who was just a friend?"

Nash considers it. "I think so. Losing a friend can make you feel that way. . . . But so could losing the love of your life."

He scooches closer.

The tips of our noses are just a few inches apart.

"Can I be honest?" he says softly.

I gulp, nodding.

"I'm sort of with my sister on this," he says quietly. "And believe me, usually I'm not with my sister on anything."

I look at him skeptically. "You two didn't talk about this earlier, did you?"

He shakes his head.

"Swear?"

He raises his palm into the air. "I swear on all stars in the universe, no, we did not."

I breathe deep.

"I can't know for sure how you feel about him," Nash says. "Only you know that, but I do know what a person in love looks like, and it looks like you when you talk about him."

The strangest sensation starts to seep into my bones. "You think?"

"Yeah, I do."

My body slowly starts to feel both light as a feather and heavy as a boulder. I can't tell if my heart has stopped entirely or is beating faster than ever before. I'm completely terrified and totally at peace. I hate this feeling and I love it, too. All at once.

And even though I'm staring into Nash's eyes, feeling things for him, all I can think about is Dylan.

"Are you okay?" Nash asks, seeing the expression on my face.

I nod, feeling hot tears start to form.

The good kind of nervous. His fingers gliding across the piano. The way he trusted me. His crooked grin. His face when he looked up at the stars.

The kiss.

Our kiss.

The one he said was fake, but felt inexplicably real.

"Did I go too far?" he asks.

"Not at all." A stream starts to flow down my cheek. "I think maybe you're right. I think I was in love with Dylan Cooper."

He smiles. "Yeah?"

"Yeah."

"Well, I—"

I move forward and our mouths touch. My goose bumps spread far and wide. His lips, moving slowly against my own, shock my system, and it feels incredible. When we eventually pull apart, his deep brown eyes are staring directly into mine.

"Sorry," I say.

"Don't be."

"I don't know what that was."

"Well, whatever it was," he says, "I liked it."

He looks at me for a bit longer and then glances over at his air mattress, deflated sadly on the classroom floor. "I guess I better go to bed."

"Are you sure you won't get cold sleeping by yourself?" I say, surprised at my own boldness this time. "It's chilly out."

He smiles. "Guess I better stay put, then."

I sit up to adjust the blankets, making sure he has enough to stay covered, when I spot the old Polaroid camera lying next to the bed. I get excited and reach down to grab it.

"What do you got there?" he asks.

I straighten back up, and he sees what's in my hand.

"A camera? How'd you sneak that in here?"

"I didn't. It was left behind from the school year and apparently got past your sister." I grin. "I found it in the cupboard over there."

"Does it work?"

"Yeah."

"We can't *not* take advantage of the fact that the universe just randomly put a camera in your room, can we?"

My heart thuds. "I guess not."

We cozy up, and I lean to the side, my head gently bumping against his. I feel a subtle sensation between our temples and am reminded that my Disk is there, reading my Orbeus. I wonder what my yellow line is doing right now. Because I certainly have an affinity for Nash.

But it's an affinity that goes far beyond friendship.

I direct the lens at us and hold the camera at arm's length. Right before the Polaroid clicks, Nash turns in a flash, his lips pressed against my cheek.

I flip over and move toward Nash, small-spoon-style. I feel his heart thundering against my back and his minty, warm breath on my neck. His thick arm wraps around my side and pulls me closer with ease—as if I'm the weight of one of his footballs—and I find myself, for the first time since Jacob showed up on my doorstep, hating that the trials will be over the day after tomorrow.

40

DYLAN

"Dylan?" Mavis asks from the passenger seat.

"Huh?"

"Did you hear me?"

I glance at her quickly. "What?"

"Are you okay?"

. . . *Am* I? I'm really not sure.

I knew she was going to do it. *I* was planning on doing it most of the day. And yet, hearing the words *break up* leave her mouth still made my entire body go numb. I take a deep breath in and exhale slowly, keeping my eyes on the road and my hands at nine and three. I guess no matter how much I know this decision is best for both of us, nothing can prepare you for the moment it becomes a reality.

"Yes," I finally say, feeling the shock slowly dissipate. "I'm okay."

"And you . . ." Mavis says, "heard what I said. Right?"

"Yeah." I nod. "I did."

She hesitates. "You're not angry?"

I look at her. "I'm not."

There's a brief pause—the only noise is the rain splashing on my windshield—and then we both let out soft laughs that shatter the tension.

"I was so nervous," Mavis says, and the relief I hear in her voice backs her up. "I didn't want to hurt you. I didn't want to ruin our friendship."

Mavis wants to stay close.

Now *I'm* the relieved one. It's like someone lifted a hundred-pound weight off my shoulders that I hadn't even realized was there until now.

I reach over and rub her knee lovingly. "You didn't hurt me, and our friendship is definitely not ruined. But can I ask why?"

"Why I wanted to break up?"

I nod, preparing to tell her that I planned to break up today, too. I wonder if her rationale is the same as mine—that our romantic spark has faded, even though the love we have for each other hasn't diminished one bit.

"I mean . . ." She suddenly sounds nervous again, which throws me off. "I don't know . . ."

"What?"

"I don't know if that's a good idea."

I look between her and the road as I approach a four-way stop. "Why not?"

The quickest way back to Mavis's house is to turn right, but even with the roads becoming increasingly slick, this conversation warrants the scenic route.

So I drive straight.

She sighs. "I guess I just feel like . . ." She pauses. "Dylan, I'm not sure I should—"

"It's okay," I say softly. "You can tell me. I won't be mad. In fact, *I* planned on break—"

"I think River is in love with you," she says, "and I think you might be in love with him, too."

She might as well have dumped a bucket of ice water onto my head.

"What?" I mutter.

"I mean, that's not the main reason," she says quickly, seeing my face. "I feel like we've just drifted apart—at least as boyfriend and girlfriend. Don't you think? I told Goldie how long it's been since we've had sex and she was shocked—though why would you even care about what Goldie has to say? My point is . . ."

Mavis continues talking, but a ringing in my ear makes it impossible to keep up.

She thinks River is in love with me?

"Dylan?" she asks. "Are you all right?"

"I don't think River is in love with me," I blurt. "That's not . . . I don't think . . ."

There were moments earlier in the gym where I thought he might be flirting, sure. But his reaction to the kiss proved that I was mistaken, that I misread the situation.

Right?

"I see the way you two look at each other, Dylan," Mavis says softly, "the way you two just . . . *vibe*. I won't lie, I thought I saw sparks during the very first Astronomy Club meeting I brought you to."

Seriously? "Freshman year?"

She nods. "I thought I must've imagined it, though, and moved on. Throughout the past two years, though, I just . . . I don't know." She looks at me. "You're really telling me there's no *there* there? That I'm crazy?"

"I'm not saying you're crazy—"

My phone vibrates in the cupholder, accompanied by the *ding* that indicates an incoming text has arrived. I can't see who it's from because the screen is facing the passenger seat.

"Speak of the devil," Mavis says, eyeing the screen. "Wait . . ."

She reaches down and grabs my phone.

"It's River?" I ask.

She looks stunned.

"What is it?"

I turn at an intersection as the rain picks up. The drops are getting bigger, faster, and louder as they slam onto my hood.

"Mavis?"

She turns, her eyes filled with tears, and shows me what River just sent. My stomach plummets as I stare at what has to be the worst-timed message in the history of messages: the photo of us kissing in the gym, accompanied with his text:

To cheer you up after a crappy day.

"Oh." My throat runs dry. "Oh, *no*."

A tear escapes her eye. "Still want to call me crazy?"

41

RIVER

The trials will be over tomorrow.

By then, Headquarters will just be the band room again, I'll be wearing clothes that *aren't* navy blue, and Affinity will have taken off with thousands of hours of boring, cringey, eye-opening footage taken of twenty teens, of which at least fifteen minutes could be used against us in criminal court someday.

As dizzying and difficult as the past six days have been, I wouldn't take them back. I made new friends after having none all senior year; I'm hopeful now that me and Mavis can turn a new leaf; and I'm grateful I got to spend almost every night with the boy who made my yellow line spike.

Then, there's Dylan.

In a certain sense, I've never wanted to go back to last June 3rd more than I do this second, and the regret burns badly. Because I'd do things differently. I wouldn't have sent that last text, for one, but I also would've told Dylan how I really felt—that I was in love with him. Sure, I'm not naive—I know it's beyond wishful thinking to believe the feeling was mutual—but still. Saying the truth out loud would've meant something, and never being able to do it now feels like a scar of my own making that might not ever truly heal.

But even if I can't rewrite history, I can at least know my truth now. And for whatever reason, I know living in that honesty will make the regretting and scarring worth the pain.

Oh, and I guess it doesn't hurt that it's seeming increasingly likely that the whole town won't know I spray-painted Dylan's billboard.

I grab a muffin next to Jacob, who's deciding on a yogurt flavor at the food table.

"Good morning," I say, smiling at him. For once, he smiles back.

He sees my expression. "You're on cloud nine, huh?"

"What do you mean?"

He scans me from head to toe. "If I didn't know any better, I'd say you snuck a boy into your room last night."

I freeze. "Huh?"

Jacob's face twists in confusion. "It's a joke, dude."

"Oh." I laugh, and it comes out suspiciously loud, as my cheeks get warm.

"Hold on." He stares at me. "*Did* you sneak a boy into your room?"

I drop my chin at him, hoping it's believable. "Who would that boy even be? Marcus? Brady?"

He considers my point. "Fair."

I grab a banana and turn to head back to the purple table, but Jacob stops me.

"Hey, just so you know," he says quietly, "I'm calling off the stipend stuff we discussed."

I look at him. "Really?"

He nods, then grins. "You have my word."

I could cry.

"From what you said about the billboard with Brady in Art,"

he explains, "and I get it now. I can't say I would've done the same, but still. I get it."

Before I can stop myself, I fall forward and hug Jacob.

He laughs. "Way to be subtle, River."

I quickly break away from him. "Sorry."

We exchange smiles.

It's terrific to think I've avoided blowing up my future over some spray paint, but it's just as meaningful to have my rationale for doing it understood.

I start to walk off. "Now let's go listen to more of Biggs making fun of Brady's ludicrous ideas about what PF could stand for—"

"Actually, I'm going to eat over there today," Jacob says, nodding toward the table where Mavis is munching on toast. He seems smitten.

And I very much approve.

I return to the purple table. Unsurprisingly, Brady and Biggs are debating the trial variables assigned to Teawood.

"I'm telling you," Biggs emphasizes to him, her tone implying she's had to do so before, "*circadian* has nothing to do with those big bugs. You're thinking of *cicadas*, Brady."

He shakes his head, confused.

Biggs turns to me for backup, but I grin and stay silent.

It's not that I'm not curious about how circadian rhythms and bereavement could be related to our Orbeuses. But knowing all the good that's come out of the trials for me, I'm not sure what could be so nefarious or misleading that the past week wouldn't still be worth it.

"How come me and Brady are the only ones who want to figure out this bomb Affinity's about to drop on us tonight before our minds are blown to smithereens?" She gives me a look. "*You're* in a suspiciously good mood today."

"What can I say?" I shrug. "A full night of seamless circadian rhythms works wonders."

She rolls her eyes at my attempt at a sleeping joke. "Jacob and Mavis no longer give a fuck, either." Her eyes find their table. "Look at them over there on the verge of making little Marvel babies."

"*Ugh*, tell me about it," Goldie says, crashing down at our table with her food. "They'd probably come out looking like that freaky little tree bark character, too, what's his face?"

Biggs, Brady, and I stare, shocked to see her sit with us without being held at knifepoint.

"What?" she says. "Those two are having a moment, and I didn't want to spoil it." She looks between each of us. "Okay, so there's no room for a Green at the purple table. Point taken—"

"Not true," I say, eyeing Biggs and Brady.

"Of course there's room, babe," Biggs says, moving her tray to create space. "We'll just have to rethink the purple thing."

"What about . . . the gred-blue table?" Brady suggests. "Rebleen?"

Headquarters suddenly goes quiet, which gets our attention. I spot the source of everyone's surprise: Dr. Ridges, striding toward the front of Headquarters dressed in a mismatched tweed suit that aims to highlight every group: a navy jacket, green pants, red collared shirt, and orange tie. He may be trying to celebrate us, but most participants seem insulted by the monstrosity.

"What in the rainbow hell is that?" Biggs whispers at us.

"*Ew*," Goldie mutters.

Brady shrugs. "I kind of like it."

"Good morning to the delightful teenagers of Teawood, Michigan," he announces happily. "Congratulations on making it to the final full day of the Affinity Trials."

He holds for applause that doesn't come until Rex begins

clapping enthusiastically and the rest of the room joins in.

"By this time tomorrow, you'll have made history," he says, his eyes hopping around the room. "Although we have mountains of data to comb through in the months to come, from what little we know already, every participant in this room has, without question, helped Affinity create the future of friendship. And as a thank-you to you all, tonight we're—"

"—giving us our stipends early?" Biggs interjects loudly to a handful of laughs.

"Not quite. You'll still be given your stipends *tomorrow* while checking out. But you will be able to participate in the very first Affinity Ball."

Chatter breaks out throughout Headquarters.

"Yes, it's exactly what it sounds like," he continues over the talking. "The Mentors and I are throwing you all a dance as a token of our appreciation for your participation these past six days."

"But I'm a terrible dancer," Brady says, his face falling.

"This is going to be awkward," Biggs notes. "Think about it. There are only twenty of us. That's . . . a small-ass dance."

"Both of you need to look on the bright side, okay?" Goldie says. "After almost a week of nothing but navy, you'll get to—*wait*." Her hand shoots up. "A ball includes better clothes than these raggedy outfits, right?"

"You beat me to it, Ms. Candles," Dr. Ridges says. "I am over the moon to reveal that Affinity has provided each of you with special attire for tonight's festivities, which you'll find in your rooms after breakfast."

Headquarters fills with buzzing.

"Good," Goldie says to us, "unless by *special attire*, he means the trainwreck he's got on, in which case, I will not be participating."

"Did you hear that?" I ask Biggs.

"What?"

"He's over the moon to *reveal* tonight's plans," I say. "Is that the big bomb you were trying to sniff out? A surprise dance?"

She glares at me, then stares at Dr. Ridges, suspicious. "Something still feels off."

"Where's the ball happening?" Marcus asks from the other side of the room.

"In the gymnasium, after dinner," Dr. Ridges answers, "and it's going to be marvelous."

The gym.

Can I do this? On day one, there was no way. But a lot has changed since then. Before I can give it any more thought, the room fills with the grinding of chairs against the floor as breakfast comes to an end.

I'm about to head to our last Fitness with Biggs and Brady, but Nora intercepts me soon after entering the hall.

"Hi," she says, making sure we're far enough from the other participants to not be heard. "How are you feeling after our Check-In yesterday?"

I nod and smile. "I'm good."

"Yeah?"

"For sure."

"Because I threw you a curveball with my question about Dylan," she explains. "I never want to make you uncomfortable."

"It *did* make me uncomfortable," I say, "but . . . I don't think that's a bad thing anymore."

I'm filled with gratitude thinking about how much she shaped my week by introducing me to her brother and asking the tough but important question about Dylan.

Nora seems relieved and maybe even surprised to hear me say that. She nudges my arm lovingly and turns to leave.

Just as she does, I think to ask, "Hey, do you know if attending the ball is mandatory?"

"I'm not sure, but I can ask Dr. Ridges." She tries to read my face. "Why, what's up?"

"It sounds fun, but I'm drained," I lie. "I was thinking about getting to bed early tonight."

I don't know if I'll be ready or not to step foot in there later, but I'd at least appreciate having more of a choice.

Nora pauses. "I think the other Blues would be bummed not having you there." She smiles at me sadly. "I'll ask, but I hope you'll decide to be there regardless."

Later that day, I head to Nora's room when it's time for our final one-on-one session. There's a note on her door that reads *River, meet me in the courtyard for Check-In. It's nice outside!*, so I do. She's not there when I arrive, though. I wonder if she'll even remember to bring my survey today.

I hear the door open behind me and turn to see . . . "Mavis? I mean . . . hey."

Mavis looks equally confused. "Hi," she says. "What are you doing here?"

"Nora wanted us to have our final Check-In here. What are you doing here?"

Her expression melts into a knowing smile. "Jade told me there's an *urgent* Orange meeting happening in the courtyard."

"I see what they did here."

She looks around the empty courtyard. "I guess this means we're allowed to talk again?"

"I guess?" I rock back and forth on my toes. "So . . ."

She laughs. "So . . ."

It's not that there's nothing to talk about; there's *too* much to talk about. Even before the trials threw our lives into a blender together, we lost an entire year of our friendship.

Where to even begin?

"Can—"

"I—"

We both start talking at the same time, and I think even the nearby bush is cringing at us, it's so awkward.

"You go first," Mavis says.

"I was just going to ask about your daydreams," I say, "or whatever we're calling them. Have you had any more with me? Or with anyone, for that matter?"

"I haven't—that I'm aware of, at least. I think they only happened during Meditation, and Jade had me stop going to those once I joined Orange."

I pause. "It's all just . . . so bizarre."

She shakes her head, clearly still a bit shaken by it all. "Truly."

I can't imagine having multiple conversations in my Meditation room with Mavis only to discover after the fact that they never happened. A thought occurs to me. "What was I like?"

"What were you *like*?"

"Yeah. Was I just . . . me?" I ask. "But with a scar on my hand? Which, by the way, the science project we worked on together . . . what a throwback."

She grins. "Yeah, you were just you, but more than that? We were just us. The way we used to be."

I pause, unsure if I should say it, but go ahead anyway. "I miss us."

She grins. "So do I."

"I saw your comic strip," I say, "*The Day I Wish We Had.*"

She turns pink. "Thoughts?"

"I've teared up at least twice just thinking about it today," I reply, "so hopefully that gives you your answer."

"I wanted to create something about that day because I think about it a lot."

"Do you?"

"Yeah. You don't?"

I think. "Well, no. I avoided those memories because they felt too heavy. At least I used to. I've thought about that day a lot more than usual this week, though."

"Same." She stares past me in thought. "Did you know he saw Mr. Babcock every day?"

"For that college prep credit or whatever? Yeah."

She shakes her head. "That's what he told me, too. But he was there for counseling."

I cock my head, confused.

"I think he went there just to talk," she clarifies. "I think he needed help."

My heart shatters. "How do you know?"

"I saw some papers from Mr. Babcock he took home from school," she answers. "I never brought it up with him. I figured he'd tell me eventually, but he never did."

I feel my throat narrow.

Dylan didn't just need me on his last day, he needed me, *period*. I could tell something was wrong that day, something more than just Summer Sign-Ups stress, and . . . I wasn't there for him. Not like he needed me to be, at least. Instead, I just sent that text—a text he felt pressured to respond to, driving through a thunderstorm at night.

"I'm sorry, Mavis," I say, as my eyes well up.

"For what?"

"That night," I say, "for causing the accident."

She squints at me in confusion. "What are you talking about?"

"He knew I'd get annoyed being left on read," I say, "but I never would have wanted him to text me back while he was driving, especially in that bad of a storm—"

"River, Dylan wasn't texting you back."

I freeze. "What do you mean?"

"I mean, he wasn't texting you back." She looks at me like I've lost my mind. "Why would you think that?"

My head is spinning. "The timing lined up. I sent the text right before the accident happened. How do you know it *wasn't* me?"

Her eyes move away from mine. "Because I know who he was texting."

It's hard for me to compute what she's saying. It almost feels like a cruel joke.

"And even if it *had* been your text he was responding to," she adds, "it wouldn't have been your fault, River. It's no one's fault. It was a split-second accident that ended in tragedy."

I know she's right. I know that's how I should have been thinking about it all along. And yet . . . the guilt I've carried driving by the billboard each morning, thinking I played a role in his *drexting* death . . . the shame of holding on to a secret that I was too terrified to tell . . . This whole time, I've been thinking that person was *me*.

Who could it have been, then?

I'm not going to press her, though. She would've said who it was already if she wanted to, and I can tell by her tone she'd prefer to move on.

But then . . . I'm trying and failing to make sense of it all. "If you weren't angry at me for that, why didn't you talk to me all year?"

She gives me a knowing look. "C'mon, River."

"What?"

She stares.

I stare back.

We both wait for the other to crack, but I couldn't even if I wanted to. I have no idea what she's referring to.

"I know that you liked him, River," she says finally.

I feel my cheeks turning pink.

I didn't even know I was in love with Dylan then. How could she?

"And I found out he was cheating on me with you that night," she adds softly.

I almost let out a snort, thinking she's making some messed-up joke before realizing she's serious. "What?"

"That's why I wanted nothing to do with you," she continues, looking at the ground. "It made losing him a hundred times worse because I was so angry at him, and then in the blink of an eye, I'm waking up in a hospital room and he's just . . . gone." She clears her throat. "I couldn't focus all that rage on Dylan, so I took it all out on you."

I rub my forehead, unsure where to begin. "Mavis, I promise, he was *not* cheating on you with me. Why would you think that?"

"You don't have to lie," she says calmly, looking up at me. "Seriously. The two of you always made perfect sense. It was right in front of me the whole time. That's what I told him that night, too, when I broke up with him. I loved Dylan, but we weren't right for each other, at least as boyfriend and girl—"

"Hold on." Am *I* the one who's in a daydream imagining a conversation with Mavis now? "You told Dylan . . . what?"

"That I wanted to break up and that I thought you two were in love," she says matter-of-factly. "Was I wrong?"

My brain might explode.

I mean, *no*, she's not. Not entirely. But . . .

"You broke up with him that night?" I ask.

She nods. "In the car, a few minutes before it happened."

I realize my jaw is practically on the ground and close it. "Was he upset?"

"No," she says confidently, "he really wasn't. Not about that, at least. Honestly, my hunch has always been that he wanted to break up with me, too."

Why wouldn't he have told me?

Dylan and I shared everything. Or at least I thought we did. But I guess Jacob *was* right—maybe I wasn't as far along reading the book of Dylan as I thought I'd been.

"So . . . you think he liked guys?" I ask.

She shrugs. "I'm not sure. But I think he liked *you*."

That day starts swirling through my head again, talking on the phone together, eating under the chronically under-construction skylight . . .

"But we weren't . . . he wasn't . . ." I struggle to find the words.

"The photo you texted him," she says, as if I should know. "The night that he died?"

I think back. *Photo?*

"You really don't remember?" she asks. "The two of you *kissing* each other?"

I inhale sharply. "Oh, *that*? No. No, no, *no*." I laugh, because if I don't, I'll start to cry.

"We were taking pics together," I explain. "He pecked me on the lips as a joke, and the camera captured it perfectly. It was totally harmless."

But was it?

That kiss means a lot to me *now*, but it didn't at the time. And I've always assumed it was just a joke to Dylan, but talking to Mavis now, I'm not so sure.

She takes a breath. "Okay, well . . . thank you for telling me."

I open and close my mouth, expecting a fight—expecting

Mavis to need more evidence, more convincing. She spent the past year giving me the silent treatment, and all it took to squash the rage that's been simmering inside her was . . . *this*?

"That's it?" I ask.

"What do you mean?"

"You've wanted to kill me since last summer for thinking I was hiding some secret love affair with Dylan from you," I say, "and now you're fine? I feel like I'm missing something."

It looks like she's holding back a laugh; as if she knows something that I don't. "I believe you when you say the kiss was a joke, River, I really do. But even if it wasn't—"

"It was."

"—but even if it *wasn't* . . . that's okay." She laughs. "This week has helped put my grief into perspective, and I've learned a lot about myself, too. We both made Dylan happy—whether as friends or something more—and I'm grateful for the time we got to have him here, you know? I'm grateful you both had each other."

I step to the side and lean against the school's brick wall, trying to absorb it all. I'm exhausted by the revelations I just learned, the emotional highs and lows that came with each, and the unanswerable questions about that day and our friend that may never stop haunting me.

Mavis leans against the wall, too, and waits a beat.

"We should go back to Mount Marigold this summer one last time," she says quietly, "before we're off to college."

I look up from the grass and smile. "Deal."

She bends her neck and squints inside to see the hallway clock. "C'mon, Gaming starts soon, and I want to kick your ass in chess."

Mavis heads inside. I follow close behind carrying my flurry of feelings.

The relief I feel from knowing me and Mavis are good again has me tingling from head to toe, even if my thoughts and emotions have been swept up in a tornado that'll be spinning for some time. Yet, through all the noise, there's one thing she said to me that I keep coming back to: *I think he liked you.*

Could she be right? I couldn't recognize my own feelings for Dylan until now.

Maybe I couldn't see his for me, either.

Nora tries to keep things light in our final Group Talk, asking about family traditions and summer plans. The Blues mostly play along, even though I can tell none of us want to. Biggs remains fixated on the idea that something bad will happen tonight, Brady's melancholy over the possibility his dream girl won't visit him after the trials end, Oaklyn still seems distant after being left out of the office break-in, and that tornado of thoughts circling my brain keeps my attention far outside the four walls of Nora's room. Ollie seems to be the only carefree Blue, as they walk us through their vacation itinerary for Seattle.

After Group Talk, I head to my room much more convinced than I've been since last June that I can handle going inside the gym. Nora was right anyway; the others will be upset if I decide not to go.

I spot the garment bag provided to me by Dr. Ridges for tonight's festivities hanging near the board. I wasn't sure what to expect, but I'm shocked by how beautiful the items inside are— all of which, I should have known, are blue. My suit jacket and slacks are navy, and they pair well with an electric blue necktie that makes my eyes pop. I try everything on, and standing in front of a small, cloudy mirror nailed next to Ms. Benson's whiteboard, I'm relieved to see that everything fits great.

I toss my dirty clothes onto the floor. They land in a heap next to the Polaroid me and Nash took last night. I smile and then reach down and grab it so I can put it somewhere safe—

I freeze. A sickening sensation fills my gut.

Because it's not the same photo. I mean, I think it is—it has to be? But Nash isn't smiling at my side in bed, like he'd been when we snapped the pic. He's not in the photo at all.

42

RIVER

"River?"

I jump.

It's Nora's voice coming from outside my door. "Can I come in?"

"Uh . . ." I don't know what to do.

I feel like I've lost my mind. There I am on my bed in the photo, leaning over toward the exact empty spot where Nash had been next to me last night. How is this possible? Could someone be playing a prank on me?

"River?" she repeats.

I cram the Polaroid into the pocket of my suit pants and say, "Coming."

I swing open my door, and Nora steps inside. She's dressed in a long, lace dress the same navy hue as my suit, and wearing sparkly silver earrings and coral lipstick.

"So," she says, spinning in the doorway gleefully, "your Mentor cleans up nice, huh?" Once she completes a full twirl, her expression fades. "What's the matter?"

I remind myself to smile. "Nothing. Why?"

"You look white as a ghost."

Chill out. I can't say anything until I've thought this through.

"Maybe Affinity should let participants spend their Free Time outdoors next summer; then you won't have as many pasty participants," I jab playfully. "My turn."

I take Nora's lead and spin in place, too.

"Very dapper." She grins.

I think I've convinced her nothing's wrong.

"So," she asks, "how did *Check-In* go?"

"Huh?"

"Didn't you get a chance to talk to Mavis?"

"Oh, right." I close my eyes and nod. "It was great."

"Jade reported that Mavis had been feeling much more like herself after skipping out on Meditation," she says. "We thought you two would appreciate the chance to clear the air."

"You thought right," I say. "Thank you for arranging that."

Nora gives me a thumbs-up and walks toward the exit. But she turns back before disappearing into the hallway. "I'm glad you decided to come tonight, River."

Finally, she closes the door behind her.

I reach into my pocket and stare at the Polaroid again. The most rational explanation as to how Nash wouldn't be in the photo is if someone digitally cropped him out of it and filled in the background seamlessly—which isn't rational at all, given you can't digitally crop a *printed Polaroid*. This isn't a prank and it's not a misunderstanding.

My confusion slowly evolves into hurt. And then . . . rage. What the fuck is going on?

I feel bad for dismissing the other Blues' anxieties about tonight and failing to help them find answers. *What are they not telling us?*

I take a deep breath, remind myself to stay calm, and walk to Headquarters for the pre-dance dinner. I'd be amazed at how Affinity transformed our former band room, if only I wasn't distracted by what's in my pocket. The space is aglow in candlelight, with golden plates and silverware arranged atop each of the tables, now covered in white linen. It's like a mini Teawood prom on steroids already.

Every participant and Mentor are wearing shades of their respective color, each with a touch of personalized flare. Mavis is by the drinks in a glittery apricot skirt speaking to Ollie, who's in a button-up blue shirt and the highest high heels I've ever seen. Jacob is already seated, dressed handsomely in a maroon jacket and bowtie, the plate in front of him overflowing with gravy. I see Biggs in a strapless, steel-blue dress by the desserts and head straight toward her.

"*Babe*," she says with an impressed dropped jaw, seeing me approach, "you look *smoking* hot, for real—"

"I need to talk."

Her mouth snaps shut, sensing my urgency. "What's up?"

I touch her elbow gently and guide us a few steps farther away from the desserts to ensure no one can hear us.

"So, I took a pic of me and Nash last night while we were in bed together—"

Biggs holds her palm up to stop me, rattling her head in shock. "None of that made any sense. One, how'd you get a camera? Two, *Nash*? Who's Nash? And three . . . you're banging a boy named Nash during the trials?"

I exhale, stupidly having forgotten she has no idea what I'm talking about. "I'll tell you the details later, but one, I found it in a cupboard in my room; two, Nora's brother, Nash, is a football player at the camp; and, three, no, but he's been staying in my room." I glance around to make sure a Mentor isn't watching us and pull out the Polaroid.

She stares. "So?"

"Nash was in this photo last night," I say. "He was lying next to me."

Biggs's face wrinkles in confusion.

"Last night, Nora's brother was in this photo next to me, and now"—I point at the empty spot where he should be—"he isn't."

"River, can we talk?"

I yank the photo behind my back immediately at the sound of Oaklyn's voice. She's sneaked up to us wearing a sky-blue blouse, and carrying a plate of meatballs and a nervous expression on her face. "I need to confess that I told Nora about the boy's voice in your . . ." She sees that my arm is behind my back. "What's that?"

"Don't worry about it," Biggs says.

"You guys are hiding something from me again, aren't you?" Oaklyn asks, wounded.

"Again?" Biggs asks.

"I know the Blues were sneaking out without me." Oaklyn starts to spiral, tears welling in her eyes. "Why wasn't I included? Is this because I made things awkward in our first Group Talk? Because I've been apologizing to you ever since, River, and I feel terribly about it, but if you're going to hold this over my head for the rest of my life—"

"What's going on?" Jacob appears over Biggs's shoulder. "Is everything good?"

Our growing huddle is starting to attract attention, I notice, as Dorian and Rex take note of us in the corner. I remember the NDA I signed, and my insides crumple with nerves . . .

Fuck it. There *is* something bigger going on here—something *much* bigger.

Not getting in trouble over the billboard felt good, but telling the truth about it felt better. And I'd rather get put in handcuffs for exposing the trials' secrets than make it to Cascara next fall as an accomplice in Affinity's lies.

I turn to Jacob. "This football player, Nash, has been sleeping in my room the past several nights—"

"The quarterback?" he cuts in.

"Yes."

"I *knew* you weren't playing with me this morning."

"He's apparently Nora's brother," Biggs mutters.

Jacob side-eyes her. "Huh?"

"We took this pic last night in my room." I show it to Jacob. "And now, he's not in it."

Jacob studies the pic like it's a calculus exam as Ollie plops an elbow down on his shoulder casually. "What's good, Blues plus Jacob?"

"Do you guys understand what I'm telling you?" I say, getting flustered. "Affinity is screwing with me, and I don't understand how or why they're doing it. I took this photo last night with Nash, and while both me *and* him were in the pic when we took it—"

"Nash Mortimer?" Ollie cuts in, their eyes doubling in size. "Sorry, but you took a photo with *the* Nash Mortimer?" They lean in. "Do the Mentors know?"

"Mortimer?" I say. "What? No. Nash Mehta."

"Nora's brother," Biggs says.

Ollie looks between us, their excitement shifting to uncertainty. "Nora's brother's name is Nicholas."

I look around Headquarters, as more eyeballs find us.

Jacob looks between me and Biggs. "Nora's brother is at the camp, but that's definitely not Nash, the quarterback at Pioneer."

"That's Nash *Mortimer*," Ollie confirms, "white guy with a man bun?"

"We've gone over this—" I pause. "Wait, white guy with a man bun?"

Biggs turns to me slowly. "Babe," she says, concerned, "do you need to sit down?"

All of them stare at me.

I feel the blood draining from my face. I'm getting lightheaded.

"You all look so lovely," Nora says fake-breezily, finding a place to stand next to Oaklyn. "How are we doing?"

"Great," Biggs says, "but a question came up about the football camp. You told us your brother is participating, right?"

Nora stares at her. "Yes."

"What's his name?" Jacob asks.

Nora stays silent for a moment before turning to me. "River, let's go talk—"

"I think River would prefer to talk right here," a voice says over my shoulder. I glance backward and find Mavis. Goldie follows closely behind.

Nora gives me her normal, casual smile, but I sense a nervousness in her I've never spotted before. "I need to show you something," she says, spotting the photo in my hand like it explains something to her, "and I promise, it'll answer all your questions."

"No," I say, "answer our questions here."

The other Mentors appear at Nora's side.

"What's going on?" Rex says, pushing out his chest, which looks comical next to Dorian.

Nora dismisses the seriousness of the situation. "I have it under control, Rex—"

"*Do* you?" Goldie snaps. "This looks under control to you?"

Nora steps closer to me and lowers her voice. "I can explain everything to you"—she glances at the other participants—"I can explain everything to *all* of you, but I can't do it all at once." She smiles at me cautiously. "Let's go chat."

I think for a moment as the focus of the room lands entirely on me.

I swallow hard. "Okay."

"Are you sure?" Biggs asks me.

"Yeah." I try to seem chiller than I feel. "It's okay. I'll be right back."

"Yes, he will," Nora says. "Now go eat, everyone. There's enough food to feed an army and you'll want fuel for all the dancing to come!"

Nora leads me toward the door.

"Have you tried the macaroni salad?" Brady asks me as I pass by, a napkin tucked into his turquoise shirt collar. "Where are you going?"

Nora stays dead silent on the walk to her room, which is a first.

If Jacob and Ollie are correct, and Pioneer's all-star quarterback is a white guy with a man bun and the last name Mortimer, *who the hell have I been talking to?*

She opens the door to her room and invites me in.

"Get comfortable," she says, pointing to the seat in front of her desk.

I'd rather stand, but I can follow instructions if it means getting the answers faster.

Nora circles her desk and grabs her laptop. Before she takes a seat, however, she groans in disappointment. "I forgot something at Headquarters," she says. "Hold tight, I'll be right back."

She jogs out of the room and closes the door.

My foot raps the floor uncontrollably. I glance at the cameras in each corner watching me. A lot of bizarre things have happened the past six days, but this feels different.

I hear the door creak open behind me, and a low voice says, "Hi."

It's Nash.

My stomach bursts with nerves as I stand. "Hey."

He approaches me, noticeably more cautious than usual. "How are you?"

"Fine," I say, guarded. "You?"

He nods. "I'm okay."

We stare into each other's eyes.

"Do you . . ." He pauses. ". . . know what's going on?"

I wait a moment, unsure, before shaking my head. "What's your name?"

He snorts. "You don't know my name?"

"Is it Nash?" I say, my heartbeat drumming my rib cage. "Or Nicholas?"

He lowers his head but keeps his eyes locked on mine, as if I should know the answer. "River. C'mon."

"What?"

"I think you know."

"Well, I don't," I say, as my blood begins to boil, "so maybe you should tell me."

He crosses the classroom and sits atop the row of cupboards lining the wall beneath the windows. "You swear you don't know who I am?"

The door opens again. Oaklyn walks in, followed by Nora, who's carrying her open laptop against her forearms. An Affinity security guard joins them, too.

He closes the door behind him and stays put in front of the exit. It makes a shiver run down my spine.

"Why do we need him in here?" I say, pointing at the guard.

Nora ignores me and then flips a switch, prompting the classroom projector screen to slowly drop down in front of the board.

"I'd hoped to get the complete data set before presenting this to you tonight," Nora says. "That way, you'd be able to really see the difference you've made. It's a shame that my Blue Crew is too smart for their own good."

The screen lights up.

Tiny print at the very top reads:

Trial School: Teawood, Michigan, United States

Below that, on the left-hand side of the screen, are four photos stacked in a two-by-two grid of me, Mavis, Biggs, and Brady. Each one is accompanied by a few stats, including our ages, blood types, and the letter-number identifier given to us by Affinity.

On the right-hand side of the screen, intentionally separated from the rest of our photos, is a pic of Oaklyn that looks like an actor's headshot. Instead of an accompanying profile noting the same stats, though, a simple line of copy reads: *Trial Artist.*

"What's going on?" I say, as I struggle to steady my breath.

"Hey," Nash says, sliding off the cupboard and walking up behind me. His hand lands on my shoulder. "Everything's going to be fine, I promise."

"Oaklyn?" I say, looking at her for either comfort or answers, I'm not sure which. But she avoids looking at me.

"Her name isn't Oaklyn," Nora says. "This is difficult to tell you, River, and it'll be even more difficult to hear, but I want to reiterate how deeply I care about you, your health, and your future." Her voice gets softer. "From the moment I saw you during your A-Test, that has, and will always be, my first priority, and I hope that what I'm about to show you highlights how instrumental you and the Blues have been to our research this past week."

Nora pauses with her eyes closed and takes a deep breath.

"Nash Mehta is every bit as real as you and me," she continues. "He just doesn't exist in the same *way* as you and me."

Nora taps at her computer, and I feel the hand on my shoulder vanish.

43

RIVER

I whip around. Nash isn't there.

But the security guard is still standing at the door. Nash couldn't have sneaked by him that quickly. I look to my right, bending to see behind Nora's desk, then duck down to see beneath her bed. He isn't there.

Nash is gone.

"He doesn't exist physically, River," Nora emphasizes. "Nash exists solely in your mind."

I close my eyes and rub my temples, feeling the Disk beneath my fingertip on one side. "I don't understand."

"I know this is challenging," Nora continues, "but if you give me the chance—"

"He doesn't exist physically . . ." I say. "What is that supposed to mean?"

"I promise," she says calmly, "I can explain everything—"

"You keep saying that," I say, trying to rip the Disk off, but it won't peel away, "yet all I'm becoming is more confused."

"Please don't do that with your Disk," Nora says. "We apply a treatment to your skin first—"

"I saw him, though," I argue. "I felt him. I *kissed* him."

"You're correct," Nora says calmly. "You did all of those things."

"Then where is he?"

"You did all of those things, but with the Nash that exists in your *head*, River."

I stare at her. This can't be real.

Am I having a vivid dream, like one of Brady's?

"It wasn't just me, though," I say, thinking back throughout the week. "Nash was in the locker room the first night of the trials, interacting with his teammates."

"Yes, he was. And I'm sure they did."

"So how can *he*"—I point at the photo of Nora, Nash, and Ruthie on her desk—"be imaginary?"

She sighs sadly, contemplating, before crossing the room. She takes the back off the frame, takes out the photo, and hands it to me. I couldn't tell from the way it was cropped behind the glass that it was published in a newspaper.

"I wasn't lying when I told you that my brother is a football player at the camp this week," she says, "but his name is Nicholas Mehta. Not Nash." She nods at the clipping, encouraging me to look.

I read the caption below the photo:

Ruthie Hook, 15, pictured above with friends Nora Mehta (15) and Nicholas Mehta (10), was one of the eight victims in Tuesday's crash on Interstate 90.

"Why would he tell me his name is Nash, then?" I pause and look up.

Nora stares at me pitifully. "My brother didn't tell you that, River. *You* chose the name Nash for your Perfect Friend."

"But . . . what?"

"You met Nicholas in the locker room on night one," she confirms, "but you haven't seen him since. Every night, you've talked to *Nash* in your room. He's your Perfect Friend."

I still don't understand. "What do you mean, my Perfect Friend?"

Perfect Friend. PF.

So if the note Mavis read on Dr. Ridges's tablet is correct—*big reveal final night of trials, no PF*—I wasn't supposed to see Nash tonight?

Nora takes a step closer to me, but I lean away.

"What I told you about your Orbeus was only somewhat accurate," she says. "That is what we're studying, but when I showed you the data on your yellow line, it wasn't spiking because Nash showed friendship potential. It spiked because that's when I turned on your Disk—or, as Affinity will call them when they go to market someday, your Perfect Friend Patch."

I run my fingers over the Disk again, wishing more than ever that I could rip it off. "So what the hell does a *Perfect Friend Patch* do?"

"It does exactly what the name implies," she says. "It creates a friend, perfected and personalized just for *you*, River." She lights up. "Think about it! Think about how quickly you bonded with Nash."

"But I thought Nash isn't *real*."

"He's real to you, isn't he? I could see in real time how you lit up talking about him, how happy he made you when I'd turn on your Perfect Friend Patch each night at 9 p.m. and he'd appear to you in your room."

"I thought the cameras weren't livestreamed."

"*These* cameras weren't," she says, pointing at the ones in her room. "In fact, these cameras aren't recording, just like every other camera in the E-Wing, except for the ones in your room, Biggs's room, Brady's room, and Mavis's Meditation room." She pauses. "In other words, the cameras we needed to document each of you when your Perfect Friend Patches were activated."

Anger simmers in my stomach. "I can't believe how much I was lied to."

"Only in the short-term," Nora says quickly. "Affinity had plans to tell you *all* of this, once our ducks are in order."

"I still don't understand why my Perfect Friend is your brother," I say. "Why would you choose Nicholas?"

"I didn't choose *anyone* as your Perfect Friend," she says. "You did, River. Your brain created Nash Mehta. Isn't that incredible?"

"No."

"*That's* why these trials are so critical," she barrels on, "That's why you've helped make history this week. We needed to learn how the patches would work on real people, not just run hypothetical models using our software."

I want to throw her computer at the wall. "So to you, I'm just like Dylan on the billboard, huh," I say, seething, "put here to be your lesson?"

"Would it be helpful to ask me some questions?"

"Sure," I say. "Can you repeat the part about how your brother"—I start to shout—"*ended up as my imaginary friend for a week*?"

She sighs, then pauses for a bit as silence dwarfs the room. "Certainly I can." She wants me to cool off, I can tell. "The first night, we turned on your PF Patch at nine—the time yours was scheduled to activate each day. But when we went to see how you were responding via the cameras in your room, we realized that you were still in the locker room and promptly turned it off. Your Patch was only activated for a few seconds. But your interaction with my *real* brother, Nicholas, left an impression on you, apparently. And that's why your brain used him—or his physical body, at least—to create the basis of your Perfect Friend."

I think back to that night.

"No," I mutter, "I didn't see Nash—er, *Nicholas*." I stare at Nora. "I saw Dylan."

Nora's eyes widen. "What do you mean?"

"I saw Dylan," I repeat, "for a second or two. Then he was gone."

Nora can hardly contain her excitement. "That's remarkable, River. It further strengthens my hypothesis about the potential of the Patch when used in the right circumstances."

"What's your hypothesis?"

"That the PF Patch can go beyond just creating a Perfect Friend," she says. "It can replicate your *best* friend."

My chest tightens.

I knew that Dylan sighting was different from the ones that came before it.

"Your mind must've known that it couldn't be Dylan," Nora says. "No, that'd be impossible. Dylan is gone, so that couldn't be true. But your Orbeus was still stimulated when you ran into Nicholas immediately afterward, and something must've . . . *clicked*." Nora's practically salivating. "Your brain created your Perfect Friend in my brother's image and gave him the name Nash." She looks at the floor in thought. "Though that part, I haven't pieced together yet."

"My dad . . ." I mutter under my breath.

Nash was the only camper's name I knew going into the trials.

I look at Oaklyn—or the person who I *thought* was Oaklyn. "You heard him, though. How could he be imaginary? You told on me for having a boy in my room."

"Cassie did not," Nora says.

"Cassie?"

"Cassie, along with the Mentors you believe to be Rex, Jade, and Dorian, are actors that were hired by Affinity to assist me and Dr. Ridges with the experiment."

What?

"I only heard your shout that night," Cassie adds in a noticeably different voice. "I didn't hear Nash because . . . well, Nash doesn't exist. To *me*, at least."

Oaklyn was an Affinity plant *this whole time*?

Rex, Jade, and Dorian are actors, too?

"If you'd like to move the spotlight off yourself," Nora says, sensing how overwhelmed I am, "I can zoom out a bit on the big picture, and explain how the Perfect Friend Patches worked with the other three Blues, too."

I just stand there, speechless, and she takes my silence as approval.

"Affinity wanted to test our Disks with a number of variables at our trial schools this summer. The two that we decided to test at Teawood were circadian interruptions and bereavement."

Nora turns to the screen.

"Dr. Ridges and myself looked for participants who, as you know, were struggling socially, but here at Teawood, we also wanted students who've been grappling with recent loss to see if they might be more or less suited for using the patch. The four of you"—she points to the photos of me, Biggs, Brady, and Mavis— "proved to be prime candidates, based on the survey and your Neuro Scores computed during your A-Tests. Additionally, we wanted to see if our Disks would perform similarly based on the time of day, or interruptions to your circadian rhythm."

She glides her finger across the trackpad of her laptop and clicks on Brady's photo. An image of his Art painting appears next to an obituary photo of an elderly woman—an elderly woman who looks like an older version of . . .

"His dream girl?"

"Brady's patch was activated in the dead of the night," Nora explains. "After a rough first day—we think his brain was adjusting to the Orbeus's initial stimulation—his patch worked stunningly well. It created a peer version—not an *identical* version, interestingly—of his grandmother, who recently passed away. As Brady described in his A-Test survey, he considered his grandma his best friend—a fact kids teased him about at school. So, although he knew the girl in his dreams reminded him of his grandma, he was cautious to tell that to any of the other participants, fearing he'd be bullied once again."

It feels like an invisible hand rips my heartstrings out of my chest, thinking about how happy Brady looked during breakfasts and how sad when he started to suspect it wasn't real.

"As Brady told me during his Check-Ins," Nora says, "the two had adventurous dreams of traveling the world together, so by activating the patch during his sleep, he was able to live out these fantasies in a much realer way. Then we have candidate D2."

The photos of Brady's grandma and the painting shrink, replaced by two side-by-side screengrabs: one of Biggs's Tether profile and one of a user named—

"Frankie," I say, remembering the Tether friend she's often mentioned.

In her profile photo, Frankie has bouncy black curls, purple glasses, and hot pink lipstick that pops off the screen.

"As we learned in her A-Test, Frankie became Biggs's first Tether friend in 2021, and the two had become best friends, inseparable for years. They bonded over their shared love of art and music, and their passion for wanting to change the beauty industry for the better," Nora explains. "Despite her outgoing personality, Biggs expressed challenges meeting friends offline, but could easily develop meaningful friendships on the platform. That's why she's been devastated ever since Frankie disappeared."

"Disappeared?" Biggs never said anything about that.

Nora moves the mouse to the *last online* figure on Frankie's profile, which reads *four months ago.*

"Frankie stopped communicating with her for no apparent reason, but Biggs got confirmation from other Tether users that Frankie's okay. The abrupt ending to their friendship with no sense of closure has been extremely difficult for Biggs to process. She compared the pain to a death in the family on her test."

Biggs.

I had no idea.

"We were interested to see how a participant like Biggs, whose friendships have been almost exclusively virtual, would create a Perfect Friend after experiencing a loss like Frankie," Nora continues. "Incredibly, Biggs's patch brought Frankie back to life."

"How?"

"We activated Biggs's patch in the mornings, between your wake-up knocks and breakfast," Nora explains. "Unbelievably, Biggs's patch created the existence of a smartphone, on which the only app was Tether. Immediately, Frankie—or the Perfect Friend version of Frankie—messaged her apologizing."

This is so cruel.

So, so cruel.

"Much like I had to justify bending the rules for you, River, so that you'd understand why Nash could visit your room each night, once we discovered Biggs's patch had generated a phone, we had to justify why another Affinity rule could be broken."

"Biggs is an influencer," I say to myself, "so she'd need the phone for work."

"*Exactly.*" Nora smiles. "She'd lose out on business opportunities for lacking access to her account. How cruel would we be for forcing that? I told Biggs that I'd slip the phone under her door each morning after my knock so she could tend to her business for exactly one hour. Then, she'd have to leave it under her bed when she left for breakfast, and never tell another participant."

My heart hurts for Biggs, too, remembering the times she brought up Frankie with a smile on her face and told us about the good video ideas they'd brainstormed together.

Nora glides her fingertip across the keypad—the Tether screen-grabs disappear—and clicks on Mavis's profile. A video fills the screen.

I seize up, anticipating what's to come.

"Candidate D1," Nora says with a sigh, glancing anxiously at me. "Mavis Meyers."

It takes me a moment to realize what the video footage is: Mavis's Meditation room.

"As you may have guessed by now," Nora says, "Mavis's patch successfully created her own Perfect Friend, and . . . well, her Perfect Friend is *you*, River."

I feel a tear leak down my cheek before realizing that I'm crying.

"How wonderful is that to know?" Nora asks softly, her voice cracking with her own emotion. "Of the infinite people her mind could have generated, it brought back to life her own past friend-ship with you."

Nora taps at her computer, and the video on the screen begins to play.

Mavis is standing alone in her Meditation room.

"Among the many things Mavis and Perfect Friend You dis-cussed," Nora explains, "there were several mentions of Mount Marigold—if I'm remembering correctly, you also included that in one of your A-Test survey responses, right?—and, of course, Dylan Cooper."

Nothing happens in the video for a while as Mavis stares at the wall smiling. Then she cracks up laughing, and laughing *hard*—the type of deep belly laughs I remember from our middle school days. She raises her hands and hugs the air—

As if I'm in the room with her.

"Please, stop," I say, looking away from the screen. "Turn it off."

"But don't you want to—"

"*No.*"

The video fades, and the screen returns to the images of the four of us.

I wipe my eyes with the sleeve of my suit coat.

"I understand that is a lot to take in," Nora says softly. "If you need a moment—"

"What about the sixteen other participants?" I ask sternly. "*Fifteen*, I guess, considering Fake Oaklyn here is a bullshitter. Who was Goldie's Perfect Friend? Jacob's? Ollie's?"

"They didn't have Perfect Friends, River."

I squint in confusion.

"Their Disks are props—replicas designed to look and feel identical to the four Blues," Nora says. "We weren't interested in studying Goldie's brain activity, or Jacob's, or Ollie's—although I'm sure we'll be able to expand our testing pool in the future." She reaches out to touch my shoulder.

But I move away. "Why include the fifteen others in the trial at all, though?" I ask. "If their patches were just props, what's the point?"

She looks at me as if disappointed. "*Tsk, tsk*, River. If you're planning to study medicine someday, you have to know that every study needs a control group," she says. "The Greens, Reds, and Oranges were ours."

The security guard's radio crackles to life, and a woman's voice starts to speak through it: "Tim, alert Mehta. We have participants becoming increasingly unruly and demanding to see D3. Mentors and Ridges are failing to contain the situation; escalation likely."

My chest swells with pride.

Nora nods at the security guard, who then replies into the radio, "Roger that."

"River," she says, drawing my attention back to her, "even among the three other Blues, I have to say, your Perfect Friend was unique."

She's speaking faster, with more urgency. I can tell she's anxious about the *unruly* participants.

"How so?"

"We only activated each of your patches for an hour each day," she explains. "That way, we could have much more control of your environment and ensure your safety. However, I could tell, both by your interactions on film and how you spoke about Nash, that your friendship with him was rapidly . . . evolving. So I decided to increase your activation period the last couple days."

That must be news to Fake Oaklyn, as I notice her face scrunch in surprise.

"What do you mean?" I ask.

"Think about it," Nora says gleefully. "The first day with Nash, you weren't a huge fan, right? But the more time you spent with him, the faster and more beautifully his personality aligned with someone else you know, didn't it?"

"Were you supposed to do that?" Fake Oaklyn whispers at her. "I thought Dr. Ridges said it was a super strict rule mandated by Affinity that patch activations couldn't exceed—"

"Who did Nash remind you of, River?" Nora ignores her.

I stay silent.

"Nash's athleticism," Nora continues, "his love for astronomy . . ."

His complicated relationship with a parent, the kindness in his eyes . . .

"Dylan."

She nods tearfully.

The security guard's radio explodes: "Tim," the woman on the other end says, panicked, as the sounds of footsteps and shouting fill the background, "participants have exited Headquarters. They're headed your way looking for D3."

The security guard turns toward the door and locks it.

"It was clear to me that you were falling for Nash as more than a friend," Nora continues hastily, "which is why I asked if you had feelings for Dylan. Your Perfect Friend was bringing back not just your best friend, but your best friend in a different *body*, and thus a different context. Befriending Nash allowed you to see that you'd fallen in love with Dylan, River."

I hear Jacob's, Biggs's, and Mavis's voices louder in the hallway. They're calling for me.

"Think about the opportunity we have before us, River," Nora barges on as if the trials aren't spinning out of control outside her room. "Think about what it could mean for the millions of people who would benefit from having a Perfect Friend to cope with heartbreak—platonic, romantic, or otherwise. Think about what it could mean for you and Dylan." A tear falls from her eye. "Think about what it could mean for me and Ruthie . . ."

The second half of the newspaper caption registers in a way it hadn't before. *One of the eight victims in Tuesday's crash on Interstate 90 . . .* No wonder Nora knew what to say to me during my A-Test. She understands the grief I feel because she's felt it herself.

"Babe!" Biggs starts pounding on the door. "Are you in there?"

"Hey, yes!" I shout back.

I hear Brady and Goldie join the other three outside as they all demand to be let in.

"Listen to me, River," Nora interrupts. I look to her. "I know

part of you hates me right now. *I'd* hate me right now, too. But . . .
I think I can bring back Dylan for you." She pauses. "Not Nash.
Dylan."

Fake Oaklyn's jaw drops. "Uh, Nora? Are you sure you're
allowed to—"

"What the hell is going on here?" Another voice joins the chorus outside.

It's Harry.

"Mehta," the security guard says with a worried expression on
his face, "that custodian is here, and he probably has keys."

Nora ignores him. "I'd like to do one last experiment with you,
River. I'd like to take you to the gym."

I swallow. "What?"

"I know it will be a challenge for you, given how much the gym
reminds you of Dylan," Nora says. "I'm assuming that's why you
had reservations about going to the ball tonight. But that fear is
exactly why it could be the ideal place to facilitate the return of
Dylan as your Perfect Friend."

The importance of the trials' location.

I recall what I read in Dr. Ridges's binder; the Patch tends to
work better if the participant is in a familiar place. What place feels
more like Dylan than the gym?

"Nora, I don't want to speak out of turn"—Fake Oaklyn steps
in, the worry on her face becoming more dire—"but that sounds
like it violates the safety precautions. Does Affinity know what
you're planning to—"

"The patch failed to bring him back after the first night, in the
locker room," Nora talks over her like she's not even there, "but
now that your mind is aware of its potential and understands how
it works, I think it could be open—not to seeing *Dylan*, of course,
but to seeing your *Perfect Friend* Dylan, if we—"

The door bursts open, and the first person I see is Harry with one of his keys in the door. The security guard nearly gets trampled as a wave of participants pours in, led by Biggs, Jacob, Mavis, and Brady.

Brady spots Fake Oaklyn. "We didn't know where you went!"

"Are you okay?" Mavis asks me breathlessly.

"Yes," I say, although I'm not so sure. "It's okay, I—"

"What's all this?" Jacob says, looking past me.

Their focus immediately flips from my safety to the screen.

Before I can attempt to explain, Dr. Ridges arrives, struggling awkwardly to squeeze his way in through the doorway.

"Please, everyone," Dr. Ridges pants, his cheeks beet red and his glasses nearly entirely covered in smudges, "let's head back to Headquarters!"

"That ship has sailed," Goldie says, adjusting the straps of her dress before looking toward the board. "Why isn't Oaklyn one of the Ds up there?"

Brady raises his hand politely, as if he hadn't just wrestled past a security guard to get in here. "Nora, would you mind explaining why my photo is there?"

"Me too, while you're at it," Biggs snaps. "Wait . . ." She looks at Fake Oaklyn suspiciously. "What's a *trial artist*?"

The room devolves into further mayhem as more participants and the other Mentors arrive. Dr. Ridges keeps failing to corral participants to go back to Headquarters, Fake Oaklyn is refusing to respond to the barrage of questions, which only further infuriates everyone asking her, and Goldie and Marcus are demanding to see "the slide with the Greens!"

Nora floats closer to me without anyone noticing. "What do you say, River?"

I almost snap at her, insulted that she'd still want to follow through on her plan—a plan that, as Fake Oaklyn made crystal clear, breaks Affinity's own safety rules. But then I think about seeing Dylan in the locker room and, even in just the blink of an eye, how real he looked. How *alive* he seemed. Will I ever get an opportunity like this again?

Another chance at first love?

"Okay," I say, my stomach filling with nerves, "let's go to the gym. I want to see Dylan."

44

DYLAN

Fuck.

I can't believe this is happening.

"That's a very misleading picture, Mavis," I plead with her. "Seriously."

"Is it?" she says, sniffling and wiping her eyes. "Because it seems pretty straightforward to me. My best friend and boyfriend, kissing in the sunset."

My insides are completely tied in knots. "I'm sorry. I can call River right now, if you want—"

"No."

"He'll tell you exactly the same thing as I'm telling you! It was supposed to be funny—"

"No." She pauses, glancing out the window. "Wait, why are we all the way out here?"

"You wanted to talk," I say, my eyes bouncing between the road and passenger seat, "so I decided to take the longer way home."

"Can you go the *shortest* way now?" Mavis asks. "And please slow down."

"Sorry, I know," I say, feeling completely gutted and taking my foot off the gas. "You're buckled up, right?"

"Yeah. Are you?"

Thunder blasts above us, and another bolt of lightning

illuminates the drenched black pavement cutting through the woods ahead.

My phone *dings*, letting me know another text has arrived. I glance down.

It's River again.

Mavis just stares out the window at the black tree trunks and limbs passing us in the darkness, too done with me to care.

I quickly read what he wrote:

Did you guys make it to mavis's house? THIS STORM IS NUTS. please text back!!

Fuck.

Not wanting River to worry, I try to text back with one hand while the other is on the wheel. But the car veers just slightly enough that Mavis notices.

"*Dylan*," she says, "will you please not text right now?"

I sigh, setting my phone down at my side as I make a turn. Incredibly, the rain picks up even more—it feels like an entire ocean is getting dumped onto southeast Michigan, I swear—as gusts of wind keep shoving my car toward the shoulder.

I take my foot off the gas when another text arrives.

I glance at my phone, expecting to see another message from River or my dad, concerned I'm not back yet as the storm worsens.

"*Shit*," I breathe.

"Who is it now?"

Mavis glances at the phone. "Jacob?" She looks at me. "Jacob Lewis?"

This cannot be happening.

"Why is he texting you?" she asks.

I think fast and decide on a white lie. "It's just for a Student Council thing."

"Jacob is in Student Council?"

No, he's not.

But he did ask to pick my brain on starting a comics club at school. We got to talking, and I found out his uncle's friend teaches the summer graphic novel course Mavis has been wanting to take. I thought I'd surprise her by paying for the class.

Jacob said he could sign her up using his family's discount code—the price of the course would drop five hundred bucks to three grand—but he'd just need to know the dates she'd take the course by June third. *Today.* I grab my phone to respond, knowing that if I don't do it now and then forget later, I'll never forgive myself.

"A Student Council text can't wait another five minutes?"

"I'm sorry," I say, my fingers tapping my phone as quickly as possible. I squint at the windshield, then my screen. "I know it doesn't sound important, but it—"

"*Dylan!—*"

45

RIVER

I don't think anyone notices us leave amid the chaos.

"How are you feeling?" Nora asks as she walks next to me, laptop in hand.

I don't respond. I'm not sure how I should feel about the spoonfuls of betrayal she fed me each day of the trials. But more critically, I'm grappling with the gravity of what might happen in just a few moments in the gym.

"Thanks for trusting me," Nora says, still misty-eyed with emotion, as the taps of her heels and my dress shoes echo down the hallways eerily. "I'm still the Nora you met during your A-Test, you know. I get what you're feeling. And I want what's best for you."

We arrive. My chest tightens as I look in through the square glass window toward the hardwood. The gym's been decorated for the dance, with a handful of small tables surrounded by chairs spaced out across the basketball court that I haven't set eyes on since our last night together over a year ago.

I get goose bumps and look away.

"Still doing okay?" Nora asks me.

I swallow hard. I'm definitely not.

But the possibility of seeing Dylan again—a living, breathing, smiling version of him, at least—is far more important than the nerves swallowing me up whole.

"Go ahead whenever you're ready," Nora says. "Give me a

thumbs-up when you want me to activate your patch, and a thumbs-down if you'd like me to stop. Okay?"

I pause. Then nod.

I might be sick.

I swing open the gym door and take a step inside. At first, I close my eyes as the nostalgic smell overwhelms me. I can't even be sure if I'm really smelling it, or if my brain is filling in the blanks of what I'm *expecting* to smell. Is the scent of the players' sneakers real? The rubbery floor mats? The popcorn from the concession stand? I don't know. I don't trust any of my senses anymore. But the bittersweetness fills my nostrils regardless, making me want to both stay in here forever and run back outside into the hallway screaming.

I can do this, I tell myself. I *need* to do this. I need to do this for me and Dylan.

Finally, I'm able to open my eyes and walk farther in. There are four big groupings of balloons—one blue, one red, one orange, one green—floating near center court. And dazzling far above me is the brand-new skylight.

It's real. Finished. And so much bigger and more beautiful than I ever imagined it could be, spanning most of the ceiling.

It's a clear evening—there's not a cloud in sight—and although it's still too light out to see many stars, the setting sun has left the patch of the universe above a purply pink that Dylan could've stared at in wonder for hours.

And maybe now he can.

I stand between the bunches of blue and green balloons near center court, hold my breath, and give Nora a thumbs-up. I see her smile and nod at me through the windowpane.

I wait. Nothing happens. Ten seconds go by—or maybe it's more like twenty, it's difficult to tell—and I begin to wonder if the patch is going to work at all. Maybe it can't now that I know the truth.

Out of nowhere, a piano appears beneath the basketball hoop I'm facing. It definitely wasn't there a second ago.

Was it?

"Dylan?" I ask, but I'm so excited and terrified that it's hardly audible.

I see a silhouette hovering over the keys, but I can't tell who it is from where I'm standing. Then the first notes begin to play, and I recognize the song immediately. It's his.

"Dylan's Song."

The notes are bouncing from wall to wall, floor to ceiling, echoing throughout the empty gym as if we're in a cathedral. It's beautiful. Almost *too* beautiful.

But then I hear it. That first missed chord. The one that always tripped him up.

I close my eyes briefly and let out a soft laugh. *It's him*, I think to myself, as another note goes awry. It's Dylan.

He's here.

My heart races.

When the song comes to an end, the silhouette stands and starts walking my way. I should be able to tell who it is, I think—the gym is dark, but not so dark that I wouldn't recognize him from here—but still. Their identity is blurred, or covered in shadows, and it's hard to know exactly which.

But as they come nearer to half-court, their features begin to materialize, and it's . . .

. . . *Nash?*

My heart sinks.

He smiles and says my name, I think. Or maybe he only mouths it? I can't be certain.

Wait . . . *is* that Nash?

It looks like him, sort of. But the closer he gets, the more difficult it is to know for sure. I start to panic and rub my eyes as my heart thunders away in my chest. Once I can see clearly again, though, I'm certain who's standing in front of me.

It's my *actual* perfect friend.

Dylan.

"Hi," he says, sporting a crooked grin. "Miss me?"

I cover my mouth with my hand, hardly able to breathe.

"Oh, c'mon," he says playfully, his grin spreading wider into a smile. "It's just me."

I allow myself to laugh as I look him up and down, completely stunned. It's him.

It actually, truly, *really is* Dylan.

"I'm glad I dressed appropriately," he says, spinning in front of me. "I heard there's a ball happening tonight."

He has on a black suit and tie, his thick mop of dark hair is the perfect amount of messy, and I've never been more certain that he's always been more than a friend to me. It feels impossible now that I ever didn't know it.

Without wasting another second, I jump forward and wrap my arms around him, pushing my cheek into his chest.

He smells like Dylan. Feels like Dylan. I can even hear his heartbeat.

He pulls me in tighter. "I've missed you, River."

Somehow, I'm able to find my voice. "I've missed you, too."

"How was Astronomy Club this year?" he asks.

I'm hesitant to tell him that I didn't attend a single meeting.

But he knows just by looking at me. "It's okay," he says, "I get it. How's Paige?"

I sniffle, trying to suck up a tear or two. "She's fine."

"Your parents?"

"They're good."

"And Mavis?"

I pull apart from him a bit, blinking away the wetness. "We're working on things."

He beams at me. "Good."

My Patch is getting warmer against my temple, I realize.

It never did with Nash.

Dylan's hand finds the back of my neck, and his fingers glide against my skin. Even the way he's standing there—his right foot staggered slightly forward—is the same exact posture as Dylan.

"I haven't gotten better, have I?" Dylan says with a laugh, shaking his head.

It takes me a moment to realize he's talking about his song. "Still a perfectly flawed performance, I'd say."

He nods smugly.

"I don't know, though," I reply. "After a year of practicing, I'd expect to hear a more improved version, I won't lie."

His jaw drops in pretend offense. "How dare you."

I shrug with a grin.

"I thought you liked the flawed version more anyway."

"What can I say?"

"Yeah," he concedes. "I know what you mean."

He stares at me as our laughter fades. I stare back.

"Thank you, by the way," he says.

"For what?"

He glances around, as if someone might be listening, then leans closer and whispers, "I loved my mustache."

I snort as another tear forms in my eye. "Yeah?"

"Of course." He straightens back up. "It needed a make-over. I'm glad you saw through the bullshit." He looks me up and down and gets serious. "You were the only one who did."

He takes a step closer.

"I'm excited for this summer," he says happily.

"This summer?"

He looks at me like I should know. "Our road trip?" He pauses. "Don't tell me you don't want to go now."

Oh. "Of course I do," I say, wiping my eyes. "I still think about it a lot."

"So do I."

But does he know that the trials are ending tomorrow and I won't have this Patch? How can we go on the road trip together without it—

Ouch. A shooting pain hits my temple for a split second, but I'm able to hide the grimace before he sees it on my face.

"It looks incredible, huh?" Dylan says, staring up. "Way better than I thought it would."

I look up, too. "It really does."

He chuckles. "Remember our last time in here? It looked like they'd just started."

The sky has already gotten darker. I can even see a few sprinkles of stars, surprisingly, despite the stadium lights blasting across campus.

"Can you imagine how much cooler Astronomy Club would've been in here at night?" he says.

"Yeah—*shit.*" Another searing pain on my temple. I rub the side of my head.

He looks concerned. "What's the matter?"

I try to smile. "Just a headache."

"*River!*"

I hear a voice, distant and faint, coming from the door to the gym. I think it's Jacob.

But I'm too focused on Dylan to care.

He looks back up at the skylight and marvels at the abyss above, his mouth slightly ajar. "So many fiery specks and pebbles out there, huh?" he whispers.

I fight to stay present as the pain gradually gets worse.

"River," he says, his eyes finding mine. "I've been wanting to tell you something."

I notice the few subtle freckles that always appear come summer. "What is it?"

He swallows hard and bites his lower lip anxiously. "I'm in love with you, River."

My knees nearly buckle. "You are?"

"Yes," he replies, "and I have been for a long time."

I have to remind myself to breathe. "I love you, too, Dylan," I say, "and I always will."

His face melts in relief.

"*River!*" Jacob's voice isn't distant or faint anymore. I can hear it loud and clear.

I turn toward the doorway. Jacob is getting yanked back into the hall by the same security guard who was in Nora's room.

"You have to leave!" he shouts, fighting a losing battle. "Dr. Ridges didn't know she took you here, and he says it could be danger—"

But he gets tugged back outside before he can finish.

I turn back to Dylan, realizing our time is fleeting. "Mavis said it wasn't my text you were responding to the night you . . ." I trail off. ". . . you know. Is that true?"

He stares at me. "River."

"What?"

He laughs. "It doesn't matter, does it? I'm here with you now."

A sharp pain blasts through my temple again.

"Are you okay?" Dylan asks.

I nod.

He reaches toward me, his hand landing on my hip, and it helps push the pain away.

"I know you're here now," I say. "It's just . . ."

"What?"

"This can't last," I say, "can it?"

His eyebrows scrunch together as he pulls me in. "Why not?"

"Because . . ."

Don't make me state the obvious.

Because I won't have this Patch tomorrow. Or the day after that. Or the day after that. Or maybe ever again.

"I know," he says, holding me tight. He leans in, his lips gracing my ear. "I get it. So let's make the most of right now."

We both lean toward each other, even though the pain is beginning to feel unbearable, until my lips touch his. I start trembling, and I feel his hands move up and down my back, helping to calm me down. Even with the Patch searing into my temple, his warm body feels too good to let go. Too right.

And all I can think is that I wish we had this moment sooner.

Like on my sofa watching his favorite documentary on black holes. Or in one of our cars after school. I wish we'd had it the last time we were in this gym together—a *real* kiss, not a joke—when I was with the real Dylan . . .

Not my Perfect Friend.

"Babe!"

I hear Biggs's voice and pull my lips unwillingly off Dylan's.

"You have to get out of there!" she shouts through the door, pounding to keep my attention. "He's not real! You're not talking to Dylan!"

You're not talking to Dylan, you're talking to . . .

Myself. I'm talking to myself.

"Is everything all right?" Dylan asks.

I take a step back. "Yeah."

"Are you sure?" he says. "Because we can go somewhere else to get away from them."

"Get away from them?" I ask, confused. "My friends?"

He thinks. "How about we go to—"

It feels like a bolt of lightning strikes my temple. I yell, grabbing the side of my head, and start losing my balance. I feel Dylan's strong arms press into my sides as he attempts to hold me up. But even so, I fall, because he can't.

Because this isn't the real Dylan.

I crash into the floor and then hear footsteps racing toward me as my head throbs in pain. I stare up into the night sky, sprinkled with faint stars, as my vision goes in and out of blurriness. Dylan appears over me with his warm smile and watery eyes, and I hear his voice one last time—*Goodbye, River*—before I start to lose consciousness.

46

DYLAN

Swirling blue and red lights.

Then darkness.

All around me.

I can't hear anything.

I can see, though. Here and there.

Then more darkness.

Suddenly, Mavis is hovering above me. She's sobbing. I want to tell her it'll be okay.

But my voice isn't working. My body isn't working. I'm outside, I think, in the rain.

A cop is yelling. I can tell by the movement of his lips. What did I do?

Then someone else is staring at me. A paramedic, maybe.

Why does she look so sad?

More darkness.

Then, thankfully, there's light. Tons and tons of it.

Bright, warm, breathtaking light. All around me.

And everything makes sense. Everything feels right.

Everything I've been worrying about is just . . .

Gone.

I'm making Mavis laugh. We're on her bed, Albert the cat nestled between us.

And I'm lying next to River in the gym, at the center of our universe.

Then I'm beneath a blue sky that expands forever, both of them at my side.

I can't wait to tell River that finally, I understand.

Finally, what felt so big is nothing at all.

Because of all the pebbles spinning around all the fiery specks,

I got to share this pebble with these two perfect dots,

at this exact moment within infinity.

47

RIVER

I hear all the beeping before anything else. It doesn't take long to place it. All the machines that either keep patients alive or monitor them to make sure nurses and doctors do as well. Why does every hospital sound exactly the same?

My eyes peel apart, but immediately close. The light hurts too much.

I suck my teeth.

"He's up." I hear a voice.

Footsteps scurry toward me. I try opening my eyes again to see who's there, but it's too difficult. It feels like someone is stomping my brain with boots on, my head is aching so badly.

"Don't worry, River." It's Mavis. "Just relax."

"We're all here, babe," another voice says. "Mavis, Goldie, Brady, Jacob, and me, Biggs."

I wait a moment and then say softly, "No Oaklyn?"

There's a brief pause before I get a few laughs.

"He's got jokes," Jacob says.

"The nurse said your parents are on the way now," Mavis adds.

I know that I'm injured solely based on the hospital beeps and horrific heartbeat pounding against my cranium, but I'm clueless as to what exactly happened. "How bad is it?"

"You're going to be fine," Goldie says.

"You fell in the gym, in case you don't remember," Jacob

explains. "You have a concussion, and you needed a couple stitches, but nothing major."

"They want to do more tests to be sure," Brady adds. "A CT scan—or was it an MRI?"

"I'm sure that's *exactly* what River wants to hear about right now," Goldie whispers, "more things reading his brain."

I feel my lips curl up into a grin.

"Hey, at least now he's in a legit hospital and not the gym," Biggs quips.

The gym. *Dylan.*

It all comes rushing back to me. His song on the piano. Being swept up in his arms. His smell. His eyes. Our kiss. The mustache I knew he'd love . . .

Except, that wasn't him playing the piano or hugging me or complimenting my spray-painting skills. Because that wasn't the real Dylan.

It was the real me.

"I need to tell you guys something," I say. "It's about the bill-board."

My voice cracks. I can't be sure if it's due to guilt or my faulty throat, but I take a moment to swallow and try again.

"I did it," I say. "I spray-painted it. And I'm so sorry."

The room goes silent.

I hate that I can't see how they're reacting.

"River," Jacob says. I feel a hand on my chest. "We can talk about this when you feel better—"

"I didn't do it to mock Dylan," I continue. "I just didn't want everyone to remember him that way. *I* didn't want to remember him that way."

"I get it," Brady says. "What you told me in Art made sense."

"I wanted people to see him as the guy who made them smile," I say, "not the guy who made them cry."

I stop talking because now I'm the one crying. Above the hospital blankets, I feel more hands on my chest, shoulders, and arms.

"It's okay, River," Goldie says.

"There's nothing to apologize for," Biggs adds.

"I get it now, too, River," Jacob says. "There are things I have to tell you, too."

There's a pause.

"I love you," Mavis says, "and I always will."

Things start to get hazy again, but this time it's warm, even comforting, instead of scary. And between the steady pressure of their hands and the comforting relief of knowing that I've been forgiven, I drift off to sleep.

48

RIVER—AUGUST 2024

I drive by my dead best friend's photo on the billboard above our town's pet groomer's, just like I did almost every day last school year. But now it's the most comforting sight on my drives through town.

It's still the black-and-white Dylan Cooper, in his favorite polo shirt that no one else knows is red, staring back at me with his crooked smile that's hiding so much.

It's still not the real him. But that's okay.

I see the faded, discolored marks where a mustache used to be, hovering above his upper lip. The purple table crew plus Mavis and Goldie tried our best at getting it back to normal last month, shortly before we hiked up to the top of Mount Marigold to watch the fireworks on the Fourth. But what can you do? Sometimes paint-removal products work a little too well.

I'm just glad the City of Teawood and the billboard company were fine with my fixing the mess without pressing charges. I think it helped that I turned myself in and explained my purpose, too. My parents, on the other hand, weren't so forgiving. They waited until I was discharged from the hospital and feeling better after my one-night stay before grounding me for the rest of June. Being grounded, I can now confirm, is much worse when you actually have friends.

Driving through Teawood is more bittersweet today than I'd have expected two months ago. I'll miss a lot of people here now. There's my family and friends, of course. But I'll also miss Dylan.

I mean, I know he's not *actually* here. I know he's gone—from this planet, at least, regardless of whether there's a Patch stuck to my temple or not. But my memories of him aren't. They're sprinkled all over this town. And I don't want to run from them anymore. I want to hold on to every piece of him as tightly as I can.

But I know how the hippocampus and amygdala work. I know that, as time goes on, even if I were to stay in Teawood, those memories will inevitably fade. Even the ones that stick with me, indelible in the three-pound sponge of flesh floating between my ears, will twist and turn as the decades progress. Sooner or later, I'll probably forget his height down to the inch, or the exact sound of his laugh. I'll probably misquote him as I retell my favorite Dylan stories to anyone who will listen, or blank on the chorus of the song he struggled to perfect on the piano.

I can't hold on to all of my Dylan memories forever. It's just not possible.

But that's okay. Because I know he'll always be with me, in some way, no matter what. Because even if my brain fails to remember, his chapter in my story has already been written, just like I've already been written into his. And those stories—*our* stories—are here to stay.

The infinite story of us.

I pull into the Meyerses' driveway. I'm running late to pick Mavis up, so everyone's already here, moseying around in the late summer heat. I step out of my car and start saying my hellos to everyone who came over to see us off.

Brady waves at me as he helps his grandpa up the front porch steps. Biggs pauses a conversation she's having on the phone—I assume it's Tether-related—to compliment my shoes.

"Loving the sneakers, babe," she whispers.

Goldie breaks away from the feud she's having with her parents in the Meyerses' garage to come give me a hug—which still feels a little weird if I'm honest. But it's a good kind of weird.

Sort of like a good kind of nervous.

Mavis's siblings Ryan and Rachelle spot me and demand that I play a few rounds of chase with them. I lose, to their delight, then continue through the house.

I fist-bump Ari, who's in a heated debate with Paige over the season premiere of a TV series they're both obsessed with, and then finally find my parents alongside Mr. and Mrs. Meyers in the living room.

"Hi," I say, interrupting my dad trying to impress Mrs. Meyers with a terrible impersonation of this comedian he loves. "Sorry I'm so late."

"You think *you're* late?" Mrs. Meyers says. "Mavis is just stepping into the shower."

I roll my eyes and grin, then walk over to my mom and Mr. Meyers, who are discussing something more serious than stand-up routines.

I hear hushed voices about consent forms and lawyers' hourly rates and realize they're continuing the never-ending conversation about what legal options we have to target Affinity Mind & Body. I appreciate that they care about how messed up what Affinity did was.

But right now, it's the last thing I want to be thinking about.

So I pretend like I didn't hear what they're talking about, exchange hugs, and dip out before I can hear more about my mom's plan to sue Nora Mehta for everything she's worth.

I haven't heard any threats about the NDA I signed, surprisingly. And to this day, I'm not even sure if it was real or just an Affinity tactic to mess with me. My thinking is, Affinity must be terrified to pursue legal action, considering that the risk Nora put me in that night in the gym has already given us a great case. Dr. Ridges knew that activating my Patch in such an emotionally charged location could be dangerous, the others told me. So did Nora. But she did it anyway.

And we weren't the only ones who had unexpected results. With dozens of trial locations across the country, it was only a matter of time before news started to trickle out about what Affinity is up to. I try not to pay attention to the reports—it seems like a new headline about it appears every few days—but it's impossible to tune it out entirely. There are already conspiracies floating around about what the Patches can do. Mostly, people have gotten it wrong, but a few have gotten it right. A few journalists have even reached out to me, asking for an interview. I've declined.

So far, at least.

It's strange. Everyone's livid at Nora, and I get why. But I also see her side, too, because I've been there myself. She knows what it's like to lose her own Dylan. She just hasn't let go yet.

And weirdly enough, maybe I wouldn't have, either, if it hadn't been for Nora.

Jacob is helping Mavis finish packing upstairs, I learn, but I don't mind the longer wait. I chat with Brady and his grandpa over burgers, get a stern warning from Goldie to "keep Mavis safe!" and hear all the cool updates about Biggs's upcoming trip to tour the Tether headquarters in London. Then I go wait by my car while Mavis is finishing up, right where the twins are drawing dinosaurs in the driveway with chalk.

With the sun falling in the sky and a cool breeze rolling in, I remind myself to savor my final moments as a Teawood resident. I'll be back after my first semester at Cascara for the holidays, of course, but it won't be the same.

Mavis comes rushing outside. "Sorry, *sorry!*" she says to everyone as she rushes by with some of her bags for our trip, hair still wet from the shower. She sets them down by my car, then doubles back to say her goodbyes.

Jacob leaves the house a moment later, carrying even more of her luggage, then heaves it into the back seat. "River," he says, wiping his forehead. He gives me a hug.

"She's such a light packer," I say with a smirk.

The look he gives me says it all.

"So, Mavis told me she needs to fly back before . . ." I pause to think. "Was it the twelfth?"

"The graphic novel course *starts* on the twelfth," he clarifies, "so the eleventh, at the latest."

"Thank you again for helping make that happen," Mavis says, appearing next to me.

"Of course," I say. "Happy early birthday. Thank *you* for coming along on this road trip when that course starts the very next day."

She hugs my side. "Wouldn't have missed it for the world."

"And to think," Jacob says with a smile, "I almost had to *blackmail* you in order to get you to pitch in."

I laugh.

I'm glad Jacob finally told me what he wanted my stipend money for, seeing as Dylan had mentioned to him that he'd wanted to gift Mavis with the course. It's funny because I would have chipped in anyway—just like Brady, Goldie, and Biggs did when they heard why Jacob wanted the funds.

When I notice what Mavis is wearing, though, my heart halts for a beat.

"That's Dylan's, right?" I ask.

She nods, smiling.

It's his blue-and-silver Timber Wolf jacket—the same one he wore the last time I saw him.

"You ready?" I say.

"Yep." Mavis, looking a frazzled kind of happy that I've never seen on her, throws a final suitcase into my trunk. "Let's do this."

She gives Jacob a kiss and hops into the passenger seat. We pull away, waving goodbye to everyone in the front yard as they disappear into the horizon.

"I can't believe we're actually doing this," Mavis says excitedly, staring at our road trip itinerary on her phone. Dylan and I created the doc last year; now me and Mavis are seeing it through.

We stop to fill up my tank, and I let Roy keep the change from the mountain of car snacks we buy for the ride. I put my key in the ignition after we decide on which chips and chocolates to eat first, but Mavis stops me from driving off.

"Before we get going again," she says, turning to face me, "I have something for you."

"Yeah?"

"I was cleaning out my closet while packing up everything last night," she says, "which is how I remembered I'd been holding on to this jacket."

She reaches into the pocket and pulls out a folded piece of notebook paper.

"I found this in his pocket," she says, "and I think you should read it."

I take it from her. "What is it?"

"Remember how I told you the actual reason behind why Dylan went to see Mr. Babcock every day?"

"Yeah?"

"I'm pretty sure this had to do with that." She nods at the note. "Go ahead."

I unfold it, hardly able to breathe. I haven't heard from Dylan—the *real* Dylan—since June of last year. Am I about to discover more of his story?

I look down nervously and begin to read:

Dear Me,

Hi, you. Yes, it's me (you). Remember when
Mr. Babcock suggested that we just start
writing without even thinking when we're
feeling overwhelmed? Well, right now I'm
feeling all the things, all at once, and I could
really use a moment to get them out of my
head and onto this piece of paper, which just
happens to be in Brady Pottses' notebook.
(Side note: I'm making "getting to know
Brady Potts a lot better" a senior year
goal. He's cool as hell.)

Anyway. So here it goes. A letter I'm writing
to myself in the high school parking lot like the
totally normal and not weirdo person that I am.

First, I hope tonight goes well for us. We're
planning to break up with Mavis. Although
"break up" sounds harsh and inaccurate.
We'd rather be friends because we think it'll
make us closer to Mavis, actually, not break
us apart. So let's go with . . . "bright up."
Yeah, we're going to "bright up," not "break

up" with her. Is that stupid? Oh well, I have
to keep writing. No overthinking. Anyway. We
love her, and we know that she loves us, too.
I hope that doesn't ever change.

Second, I hope whenever future Us is reading
this, we're still playing basketball, but not
because we have to, or because people in
Teawood expect that of us, or because some
college scholarship depended on it, but because
it's still fun. Or maybe we're not playing
anymore because it's not. Either way, I hope
we're still playing (or we're not) just for us.

Third, we better still be learning piano(!!!). I hope
that we've mastered "Dylan's Song," as Mavis
and River have been calling it. I hope we're not
having to sneak into Mavis's church to practice
so that our dad doesn't find out and get angry.
I hope we can play anywhere, anytime, and if he
doesn't like that, that's his loss, not ours. I hope
we're still playing, just for us.

Fourth, I hope we told River how we feel.
Because we're pretty sure we like him as

more than a friend. Actually, we're more than pretty sure. We're pretty positive. And that's probably the scariest thing we're going to write in this letter tonight because we don't even know what that means for us, let alone what that means for us and River. But it's the truth.

Future Us wishes we could tell past Us that it'll all be perfect. That the future will be awesome. That it'll all work out with basketball and college, with piano and Dad, with Mavis and River. But we don't know that it will.

Hopefully, though, no matter what, we'll get better at pausing when things get scary. When things feel like too much. And we'll marvel at the fact that, of all the pebbles spinning around all the fiery specks, we got to share this pebble with these dots at this exact moment within infinity.

Love,
Dylan

ACKNOWLEDGMENTS

Of the four novels I've written, *Another First Chance* challenged me more than the others in just about every way. It's the first book I wrote with multiple first-person perspectives; my initial draft was about twenty thousand words over my editor's target (I'm so sorry, Alexa), and I spent way too many hours reading about the brain on Wikipedia. But more than that, this book centers a teenager who's grappling with a form of heartbreak that most of us won't have to endure until much later in life, if at all: the anguish of losing a best friend. I knew that I needed to get it right.

Luckily, there were a few people who had my back along the way.

Alexa Pastor, my editor at Simon & Schuster Books for Young Readers: when I couldn't see the forest for the trees, you stepped up in so many ways to help my messy vision board of a book become *Another First Chance*. Thank you (for real).

Moe Ferrara, my agent and publishing partner-in-crime: you continued to be my fierce advocate—and, just as importantly, my levelheaded voice of reason—when it mattered most. Thank you, thank you, thank you.

And, as always, to the friends and family who recharged my human batteries in ways you'll never know: I'm the luckiest for getting to share this pebble with you at this exact moment within infinity. Love you.

1
I
w
s
b
ə
w
l